GILCHRIST

Maurice Leitch was born in County Antrim and educated in Belfast. His first novel, *The Liberty Lad*, was published in 1965, followed by *Poor Lazarus*, winner of the 1969 Guardian Fiction Prize. *Silver's City* won the Whitbread Prize for Fiction in 1981. He has also written radio plays, short stories, and television screenplays and documentaries. He lives in North London with his family.

MAURICE LEITCH

GILCHRIST

A NOVEL

Minerva

A Minerva Paperback
GILCHRIST

First published in Great Britain 1994
by Martin Secker & Warburg Ltd
This Minerva edition published 1995
by Mandarin Paperbacks
an imprint of Reed Books Ltd
Michelin House, 81 Fulham Road, London SW3 6RB
and Auckland, Melbourne, Singapore and Toronto

Copyright © 1994 by Maurice Leitch
The author has asserted his moral rights

A CIP catalogue record for this title
is available from the British Library
ISBN 0 7493 9655 5

Printed and bound in Great Britain
by Cox & Wyman Ltd, Reading, Berkshire

For Sandra

With every day, and from both sides of my intelligence, the moral and the intellectual, I thus drew steadily nearer to that truth, by whose partial discovery I have been doomed to such a dreadful shipwreck: that man is not truly one, but truly two.

Robert Louis Stevenson,
The Strange Case of Dr Jekyll and Mr Hyde

GILCHRIST: From the Gaelic, meaning a "servant of Christ"

ONE

The setting sun, edges frayed and smoking slightly, hung suspended over the crest of the great headland and its solitary white hotel rearing straight up out of the rock. At this hour the pale walls were a delicate, litmus-paper pink, all brutalities softened, made mysterious by the dying light. Advancing towards it Gilchrist kept his gaze fixed on the pulsing, fiery disc in front as though it might suddenly plummet from sight if his attention chanced to waver. Nature was given to such tricks, it often occurred to him, sly, little, waylaying acts of treachery when least expected. Or when your guard happened to be down.

Most men have a secret, sustaining image of themselves and Gilchrist was no exception. Lying on his hard mattress in his apartment on the fourth floor of the Miramar, he liked to think of it as the couch of a warrior, one whose eternal watchword was vigilance. And something of that same obduracy he cherished in himself – or had, until recently, he reminded himself bitterly – seemed to be found here in this country he had sought refuge in. All about were the reminders of a hard-fought, continuous battle against a landscape refusing to yield.

On his frequent walks into the countryside beyond the confines of the town, past the bull-ring and the encircling Carretera Nacional, it was as though he had strayed into the Biblical desert. Scrubland, blackened by weekend cooking fires, rapidly gave way to scree and then sheets of grey-fissured rock running off and up to the distant *sierra*. Saw-toothed, his little book of the lingo informed him, was the derivation. No other language, it struck him, could have come up with quite so cruelly apposite an image.

One afternoon he had taken up the challenge of all that heartlessness, as he saw it, by striking deeper and deeper into the upland wastes. The sun beat down on the crown of his panama and across the thin shoulders of his linen suit. He kept wiping sweat from his brow with a soaked handkerchief. It was the only concession he was prepared to make.

Toiling along a dried-up river-bed he saw a distant bird of prey outlined high against the blue. He watched it for some time, pitting himself against that, too. There seemed no end to his appetite for some form of confrontation. Mortification, as well, for his feet and body ached, while his throat felt parched. He had brought along nothing to drink.

At one point he stumbled and a sharp rock tore through his trouser-leg. He felt convinced he must be bleeding beneath the cloth but a fierce satisfaction only drove him on to greater excesses. The sound of his own breathing was all that could be heard. Not a solitary insect whirred in the dry heat. Nothing lived up here except that black-winged cut-out drifting far above watching him crawl below. Borne high on the thermals, it hovered effortlessly, and he began to have visions of its dead, unblinking eyes fastened on him. Mopping his brow he dropped down on to a flat-topped boulder. All around the speckled stones shimmered feverishly in the heat.

But, no, he berated himself, *no, it was a delusion all his shortcomings could be conveniently erased at a stroke, even several strokes.* The image was one he had often employed, that of a giant Divine Hand ponderously moving across "The Blackboard Of Life" wiping clean a catalogue of sins. On occasions he had even gone in for the real thing, chalking up a list in bold capitals that could be read by every person in the gathering. PRIDE. COVETOUSNESS. LUST. ANGER. GLUTTONY. ENVY. SLOTH.

"Each one a deadly virus eating away at the soul, poisoning the conscience, rotting the will to salvation. Certain among you may well be suffering side-effects at this very moment. Believe me you don't have to be a medical man to recognize the symptoms of severe Toxic Transgression. But it doesn't have to be Terminal, dear friends, because there also happens to be a simple little word with the power to relieve those symptoms. Look, I'm writing it up for you now. REMISSION. And now two further words. REMISSION OF SINS. Three ordinary little words with the power to change history. Yours and mine, dear friends."

And there and then, overcome by the power of his own remembered words at their most persuasive, he sank to his knees baring his head to the brutal Andalusian sun.

"Lord," he prayed, "do not desert thy servant in his hour of need. The turning he took was a wrong one and the harm done to those people back home who gave their trust as well as their money must weigh as heavy as lead with any hope of redemption. Vanity played a major part in his downfall, but he would be a fool and liar if he didn't admit to most, if not all, of the other temptations as well. Lust raised its ugly head, as did greed, not to mention envy. Lord, behold a poor and penitent sinner prostrate before you in this barren spot. But then, perhaps, thy heavenly hand has directed him to such a place as was the case in Bible days of yore when thy voice spoke to the chosen few in the raging wilderness." And for the first

3

time in weeks, if not months, he did feel he might well have broken into the light after being kept so long in darkness.

He blinked up into the cloudless sky but the vulture had disappeared. It might have been the effects of the heat but for a moment he did believe that perhaps the evil one himself had brushed him briefly with its wings.

As he knelt there he began to notice tiny growing things in the crevices of the rock, something he hadn't spotted before. And as though some kind of starvation of the senses had occurred because of his state of mind the scent of freshly crushed herbs now, too, wafted his way. He saw a lizard blending with the grey and russet of the stone, and various insects could be heard. The tinkling of distant goat bells added its contribution until the man on his knees – they ached intolerably – felt as though he might not be able to withstand such an onslaught much longer. His head swam. He was most definitely feeling his age. For someone in his fifties, despite having kept himself fit, being out here like this under such a merciless sun implied some form of wantonness, if not out-and-out derangement.

And it was at this point as though to reinforce such feelings that he became aware of someone standing watching him. Slowly turning his head he saw a young boy some little distance off beside a rock as tall as himself. He was wearing what looked like cast-off clothes and had a length of burnished metal tubing in his grasp holding it like a staff. Slung about his neck on a piece of rope was a battered transistor radio. Everything about him, his dress, the rod, and the rough tether supporting his ancient transistor, suggested a makeshift life of hardship in the open. His face was black as a gipsy's.

They stared at one another in silence, Crusoe and Friday, until Gilchrist smiled and rose awkwardly to his feet. The boy, however, seemed to take it the wrong way for, recoiling, he gripped his rod even more tightly. For the first time Gilchrist noticed how badly mauled it was, that incongruous piece of plumber's pipe. Aware suddenly of his unprotected pate he bent to retrieve his panama and, as he did so, the boy stooped too. For the briefest of moments that mimicry seemed genuinely amusing to Gilchrist until he saw that the boy had picked up a rock in his fist the size of a cricket ball.

Some old, buried instinct made him fall back on the only language he knew, the one which had always helped him out of trouble in the past. Sinking to his knees, and with hat pressed to his breast, he began, "Dear good and all-forgiving Father, breathe your fire into the heart of this simple peasant lad that he may find the true path. He and I, we speak a different language, but it is within thy power to join our minds in heavenly harmony. Look down on our strange meeting in this place and bless our communion. Hear thy servant, O Lord, and grant him thy continuing support in the work he carries out in thy Holy Name. Amen."

Opening his eyes the man in the crumpled linen suit was dazzled for a moment by the rays of the sun, then he realized there was no sign of his young listener. However, he had attracted another audience, for now the goatherd's flock stood carefully regarding him.

Gilchrist confronted that assembly of chewing, animal masks. Reflected in their narrowed black eyes he suddenly saw himself for what he was, someone who had lost his grip on reality. Whatever had happened to him in his recent past, the series of calamities in his public and private life, the subsequent flight to exile, his soul-searching and loneliness, all of that had brought him to this sorry pass. He shivered a little then, thinking of the risk he had just run virtually offering himself up on the altar of this primitive land. His own particular creed couldn't help but remind him that a century or so earlier he might have been burned at a stake on account of his behaviour.

In some of the remoter parts he might well be stoned for it to this day.

On the coastal strip far below where holidaymakers' bodies darkened the beaches and speedboats slashed the warm, blue fabric of the Mediterranean – he could see that pale and intricate scarring from here – another world existed, a world where, for the first time, he felt infinitely safer than he did in this God-forsaken place.

The goats kept him in their sights. It was as if he had now become *their* captive. His brain hammered at the crazy notion that they were guarding him until their young keeper returned, but the kneeling man who had once tended his own human flock knew he must not hang around for that to happen. He thought of reinforcements arriving, more ragged hill-folk like the boy, all clutching rocks in their dark hands. Very carefully he began to rise from his knees not once taking his eyes off his watchers. The oldest billy – curving horns as sharply pointed as skewers – eyed him with more than normal suspicion, it seemed to Gilchrist. "There, there," he murmured to it feeling both ridiculous and fraudulent at the same time.

Finally he managed to reach his feet, settling his panama tenderly on his head as he did so as if it had all the potential provocation of a steel helmet. The sun, even hotter now, beamed cruelly down. He was dying to wipe his brow but didn't dare in case the sight of a spotted handkerchief might trigger off a stampede.

When he was several paces distant he risked turning his back and as though walking on eggshells proceeded to make his way back down along the path he had come. He felt he'd had a narrow escape from something he knew he could never put into words or explain to another living soul. But then so many things in his life these days were like that.

About fifty yards or so into his descent Gilchrist looked

over to his far right and saw the young goatherd standing motionless on a boulder. He had a hand cupped over his eyes following his progress. Gilchrist stopped to look at him. He felt he needed to explain himself in some way. Some kind of parting gesture was called for but there was nothing he could think of, no universal semaphore that he knew would not be misinterpreted. Instead he called out, *"Vaya con dios!"* realizing almost immediately it came from some silly, half-remembered, popular song.

The last thing he saw as he went slithering down the slopes was the boy on the rock energetically crossing himself. And Gilchrist knew it wasn't a response to his words that prompted him to act as he did but something far more elemental than that, some ancient exorcism as old as the stones themselves. It left him with the feeling he had been effaced as easily as if he had been something scrawled on a wall. He might never have existed.

Which was something the man in the straw hat with the faded maroon band was growing used to by now, he mused, as he walked along the deserted beach into the setting sun. But then, perhaps, the past which tormented him was his own invention. Indeed there were times when it was as if the life he'd once led actually did belong to someone else, some other person bearing no more than an uncanny, outward resemblance to himself.

His tracks spread evenly behind him in the firm, damp sand. When he made his return journey he was careful to stay within that first band of prints. He had always been a creature of tidy impulses at the best of times but since he had come here he seemed to have grown even more resolute in his habits. The more his inner world swung out of focus, the greater grew the need to regulate his day-to-day routines.

He looked down at his watch now. At this precise hour

7

every evening he would come upon the solitary woman on the beach mat, her face held up to receive the last, lingering rays of the sun. She was always the last to leave this stretch of sand and Gilchrist felt he recognized some deeper obsession there which went beyond the straightforward desire of achieving a healthy tan. Already she was the colour of oiled teak, her straight hair bleached to straw. In her late thirties, with a lean, athletic build, she might well have been of Nordic extraction. Finnish, thought Gilchrist. Just why he should be so specific he had no idea, beyond the fact he felt she must come from a country where the winters lingered at their longest and darkest. Some inner loneliness was also present there, it struck him, something he felt attuned to because of his own origins.

Not once had they spoken, or nodded, even, but Gilchrist felt convinced he must certainly have crossed her mind, just as she had his. That, of course, was old vanity at its work again, but he was still a striking-looking man who carried himself well. Why deny it? All those years spent engaging the attentions of the crowds had left their mark. He recognized it in himself, the way he had of meeting people head-on, eye-to-eye, like an actor or politician, sure in his powers, and ever eager to try them out on anyone or anything within range as though they might wane through lack of exercise. At times it could be an appetite as raw and powerful as any, but on this occasion as he drew closer he purposely kept his gaze fixed out to sea.

But he could still smell her tanning lotion, some heavily-scented coconut preparation, and he began to tremble, his mind filling with images he had no wish to entertain. He knew she wore a mere wisp of something below the waist, nothing above, and now he visualized the oiling of herself with slow, steady strokes of her gleaming palms, a look of animal impassivity on her face as she did so. Gilchrist couldn't help thinking of Eve, the serpent, those same gleaming, sinuous

8

bodies and that expression they must also have shared, the one they turned on Adam, lazy, unblinking, yet at the same time infinitely knowing.

Away on the darkening horizon a powerful motor yacht kept up a dull roaring as it headed for its evening moorings in Marbella or Puerto Banus. Gilchrist experienced a pang of loneliness as he thought of those rich pleasure-seekers on board whose preoccupations were so different from his own.

Then a voice called out, "Good evening!" and it was none other than his bleached blonde on her rolled-out mat. Just to upset his expectations she wore a faded grey singlet with the letters YMCA printed across it.

Gilchrist stopped short, removing his panama. Smiling, he replied, "The nicest time of the day."

"But it is when the sun goes down. So melancholy, don't you think?"

Her accent was faultless, yet something in the construction had that faint textbook ring to it. They were about a dozen paces apart. The sand where she had spread herself had a grey, used look and Gilchrist felt oddly reluctant to leave his own firm causeway for that lifeless zone. Hadn't he read or been told somewhere that many of these beaches were, in fact, man-made, endlessly raked and sifted? But he realized he must go closer for he was embarrassed to be raising his voice in this manner. The woman was smiling back at him, invitingly, it would appear.

"Please correct me if I am wrong, but I think your face is familiar to me?"

Gilchrist lowered his head, carefully wiping the sweatband inside his hat with his blue and white spotted handkerchief. The words didn't alarm him as they would certainly have done when first he got here, sweating profusely in the wrong kind of suit, made even bulkier by the money-belt underneath. For almost a month he had kept himself to himself in his apartment,

9

rarely venturing out except after dark and then only into those areas free from tourists. Gradually, however, common sense prevailed, for who among the good canny folk he had ministered to back home, he asked himself, would ever find themselves among the topless bathers, the sun-scorched drunks, the transvestites lined up for trade in the Plaza Costa del Sol as the nights slid into the pale grey early hours.

Moving amongst all of them, as he found himself doing more and more now, it came to him that the reason he stayed on in this truly terrible place was because of that very fact. He had begun to feel safe again, swimming alone among all these denizens of the night too concerned with their own affairs to pay attention to the passing man in the panama. Yet, occasionally, as he happened by some pavement table or skirted a throng of revellers entering or leaving a club, someone might look at him with a hint of half-recognition in their eyes. *Aren't you . . . ?* The question would hang in the air before he ducked his head quickly, making his way on into the scented night.

Back home there happened to be a celebrity who had an afternoon television show, an agony uncle with perfect teeth and boyish grin belying the prematurely grey mane which gleamed like platinum under the lights. Clambering amongst his studio audience of housewives like some elegantly suited chamois he jabbed at them with a hand microphone, alternately hectoring and cajoling. Often there were tears, and always heightened emotion, but the talk-show host with the noble profile never lost his composure or his smile. He had a huge following and photographs of his house and lovely family were regularly featured in all the magazines. At first Gilchrist couldn't see the resemblance himself, but after so many had remarked on it, he, too, was forced to recognize it as a phenomenon over which he had no control. He felt like that now, deciding to go along with the deception just to see how far it might take him.

The woman said, "I have been thinking to myself where it is I have seen you before."

Gilchrist smiled back at her giving nothing away. He had moved closer so that now he could see her burnished shanks in finer detail. She clasped her knees, chin propped on her arms. There didn't appear to be an ounce of spare flesh anywhere on that uniformly tanned frame.

Gilchrist pulled his own stomach in like some would-be suitor. How ridiculous he had become, allowing himself to play the part of a man he had never even met. Yet, where was the harm in it? And he still hadn't actually *lied* – at least, not directly. He thought of that motor cruiser out at sea heading full throttle for landfall, its complement of rich and jaded passengers on board. For some reason he pictured them like that, lolling about, while a young crew in whites raced tirelessly after their every whim. The growl of the turbines could still be heard, alien and uncaring as the people on deck. Why then shouldn't he, too, enjoy a little of that same status even if his credentials happened to be bogus? But were they? After all he and the man on afternoon television did have more in common than merely their looks, for Gilchrist was recalling all those faces from his past – his quite recent past – and the way he, too, had of kindling emotions, standing, arms uplifted there under the taut, curving slope of his "canvas cathedral". Once again he smelt that hot, green expanse of fabric above and grass beneath, shot through with scent rising from more than a thousand young, yearning, female bodies. His real appeal had always been to the fairer sex just like his celebrated double.

"Are you here on holiday?"

There was something serious there, in the line of the jaw, the mouth, too, with its tendency to straightness. Her eyes were greenish with tiny flecks of a darker hue. They looked smaller than average but then most women's were without make-up. Even he had noticed as much.

11

"Yes," he replied. And then some perversity seemed to take him over, an inner voice not his own making use of him for its own mischievous ends. "I'm here with a party of friends," he heard himself lie. "That's their vessel out there, oddly enough," and he pointed to where the rays of the setting sun were turning the lines of the distant craft to precious metal. "However, I have to say I much prefer terra firma to a life on the ocean wave."

He watched her brow wrinkle as she tried to take in the unfamiliar expressions.

"Yes," he continued, warming to his task, "there's nothing I like better than walking by the shore after the fierce heat of the day. I find it the best time to let one's thoughts wander at will, free from distraction. If you can recall, even our good Lord himself enjoyed his evening stroll by the Galileean shore." That, he supposed, was the real Gilchrist talking and not this impostor with the lying tendencies.

Then he asked, "Are you from Helsinki by any remote chance?"

She didn't bat an eyelid, this woman in the faded grey athletic vest, her breasts barely disturbing the printed legend across its front. YMCA, he thought to himself? Her age might be closer to forty than at first surmised, perhaps even a little on the far side of that.

"Amsterdam is my home. Have you been there?"

"Sadly, no," he said. "I hear it is very beautiful. Water everywhere?"

She permitted herself a tiny smile. "Not only in the canals, I'm afraid. We do have a lot of rain. As in your own country, I think?"

Was his accent showing, Gilchrist wondered? And again he thought how absurd to be going along so readily with this masquerade. Yet the thing was he really did seem to care desperately now for this stranger to believe in him. It was as if

12

he had lost sight of himself and needed to catch a reflection in the eyes of another human being even if it were a foreign forty-year-old the colour of tropical hardwood. By now she had relaxed her grip on her knees and he could glimpse the bright orange vee of her bikini bottom. It felt odd for him to even *think* such words.

Quickly he asked, "Are you staying in one of the large hotels?" gesturing along the beach in the direction of the Paseo Maritimo and its high-density blocks.

"No," she replied. "I have a place nearby," and it was her turn now to motion over her shoulder in the direction of a row of apartments, newly-built and seemingly unoccupied, where the sand ended and the rocks began. Their large, square picture-windows returned the glare of the setting sun as they stared together in silence up the slope.

Gilchrist felt the moment had come to say his farewells yet some desire to prolong events kept him standing there hat in hand. It must make him look as though he were paying court, he thought to himself, and panicking at the idea he jammed the panama back on his head.

Then the woman said, "Could I offer you something to drink – even some tea, perhaps?" and he heard himself reply, "That would be most pleasant – if it isn't any trouble, of course."

At the steps of the apartment – he had been right, hers was the only one that appeared to be tenanted – she took a key from her canvas knapsack and unlocked the door. Gilchrist followed her inside. The place held no surprises, a clean, cool, uncluttered, three-room arrangement with a small paved area beyond some sliding windows at the rear. He sat on a settee with white tubular metal arms and a hard base while the woman drummed water into a kettle in the tiny kitchen. Across from him two open doors led to the sleeping-quarters,

13

for he could make out a bed in each. One had recently been slept in and was strewn with belongings. The other was as tightly made up as a hospital cot.

As he rested there, hat in place beside him on the pale grey covering of the couch, Gilchrist felt as anonymous as the furnishings, or the very room in which he now found himself. Invisibility had claimed him yet again – passivity, too – for he waited meekly for whatever fate might have in store. Perhaps he would get to enjoy the sensation, he told himself, just as his female flock always seemed to have done. It was something he had often envied, that willingness with which they would surrender themselves to the sword of his rhetoric. It was not unknown for some to fall down on the trampled grass between the seats, or near the front, when the time arrived for them to come forward and give themselves up to the Power of the Blood. At such times he knew it would never really be possible for him to participate in that great wave of compliance sweeping through the tent. He was there merely to direct, to channel it. That was his mission and there could be no thought of him ever behaving in any other way.

Then she came out of the kitchen carrying a tray and, after pouring tea for them both, excused herself and went into one of the bedrooms. Gilchrist could hear the roar of a shower as he sat there munching a biscuit. On the low table in front of him was a pile of foreign fashion magazines labelled with a subscriber's address in the Netherlands. Her name was Renata Kooning – or, at least, the name on the magazines was. Gilchrist wondered if he would have to compound his own deception further by supplying a bogus introduction if and when the occasion arose. He wasn't quite sure whether his new-found *friend* could be trusted to carry it off or not. He had a feeling the old Gilchrist certainly was not up to it.

She was wearing a kimono and her damp hair hung in rat's tails when she returned from the bedroom. It was the one with

14

the untouched bed in it. They took tea together and talked a little about the usual things, the climate, the country, its food and drink, the escalating cost of both, the new rudeness. She had been coming here for ten years, she told him, perhaps a little longer. *Always alone?* He had no idea why he'd said it for they could have gone on like this indefinitely, two mayflies stitching patterns in the air around one another. She poured more tea and he watched the pale stream enter the cup. It was weaker than he was accustomed to.

She said, "This time my son is with me. He is studying art history so he has gone to Granada to look at the Alhambra. His father and I, we divorced when he was little."

Seeing him glance across to the bedroom with its perfectly made-up bed she said, "Please do not look too closely at the *other* room." She was smiling again. "Like most young people his age Rudi can be something of a slob."

They laughed together, two people of a similar generation sharing a joke at the expense of another. Gilchrist felt flattered to have been granted membership of the club, emboldened, too, for in his best counselling tones now he murmured, "It cannot have been all that easy bringing up a son on your own."

The woman in the patterned blue and white Japanese robe looked directly at him, then said, "But now he is grown up, you see. He has his own life and I have mine. Each of us is free to take our pleasures as and when we care to."

Gilchrist lowered his head in what he trusted was the modest attitude of someone who has seen it all. Preacher and television pundit were now interchangeable. The process was one with which he was familiar. How many times had he experienced that sudden slippage of personality, felt himself being taken over by another's voice and mannerisms – even thoughts, he had convinced himself on occasions. Now, as he perched on the edge of that hard settee, cup and saucer balanced on both knees, he decided not to tempt fate by looking at his reflection in the glass patio doors across the room, just in case the ultimate in transformation might indeed have come about.

"Are you married?"

"Oh, no, no," he said quickly, regretting it the instant he'd said it in that way in case she might think he was one of *those*. "Never really got around to it, I'm afraid. Much too busy with other things."

And it was at that point when he heard his own laugh that Gilchrist was to realize something odd was about to happen in this room, unaccountable as an episode in a dream, and just as disturbing. He found himself watching events as though on a screen of some kind and one large enough to accommodate every possible permutation of activity, although at this early stage in the proceedings there was only a cast of two and they were sitting still and facing one another as though composing themselves for what lay ahead.

Once Gilchrist had found himself inside a car in a back-country drive-in movie lot – it was the time of his first real trip to "the land of the mighty dollar" – and through the windscreen he could make out that other oblong expanse at a distant remove where lit faces loomed as big as those on a billboard. They must have been quite close to the front, those three young church elders and himself. He remembered feeling acutely embarrassed in such proximity. The smell of mouthwash was overwhelming. Victor Mature's dark liquid eyes seemed to be fixed reproachfully on his own – it was an early Biblical epic in bleeding, livid Technicolor – and the experience was close to the one he seemed to be having right at this moment.

The absence of any sound was a further similarity, for he remembered they sat through most of it in silence not realizing they were meant to shackle their car to the short metal upright planted alongside. His companions with their crewcuts and wash'n' wear suits seemed to be almost as green as he was when it came to the ways of their own country. They had Bibles in their laps – he had a feeling the purpose of the outing might well have been to check out the film for possible blasphemy, yet, all around them in the other cars, it was obvious two at least of the other commandments were being broken more energetically and with greater licence than anything portrayed high above them on the big open-air screen.

And so Gilchrist sat waiting for the action to get under way, feeling as removed from it all as he had done then on that insect-laden summer night deep in the sleeping heart of Kansas thirty years earlier.

He saw a man on a modern, functional settee, a cup and saucer planted on his knee. The man was smiling sociably at someone across the room from him, someone whose face was hidden. The object of his attention, a woman – that seemed apparent because of the back of the head – kept patting, then teasing the damp ends of her hair with the fingers of one hand while the man looked on. She could have been speaking but there was no way of telling because the soundtrack, as on that earlier occasion, had gone dead. Yet that didn't seem likely judging by the manner in which the man was now watching her. His attention was fixed on what she was doing with her other, unseen hand rather than her lips. A look of fascinated disquiet had settled on his face. Now, he half-rose, then sat down again. He loosened his tie in a way which seemed crudely out of character.

All of this Gilchrist studied avidly. Some of the stranger's agitation was evidently affecting him as well for he could hear his own breathing start to quicken. In some odd fashion it seemed to agree with what was being mimed in front of him there on the screen. Gilchrist could feel his clothes stifling him. But the man on the settee appeared to be ahead of him in that respect for already his shirt was unbuttoned to the waist. And,

17

continuing to stare with fascination, Gilchrist saw him start to fumble with his belt buckle, then the top of his trousers.

Gilchrist found himself struggling hard to keep up. It reminded him of that business when they were young, that manic school-yard exercise – O'Grady's. Faster, faster, they would follow each barked command. *O'Grady says this, O'Grady says that.* It was always an ordeal and now, as then, Gilchrist felt himself falling behind. The mythic drill-sergeant kept remorselessly on. He was the stuff of remembered childhood nightmares, a crop-headed giant with military moustache and cruel biceps, perpetually displeased, for that, for some reason, was how he had always imagined him to be.

Now the woman was caught up in the work-out as well, the kimono slithering free for greater ease of movement. Fragile, dark-toned, her shoulders gleamed. By contrast the man's body didn't fare so well. He was sitting close to a lamp and Gilchrist felt for him and his pale, unlovely flesh.

And now the woman was rising up and out of her chair until she stood facing the seated man on the far side of the room. Reflected in the glass at his back the white globes of her buttocks stood out startlingly pale against the rest of her. Slowly she began to move closer into the foreground and as she did so Gilchrist experienced a troubling loss of perspective for it was as if she were advancing out of the screen and straight towards him personally. *What had happened to the man on the settee?* There seemed to be a blur in his vision in that area. The blur became a void, an emptiness, until, dominating the whole scene now, as big as one of those celluloid giants in that Mid-Western car-park under the stars, the woman's full nakedness swam into close-up as though for his attention and his alone. Yet he didn't feel shocked or put out by it in any way because all the time he kept thinking, *None of this is really happening and even if it is the man on the settee is the one who must deal with it.*

He gazed at the nipples, twin dark berries, while much lower, miraculous confluence, that shadowy delta, equally perfect in hue and definition.

Once more the focus began changing. The woman's features now gradually filled the screen, eyes intent, lips parted slightly. The definition was life-like, almost miraculously so, for he could detect minor blemishes, the merest hint of oiliness across the forehead, a small white scar which followed the ridge of one eyebrow. Nearer loomed the face, the mouth wide open now, and Gilchrist, for his part, also felt as if he were heading towards some form of gentle collision – even more fantastical, fusion of sorts with the image swelling on the screen.

He kept waiting for the moment of truth to arrive but not in any urgent or anxious way for he was relaxed now as if all responsibility had been removed from him. He thought of those swooning female converts in the great tent. This must be how they felt. After all these years and now for it to be happening to him. Such sweet surrender. With closed eyes Gilchrist gave himself up to the sensations breaking over him in warm, successive waves, each more deliciously variable and enervating than the one preceding it . . .

Later. He was in darkness, total, black, and not that other earlier, self-induced eclipse, for his eyes were wide open. And it was as though he had also broken free from a dream he'd had, for remnants still clung. First he imagined he might be the last person left – he almost thought *alive* – in that distant, drive-in movie park, all the cars gone and the big screen invisible and silent out there in the night somewhere. Then he had the strong impression of water near at hand, convincing echo of his final moments of consciousness before that other tide-race of sensation had sucked him off and away.

But the water was real this time, both his feet were wet,

immersed in the stuff, the salty tide foaming in around him out of the blackness. He could also hear music. It came from the piano-bar in the great hotel high on the cliffs for, somehow, that was where he seemed to have fetched up, directly under its walls where the headland tumbled into the sea. The curve of the bay stopped at this point. It was also as far as his evening walk took him for he would turn just here, retracing his spoor in the sand back along the empty beach in the direction of the main resort. But never had he left it as late as this, never allowed himself to be trapped by the onset of night in this way. He felt apprehensive out here alone at such an hour, even though people were dancing and drinking cocktails a hundred feet or so above his head. For a moment he thought of scrambling up to the lights and the music by way of the cliff-face but, remembering the look of that sheer drop in the daytime, he put the idea out of his head.

With the solid rock at his back Gilchrist took stock of his situation. It seemed an appropriate moment, not merely because of where he now found himself, but also because of what had happened earlier. *But had it happened?* Already the details were fast unravelling in his head. Soon nothing would remain save a few threadbare scraps of something vaguely disturbing involving someone else, a stranger.

The man on the settee, he told himself. For some reason he seemed to have formed a violent antipathy to that someone who had sat there in that room and gone along so compliantly with everything which had taken place. There could be no real remission in such a case, despite what he used to tell his followers in that big tent. Someone like that was beyond redemption. Standing in the darkness there, suddenly he felt as hard and unyielding as the stones at his back, exulting in his newly restored convictions. Already the couple and their antics had faded to a featureless blur.

"Lord," he prayed to the invisible, murmuring sea, "yet

again hast thou delivered thy servant from the gaping pit. Others, also, have wrestled with temptation and seen visions in the desert places. Forgive a poor, deluded soul for including himself in such a band – no one knows better than he the extent of his unworthiness – yet, surely, this humble follower deserves some credit for past endeavours. Think, for example, of all those penitents brought forward to the Mercy Seat through the power of his persuasion, a gift, which originally must have been heaven-sent.

"Your good intentions, I realize, were with me when I struggled against my enemies closing in like a pack of wild dogs scenting blood – *mine,* Lord, *mine* – but couldn't you have considered, perhaps, felling a few with something sudden and debilitating? These are grave Old Testament remedies, certainly, but then the message I delivered in my big tent was never the watered-down version. Hellfire and damnation are all very well in the hereafter but might you not have seen your way to a tiny foretaste of that just then to keep the hounds at bay, or until I managed to get my affairs in order?

"And one final thing. Why couldn't a Divine Deflecting Hand have been deployed when into my life swam that *innocent* little redhead who was to cause so much heartbreak? Where, oh where were you, then, I say?"

His cry, real, heartfelt, rang out in the void. High overhead the music seemed to falter then die for an instant as though his voice had somehow, miraculously, carried to where the diners sat flushed with food and drink. But, after a pause, the piano player resumed his work and the man on the shore was left once more with lonely reality. His feet felt wet and very cold. Both palms burned as though he had clawed his way over the rocks to reach this point of no return.

He couldn't remember any of it, but then such lapses were not unusual. In some odd way they were even reassuring, a reminder of better times, nights, in particular, when the full force of that mysterious charge would seize him in its grip, later to release him spent and sweating and never completely conscious of what he had said, or how, up there in front of his congregation. All of that was acceptable as long as the Power was still with him, for he saw it like that, something under pressure waiting to be released, as real as blood or marrow, the very essence of himself.

Still, the symptoms were reassuring. He recognized that old lassitude, always pleasurable in some curious way. He had also been perspiring heavily, the night air now chilling him to the skin. Even the front of his trousers felt damp, something which he couldn't recall happening before. It seemed he had nothing to fear, the force was still intact, the wellspring undiluted. He felt at ease with himself propped there against that dry, flat slab of foreign stone, invisible, but now almost friendly to the touch. He had made contact. Better still he had put his case and strongly, at that, without fear or favour . . .

Far out on the distant horizon a ship appeared sliding slowly along as though on a stretched, invisible wire. To Gilchrist, in that moment, it appeared exactly like a fallen constellation. *Could it be a sign*, he wondered? But, standing there, watching that dream-like craft pass by with its tiny, pulsing pinheads of light he began noticing for the first time there were other random clusters pricking the blackness. High above and across to his left hung the Great Bear, or Plough, as it was known back home, he supposed because the implement was one they were all familiar with compared to an animal bordering on the mythic.

He thought of the place now – not *them*, not the people – with something akin to homesickness. The memory of tramping home alone along dark Antrim roads as a boy welled inside. Night fears were always to the fore because the fields and ditches rustled with hidden life but, even if there was no moon and he had to hold nervously to the middle of the track, there was always that six-pointed talisman overhead to keep him company. Now he sighted along the last two stars in the configuration. They led him on to the brightest gem of all, his very own guiding star on those country nights when nothing broke the silence save the sound of some far-off farm dog. But why should due North be at his back instead of out there across the invisible ocean where his instinct directed him? Head, not heart, told him then those waters led to Africa, not to his own distant land, and at the thought he felt even more displaced and alone.

Arms outstretched like a blind man, he began picking his way back across the rocks. Yet the darkness didn't seem quite so black or intense now. He could make out shapes close at hand and off to his left along the bay could be seen the confused, pink glow of the resort. He smelt the sea and some plant nearby with a scent like fresh pencil-shavings. All his senses seemed highly charged as he moved to safety and a footing at last on flat, firm sand.

As he passed the woman's apartment set back on its rise from the beach, he didn't send a single glance in that direction to see if a light was on or not. Everything that had occurred there earlier or, perhaps not, as the case might be, had faded from recall as easily as smoke might disperse, or one's breath on some hard clear morning of frost.

Gilchrist wept a little at the homely image for it seemed so real to him, yet at the same time so foreign to this place where no one cared whether he lived or died. Trudging back along the deserted strand to his apartment and his solitary bed he continued grieving for his lost innocence and those grassy arenas of his youth where first he had discovered his mission in life.

TWO

In the beginning was water. The Word followed much later.

Now they are one – or will be soon – thinks the man gazing down into the wavering blue shallows. The swimming-pool seems vast, empty and silent save for the tiny trickle of an overflow somewhere. *Churchlike.* Already the old connections are welling up. It's at the heart of how he operates after all, words given rein when the time comes, images spilling out like conjurers' scarves. Holding forth. And afterwards so little recall. But that, he supposes, is the price he must pay for his "gift of tongues", that and the subsequent fatigue, the headaches, the drenching sweats. Mercifully, today, he should be spared that.

Kneeling now, he trails a hand across the flat, tinted surface. Warm enough. Barely. The caretaker had promised to leave the heat turned on after it was pointed out to him just how fundamental a stipulation that was. The man had stared back at him, a puzzled expression on his face.

"It's not exactly the River Jordan, you realize." His little joke. Beyond the windows pale, bunched clouds scudded across a sky the colour of the water at his feet. Cruel March.

"Ach, sure, I'm with you, pastor," returned the man, grinning now.

It hadn't occurred to him, you see, that these strange celebrants with their equally odd rites might feel the cold as other people do. For a moment the man on his knees by the still depths suffers a pang of something, not quite self-pity, not quite resentment. Mocked. Misunderstood. But then, sighing – wasn't that always the way of it?

Prickly wet, his hand bears the scent of something chemical. He remembers the streams of his childhood, pure, self-cleansing. If he closes his eyes he can hear, taste, smell, see them as clearly as if it were yesterday. His earliest memories are all of water. In the beginning . . .

His father's work was patrolling their stretch of river and its weirs, dams, sluices and various tributaries. He carried a long, metal-shod pole and his waders were blistered with medallions cut from an old inner tube, for he was someone who could never bear to part with anything no matter how old or worn-out it might be. Everything in their house was like that, even the very clothes on their backs, all patched, mended, salvaged. The river itself spewed up a rich harvest of pickings. After each flood-tide they went gleaning along the banks and sand-bars, bent double like some infirm, purblind beggar family, his father in the lead turning over the pale crust of debris, followed by his mother, then his twin brothers and, finally, himself, at the rear with his own little child's staff.

His eyes must have been keener than the rest or, perhaps, he had a different view of things even then, for always there would be some overlooked trifle, some minuscule object only he could find value in. A scarlet cartridge-case, the tiniest of brown bottles, an animal skull scoured clean by the elements, a broken harmonica, a bed-knob, once a carved cuckoo separated from its clock. Such treasures he kept in a cigar-box

25

under his bed. Inside its lid was pasted the portrait of a Cuban national hero and the scent of leaf tobacco and cedar wood still lingered despite having been so long afloat. He must have been quite young then, eight or nine, although the foraging continued well into his teens. It was an addiction too deep-seated to shake off.

Looking down into the unnaturally blue depths now he catches sight of something lying at the bottom of the pool. It's a diminutive yellow submarine, sunken and forgotten in one corner, and the sight of that little plastic trinket reminds him even more poignantly of a time in his life when he never had a new toy of his own. Yet his father wasn't a miserly man, merely someone with a passion for independence which had got out of hand. He was also shy to the point of paranoia, which may have accounted for it. Often he would hide whenever strangers came to their forgotten reaches to swim or fish in its pools. As a water bailiff he seemed singularly unfitted for his post and the stretch of river he was paid to patrol must have been a paradise for poachers.

And so they grew up like that hidden away from the world in their backwater, a family of castaways, it often occurred to him and, in that same story-book fashion, almost as self-sufficient for the river provided them not only with firewood and most things about the house but with fish and fowl for the table as well. And when the American GIs built a base camp upstream, for that was the war-time, their bounty came bobbing downstream like floating manna. Great dented cans of tomatoes, peaches and pressed meats, jars of coffee, jam and ketchup, and something called peanut-butter, were fished out and carried home and opened in wonderment at the kitchen table.

For a moment the man by the swimming-pool feels a conflict of emotion, recalling, as he does, all those homely tastes and odours, for it was the very placidity of that existence by the river-bank that finally drove him out. He was seventeen when he stole off like a thief in the night, although taking with him little more than his few childish keepsakes in that old Havana cigar-box. Now he thinks of them there in that house crammed with flotsam, three grown men eating silently together off what little remains of his mother's good ironstone dinner-service, the only thing she brought with her as a young bride.

Ten years after his flight he went back for her funeral, and the sight of those mottled old thigh-boots of his father's hanging down like two amputated limbs from their straps on the back of the door made him want to weep far more than the woman laid out in the big front bedroom upstairs. *Forgive me, Lord, for my odd and contrary heart.* He hadn't returned since, for everything changes and decays. Everything except water. Water, the constant . . .

Which returns him to the here and now and the task ahead. The clock on the facing wall directly above the high board reads a fraction after two. Carefully he checks it against his wrist-watch. Almost an hour to kill. But then his timing is deliberate, something he has cultivated over the years, this business of arriving early, leaving late. First and last. His little conceit. For a moment he savours the stillness, more important, his own solitariness in the heart of this echoing, vaulted place with its floor of unmoving, tepid water. *Cathedral*, he thinks for the second time that day. Only he would see it in that light, he tells himself. Nevertheless, that's what it is, or will be in about sixty minutes from now. Recalling the caretaker's rascally grin he can well imagine his reaction to such an image.

As he stands there on the gleaming tiles, *his* handiwork, no doubt, his resentment is directed not just towards the man and his mocking deference, but to all his cronies in the pub as well, for his breath had a distinct chemical overlay put there almost certainly to disguise that other tell-tale odour. Kissick is his name and the sound it makes suits him. Murmuring it quietly to himself a couple of times just to prove the point, prolonging the first syllable more than is natural, sure enough, he can feel his lips draw back in that selfsame sneer the caretaker had used towards him earlier.

"Well, we've had water-polo and life-saving classes and once, I remember, an evening of that synchronized swimming you see on the television, but never the like of what you good folk have in mind."

They were facing one another across the breadth of the pool because that was where he had been forced to seek him out, Kissick interrupting his business with the long-handled net and a plastic bucket in institutional green the same shade as his wellingtons.

Raising his voice to make it carry, he'd replied, with as much irony as he could muster, "Every little infant is familiar with what we have in mind, Mr Kissick. Even you, yourself, must surely have some recollection of what you once learned in scripture classes."

The man on the further side tapped the butt-end of his dripping net on the tiles as though applauding.

"Well put, pastor!" he cried. "Well put! Still, you have to admit there's more than sufficient water for the job." With his free hand he gestured across the dimpled expanse separating them.

"Not for our purposes, Mr Kissick, not for our purposes. But why don't you stay and find out for yourself? Who knows, you might even derive some comfort from our simple little ceremony."

Even as he spoke he knew it was a lost cause. Not that he had ever held out the slightest hope for this grinning creature, anyway, now trawling his net through the water as though their business with one another was at an end, last word on the subject well and truly spoken. But in his heart he knew that not to be the case, it still had to come, and where else but later in the confines of the Market Bar? How they would relish the topic there, he thought, imparted over the wet mahogany, the great, bare, mottled arms of Mrs Rath herself plumped down on a spread beer-towel the better to enjoy the details.

He'd had occasion to go into the place only once. It was in connection with a collecting-box that foolishly, somehow, had found its way there and now none of his helpers had the courage to retrieve. But once was enough. The fumes of drink, tobacco and a coke fire had struck him like a blow, even though trade was at a lull. His visit had been chosen carefully with that in mind. Behind the bar the legendary widow was screwing a fat plug of soiled cloth into a pint glass.

"And what can we do you for, pastor?" she said, large china-blue eyes fastened on his. Her tones were soft and breathy and he remembered staring at the slow movements of her freckled fists as though some deeper, shameful suggestion was being put to him if only he could read the signs right.

Stammering out something about his errand he stood there while she held up the tumbler to the light, exhaling on it as she did so. Through the curve of the glass he saw a great, red mouth shockingly magnified.

"Will you take something? Something soft? On the house?"

Again it was there, the coded invitation, or so he imagined anyway.

"We're all Church of Ireland here," she said. "No offence, mind," and reaching down the collecting-box from a high shelf she blew the dust away before handing it over the counter to him. Shaped from reinforced card, it had a light plywood base and was a replica in miniature of the big Gospel Tent, the design his very own, down to the gold, embossed *Awake* let into the curving spread of the roof. Now it looked merely abject sitting there in a cleared space among all those upended glasses. As he took it in his hand he hadn't the heart to weigh, let alone shake it, knowing full well what the result would be.

How puny his efforts were, really. That little pasteboard edifice squatting on the wet wood seemed to symbolize the meagre extent of his influence. He might as well toss it on those glowing coals this instant, watching it turn to ash before his eyes, for all the relevance it represented.

The fire in the grate was banked high, throwing out an awesome heat. Everything in the place suddenly it struck him shared that same profligacy, the multi-hued array of bottles, augmented two-fold by the mirror at their back, the polished beer engines let into the carpentry of the bar, the cartons of cigarettes, cigars, nuts and potato crisps, a giant jar of pickled eggs like a medical exhibit. The walls, too, bore their bounty, photographs of football teams, their pennants and rosettes, shelves of shields and sporting cups, a rash of seaside postcards, newspaper clippings, souvenirs, framed messages similar to those people put in the back windows of their cars. *All Water Used In This Establishment*, he found himself reading, *Has Been Personally Passed By The Proprietor*.

He remembered feeling weak in the heavy atmosphere, the lazy tick of the American clock measuring out the long, unhurried seconds as he stood there as though held against his will. The woman behind the bar continued her slow task of drying with her thick twist of rag. She smiled knowingly, content in her world, and he watched.

"People come from all over to your meetings, so I hear tell. I've seen the cars myself. Big, shiny, *new* cars."

"No price can ever be put on salvation," he said. "The Lord turns no one away."

She held up a glass for its final inspection. "Miracles cost money. These days, they do."

Vainly he tried to protect his puny cardboard toy by

30

shielding it with his arms. "It was a mistake," he said, merely drawing attention to what he hoped to conceal.

She laughed at him, showing strong white teeth, unnatural in a woman her age. He could just hear her announcing to the assembled bar, *yes, everything's my own*, with that same sly ambiguity he felt certain he had detected earlier.

"Stick to your fat farmers, pastor. We're all too far gone in this place for second chances."

And she was right, of course. He had no power here in this overheated emporium of vice, presided over by this bulky madam in her flowery wrap-around apron as if she were in the privacy of her own kitchen. Recognizing defeat, he backed out then, thinking desperately of a parting tag, but none came, not until he was standing outside still clutching his sorry husk of a collecting-box.

"Woe unto them that rise up early in the morning that they may follow strong drink!" he declaimed to the empty air. "For they regard not the work of the Lord, neither consider the operation of his hands. Isaiah Five: Eleven!"

His face burned as he searched for his car keys, transferring his lightweight burden to the roof. There it sat on the sweating metal as cruelly out of place as it had been inside earlier on the woman's bar counter. What did it signify to anyone other than himself anyway? For he was remembering what he had to endure before the Mission committee to convince them to have it fashioned in the first place. Those red-necked elders in their stiff, dark suits pondering over his sketches as he passed them up the long table. Fighting for every penny his own eloquence had wrung from the crowds in the big green Gospel tent whose reproduction stared back at him now as if in rebuke.

Taking down the box from the dome of the car he proceeded to empty his pockets of all change into the slot cut into that sloping cardboard roof. Then he drove off with it sitting square and newly-freighted on the seat by his side. In some strange way he felt himself charged afresh as well, although another might say he was deluding himself. And not for the first time either.

All of this he's remembering now as he continues to observe the slow sweep of the pool, the caretaker Kissick intent, handling his long, slick pole with surprising delicacy. The word *love* also comes to mind, oddly enough. Yet that is what's involved, thinks the watcher. These people with their affections, sly, yet stubborn at the same time. He knows he'll never be able to capture any of that for himself, or his mission in this place, yet still he hungers after it like some pitiful swain unable to take no for an answer. The woman in the pub had told him as much, sniffing him out as easily as if he had confessed all to her, in much the way he imagined other men must do in that place, their tongues loosened by the drink she pours out for them.

Kissick by now has completed his performance with the net. The water settles gradually until it lies as still as jelly in a mould. Both gaze down for a moment as if taken by surprise at such perfection, then, away at the deep end, the caretaker grounds his pole with a flourish, saluting jauntily. He's grinning at him once more and the man a length away despises him for it. How could he ever have deluded himself he might minister among such people? Snakish, they leave nothing but their slime on the empty nets of the Word, their sly, pagan ways bred into them.

The widow Rath had advised him to cultivate his "rich farming friends" but the truth is he is heartily sick of preaching to the converted. There they sit, row upon row, like the beasts they tend, while he pours out his soul. He gives them pearls but they might as well be those bran nuts they feed their cattle for all the value they place upon them. Him, too, for that matter.

Kissick calls out, "I'll look in later and lock up after you've all done. The place'll be in good hands with you, pastor." He salutes a second time as if requesting dismissal from a superior but, of course, they both know the mockery of that.

"There's a mixed party of blind folk coming tomorrow morning first thing. Never a dull moment, as they say. This job's getting to be a regular education so it is."

At the exit doors he turns for a parting shot. "Good luck with the dippin' then!" He makes it sound as if they're a breed of sheep and not the human flock shortly to arrive with the promise of redemption in their hearts.

The caretaker disappears leaving the place to the man and his resentments, the other's odious presence, as he sees it, lingering like a curse. Convincing himself of the man's essential depravity – he believes he may well be being spied upon at this very moment – he visualizes the boring of peep-holes in the soft wood of the changing cubicles, imagines a rheumy eye pressed close to spy on the town's schoolgirls at their undressing.

Lord, he mouths silently, *cleanse this place from every rank and rotten thing that it may be fit for thy sacramental purpose. Let this water in its purity symbolise thy sanitizing power. And wash away, too, thy servant's own imperfections. Soften his heart towards those who would mock and deride. But, above all, continue to bless the healing work these hands carry out in thy glorious name.*

And, stooping low, he gives them a parting rinse in the blood-warm depths before going out to his station-wagon sitting where he's left it in the car-park.

Minutes later Harold Drummond draws up alongside in his cherry-red Nissan and, rolling down their windows in almost perfect accord, the two sit gazing silently across at one another. Harold is the first to speak.

"I went on ahead of the coach. I hope they know the way. He's a new driver."

"The Lord will guide them to us, Harold, never fear."

That's insufferable of him and he knows it, but the man in the other car manages to bring out the worst in him without really trying. Young, balding, a worrier and family man, he likes to think he's indispensable. In many ways he is, but only because of his passionate commitment to being regarded as such. Pasted to his nearside cheek is a scrap of toilet paper masking a shaving cut. It looks like confetti. And his shirt collar is uncomfortably tight. He exudes heat, panic and a liberal application of the wrong aftershave, even at this distance.

"I hope they all remember what to do."

"What is there to remember? Even babes in arms take to the business like ducks to water." And he permits himself a laugh at his own little joke. For a moment the other looks at him as if he's mad. Perhaps he is.

"Anyway," he resumes, "that's your department. You've taken them through it, I trust?"

"Over and over and over. But how can you ever be certain? There's a new girl. I meant to tell you about her."

Just then the coach comes rolling up, a brave show of millinery – picture and straw, for the most part – decking its side windows. The air-brakes gulp and sigh sending a ripple through the human floral arrangement within. Inside their cars the two men sit watching and waiting for the doors to swing open, spilling the harvest out on to the asphalt.

"Eric . . ."

"Yes, Harold?"

The other looks at him out of that young, blemished moon face of his. *Yearning. Always yearning.*

"Donna. Her name is Donna. Donna Brady."

"Later. Details later. When we're inside. Right now, let us pray for full nets and a mighty haul for Jesus."

Closing his eyes is a tremendous relief, so much so he feels

34

like keeping them that way indefinitely here in the stuffy confines of the car. But shutting out the visible world only seems to summon up demons of a personal nature, those normally kept hidden in the dark. His familiar, the impostor, for instance – the one with never enough answers when the time comes for him to do his stuff. The evocation is so real he feels certain if he opens his eyes there he'll be grinning back at him out of the driving-mirror.

But the moment departs, as it usually does, and he climbs out, smile fixed firmly in place. He walks towards the party of celebrants accompanied at a distance by their nearest and dearest. With eager little cries they come rushing to meet him, an unexpected flurry of early blossom in that wintry place, in their peach and apple, apricot and lime. Easter, after all, is only weeks away. And his own suit is in keeping with those soft pastels. Today he's wearing a pale blue seersucker, faintly striped, purchased that time when a guest of the Biff Brown Gospel College, Concordia, Kansas, Pop. 68750. He also brought home with him an honorary doctorate and the framed scroll to prove it.

Now he's raising his arms in a gesture worthy of the great Biff himself – *Jesus Loves You and So Do I* – stationed in a car-sized rectangle of speckled tarmac. Framed by white lines he stands there while his little, loving flock race nearer. It's a genuine emotion as far as he's concerned. He feels like a bridegroom. Who would wish for a sweeter union, he tells himself.

Then they are all about him clutching testaments in their gloved hands, red ribbons marking passage and text, private and most personal to each one of them.

"Pastor! Pastor!" they keep calling out, which is the form of address he personally prefers. The almost mandatory use of christian names in his chosen line of work has always for some reason made him deeply uncomfortable.

35

"Oh, Pastor, Pastor!" they cry. "Please tell us again. How our sins will all be washed away. Forever and ever?"

"Amen."

"You promise you won't let go," a round-faced innocent whispers, and they all laugh.

Laying a palm to the child's cheek for a bare second, no more, he feels the blood-heat leap across with such force it's hard not to flinch. The eyes stare into his yearningly until he makes some harmless quip or other, distancing himself from so much ardour. It's all a risky business and he knows it. He has a genuine sense of being under siege. They're so close the hot scents they throw off have his head swimming.

Keeping their distance and knowing their place are the others, the odd parent, a brother, sister, a concerned aunt or two and, of course, the remaining handful of celebrants. The girls are plain Janes for the most part, while the few men and youths there are look anything but joyous in their heavy, dark good suits, raw, red hands hanging down like butcher boys'.

Am I failing these others in some way, the man surrounded by his perfumed little bevy asks himself. More truthfully – and he's ashamed of himself for thinking it – *will they hold it against me?* And, then, almost as an afterthought – *when the time comes* – as if some premonition of subsequent events had crept momentarily out of the shadows to put its paw on the proceedings.

"Follow me!" he calls out. "And please make sure all your belongings are with you before we go inside!"

A shrieking rush back to the bus ensues. Patiently he waits until everyone has retrieved their things. Some clutch ordinary plastic carrier-bags; others, most of the girls, seem to have proper weekend cases. Again he finds himself unaccountably moved by the sight of those dainty containers. He can't help visualizing their pale, ruched insides in watered silk, as softly vulnerable as their owners. His heart goes out to all of them there shivering in their thin frocks. So much trust, so much innocence . . .

Away across the windswept expanse of tarmac Harold Drummond can be spotted busy at the back of his car. Only his legs are visible. The rest of him is buried deep inside the boot as he hunts energetically for something mislaid. The scene is a familiar one, almost ritualistic, in fact. It's best not to look, yet in spite of everything he finds himself mouthing the words of the latest text Harold has pasted in a stripe across the breadth of his rear window. *Behold I Come Quickly*. He cannot really help it but for a moment it brings to mind those horrible framed inscriptions he caught sight of that day in that public house. Poor Harold.

Without delaying further he marches his little army briskly across the car-park and up the steps of the Thomas P. McGladdery Leisure Centre. A plaque above the double doors in expensive foreign marble commemorates the opening ceremony by a minor royal the previous year. The McGladderys still own most of the town. Old Daddy Tom, stern Sabbatarian and pillar of the established church, would surely rotate in his grave if he could see who was blithely tripping under his sculptured profile at this moment.

Up until a few months ago the swings in the park were chained and padlocked on Sundays by council decree. The same religious curfew extended to most other things in the town, except in the stews close to the river still known as the Dardanelles, where the godless elements proliferate. The Market Bar, incidentally, happens to be down there. But then the terrible abomination occurred, the unthinkable, oh woe, oh woe. Some English civil servant from the department responsible for financing the upkeep as well as the building of the Centre ordained it should be open to the public all seven days of the week. The town still doesn't seem to have recovered from the shock and shame of it. The swings and roundabouts have long since had their shackles struck off. This place, too, stands invitingly open, yet no one ever appears to come except for a few tattooed, Waterside roughs with their rolled-up towels.

Now, as he stands just inside the entrance ushering in the last of the stragglers, the man in the American suit experiences a quiet moment of satisfaction. The occasion represents, surely, something of a small victory over those who would despise and even try to hamper him and his work. Not just shades of that old tyrant, either, outlined in veined Italian marble above his head, but all those others, too, still alive and very much in control of things. Staring back at him now from the reflecting glass of the door he sees someone who cuts a romantic figure – a subversive, even, boldly courageous in his mission against closed minds and moneyed hypocrisy. Once again that day a rush of love for his loyal little band sweeps over him.

"Good, good, good," he catches himself murmuring. "Fine, fine, fine," like some proud parent.

They come to an open hatch let into the bare, plastered wall and leaning on the sill gazing out at them is a young bottle-blonde with heavy graveyard make-up. She's chewing with a doped expression on her face while her Walkman hisses on a high and steady note as if recording the activity *inside* her brain instead of the other way round. She also looks as though she might well be waiting for her tough friends from the Waterside to show up.

At the changing-rooms they go their separate ways except for the relatives in the party who continue on up some concrete stairs leading to the raked seating-area overlooking the pool. However – and this is most odd – the moment he himself sets foot in that long, white, tiled basement room with its row of hand-basins and facing cubicles like horse-boxes, because of their lopped-off doors, he feels inexplicably ill at ease. His four male companions look at him in silence. They're waiting for him to carry them through the next stage, he knows that, but suddenly he finds he isn't up to it. The place smells of something strongly citrous, masking the deeper reek of disinfectant. There's also more than a passing whiff of overripe cheese even though no one, as yet, has started to remove their socks and shoes. Catching sight of himself in one of the mirrors he concludes that he's looking decidedly shifty, that old impostor at a loss for words returned to haunt him once again.

One of the youths, Wendell by name, is seized by a sudden choking fit. He has flaming red hair and a great knob of Adam's apple. Rushing to one of the basins, he ducks, drinking rapidly from the tap, and the brutal sound immediately releases the tension.

"Lord, Lord, look kindly down on our little undertaking here today," their leader intones rapidly and smoothly, finding his voice at last. "Set thy sacred seal of approval on everything connected with this place and its ceremonial use by those of us about to be washed by the deep-cleansing Power of the Blood . . ."

It is something he can turn on as easily as that tap over there, while his listeners stand transfixed, eyes closed, faces piously frozen. *Just see how easy it is to turn people to stone*. Even more shaming, his mind seems bent now in some horrible way on what is taking place next door. A muffled outbreak of giggling is to be heard and as if on cue a rush of images – scents, too – assails him as he babbles on faster, faster. *My God, and to think I was so ready to accuse that caretaker earlier of this same sort of filth.*

"Amen." Finally he manages it. Amen. Such a tremendously useful word. On this occasion it carries him as far as the doorway itself. A quick palming of the air in blessing – or is it betrayal? – and he's free. The door bangs at his back. As it does so there comes a renewed burst of girlish glee from the adjacent changing-room. For the first time, really, he takes in that dainty silhouette fastened to the wood. She looks distinctly coquettish up there in her little crinoline, as if daring him to enter, join in the fun. He stands there a moment longer, then the caretaker and his grin come floating back to plague him.

Rapidly, purposefully, he walks off in the direction of the outside air and the car-park. By the time he gets back, hopefully, he will have the changing-room to himself. And so indeed it turns out. Everything, in fact, so far has gone – *is* going swimmingly. Forgive him his little jokes, Lord . . .

> "Thousands stand today in sorrow,
> Waiting at the pool,
> Saying they will wash tomorrow,
> Waiting at the pool."

The strains of the old redemption hymn rise up like – incense, he is about to say, but the word is an affront. No, something pure, innocent, like early mist, perhaps. That way it had of smoking upwards off the surface of the river on those summer mornings from his childhood. Melting to invisibility. Just as the sound now seems to do before it reaches the high vaulted ceiling and its exposed beams. Everything is like that, raw, unadorned. Tile, glass, steel, concrete, even the little timber there is, appear unfinished. He warms to the look and feel of it all. It's only a dream as yet but when his own church becomes reality – he sees the tent as merely a temporary phase – this is how he imagines it to be.

The site is already promised. A grass-domed hill a mile outside town. Like all such places it is reputed to have been an early settlement and burial mound, a fairy thorn allowed to grow on the summit untouched and solitary like some misshapen, indigenous *bonsai*. According to hearsay their roots jealously cradle ancient bones. He grew up half-believing those dark, old tales. On the spot where that pagan shrub stubbornly writhes will rise his own symbolic burning bush in the shape of a clean, well-lighted house of worship where voices will lift and testify. As now.

> "Others step in, left and right,
> Wash their stainèd garments bright,
> Leaving you in sorrow's night,
> Waiting at the pool."

The McClung sisters, Freda, Joanne and young Renée, gently fluttering their tambourines like hand-held haloes, sing sweetly to Darren Dougan's accompaniment. A serious youth, who lives for his music, he crouches over his Yamaha keyboard while a little red eye winks on, off, off, on, monitoring the sound-level. They're lucky to have his services, for he does bring something very professional and stylish to all their proceedings. Now, as the final chorus of the grand old spiritual rings out across the watery expanse, he segues into a tasteful rendering of "Shall We Gather at the River?"

For the man standing at the shallow end dressed in white from head to toe it's a moment that comes close to perfection. By his side Harold Drummond waits, similarly attired – spotless cricketing shirt, trousers, tennis socks. *Socks?* His own feet are bare. It seems only fitting, a touch of humility, with the obvious Biblical precedent as well. But obviously not to Harold. Together now they climb down into the still pool. A strong smell of chlorine is stirred up by their passage. When both are positioned about a dozen paces or so out and up to their thighs facing the short, gleaming, metal ladder he extends his arms slowly and dramatically.

"Except a man be born of water and the Spirit, he cannot enter the kingdom of God."

It's their pre-arranged signal for the first of the group to emerge, blinking and nervous, on to the tiled apron. Harold wades forward to assist the girl into the water, a stout farmer's daughter with blonde braids. She lowers herself with a panicky expression on her face as though she might well screech at the moment of impact. Momentarily her ankle-length dress balloons then falls straight and weighted, absorbing moisture like the wick in a lamp. The man watches all of this avidly. He can't help but register the outline of her wetted underthings, and when she turns about in the water to face him it's hard to drag his eyes away from the now clearly defined mound of her sex. At the same instant he also realizes his associate is wearing what appear to be patterned red and white boxer shorts. *Oh, Harold, Harold . . .*

They take hold of one bare, freckled arm apiece. Her name is Myrtle, she whispers, as though begging them to be gentle with her. Myrtle Gault. He smiles reassuringly, squeezing the soft, yielding flesh as he does so. She gives off a baby smell, milk and sap and perfumed sweat.

"With the blessing and full authority of the Church of God The Redeemer, and your own willing consent in the matter, Myrtle, I now baptize you in the name of the Father, the Son and the Holy Ghost."

And inhaling deeply, as if it's they who are about to be immersed and not this sturdy farm girl, they thrust her under. He and Harold, they strain as one, legs splayed to gain purchase on the floor of the pool for now quite suddenly it's a dead weight they're handling. No matter how many times he does this the shock of it always catches him unprepared, this startling transformation to inert mass. For him it's the worst moment of the whole business – he has never discussed it with Harold. Below in the water between them as the seconds stand still they seem to be holding a lifeless thing. That's how it strikes him. And nothing can dislodge the feeling.

An occasion a year or more ago may have something to do

with it. Again the participant was a woman, not quite so young this time, but grossly overweight. Because of it they nearly came to grief. Nothing could have prepared him for that terrible, dragging pull. Something seemed bent on taking the two of them down with her as in some grotesque parody of the sacrament itself. God forgive him, but each time he feels he's been involved in an act of violence of some kind – people have been known to stain themselves – and, indeed, when they do bring the girl up streaming and he touches her on the forehead, once, she jerks in their arms as though she's been given an electric shock. Her eyelids roll upwards, her mouth falls open, the rest of her goes limp. Harold is giggling. It affects him that way, he's noticed.

"Hallelujah!" he calls out now. "Hallelujah!"

And his cry is taken up by those watching the proceedings from the tiered seats. One of the women is weeping, a handkerchief pressed to her mouth. She looks like a sister, certainly not a mother.

Together, he and Harold, they navigate their waterlogged craft towards the edge of the pool where someone is waiting with an outstretched towel. For his part he feels drained, legs quivering a little with a life of their own like a runner's after a hard race. The warm ripples lap groin-high as he steers for the ladder, the sensation vaguely pleasurable in an unsettling way, not strictly appropriate for the occasion.

As they hoist the girl's dripping bulk up the rungs to the relative above, the great, globed behind brushes his cheek, all that young, lusty blood-heat leaping to meet him in the instant. Perhaps, he thinks, some transforming miracle has taken place underwater after all, something generated, an exchange of energy. He is merely the conduit for whatever power is discharged at the moment of contact. At such times he imagines himself as a scientist might, cool, dispassionate observer of the results of what he has merely set in motion.

Swathed in a bath towel, the girl is ushered off to the changing-room. It's as though she's never been, the water flat and still as before. The organ ventures a hesitant, muted rumbling away at the deep end, Darren's brave attempt to bridge the moment, for the next person hasn't appeared. Harold and he stand waiting, waist-deep, like a couple of those Highland cattle in that picture he has sat facing so often in so many parlours, and he suspects with much the self-same look of stunned stupefaction about them as well.

Then the youth named Wendell does appear, he who was so nervous earlier. He hangs in the opening beyond which lies the shallow, water-filled moat through which everyone must wade. His thin, white cotton trousers are skimpy beyond belief, laughably so, and his great, bare, bony feet and ankles bluish with the chill of their compulsory dip in disinfectant. All eyes are trained on this spectacle and the man in the pool glances up in spite of himself at the watchers for some sign of hilarity. What does he see, then, but a file of strangers making their way along the top tier of seats. Only they're not completely unknown, are they, this silent procession of young people in their soiled T-shirts, mutilated jeans and concentration-camp haircuts. Unfortunately he recognizes them far too well. *But what can they be doing here, and at this time?* Surely it was agreed the pool should be kept strictly private until he and his flock had completed their business. Kissick the caretaker had made that clear. More accurately, he had made that clear to Kissick.

Then, as though to clear up this mystery, the boiler-suited hero himself emerges from his underground lair at the back of the diving-boards. He leans against a pillar, grinning, a life-belt in his hand, and a look passes between him and the teenagers in the gallery that cries out *collusion*. At least it appears that way to the man up to his middle in the pool.

"My friends, let me remind you once again of John's crucial message as contained in the Gospels. I baptize you with water, he told his followers, but One who comes after me shall baptize you with the Holy Ghost and with fire. You all have that choice, dear friends, and even if you don't take up the first option here today, I beg of you to consider it most seriously in the near future, for your eventual salvation."

And he scans those closed young features up above under the roof, not for any trace of contrition, never would he be that gullible, but for the tell-tale grin, the nudge, the hand over the mouth. Instead, they stare back at him, hard-eyed. Like a jury, it comes to him.

"Now! Now!" he calls out in something of a panic to the waiting suppliant, and Wendell, equally affected, stumbles forward to take hold of the curving metal of the ladder. Harold, meanwhile, is staring sideways at him as if he's not himself, and the poor fool may be right, such a rage consumes him now. Most of it is inwardly directed, but enough is left over for him to yearn to be able to call down just this once some form of retribution – heavenly napalm is what he has in mind – on those cropped heads and their owners for daring to outface him in this way.

Taking their great redheaded gawk by the wrists they lower him into the pool, not quite so lovingly this time, he's bound to admit. Harold is a little rough, too, it strikes him, but for a different reason, reserving, as he always does, his gentler side for the womenfolk. They tow the trembling youth out into deeper water. He looks at them both as though they might be intent on a drowning between them and, indeed, when the sacramental words are said over him and he goes under, a moment of suspension occurs almost as though they might be holding him there longer than is safe simply because their minds are elsewhere. In his case he can't help himself, a part of him still painfully attuned for some movement, a change of expression, a sound, from those young wretches sitting aloft in judgement on him.

Then he hears Harold hiss, "Pastor! Pastor!" and below in the water a single, fat bubble forms, followed by a glistening string of smaller ones raggedly coiling out and upwards from their victim's open mouth. *Victim*, he thinks wonderingly to himself. *Dear God*. And they hoist the gasping creature up and out into the air.

Suddenly contrite, he touches that poor inflamed brow to make amends. These are his flock, after all, pitiful, even laughable though they may appear to certain people. He's thinking, of course, of the delinquents in their cock-loft still watching events in silence. *But why are they that way? What are they waiting for?* It makes him very uneasy. May God forgive him, but it also makes him eager in some perverse way to race through the remaining three or four names on the afternoon's roster, impatient for the moment of reckoning to arrive.

Poor Wendell is helped up the ladder faster than he came down. Still in a shocked state he makes his way back alone, cold and dripping, to the changing-room with no one to help him or offer a dry towel. One of those lost souls who turn up every so often at the tent services, he seems to have no kith or kin or connection of any sort with the locality. And as he disappears through the opening to paddle sadly back through the disinfectant one last time that day, he might just as well be vanishing from their lives for ever.

But now his place is taken by someone very different, someone who looks as if she may have arrived to redress the balance. A woman in her middle years stands there, feet apart, sturdy, beaming. She has an immediate effect on those sitting in the lower rows for they break out in smiles at the sight of her, while one or two clap their hands. The organ joins in the joyful mood and Harold, too, seems elated.

"It's Rose," he whispers, adding as if to a slow child, "You know, Rose, the lollipop lady. Outside the infants' school in Castle Street?"

And, of course, he does recognize her then despite the absence of the yellow oilskins, the man's cap, peak back to front, the all-year-round wellingtons. She looks scrubbed and virginal like one of her own charges at bedtime fresh from a bath instead of about to take one as she is now, and suddenly his mood lifts. They move forward to receive her. The scent of lavender greets them. He notices also the fanned ends of her hair have been crimped with old-fashioned tongs in that same way his own mother used on hers.

"The Lord loves you, Rose," he tells her. "And so do we." And he means it sincerely.

Between them she half-crouches in the shallows as if she might strike out on her own in some awkward and long-forgotten stroke. He remembers country people from his youth who had that same way of embracing the water as though it might betray them.

"Let the Saviour wash away your sins. If you believe in Him, then they will fall from you as easily as drops of water. You do believe, don't you, Rose?" He really doesn't need to ask, the answer is plainly there to see.

From that point onwards everything seems to swing into focus, just the way, in fact, he had imagined it would be. The light from outside streams down as from an arranged source enclosing all the participants in its broad beam. Harold and he work effortlessly within that bright expanse of water in a mood of controlled fervour. Both feel energized. Every so often they glance, grinning across at one another like a couple of conspirators. He has the clearest image possible of the water acting as conductor for their own dynamism, ripples of the stuff spreading, spreading, so that not one soul in the place remains untouched by it. For some reason he has completely forgotten the watchers under the rafters. The caretaker, too, no longer seems a threatening presence. On the contrary, he appears to have a serious, even thoughtful look about him now.

47

After Rose comes a man of much the same age, a bachelor farmer, with his elderly mother in attendance. He flails the water with sinewy arms still burned black from last year's fierce summer. They can feel him putting up a hard fight under water, but he's no real match for the combined power of the Lord and their zeal.

"*Hallelujah!*" he cries, spouting like a whale on reaching the air. "*I'm washed in the Blood of the Lamb!*"

"*Hallelujah!*" they echo, and the sound seems to expand to fill the glassed-in dome high above their heads. This place will never see another day like this, it strikes the man holding the streaming convert. *How can it ever be the same again, for between us we have filled it with the breath of the Holy Spirit, purifying, sanctifying.* And he has a sudden and startling image of himself doing the same thing all across the country in the most unlikely of settings, billiard-halls and bingo parlours, football pitches and fair-grounds, oddest, yet most appealing of all, for some curious reason, the open deck of one of those weekend pleasure-boats carrying its complement of trippers, many the worse for drink, across the immensely broad, flat waters of Lough Neagh, a matter of only a few miles away. Incidentally, their very own inland Galilee. That is something which had never really struck him before, and he rejoices in the sudden gift of it.

"Just one more to go."

It's Harold, close by his side, and looking strained for some reason but, then, perhaps, this day's work has taken it out of him. He's young, after all, hasn't learned as yet how to channel his energies in a controlled manner. When he started out his own legs would almost buckle under him with undischarged tension, a seepage building up, it often seemed to him, something dark and deadly like the poisonous lees at the bottom of a barrel. Some of that still does affect him, the sweats and the headaches, the direct consequence, almost certainly, but he has conditioned himself to keep them at bay, at least until he has found a darkened room in which to lie down. His own mother would rest in that same way, a vinegar-soaked rag laid flat across her temples. It may have had more to do with her time of the month, he sees that now with adult hindsight, but still he can't quite rid himself of the idea that the pull of blood cannot be ruled out. He likes to think of something long-buried and forgotten in the hereditary line putting forth a late shoot in himself, even if it isn't exactly something to be thrilled or proud about.

"It's the girl I told you about earlier. She asked to be our last one today."

"So where is she, then?"

It's hard to keep irritation out of his voice. Already some of the people by the fringes of the pool are glancing at their watches and moving restlessly around in the hard, shallow, plastic wells of their seats.

"Has she brought no one with her?"

He's beginning to realize now he should have organized this whole affair himself instead of leaving it to the man up to his fly-buttons beside him in the water.

"She's a special case. I meant to tell you. Truly a lost lamb. Donna Brady. From the Riverside."

A premonition of something disastrous waiting to happen is forming within like ice. The water, too, seems much colder suddenly. Harold is avoiding his eye.

"Harold," he hisses, "who is this girl?"

"She's, she's – "

But the revelation remains unspoken, unguessed at, for in the doorway she appears now, this mystery from the slums, standing there barefoot and pathetic – really, it's the only word – and glancing all about her like a sacrificial victim.

Much later he is to recreate this precise moment, trying to freeze not only the image but also his instant reaction to that first sighting of someone who is to change everything for him and his life in such a catastrophic way. It's to become something of a torment.

But all of that is in the future now, and he looks and sees someone in a plain white dress, someone ordinary in every sense except for her fierce red hair. It brings to mind a particular shade of autumn, that last almost violent flaring of colour, always one bush at the heart of other quieter-toned clumps which draws, then shocks the eyes. Just as now, because there is definitely a sudden mood of suspense in the air.

Up under the roof even the uninvited visitors seem more intent. The seven – four boys and three girls – although it's hard to tell much difference, lean sharply forward, while the one he takes to be their leader has risen from his own seat, strongly gripping the back of the one in front. An intensely freckled youth with faded blue tattoos disfiguring both forearms, he has a fuzz of russet hair not so very unlike that of the girl who stands below. She looks directly up at him for some reason, thin and nervous as a reed in her simple white shift, and the man in the water has a sudden unexplained rush of feeling for this young, oddly sexless creature hesitating on the wet tiles. He finds the urge to capture her attention all for himself quite overpowering.

Arms outstretched, he cries, "The Lord calls you, Donna! Whatever you do, don't keep him waiting, Donna, for only he is able to wash your sins until they be whiter than the driven snow!" Even though it must be plain to everyone that this shivering innocent has nothing to confess or feel contrite about.

"Come, Donna. Come."

Already how sweet the name sounds on his lips, in his ears. *Donna*.

Harold makes a jerky move forward in the direction of the ladder but he beats him to it, wading swiftly and surely ahead.

50

The girl edges a single step closer to the brink. Never has he felt stronger or more alert to his own powers. On he draws her with all the dominance at his command. Harold is right, he is thinking, truly she is a lost lamb, but now she is found, so praise the good Lord for leading this little one out of the darkness and into the light.

He can see her very clearly now. It's to be another of those instantaneous, flash-lit impressions to be stored away for future reference. Pain will be associated with it each time he recalls the moment. Even now there is an element of that same distress for him in the sight of that painfully thin figure with the white skin flecked a paler shade of the same carrot colour as her hair. She has large greyish-green eyes and a smallish mouth, with lips on the thin side. About fourteen years or thereabouts, he's prepared to hazard, a child, or one just about to leave that behind for he sees she's wearing a cheap chain about one slim ankle. Somehow, the sight of that tawdry gold filament jars the image the man in the water has formed in his mind of someone so artless, so virginal. An old prejudice, one he had forgotten he'd even possessed, comes to recall, about the sort of women reputed to wear such things. Still, he puts it out of his mind as rapidly as it arrives. This poor child must truly be alone in the world if there's no one to advise her about such things.

"Take my hand. Don't be afraid. Jesus is your friend, Donna."

The words are for her ears only. They are now only a yard or so apart. She has, he notices for the first time, a mole the size and colour of a penny-piece on the soft, vulnerable flesh of one upper arm. By now she's right up to the ladder, yet still she keeps on shooting glances up at those seats and their occupants in the topmost row. *Why?*

"Almost there, Donna, almost there."

He stretches out a hand and takes hers in his. It's throbbing, hot as fire. The silence in the entire place is profound. Even the murmuring organ has shut down. She twists her body awkwardly, reluctant to let go of his hand, backing, backing, in her agonizing descent. He finds he's mouthing sounds barely intelligible, meant to reassure. Her left foot, the one with the chain, touches the water first. Reaching out, he places a palm, butterfly-light, on her flank because he fears he might very well lose her at this crucial point. Then she sighs, surrendering to the embrace of the water.

"Come," he tells her, taking the thin wrists and beginning the slow and loving tow out into deeper parts. As he does so he's also trying to manoeuvre her around so that she no longer faces the watchers in the gallery, those silent ones, but, strangely, she resists him.

Harold edges into the picture now, causing a minor swell that laps briefly about all three of them. He grabs the girl's hand and for a second she looks at him oddly in startled fashion. She glances between the two of them like someone caught up in a contest of some kind. *Tug of love* is the phrase that floats into the man's head for some reason, that current expression that seems to be in all the papers.

His mind seems to be full of the oddest of distractions. And he finds he's irritated still, in spite of himself, by the girl's continued attention to the upper gallery instead of on what should really concern her down here. An expression of almost paralysed dread is on her upturned face.

He looks quickly across at Harold to signal his intentions. Harold returns his glance while shifting his grip on that pale young stem of an arm.

He starts to intone, "In the name of the Father, the Son and the Holy – " when an object flashes through the air landing dully in the water just a dozen feet away. At first he takes it for something that has fallen from the roof and missed them – God be praised – some structural component loosened by a workman's carelessness.

The thing itself is metallic, it catches the light, but why does it float as it does, half-submerged, in that odd way? He peers more closely at it. Bobbing gently, the burnished cylinder drifts towards him, coquettishly, almost, presenting a concave base for his attention. *Dear God*, he thinks to himself, *it's a beer-can*, as if his brain has gone into slow motion. *A full, unopened can of beer!*

And at that point the expression on the girl's face finally brings home to him the full enormity of what is taking place at his back. An animal roaring has broken out high above, made more terrifying by its very wordlessness. The girl's eyelids begin fluttering faster. He feels her turning to dead matter in his grasp. Harold, meanwhile, has a look of stupefied panic about him. Thrusting him aside and encircling the young waist before the rest of her goes under he manages to wrest her about and to him, away at last from the sight of her tormentors.

More beer-cans start striking the water, mostly empty, he notes, the surface dotted with them, a bizarre flotilla of crushed and glinting metal seemingly as light as paper. At the far end of the pool he sees the caretaker Kissick racing for the stairs. The grin has gone from his face – forever, judging by the expression of disquiet now in its place.

He hears himself shout, "*The Lord won't forget this – and neither will I!*" realizing with some shock his words are directed at the man in the boiler-suit and not the baying pack ranged along the back of the gallery.

The redhead is leaping up and down on top of his seat like an orang-utan, face contorted. He hurls yet another clenched beer-can to join the collection in the water, paying no heed to the man racing up the concrete ramp towards him.

Far below, in what has turned out to be a watery arena of the worst sort, the preacher clutches the target of all this wrath to his chest. *Why?* he asks himself, *why?* rocking gently in what he hopes is a comforting motion. *What can a poor, palpitating creature such as this have done to bring down such a barrage of rage?* But the question seems irrelevant suddenly, given the urgency of the situation. For the first time he realizes he has forgotten the rest of the people there, despite their presence at eye level. Most of them look as bewildered as Harold does, up to his waist and with his mouth hanging open like some stupid cur. *Useless*, he thinks. *A broken reed.* Then, startlingly, the girl speaks, barely a murmur, really, lips close to his shoulder.

"Save me, Pastor, please save me."

For the tiniest moment in his confused state the man holding her fast believes she means it in the scriptural sense, the very reason for her presence here this day, after all.

"Please don't let them get me, please, mister. Promise me. Promise."

Her voice with its thin, slum-dweller's whine comes as something of a shock. He realizes he must have conjured up a very different intonation for her in keeping with the romantic projection in his head, but nothing can take away from the powerful desire he has to protect this waif from her foes. Fixing a look of defiance on the redheaded villain of the piece sidling almost nonchalantly now along the row with his followers in train, that same look, it seems to the man in the water, is returned with a vengeance. *Unfinished business*, it says clearly, *unfinished business*.

Kissick by now has reached the top of the steps. Dishevelled and panting heavily, he looks his age, heart no longer in the chase. Aware that he poses no real threat to them – no one in the place does – his tormentors laugh as they leap-frog down over the backs of the raked seats. A row or two from the front they all file smartly to the right kicking the chairs in front on their merry way.

Clenched fists raised high, they break into a parting hooligan chant, "*Here we go, here we go, here we go!*" the sound lingering like the throb of a wound long after they have disappeared from the building.

Everyone is looking down at the man in the water still clasping the girl to him in her soaked white dress. It's like holding a young animal, he's thinking to himself. She's murmuring something he can't quite catch. It sounds like, "Our Damian is the worst. I can't go home," something like that, but no alarm bells ring as they should and would have done if he weren't so smitten by these powerful, new feelings raging through him. All his senses are at full stretch.

Gazing about, he notices, for instance, that the water in the pool seems to have changed colour and quite dramatically at that. Then he sees that the sun in its slow descent is level now with the lowest line of windows and that ruddy tint flooding the surface is merely a trick of the light. But is it? Without altering his hold on the girl, he cries out, "*Blood!*" repeating it a couple of times more for good measure.

"The Lamb of God spilled his own precious blood so that we might be born again under its deep, cleansing power. Like this young person you see before you here. Some have tried today to make a mockery of our sacrament, our sacrament of *blood*, friends," and here he dabbles a hand in the water just in case the connection hasn't struck home.

"But I tell you these godless ones will not prevail. They have failed in their mission of desecration, routed by a Power far greater than anything they or their puny imaginations could ever hope to comprehend. Never fear, friends, the good Lord will deal with them in his own way. Never you fear."

And he smiles reassuringly at them sitting there. They stare back with dulled eyes. Then a woman in a cerise-coloured hat and a tight, punishing two-piece stands up. She has a small child with her and, jerking it to its feet, she walks angrily off in the direction of the exit doors. Another woman follows her, another and another, then they all seem to be heading off in a mass exodus.

55

"Friends!" he calls out after them. "Friends, the work of the Lord isn't finished yet! One lost lamb remains to be saved! Look! Here she is, friends! *Here!*"

But his words no longer have any effect. Even the youth with the organ has unplugged his instrument by now. And the caretaker, too, is busy trawling for beer-cans along the lip of the poolside as though his life and job depend on it. He has the grace to keep his head lowered while he manoeuvres his straining net along the scuppers.

Still gripping the girl to him like a dancing partner the man in the water turns his head to look for Harold. He sees he has managed to get himself off into a far corner of the pool, his back jammed against the tiles, half-crouching and with a hangdog expression on his face that says it all. No support can be expected from that quarter.

"Donna," he murmurs to the child in his arms, "put your trust in the Lord and the Power of His Redeeming Blood. Believe in him and no one can harm you. I give you my solemn word on that. You do believe me, don't you, Donna?"

Looking up at him out of those sea-green eyes of hers that would melt the hardest heart she whispers, "Oh, Pastor Gilchrist, I do. I surely do."

And, barely bothering with the words or the form of the rite, he plunges her under rapidly and cleanly. Hands crossed on her young bosom she comes up streaming like a figure-head.

"Your new life begins here," he tells her. "And I will be by your side, no matter what," little realizing just how fateful the consequences of those words are to be for them both.

THREE

Towards the end of September the weather took a sudden, unexpected turn for the worse. High in his apartment block Gilchrist looked down on the Avenida Montemar and its streaming palm-trees. His balcony was sheltered by the one above and he would sit in a cane chair among the dying plants inherited from the previous occupant listening to the hiss of tyres far below. He had entered an inert phase, barely moving from bed to balcony and back again, with occasional forays to the tiny kitchen and bathroom.

The couple directly overhead, retired, with a champagne-pink poodle whose nails clattered as busily as castanets on the tiled floors, were house-bound as well. Guzman was the name on the battery of bellpushes in the tomb-like vestibule. They came from the distant capital, but how he had picked up something like that he had no conception, just as he also knew they were resented like all *madrileños* in this part of the deep South. She was a short, dumpy, unsmiling woman with hair dyed the same rosy tint as her beloved Pepe. The husband appeared to have no name, for it was Pepe this, and Pepe that, as her high heels echoed the lighter, more excitable tattoo of the dog's across the ringing terrazzo.

At night their television roared but, then, so did everyone else's, police sirens and bursts of gunfire punctuating the harsh, dubbed tones of the actors. Everything in this language, it occurred to him, was twice as loud and urgent as in his own.

Stetched on his bed, or out on the balcony, listening to the rain, he experienced the full force of being a stranger in a strange land. It was as though this enforced captivity along with everyone else in the ten-storeyed block only served to heighten the feeling of being anonymous, invisible. For the briefest of moments he caught himself missing the small country town he had fled. His own people were neighbourly by instinct, he reminded himself, involved in one another's lives. They were also soft-spoken and smiled frequently as they conversed on the street or in the shops. He permitted himself his customary little weep then as the rain fell like stair-rods beyond the open mouth of the balcony.

On the opposite side of the Avenida a new building was rising. Each morning with the hot sun came the clamour of picks, hammers, shovels and drills filling the apartment the instant he pulled back the sliding glass screens. It became a source of wonderment to him that such flimsy materials could frame such an impressively solid-looking block, for plainly that was what it was destined to be, a reflection of his own. The bricks were mere husks of baked clay, honeycombed, light as air, but it was the scaffolding the men were using which somehow disturbed him most, for those misshapen billets, hewn straight from the hillside by the look of them and not much taller than the workers, looked only fit for the bonfire. He would sit watching the Moroccan labourers in their woolly hats swarm over the structure handling these well-worn props while somewhere a transistor whined eerily, non-stop music from the facing continent. Above their heads he was able to make out a broad ribbon of the Mediterranean.

Today it had disappeared but he could imagine it still out there somewhere lashed to a khaki-coloured broth.

As the building rose so his view of the sea diminished. Just how high the block would eventually go was a question he asked himself, how long before that distant stripe of ultra-marine narrowed to a ruled feint and, then, one day – nothing. It wasn't really a major worry as far as he was concerned because he had no intention of settling in this place, but he did sense his neighbours cared passionately. Their voices told him so as he listened and watched them pointing across the way. The language they spoke still meant little to him but inflection and gestures did, increasingly so. After a day spent reading faces as well as shop signs his eyes would ache from the strain of simply *looking*.

Through the falling curtain of rain he continued to study the raw, dripping shell opposite. What he could see was some-thing which might just as easily be a building half-demolished instead of the direct opposite. The effect, oddly enough, was identical. The outer, facing walls were not in place as yet, but, exposed to the world was a series of bare lime-washed cells with wires hanging down in which people soon would sleep, eat, make love, laugh, quarrel, even sit staring out, solitary, just as he was doing right at this moment.

He couldn't help remembering another building at home on the main street that really *was* being torn down and how all its pathetic little secrets kept hidden up to then were suddenly opened up for everyone to see. Rotting scraps of carpet and old lino, wallpaper in patterns not seen for a century or more, fire grates barely the size of a bird's nest, ancient bell-pulls, even pictures left crazily hanging, all waited for the breaker's ball to come and put an end to their shame.

Here that process was travelling much too fast. The proof was staring at him. And people couldn't cope. He saw it in their faces, that jittery look which said *faster, faster, ever faster* or be buried under concrete as another apartment block went up. Already the one across the way had its name on a painted board. Los Alamos. The Poplars. But where were they? Still in their plastic tubs, most likely. In spite of everything he had to laugh, feeling a sermon coming on.

"Living on the shore,
I'm living on the shore,
I'm living where the healing waters flow."

Then he sang "Homeward Bound For Glory", "Honey In The Rock", "Who Shall Roll the Stone Away?", and finally "Crimson Waters". Throughout the recital the dog upstairs ceased its restless pattering. The instant he finished, however, it began a mournful howling as though the music had somehow pierced through to something deeply elemental in that canine breast.

Out on his balcony Gilchrist listened to the sound. The rain hissed past mere feet away gaining force until it struck the torn crowns of the palms far below. He couldn't really sink all that much further, he told himself, reduced to a congregation of one and a neurotic pink-rinsed poodle at that. Once more he felt elated by the sheer absurdity of what had entered his head.

So, he thought, *so*, and going through to the living-room and into the kitchen beyond – it had a lingering, sickish, sweet smell which came from the butane cylinder – he found a large refuse sack in a cupboard under the sink. Into it he proceeded to pitch all the cheap plastic pots with their dead plants that lined the balcony. Nothing could ever call those back to life again even if he wanted to, and so he continued in this fashion going through the entire apartment systematically disposing of everything that was ugly, depressing or useless to his needs. The olive-green bag bulged satisfyingly, the colour reminding him somehow of England. He decided his predecessor must have brought it from there. The name on the contract papers he had signed was Peploe. Robert James Peploe.

60

Finally he tightened a length of string about the gathered neck and placed it in the centre of the living-room floor where he stood contemplating its squat contours. It was almost as though a weight had been taken from him and transferred to that glistening, swollen bundle.

He couldn't help recalling what used to be known at his tent-meetings as the Sin-Bin. At his urging people would come forward with various personal objects which they would drop into the open mouth of a big plastic container. It was something he had picked up on his trip to the States that time, for the Bible Belt was a fertile source of such gimmicks, many of which, he had to admit, he had embraced all too avidly. Quite often at the end of those services under canvas when everyone had left he had longed to discover drugs, weapons, items of pornography, stolen goods, perhaps. Sadly, the haul was always much tamer than that. Cigarettes, matches, a packet of Rizla papers, a betting-slip, lipsticks, a silver ring, once a pair of women's panties, but of a large size and certainly far from sheer or even see-through, his catch was hardly one to get excited about.

In the apartment above the dog was restlessly quartering its confines again. Why didn't they get its nails clipped? There was an actual poodle-parlour less than a block away adjacent to a hairdressing salon used by the pets' owners. The assistants in both establishments wore identical smocks in palest magenta. As he passed by he was struck by the similarity in the clientèle, a kind of beady-eyed self-absorption as the sleek, pomaded girls ministered to their upright charges.

The sight of the bag squatting in the middle of the room like that was beginning to bother him. He knew if he sat here long enough allowing it to assert its presence it might easily become a fixture. He had a raincoat hanging in the hallway – it was the first time he'd worn it since he'd left home – so, draping it about his shoulders in that way he'd seen these continentals

61

do, he left the apartment lugging the weighted sack behind him. It created barely a whisper on the polished marble of the corridor, which suited him, because for some reason he felt guilty as though at any moment a door might suddenly open and someone would be standing there to berate him for something he hadn't known he'd done in a language he couldn't understand.

When he backed out of the lift downstairs dragging his burden and traversed the melancholy lobby – its tiny bulbs burned feebly day as well as night – he discovered that the rain was beginning to slacken off. Already a patch of pale nursery blue lightened the sky beyond the glass doors with a promise of more to come.

A fierce odour of vegetation hung in the outer air. The trunks of the trees, rearing straight up out of the flower-beds, glistened, running with moisture. Normally they looked dry as elephant-hide and as he rounded a corner of the building he came upon the dog from upstairs squirting its own lemon-hued little contribution on to the base of one of these. Close by, fondly watching, stood his mistress. She was wearing a transparent plastic rain-outfit embellished with a daisy motif with hat and galoshes in the same material.

For a moment Gilchrist stood where he was. How had they managed to get down without his knowing? It was, he noted, *them*, as though the still-straining Pepe was equally redoubtable. Then the woman turned as if sensing his presence. It should have been the animal, of course, but he was far too preoccupied with his daily *pee-pee*. They faced one another, she, staring unashamedly, taking in his misshapen bundle, grotesque suddenly, as well as sinister, and he, smiling back, showing his teeth. He also raised his hat a fraction with his free hand, overcome by a powerful desire to say, "Sorry," for these people seemed to have that effect on one.

Instead, he heard himself murmur, "*Buenas tardes, señora,*" and to his great astonishment her face softened and she smiled, returning the greeting. It was the first words they had exchanged and a foolish joy filled him. He kept nodding like some tongue-tied emigrant who has used up his meagre vocabulary, which was close to the truth.

He and Señora Guzman – oh, the cosy familiarity of it, already – stood watching as darling Pepe finished relieving himself. A shiver passed over that curly pink pelt. He yawned deeply. His incisors were the colour of old bone-handled knives. He stretched each of his shaved rear legs in turn. A dear little dew-drop glistened at the tip of his woolly penis. Then he ambled off to inspect the bole of the next tree.

The lady from upstairs shrugged, spreading her palms, and he reciprocated as accurately as he could without letting the coat slide from his shoulders. *Ah*, she seemed to say, *we all have our little weaknesses, don't we?* and he was inclined to agree. It felt good to rejoin the human race once more, and when she went trotting off with a rueful smile to catch up with her pet he was experiencing a jauntiness he hadn't known for an age.

His mood would soar even further when the sack he was holding went from his possession. Observation had taught him rubbish here was simply left in the street, reasonably contained in plastic, of course, bins appearing never to have caught on. In the gutter at intervals clusters of these bags would appear as if by some curious, self-progenitive process, for never once had he seen anyone adding to them. So mystifying was the whole business he had fallen into the habit of taking out his own refuse after dark. But now he felt confident enough to place his own green giant beside a little mound of the local, home-grown variety without fear of being challenged. And, indeed, why should he be? He had nothing to hide, and even if he had, his secrets were safe, encased as they were in stout English-made garden polythene. For an instant he thought of raked leaves, the reek and drifting smoke of autumn bonfies, and felt those old pangs of displacement again. Then his newfound cheerfulness re-asserted itself. Turning his back on his own personal sin-bin he walked off feeling lighter already in every sense.

He passed the Bar Valladolid with its scalloped orange awning where he often selected and ate from the excellent *tapas* displayed under glass. An army barracks was not far off and the family-run bar had become a second home for all those sad-faced young conscripts in coarse khaki. They had the same look about them as that goat-boy he had encountered that strange day out in the stony wastes beyond the bull-ring. A group of them was gathered now about the flashing fruit-machine as he went strolling past. It always struck him as curious they never seemed to laugh or raise their voices like others of their own age, not even when out of uniform, which made them even more impoverished in all that hideous, stone-washed denim. But they never bothered with him which was all that mattered as he sampled the *tortilla* or the Russian salad or, best of all, those little baby eels swimming in *vinaigrette*.

The rain had all but ceased by now and it was good to feel the newly released heat in the air intent on sucking up every last remaining trace of moisture. Soon it would be back to normal, sprinklers pulsing in the borders, with the tough, indigenous turf glittering like new-painted metal under the rays of the sun. The raincoat felt constricting about his shoulders, ostentatious, too, in a vaguely theatrical way, so he took it off and carried it over his arm. Buoyed up as he was he had no desire to draw attention to himself. Especially after what had occurred a week earlier.

One afternoon – it must have been by chance – he had strayed into the narrow, packed *calles* of the San Miguel quarter where the tourists came to window-shop.

As summer slid towards autumn, the year ageing noticeably now, so, also, did the visitors. Saga Holidays had entered its busy period and more and more pensioners were arriving to winter here. He saw them everywhere, heard the accents of Bradford, Liverpool, Glasgow, Birmingham, occasionally his own region, but that was rare, thank goodness. They moved around in groups or sat in the sea-front cafés, row upon row, like flocks of greying migrants. They left him feeling depressed and the more they carried on – some were incorrigibly sportive – the gloomier he became. But then, there but for the grace of God, he thought to himself, fiercely confident in his own uniqueness as always.

But that very pride was to suffer a serious blow that was to keep him indoors for some time away from the sight and sound of anyone who spoke English. His past caught up with him in those narrow streets, his guilty past. It happened in this way . . .

On his wanderings he had turned into an alleyway which branched at right-angles off the main thoroughfare. Here the shops seemed far from fashionable. Most were darkened caves piled high with haberdashery, kitchen goods or cheap shoes, presided over by some crone sitting motionless in twilit gloom. None of their wares interested him, he simply passed by barely registering their presence. A smell of suspect drains and rotting fruit hung in the air.

Several of those awful cats, large-eyed, skeletal, vaguely Egyptian-looking in feline terms, nosed about the gutters. He hated their hoarse cries and the way they followed you about. At such times he yearned to have his foot connect with one of them but was afraid to because of his foreignness. The locals mistreated most forms of animal life with almost cheerful callousness, but that was their custom not his. Already one of the sinister creatures had singled him out for attention. Dragging crippled hindquarters, it left off its half-hearted scavenging to come after him. He quickened his pace despite the clammy heat.

He had the alley to himself, but as he made towards the distant opening where streams of souvenir hunters pushed past, a couple unexpectedly broke away, heading in his direction. Stopping short he could hear himself wheezing. Or was it the cat? The sound certainly seemed to be coming from someone else. He also found he couldn't move, rooted there in the heart of that foul-smelling passageway.

The man and the woman were coming closer. He could see them both in chilling detail now. But had they spotted him? He knew he had to act quickly and decisively if that were not to happen. Ruling out direct flight, for that must surely draw their attention, he looked over at the nearest shop doorway. Women's underwear filled the window, an array of such astonishing profusion and intimacy he felt horrified merely glancing at it. Yet the die was cast. With the brim of his panama pulled down he sidled rapidly across the cobbles and into the dark interior. Sure enough an ancient grandmother was seated in the recess walled in by ceiling-high ramparts of cardboard boxes. They stared at one another.

Behind him he could hear the cat in the doorway. The noise it made could hardly be described as purring. That was much too cosy and domesticated a word. Instead it rasped terrifyingly like some asthmatic breathing his last. The old woman looked at the creature, then at him. For some reason he was beginning to feel responsible for the damned thing.

"*Qué? Qué? Qué?*" granny cawed in a hoarse voice and frantically he sketched something shameful in the air. All the while he kept listening for the sound of approaching footsteps. Sweat was breaking out on him. He swabbed his temples with his blue and white spotted handkerchief and the old woman eyed it suspiciously as though now he were semaphoring something even more unspeakable.

On a poster on the wall a ripe young brunette modelled a brassière and matching lace underthings. Gesturing in her direction – she continued to smile exclusively for him like all her kind – he croaked, "Pan-pan-pant-*ees*" like some breathless degenerate in the grip of his vice. And it came to him that if his two avenging angels could see and hear him at this moment all their worst suspicions would be realized. He could hear them quite plainly now, their footsteps distinct and separate, the man much more heavily-shod than the woman. Despite the heat he seemed to be wearing old-fashioned boots judging by the rasp of metal on the paving, a detail which only served to reinforce Gilchrist's deepest fears.

Keeping his back to the doorway he continued with his desperate mime, the hag on her kitchen chair offering no help whatsoever. She had lizard eyes and a mouth like a shrivelled purse. With murder in mind Gilchrist grimaced and gestured. The couple were not too far off. He kept listening for a word, a murmured aside, anything to torture himself further, but nothing was forthcoming, just that slow, steady, unhurried trek in his direction. They ambled like a couple of country people – but, then, he knew that to be true, didn't he?

The old woman must have grown tired of the dumb-show for she called out, "Dolores! Dolores!" and through a curtain at the rear of the shop appeared a young girl wiping her mouth on a paper napkin. She seemed to take in the situation at a glance or, perhaps, she had been spying through the curtain all along, for in very passable English she enquired, "Something for your wife, *señor*? Or . . . girlfriend?" and Gilchrist found himself blushing at the way she looked at him as she said it.

"For my niece," he insisted. "Niece. Some – some . . ." and once more he allowed his hands to complete the sentence. "About your size."

The girl propped a short metal ladder against the wall of cardboard and, mounting rapidly, pulled out one, two, three of the cartons leaving gaping holes in the edifice. She caught him glancing at her trim rear end as she did so – she was wearing skin-tight denim jeans, of course. This time she didn't bother to hide the smile on her face.

By now the boxes were gaping open on the counter, tissue paper peeled back from their contents for him to admire and, perhaps, fondle if he so desired. The two women watched him. It was hard to know which was worse, approaching nemesis in the alley outside, or the look on their faces, a look as old as time, sly, knowing, with more than a hint of derision. Or was all this just in his head? For some time he had convinced himself the entire female persuasion could detect the reek of guilt about him at twenty paces and was hell-bent on making him pay for his supposed crimes against their sex, specifically, one of their number whose young memory he was invoking at this moment.

"No, no, *niece*," he lied. "Schoolgirl – young – *young.*" *Why was he babbling in pidgin when the girl in the shop could understand English perfectly?*

"Fifteen," he persisted, palming the air thrice, and the instant he signalled that precise age group he knew his sins had truly found him out.

"Ah, *mujer joven*!" exclaimed this other teenager with a laugh, pouting and lowering her lashes in an obscene parody that made Gilchrist's blood run cold.

"School-*girl*, school-*girl*!"

The old lady, too, came briefly to life, cackling and exposing her ancient gums. The noise both were making drowned any sound from the street. Gilchrist edged further into the shadows away from the open doorway.

Grandma in her kitchen chair gave off a strong scent of aniseed, or it might have been liquorice. Two good old-fashioned remedies, whatever they were. His own handkerchief reeked of the oil of cloves he had been using for a troublesome tooth – he was much too terrified to seek out a Spanish dentist and all that might entail. He could smell the essence now in the narrow confines of the shop as he mopped his brow, a pungent, troubling aroma that brought back childhood, his mother treating them with rubs and inhalants that always seemed to burn, sting, or choke alarmingly.

By this time the girl had swept away the first selection of boudoir garments. He had been given a tantalizing glimpse of them nestling in their tissue like so much silken froth, and in their place now she unveiled for his tastes a very different set of items. Once more the two of them were eyeing him like a couple of conspiratorial madams as though urging him to handle, to sniff, even, and it was difficult to resist, for these it seemed to him were in the identical style *she* had favoured down to the tiny, sprig-like motif in pale blue worked into the soft cotton. He recalled how she would dutifully wash them out each night in that English boarding-house on the South Coast before getting into bed, laying them out to dry on the radiator or on a line above the bath. They always looked so touching, so virginal, hanging there. In the washstand mirror his own reflected face was that of a criminal, or so he told himself, if ever they were discovered, two runaways from an unforgiving past.

And as he bent now to inhale the always curiously moving odour of new cotton a shadow passed slowly across the doorway, a vengeful shadow which had followed him over a thousand miles from that same past to finally catch up with him. For a moment he held his breath, reconciled almost to being discovered up to his old tricks, but then the harsh sunlight came flooding back and the footsteps passed on.

Cash at the ready, he completed the transaction. God knows he didn't need to, for what use to him were two pairs of young girl's underpants? But there seemed no other way out of the shop. The women appeared disappointed at the brisk conclusion of all of this, and the younger one made an elaborate package of the items while grandma clucked advice. Impatient to be gone Gilchrist felt like snatching the soft, flat parcel out of the girl's hands but, finally, wrapped in paper patterned with pink fleurs de lys, it was handed over and murmuring a string of "*Grácias, grácias*" he lunged into the alleyway in the hope of catching a vanishing glimpse of his two mythical tormentors.

The street was deserted, save for the cat who waited patiently panting in the shade, ribcage fluttering. It turned its desperate yellow eyes on him but before it could get close he had set off up the alleyway at a rapid pace to lose himself among the passing crowds.

The experience had affected him badly and his mood remained nervous as he allowed himself to be swept along clutching a purchase he didn't want or need but which he couldn't bring himself to throw away. That would have meant a betrayal of some sort. Yet he couldn't explain it properly.

Back in the apartment behind closed doors, unwisely he unwrapped his little gift. Potency undiminished, there they lay folded neatly in softest tissue and, taking them up out of their nest and holding them to his face once more, he breathed in all of that rich, pure newness which was like a drug to him in his state, opening up memory as well as old wounds. He was thinking of the girl again and the way the water in the baptism pool that day had so cruelly outlined her thin young form. He also remembered the heat from that unformed body almost feverish to the touch. Some of that same fever still ran in his own blood despite all his efforts at self-healing.

At this point he wept a little for himself, wiping his eyes on the soft cotton which had set off all these emotions. Then he returned the double set of young girls' pants to their pink paper so that it looked as though they had never been unwrapped in the first place. Under a pile of his shirts he found a hiding-place, for out of sight out of mind seemed to be the sensible line to follow. At the same time he had this other notion about guilt and being caught with the evidence. Somewhere out there they were searching for him, he was convinced of it, even though he hadn't really seen them properly, just a glimpse in an alleyway of two oldish, dowdy people who looked as though they might have come from his own distant part of the world.

He sat on the edge of the bed staring at the varnished wooden chest which hid the proof of his crime. Already in his mind they were in the foyer below studying the name-plates in the half-light, sniffing the air like a couple of human tracker dogs, long in the tooth, admittedly, but still hell-bent on retribution. Almost certainly their connection with the girl had to do with blood, he felt positive of it. Perhaps the closest there was – although they appeared a little on the elderly side for the parents of a fifteen-year-old. Yet she did come from a very large family . . . His breathing began to trouble him as all these thoughts poured through his head. He rose from the bed, he paced the room, he gulped down some water, he threw himself on the coverlet again.

That was the day the rains came. He did find some consolation imagining what it must be like for his pursuers out there in those flooded streets, or behind glass in some bar somewhere, waiting and watching for the trail to come alive again.

But now the fear seemed to have left him. Perhaps he had managed to tame it by dint of all that agonizing in his apartment while the deluge hissed like serpents past the open balcony on to the palms below. He skirted one of these now. From its crown, drops the size of fifty-peseta pieces descended, bursting, then evaporating almost instantly as though on hot iron. A lush triangle of green lay just across the way from the traffic lights at the bottom of the incline which led past his block. He waited for a lull in the line of cars – the rain had made them showroom-fresh – then he crossed over and was swallowed up by moist, cool shade.

Now he was on an avenue as soundless and exclusive as any to be found in the better-off areas of the town he once had lived in. A monkey-puzzle tree caught his eye, a specimen which would have been equally at home in one of those distant drives with their privet hedges, their painted wrought-iron gates bearing the names of Irish mountains, lakes and rivers and, of course – a powerful memory – that locally quarried gravel spread on each driveway which a shower could turn to jet.

It was to be the start of a long, leisurely ramble past shuttered villas set back from the road in perfect, watered gardens. Barely a sound could be heard save the whisper of sprinklers or the soft murmur of the invisible sea. Silence like this cost money no matter where you lived. But, eventually, feeling like a potential burglar, he swung back to those more familiar parts of the resort.

It was late afternoon. Skewers of light darted off metal and glass from the line of cars idling on the curving through-route to Benalmadena, Fuengirola, Marbella, Estepona, places he still hadn't visited even after all this time. A little coastal railway ran closely parallel to the sea, emerging into the light from the station under the Plaza de Andalucia. It seemed perverse not to have ventured down those marble steps to buy a ticket to see such places, especially on a day like today when his confidence was running so high.

He entered the square, passing the small, underground cinema. Clint Eastwood in *Un Punado de Dolares*. An outsize billboard close by advertising Jesus Jeans delivered a momentary shock, but any outrage he might once have felt seemed very distant. He could still muster the occasional prayer in private but his faith, once a mighty torrent, of late barely trickled. Those "heavenly head-waters", as he often used to refer to them, would appear to have almost dried up. How long must it be before he felt fit again to take up the flaming gospel-brand? And when would he be ready to go down once more into the pure and crystal waters with healing hands outstretched? Fire and water. Those two essential elements for his work.

He waited for a sign. He would know it when it came, or so he told himself. That day on the foreshore, the woman, and then later on in her beach apartment, the two of them together in that animal way. Something momentous had happened then, he was convinced of it, a rite of some sort, a testing to see if he was ready. He was thinking of her now as he passed the pouting sex-pot high above on the hoarding – she looked like the same girl in that poster in that backstreet shop – and felt as though suddenly he were melting below the waist, a sensation as startling as it was unexpected.

For some reason his path led him in the direction of the *mercado*, as it was known, again, underground, the stalls lit by bare, hanging bulbs which threw a ghastly glare on the cuts of meat and strings of sausage, the still-writhing fish on their beds of ice, the mounds of peppers and aubergines like glistening, purple-black tumours. As far as Gilchrist was concerned the place had all the allure of a charnel-house so he kept on going past the crypt-like entrance. The area itself was where the hidden Spanish lived, the working people of the town, who had been here long before any tourists arrived.

The square where he found himself, Plaza de las Mercedes –the name had a hint of the religious about it; the quarter near the bull-ring was called El Calvario – was bounded on all sides by peeling, ochre-coloured apartment blocks seemingly crammed with excited humanity. Washing hung from every balcony. The noise of motor scooters, radios, street-sellers,

73

cagebirds, yelling children, was like an invisible haze in the air. Gilchrist strolled into all of this like someone who has ventured by mistake on to a film set. A series of small-scale but remarkably intense dramas seemed to be unfolding all about him and all connected in some way, yet he knew he would never get to understand the plot.

A police-car with its navy stripe and dead roof-light was brutally parked centre-stage where a scattering of dusty plane trees offered some much-needed shade. The driver and his partner leant against the roof smoking grimly and, with their belts, guns and clubs, looking every inch what an imagined Latin police-officer should look like. There was definitely something stagey about that stance, Gilchrist told himself, as though assumed for the benefit of people like himself.

But then, he supposed, he too had his own walk-on part, the nervous foreigner in panama and lightweight "tropical" garb about to make his, mercifully unannounced, entrance from far left. And it was his firm intention to thread his way through the milling cast of extras in just such a fashion as quietly and quickly as he could. There were several bars and cafés complete with outside tables where he could have found a seat to sit and watch the show but too much was going on for his taste. Everyone appeared to be distracted to almost breaking-point. It was in their faces and, certainly, in the pitch of their voices.

As he hesitated on the edge of things a child's ball fell from a balcony and bounced at his feet. He pretended to ignore it, as he did the cry which followed its downward flight.

He decided to cut across the square, for there seemed to be less happening over there. In the centre the trees were shedding their bark. They looked leprous, abused, infinitely different from those earlier specimens he had seen in the richer residential parts. Avoiding the litter and dog-droppings Gilchrist threaded a route across the thin gravel. Benches were here and despite his earlier intentions he sat down to rest in the shade. Medallions of filtered light dappled his hands and thighs. It gave him the illusion of being camouflaged in a ridiculous, childish way and for the first time he felt able to watch without being observed in return.

His travelling gaze had alighted on a bar directly opposite with a single zinc-topped table pushed against its outer wall. Solitary, it seemed placed there as an afterthought out of some half-hearted recollection of hospitality, for the dark interior was jammed with workmen intently following football on a television set. From his bench Gilchrist could make out the kaleidoscopic blur of blue-grey images shifting and breaking above the drinkers' heads.

His real interest, however, was centred on the table and, in particular, the couple sitting there, a bottle and glasses in front of them. The man had his back towards him but Gilchrist could see his companion clearly, a slatternly blonde in halter top and cut-off jeans. They didn't look part of the *mise-en-scène*, yet somehow in an odd way did. It was hard to explain but Gilchrist in his bower felt he must not take his eyes off them in case he missed their cue for action when it arrived. Whatever the outcome he felt a deepening curiosity about the two. German? English? Scandinavian? There was no way of telling, certainly not at this distance.

The girl was doing all the talking while the man sat hunched and immobile as though part of his chair. She kept stubbing out cigarettes with a rapid, pecking motion. Were they quarrelling? Her shoulders and arms were the colour of oiled teak. If it weren't for that bleached hair and those pale eyes she might almost be negro. Like a negative, Gilchrist thought. He continued studying the pair, though why, and with such dedication, he found it impossible to say.

Something vaguely familiar about the man's neck and torso was nagging at him, but the memory, if it could be called that, was far too frail to amount to anything. He had on an Hawaiian shirt in livid greens and yellows and his hair was gathered in a pony-tail, but it was his face which Gilchrist longed to see. He found himself willing this perfect stranger to *turn, turn, turn around* and put him out of his misery.

And then the man's arm went lazily into the air and Gilchrist heard the words, "*Tinto!*" and "*Favor!*" ring out. The utterance, as well as accent, gave nothing away, the voice merely strong and authoritative.

A waiter appeared, still arguing with someone inside, and slid a full bottle of red wine on to the table as though by the merest chance. It was something Gilchrist never tired of watching, that offhand yet elegant way they went about their business. Even when it came to scooping up cash at the end of a meal they never seemed to count it, as if such a thing was beneath their dignity. He suspected they despised their customers – well, the foreign ones, anyway – so the sensible approach would seem to be to counter arrogance with some of the same, something which the man in the patterned shirt appeared to have mastered. Already Gilchrist was seeing him as a self-confident character not readily deterred. Someone not unlike the man he used to be himself was the notion which came strangely to mind.

As he continued to spy something occurred which served to reinforce his theory. The girl reached out to intercept the full bottle and the man gripped her by that thin brown wrist, causing a look of pain to cross her face. Then he leisurely filled his own glass to the brim, and she seemed to shrink away with a cowed expression on her tanned features.

He decided he'd seen enough. There were no more mysteries. Well, one final one, and that would easily be resolved the instant he strolled past the table. A look, one swift look was all it needed and he could go home content.

Leaving the trees he proceeded in the couple's direction

without haste as though out for a leisurely stroll. The sun was sinking now, flooding the walls of the buildings in the square in that pale pink wash he enjoyed so much.

As he drew near the bar and its solitary table, padding along softly on rubber soles, the girl looked up out of her misery directly at him. Instantly he lost all composure, such shock was apparent in that look, startled recognition the only way to describe it. For a second he felt himself on the brink of faltering, even coming to a dead stop, but then he became afraid, moving quickly on past the back of the girl's motionless companion.

He felt confused like someone whose memory has suddenly let him down, desperately needing time to fathom out just where and when she must have seen him before, for that seemed obvious. He thought, too, of the old couple a week earlier in these same streets. Was this, then, a further manifestation, one more demon conjured up out of his own head?

At the corner he turned to look back. The girl was leaning forward, an intent, almost hungry expression on her face, her turn now to grip the man by the wrist. She was telling him something, something urgent, compelling, and Gilchrist knew it concerned himself.

As he watched, her listener turned in his seat to face him and Gilchrist's curiosity was finally laid to rest. But, at what cost, for, as their eyes met across that dusty stretch of pavement, it was not as either of them expected, a simple case of two strangers exchanging glances but, instead, doubles, twins, an optical illusion, but without the intervention of any mirror. The man in the lurid shirt was *himself*, some years younger, perhaps, heavier, too, but very recognizably *himself*.

This was no self-induced delusion either, for the girl had seen it, as had his *alter ego*, judging by the way he now stared back at him. He was smiling as if recognizing an old friend. It was that smile which caused Gilchrist's nerve to crack and, ducking his head beneath his panama's brim to hide the evidence of their unholy bond, he hurried away from his fate.

Morning. The builders were back in force once more drilling now in short, vicious bursts. Listening to them, even behind drawn curtains, was like being tortured by so many frustrated woodpeckers, for they were sounding every inch of the concrete, it would seem, for that magic response, a tell-tale change of pitch when and if hot metal hit home. He waited, but it never came. The idea had become mildly obsessive, respite, at least, from that other anxiety which had kept him terrorized and awake much of the night. Yes, he told himself, that concrete carcase opposite must be like gruyère by now judging by the racket going on.

And while on the subject, a little cheese would not go amiss right now, even the Spanish variety which was like rubber. He ran through an inventory of what he had in the larder. Some sausage, a tin of sardines, a single curling slice of ham (were there still eggs?) an orange, crackers, an unopened jar of olives, one tomato, some breakfast cereal. No milk, butter, cheese. All three tasted strange to his palate, ersatz. Had they no real cows in this country? Only bulls, it would appear.

He lay there considering. If he were in for a state of siege – for he felt convinced now the real nightmare lurked in the streets, and not in his head any more – how long could he hold out on such pitiful rations? Three, four, five days? In the longer term he knew he would have to brave the outer air at some stage, ideally heading further afield well away from this place. For safety reasons most of his money was distributed locally between three banks, so there was also the business of getting it out smartish without too much fuss. Putting it in had been simple. The reverse might not be. God forgive him, but one of the principal reasons he had decided on this refuge in the first place was its reputation as a safe haven for people like himself who valued discretion when it came to starting afresh.

Stretched under his thin sheet he watched the light burn above the curtain, a searing stripe intensified by the glass beyond. What a hypocrite he had become. *Haven, discretion, fresh start.* There spoke the true con-man, swindler, fraudster, whited sepulchre.

In the midst of this litany of self-disgust the din outside ceased suddenly, every drill stalling in unison. Silence followed. For the first time in weeks even the drifting cries of gulls could be heard, then voices started calling out, angry, accusatory. One of the labourers had struck a power cable, that had to be it. Perhaps this sad-faced Moroccan with his big brown fingers had blacked out the entire neighbourhood. Almost gleefully he waited for confirmation.

Directly overhead the poodle had gone into a clacking frenzy, his first of the day so far, intimidated by the competition outside, and Señora Guzman began yelling at her spouse. He could hear him groaning and, yes, the accompanying complaint of bedsprings. Their marital couch must be of the old-fashioned kind. So many sounds now. It was as if the entire block was coming out of a long, deep sleep. Water gurgled, a telephone burred softly – was that a cagebird? – a clock ticked. *My God, somewhere a baby was crying!* For the first time Gilchrist felt as though he hadn't been living in a tomb after all. A distinct correlation appeared to exist between the luxury of the building and the actual noise quotient. He was thinking, of course, of those run-down tenements he had seen in that square the day before. Human ant-hills.

Which brought him back once more to his personal bugbear, his double in the tropical shirt. He was able to confront the idea of it, of him, with relative equanimity now considering his state of funk in the early hours. He kept seeing that smiling face and then his own terrified expression superimposed like one of those two-sided trick playing-cards, switching faster, faster, until it was impossible to tell who or which was which. That, of course, was what had panicked him, a notion gnawing at him so outlandish, so bizarre, that he couldn't bring himself to admit it even to himself. Yet undoubtedly it did exist somewhere in those deeper recesses curled up for the moment like a sleeping beast, a panther, perhaps, black as sin and twice as deadly.

Lord, he prayed, *protect thy servant from that other darker side which lies within us all and help him to be ever-vigilant whenever and wherever it shows its sly and knowing face.*

The prayer was only a very short one, nevertheless it was the first occasion in a very long time he had been able to express himself in the old, familiar way.

He felt much better for it and some little while later he rose, washed, shaved. The water was still hot enough for his needs, but he had been quite right about the power failure. The lightswitches failed to generate anything more potent than a click, even though the noise echoed like a whiplash in the silence of the apartment.

To his surprise he found himself humming to his reflection in the full-length mirror on the wardrobe door. *Really*, he admonished the distinguished stranger in his pale blue seersucker gazing back at him, *really, allowing yourself to be terrorized by a ghost in this way, a chimera*, for that seemed more and more likely now, a creature of his own conscience.

And while on the subject, why should he feel guilty about that money in those bank accounts, all of it hard-earned by the sweat of his brow? Not once had he asked for, or been offered, his rightful share of that collection when it came spilling from the buckets to be counted out on the table after everyone had gone off on fire, filled with *his* fervour, *his* energy. Certainly no one else's. What had they expected him to live on, for God's sake? Manna? Any little which did happen to come his way, he recalled, had always been tendered grudgingly, notes peeled from a wad with the reek and grime of the cattle-mart still clinging to them.

Standing facing them in front of that table he felt like one of their hired hands. "Keep up the Lord's good work, pastor," all the thanks he ever got for draining himself, *tithe* a word which never seemed to have occurred to them, and if it had they would merely pronounce that it smacked of corrupt, Established practices.

As he stood there adjusting his necktie, striped red and navy poplin, he recalled the powerful scent of mothballs and peppermint they gave off, a combination always associated in his mind, somehow, with narrow-mindedness and cant. They would drive away then in their Volvos or new BMWs with stickers in the back window proclaiming their state of grace. Why had he put up with it all those years? And then to have them turn on him when he found himself in trouble.

By then, of course, he was banking the takings himself. Some sort of tax fiddle had made them decide to trust him to open an account in his own name or, rather, the name of the church. He had become a limited company. So when catastrophe struck he was able to take the money – *the Lord's, the Lord's* – and run with it. He thought of it now gathering Spanish interest in three separate locations and although the emotion was unworthy he rejoiced a little in the manner in which, finally, he had wrested his rightful ten per cent from all those tight God-fearing farmers almost a thousand miles away.

He left the apartment in quite the sunniest mood he had experienced in an age.

That day and the next and the next, too, deliberately and almost serenely, he made a point of avoiding the square where he had seen the couple. He felt no urgency about re-creating

81

the encounter for by now he was convinced they were regulars in that bar with its solitary table. The other thing, of course, was that fate played a hand in all of this – he knew it – and so he was content to drift about the streets, promenades and beaches, aimlessly, almost, like flotsam waiting for the pull of the current to carry him towards landfall.

On the fourth day – it was a Wednesday, bright, hot and a feast day of some kind; the streets were full of the "real" Spanish in their own restrained version of holiday attire – he set off to confront his destiny. The tide of his affairs had finally quickened, he had decided.

He was wearing his best clothes, a lightweight English-made suit in pale tan, well-polished black Church's shoes and his other panama still smelling fresh from the hat-box. The eager crowds swirled about him gorging on ice-cream. He could hear thin, screeching band music and the first of the fireworks. A procession was to follow later that evening. Portraits of the local Virgin were plastered everywhere. In the mood he was in the sight of those limpid doe eyes, infinitely compassionate and knowing, pursuing him wherever he went, induced a feeling not of disquiet mixed with disapproval as he would expect but one quite the opposite. He felt himself open to each and every influence no matter how irrational or superstitious. The idea of being abroad in this way in his formal clothes, so staid, so *Protestant*-looking, while underneath there lurked someone wide open to miracles, caused in him a degree of private amusement.

He also felt, finally, he was taking the fight to the enemy, for in some strange way that was how he now saw his quarry. That other couple he had hidden from that day in the alleyways of San Miguel held no terrors for him any longer. Curiously enough, it was this younger, more dangerous duo he decided he needed to confront if he were to prevail. In his fine West of England hopsack he felt armoured against anything this new foe might care to direct at him.

Arriving at the square, however, he suffered a momentary setback to his plans for he found a village band had taken over the gravelled space at its heart obscuring his view of the bar through the trees. Their open peasant faces – many were young girls – looked out of place in that drab setting. Their uniforms, russet and green with scarlet facings, and the fire glancing off their instruments strewn among the roots of the trees like treasure trove, brought a rare vitality to that run-down quarter.

The police-car, he noticed, was parked in the same spot, although the occupants were now slumped inside. He could see two dark, greased heads lolling against the head-rests. They may well have been dozing or, even, asleep, for it was coming up to *siesta* time – at least, here it was, despite the festivities going on in other parts of town. On the balconies the washing hung straight down in the heat, children, dogs, cagebirds all were silent, and when he finally managed to get an unobstructed view of the bar between the trees, it, too, looked deserted. The table outside had its two chairs tilted against the metal rim.

He moved closer picking his way through the sprawled musicians. A handful were drowsing, handkerchiefs over their faces as if in a hayfield and not this dusty wasteland with its litter of rubbish and crushed cans. The younger members were drinking from some of those same cans, but he saw one or two of the older men directing thin, purple streams into their open mouths from wine-skins, the sort the tourists love to misuse in restaurants along with castanets. Country eyes followed him. It didn't bother him. In fact he felt quite gratified, accepting it as his due, as he might have done in the old days making his entrance up those grassy aisles between rows of worshippers.

But then he emerged from the trees and he was in a desert, footsteps echoing in the emptiness of the street. At his back the cicadas kept up their monotonous chorus, breaking off every so often in that unsettling way of theirs. He kept imagining a myriad tiny insect heads all turned in his direction and holding breath until he passed.

At the open door of the bar – the Mariposa – he hesitated, glancing inside. Secretly he must have been hoping to glimpse a face he knew, a reflection, and for a second it did seem to be that way, for someone familiar appeared to be staring back at him from the gloom. Then he saw it was his own face in a mirror at the far end of the bar, the name of a beer blazoned across his features.

Pulling out one of the chairs he sat down at the circular zinc-topped table. Here he would stay for as long as it had to take, he told himself. This tiny section of pavement, this table, would be where he would make his stand. And so he waited, a solitary and, possibly, eccentric figure in his panama and formal suit.

The acrid reek of onions frying and, closer at hand, something rank and neglected within the bar itself assailed his nostrils. Smell had never really been among the most potent of responses for him. Still, he wasn't completely immune. Woodsmoke, certainly, and, yes, paraffin, rotting apples, damp wallpaper, the sooty smell of rain barrels – any of these could bring back childhood in a flash. All were the scents of winter, it came to him, his early young life spent in a perpetual tundra of the senses. His thoughts were slowing in tempo with the invisible cicadas in the trees. They sounded much less active now . . .

He must have dozed off about this point for the next he knew he had started up awash with sweat, the band of his panama biting into his brow. A taxi had turned into the still lifeless square and was drawn up ticking over a few yards away. Both rear doors were wide open and Gilchrist could see a pair of straining young buttocks tightly defined in faded denim shorts. Their owner was bending to help someone out of the back of the taxi. Some sort of tussle was going on.

The blonde – for it was she – as brown and lithe as a whip, continued to wrestle with her reluctant partner. For a crazy instant Gilchrist felt the urge to get to his feet, for suddenly he felt he was involved. But then this slip of a girl in her ragged cut-offs and black singlet turned, seeing him for the first time. They looked steadily, directly, at one another. He raised his hat. It had become an automatic gesture by now. Regardless of the consequences he rose and walked towards her.

She was pretty in a cheap, faded way, despite the ferocious tan, he saw that instantly, eyes of cornflower blue, a tiny mouth and nose. A small circular tattoo marred the chocolate perfection of her left shoulder and she had a fine bracelet of white beads wrapped twice around one thin wrist.

"Allow me," he murmured.

Then it was he leaned foward and reached into the depths of the taxi like some crazy fool reaching into a cage, supremely and cheerfully oblivious to what type of wild animal might be inside. A rush of stale drink, garlic and tobacco fumes engulfed him; he found and grasped a hot, moist paw. It felt comfortingly familiar in size and texture despite the sweat. And now he was hauling this uncouth version of himself, grunting and perspiring, into the sunlight. His younger self – he felt nothing odd about thinking of him in this way any longer – stood swaying beside the taxi, a lopsided grin on his face.

"Cheers," he announced, then hiccupped. He was trying his utmost to focus on his rescuer.

"Have we met, old chap?" he enquired sweetly in an accent clearly not his own, and Gilchrist felt unaccountably saddened that the other had not recognized him at this crucial first moment of meeting.

The girl spoke. "Don't keep him waitin'. Pay the bleedin' taxi, will you?"

Both men looked at her in much the same way, surprised and just a little hurt. Thrusting both hands into the pockets of his baggy surfer's shorts her companion came up with nothing but empty lining. He shrugged, still grinning.

The girl said, "Trust you. Oh, trust you."

The taxi-driver switched off his engine. Through the trees Gilchrist thought he could make out movement in the police-car.

The girl said, "Don't look at me. I'm down to me last five hundred. Who would go an' leave a whackin' great tip, eh? Even when I told him not to."

For the second time Gilchrist murmured, "Allow me," producing his wallet, and peeled off a series of notes in varying denominations without really bothering to examine them as closely as he should have done.

The taxi-driver accepted his good fortune without the slightest sign of animation or gratitude, which of course was normal, then drove off leaving them standing there conspicuous suddenly in that dead and dusty place.

As the car disappeared Gilchrist saw his two companions staring at the wallet still gaping in his hand. It was a look of open, unabashed appraisal, surprisingly united in its intensity, but Gilchrist was far too elated to let that affect him. A rush of almost childish gratitude had enveloped him at the way in which this meeting had finally come about. His rôle had been made so very easy, he told himself, and as he put the wallet away it occurred to him that even if he emptied it, that would be a small price to pay for this warm, almost sensual feeling he was experiencing.

Seemingly something of the same was affecting his new-found familiar, for, with palms spread flat on the table, he announced loudly and with great good humour, "Let's have a little drinkie-poo, shall we? To celebrate. Tell that bastard José he has customers. Custom! *José!*"

But the girl appeared nervous. She kept throwing glances across the square in the direction of the parked police-car.

"Oh, forget Cagney and Lacey. They're in love, I keep telling you."

"Keep your voice down."

"Well, if you won't flush out that lazy sod wherever he's hiding, then I will," and he attempted to straighten up with the intention of heading towards the open doorway.

Gilchrist and the girl moved simultaneously. Between them they manoeuvred him into a chair, for it was obvious that was where he belonged. With the same sunny expression on his face he accepted their ministrations, beaming up at them.

"Please be good enough to tell José an old friend has arrived from – from . . . God knows where." He gave a laugh. "And only a bottle of his very finest will do."

For a moment the girl looked at Gilchrist beseechingly, but no assistance was to be forthcoming from that quarter, not while this present mood was on him. She went inside then and the two men were left facing one another across the painted lacework of the table.

It was an important moment. Gilchrist stared hungrily, all etiquette forgotten. Indeed, even as he sat there, feet away from his similar, he could feel himself going slack in mind as though merging in some miraculous way with that unshaven, grinning replica opposite. They continued to examine one another. The man in the lurid shirt – palm-trees figured strongly, along with sunsets and sail-boats – had an unfocused look about him. Gilchrist experienced a momentary twinge of disappointment as it came to him that, perhaps, the other still hadn't fully realized the significance of their bond. He took his panama off as though to reinforce their likeness. He also loosened his tie, a little too strenuously, for a button plopped on to the metal in front of him. As he stared down at the tiny bone disc it wavered in front of his eyes disappearing into the white-enamelled expanse. His vision felt blurred, he dabbed his brow with his handkerchief. Then he saw a paw outstretched towards his.

"Jordan," said the man opposite and they clasped hands.

"Gilchrist."

Later he was to learn it was a Christian name, but that was only a minor detail, something to laugh about like a couple of schoolboys while the girl looked on uncomprehendingly. Her name was Angie.

A moment later she emerged with the waiter he had seen that first time, although now it turned out he owned the bar. Yawning and reeking of interrupted sleep, he stood there only half-comprehending as Jordan subjected him to a stream of good-natured abuse. Gilchrist revelled in it all, recognizing, as he thought, something of his old self in the other's gift of the gab. A certain coarseness of expression did, unfortunately, mar the performance, but something close to a thrill of pride at his new-found double's handling of the situation, drunk as he was, made him feel a partner in all this badinage. The tousled-haired proprietor – he looked very young to have his own place but, then, he had a perpetually worried look about him that spoke of unpaid bills and daily setbacks – hung in the doorway, head bowed before the barrage.

The girl, too, looked down. She kept toying with her purse which lay before her on the table, pink, heart-shaped, with a thin, writhing, gold strap. Gilchrist sensed what she was doing would eventually irritate the man opposite. He also realized she might easily produce a similar reaction in himself. She hadn't smiled, not once, since their meeting. Her fingernails were bitten to the quick and there were indigo-coloured bruises about the base of her throat which he understood were known as "love bites".

"Let's go somewhere else," she pleaded. "Please, Jordan. You know what they're like." She was looking over towards the police-car again.

"You worry too much. This is a free country, I tell you. Isn't that so, José? *Libre*. Eh? *Compadre?*"

For the first time the man leaning in the doorway permitted himself a wintry smile, but merely for a second.

Jordan said, "Three glasses. *Tres. Tres.*"

Gilchrist wondered why he persisted in sprinkling his delivery with beginner's Spanish when it was obvious the proprietor understood English perfectly. No one had told him so, but he felt certain of it. But then, he decided, it was because the other was drunk and it was something people did when they were like that. It didn't bother him. On the contrary, it actually seemed to make the man opposite in some curious way more endearing.

Some moments later an uncorked bottle of red wine arrived on the table. It looked like blood to Gilchrist despite the beads of moisture coursing down its sides. He knew it was customary to drink it icy cold here but he still couldn't keep a flicker of distaste from his face as the first glass was filled with the purple stuff.

The man pouring must have spotted his reaction, for he gently suggested, "Some other poison, perhaps?" and Gilchrist, who was no drinking man, mentioned the only one he could think of.

The sherry when it arrived was also chilled and drier than he could have possibly anticipated. They raised glasses – the girl left hers untouched on the table – and Jordan said, "You've picked up the local custom, I see. The old *fino*, eh?" and Gilchrist, feeling flattered, swallowed a little unwisely. The pale, straw-coloured liquid tasted like lighter-fuel but almost immediately a warm and spreading glow dispelled any such comparisons.

89

Relaxed in his chair, with loosened tie, and hat before him on the table, his perception of the square and its inhabitants began to take on a more favourable aspect. Among the trees the band had begun to rehearse something restrained and lyrical to further complement the mood. He realized he was smiling quite a lot and when the bar-owner returned with a bowl of olives and a fresh ashtray – the girl, of course, was smoking ferociously – he felt like complimenting him on his place. Gratitude was the overriding emotion, but for what and why he had no real idea.

As he was leaving the table the waiter-cum-proprietor made some remark in Spanish to the girl and they both looked at him. When he had gone Gilchrist asked her what it was he had said, for he was curious, emboldened, too, by the *fino*. She hesitated, glancing at her companion.

"Go on, tell the man," he ordered her. "You're the one with all the patter, not me. Quite the little bi-lingualist, aren't we, baby? When we're in the mood."

And he reached across and took the cigarette from her, putting it in his own mouth. Eyes closed, he inhaled deeply, and for the first time Gilchrist received the full force of the powerful herbal reek of the local tobacco. Then the man across the table from him did a curious thing, for he offered the half-smoked cigarette to Gilchrist who looked down at the loosely-packed tube a trifle bemused as how to react.

"No?" murmured his similar and, mercifully, he was spared any further embarrassment as the cigarette was returned to the girl once more. Now, she, too, sucked avidly on its ragged, moist tip, lips puckered in disturbingly sensual fashion. Gilchrist watched all of this conscious there were undercurrents here that would take him some time to fully comprehend. Yet he thrilled to such a quest. He sipped his sherry in its chilled, tulip-shaped glass, beginning to feel just that little bit heady himself.

The girl – Angie – spoke. "José wants to know if 'your brother' will be staying or not. He has an extra room, he says. No problema."

Her accent was North Country, whereas Jordan's was much softer-spoken with a recognizable rural burr. He had the hands, too, of a country man and Gilchrist couldn't help comparing them with his own as they cupped their separate glasses of very different drinks, the one raw, red, earthy, and his own, pale, almost anaemic. There seemed to be something of deep significance there, but, again, something to be analysed at a later time.

"Well – *brother*?"

Gilchrist said, "I already have a place of my own. An apartment, actually," and noticed for the second time how their gaze converged on him in that selfsame, quick, appraising way.

They sat there in silence like three people who have exhausted all curiosity about each other, although a million questions remained unanswered, particularly that central, most incredible one of all. Yet Gilchrist felt there was no real urgency.

The light was draining fast from the sky giving way to deeper, denser shades of blue. He was amazed at just how swiftly the transformation had come about without his actually noticing it. The trees at the heart of the square had coalesced into an unmoving, inky mass. The band had long since gone – again, without his knowledge. Swallows, or they may have been bats, stitched complicated, swooping patterns in and out of the shadows. He could smell the evening cooking-smells as if a myriad appliances had come on suddenly in one orchestrated surge of power. It made him realize he was feeling quite ravenous. He was about to suggest they have a meal together – on him, of course, why not? – when the man opposite sighed deeply, mournfully, and his head began to dip towards the table. Gilchrist managed to move his glass out of the way before his forehead made contact with the painted metal.

The girl said, "Oh, shit, *shit*," stubbing out her damp butt. "I can't do a thing with him when he's like this. He's his own worst enemy."

Gilchrist sat contemplating the head resting before him. There was the definite beginnings of a bald spot there where the coppery strands were drawn back tightly over the scalp towards the twisted band binding the ends together. It looked like something a child might affect, a little girl's elasticated hairband flecked with tiny, glinting bobbles. Somehow that touched him, the vulnerability of the thinning patch, allied to the vanity of the hairstyle in someone of his age. Although he had determined to put off all such speculation for the time being it was obvious a matter of only ten years or so separated the two of them in age. Perhaps less than that.

"Jordan," the girl said with some harshness in her tone and looked as though she might well shake him.

"Let him rest a bit," murmured Gilchrist, which was presumptuous of him he knew, yet, in some odd, unexplained way he felt he had a protective right.

The girl cried out, "*José! José!*" but there was no sign of movement within. "Bastard!" she hissed.

Clearly she was becoming agitated and Gilchrist, again surprised at his own daring, reached out and took her small, hot palm in his in what he hoped was a calming gesture.

"Let me help. Please."

She looked down at the conjunction of their hands on the table. Her pale blue eyes – they seemed to have shrunk piteously – were filled with tears of frustration.

"Let's get him upstairs," he suggested.

Together they lifted the sagging form up and on to its feet. For a moment there was a brief spasm of animation, but it passed quickly and the head fell forward once more. A sort of liquid, whistling noise came from the lips anticipating the full-blooded snoring which could be not all that far off.

Manoeuvring him through the darkened bar was easier than expected – there was a certain mobility in the legs still – but the hard part came when the stairs were reached. Gilchrist pushed from behind, his arms wrapped about the surprisingly soft midriff, the girl pulling on a handful of shirt-front. The stairs were marble, cool and deadly – there was danger here, a slip was unthinkable – but somehow they managed the ascent between them, steering their burden into a room off the landing, where, very carefully, they felled him on to a bed.

The girl lit a lamp. It had a tasselled, blood-red shade, and Gilchrist felt embarrassed at the sudden intimacy it revealed, the disorder so unashamed, so widespread in its ferocity, that for a moment he felt almost swamped by the sheer volume of personal effects strewn like debris about the room. In vain he found himself looking for a solitary oasis but there was none. The room was also airless and very quiet save for the breathing coming from the bed. Gilchrist stood there as though in a vacuum, ill-equipped suddenly to deal with the situation.

The girl's proximity posed a grave threat to his composure. He could smell her scent, musky, uncharacteristic, but perhaps it came from the array of bottles on the dressing-table, many left unopened. It was also hard not to notice the various items of underwear scattered so carelessly in different parts of the room. None of that appeared to bother her, however, and for the first time he felt the reality of his age and situation, someone with outmoded attitudes from another time and place deluding himself for a little while that he had genuinely shared something with this couple.

"Not a pretty sight, eh?" she said and in the instant all his old illusions came flooding back, for how could he agree with that when, lying spreadeagled on the bed, a contented smile on his face, was someone, if not himself, then someone in his own image. The phrase set off in him a tiny frisson, faintly blasphemous.

"Shall I give you a hand with him?" The girl gave him a knowing look.

"With his clothes, I mean."

It – he sounded suspect, he knew that, but he was thinking suddenly of his old appendectomy scar. *Could it possibly – ?*

"No," she said, "I can manage, thanks. It won't be the first time," and something in her tone seemed to penetrate the layers of insensibility for the man lying on the bed said quite distinctly, "King's Cross."

His eyes were closed, he appeared to be unconscious, but the words were clear.

"Oh, for Christ's sake, Jordan. Not that again. Not now."

She had sat down on the edge of the bed, her back to them, and began to unlace her sandals. His double was snoring steadily now, a babyish dribble of moisture trailing from the corner of his mouth.

"What did he mean?" he asked the girl.

She stood up and kicked her sandals off into a corner. "Don't worry," she said. "It'll keep."

Then, fixing her eyes steadily on his, she began snapping free the metal buttons on her shorts. There were at least a dozen – it was that busy, current style – and Gilchrist remained paralysed mentally counting off each tiny, intimate plop, perfectly resigned, it would seem, until the last one broke clear from its fastening. Only when he caught sight of a taut, black triangle – silk, at a guess – did he gulp and make a retreat for the door. His forgotten hat he returned to his head and settling his tie to rights he made his exit from that hot and over-powering room.

Outside the air felt just as oppressive, but stars now pricked the velvet blue of the night sky. They looked cool up there, inspirational in time and space.

Making his way back to his apartment his mind continued to sieve everything which had occurred or been said since the taxi first drew up in the square and his hands had met those of his likeness for the first time. The waiter had called them brothers, but that wouldn't do. It might for other people, José, or even the girl, but they, the two of them, knew differently – *they did, didn't they*? He recognized, of course, that the man lying back there on the bed could not answer for himself, not in his present state, but, he, Gilchrist, felt justified in speaking for both of them. He had this wonderful new confidence as though bolstered by the very idea of duplication.

But then he put a brake on his fantasies. He thought of what the girl had said. "It'll keep," had been her words. *Yes*, he told himself, *there was all the time in the world to get to know one another*. Past as well as present.

As he passed the row of painted, transvestite whores who came out each evening at this time like so many perfumed night-birds, he was immune to their hoarse blandishments.

"*Buenas noches, señoritas*," he murmured politely, tipping his hat to them and passed by smiling to himself, for, already, he was recalling scenes and faces from his past now that he had someone, someone like-minded, to share them with.

FOUR

Blackened tin kettle in one hand, wrecked umbrella held upright in the other, Max Buckingham comes high-stepping into view across the sodden field. He is wearing an ancient, frogged dressing-gown, ankle-length, glazed with dirt, and a hair-net. On his lips and cheeks can be seen caked traces of last night's slap.

Like so many of these puzzling new expressions he's been coming up against the word still has the power to unsettle the boy watching The Great Man through a tear in the tent. Certainly he can *think* it, but as yet he cannot bring himself to say it, not in the easy way the others do with that carelessness which comes from long and confident usage.

At this moment he's in his dusty nest of old stage curtains given to him for bedding, bare boards below and, high above, the sloping fabric of the great tent, drumhead tight, because of the night's rain. It's just beginning to give off an underwater, greenish glow as the early light penetrates. There's a fierce odour of trampled grass, cigarette-ends and, of course, canvas but that's not quite so insistent at this time as at noon when the sun beats down full upon it.

Sometimes at night curled up beneath his claret and gold coverlet all his senses seem to vibrate at full pitch because of the exotic scents and sounds surrounding him. Lying awake he can also make out stars through the roof. When it rains, as it did last night, those same holes up there keep him roving restlessly about from one dry patch to the next. But he's seventeen and everything is still an adventure, even the wildlife he can hear outside in the small hours through the patched walls.

Old "Rajah", the one with the little performing dog, told him how in one place down the country somewhere he, himself, would often attach a cymbal to one leg at night to deter rats. But then they all enjoy recounting such stories to the josser. That's what they call outsiders, people like him. They make it sound like a failing.

"You must never, *ever* take it personally, dear heart. *I*, certainly, haven't, and I've been in the business – oh, an eternity."

That's The Great Man speaking, the words booming out as though amplified. He's never heard him lower his voice, never, not for anyone or anything. Like the genie out of his bottle.

He watches him now slanting across the wet grass, still relatively unmarked. Yesterday it was pasture. The cows, spurting khaki streams, had to be turned out when they arrived in convoy. The Great Max – in his time he has appeared before many of the crowned heads of Europe, or so the posters have it, *but what exactly does it mean* debates the young watcher in the tent – is fetching his morning shaving-water from old Fay's caravan. The ritual is equally baffling. Can he not even boil a kettle for himself, great man and all as he is? And why does Fay, so willingly, go along with it? They say she never sleeps, the old woman with the smoked face seamed with a million tiny lines. It gives her the look of some ancient squaw. But do they mean it literally? There are so many things he still has to puzzle out for himself about these people.

Now he resumes his surveillance, for Max has disappeared inside his own caravan and his next move will be to take up position at the uncurtained window as though performing for an audience. Holding his nostrils between finger and thumb in exaggerated fashion he draws down the angled cut-throat with his shaving hand.

Elbows propped on the velvet layers the boy watches with the utmost concentration. It's as if he's possessed by some hunger of the eye which cannot be appeased, and the man at the window seems to be aware of the effect he's having. But then, the boy reasons, isn't that how he behaves most if not all of the time, with or without witnesses? He has this certain way of smiling, head cocked to one side like some raffish jackdaw expecting approval.

Of all the people in the troupe he is the one who has affected him most. Old "Rajah" Brooks, Fay, her two sons Gus and Sonny, Connie Carr, Maureen, Gus's wife – each of them is worthy of close study, but The Great Max, Max The Incomparable, beams forth with planetary force from the heart of that little constellation.

"One of these days, dear heart, one of these days I must take you aside and tell you a little of how it used to be for this humble player in his golden years. Alas, most of my precious scrapbooks perished along with so many other mementoes in that dreadful fire I suffered a year ago, but I'm sure you'll take my word for it. Everyone in the profession knows Max Buckingham. His reputation precedes him wherever he goes." And here he flung a hand heavenward, laughing in a way which made the boy confused as well as uneasy for some reason.

Shaving completed, and not too carefully at that, the man framed in the caravan's solitary window scrubs his face now with a soiled rope of towel. The dressing-gown drops from his shoulders to reveal a dingy string vest almost as grubby as the towel, and he poses for a further moment before the unseen mirror, turning his head this way and that. Even at this distance it's obvious he's enamoured of the reflection before him in the glass. It's a source of wonderment to the watcher, this unflagging self-esteem. Certainly he is a long way from what might be considered fetching with that great, pitted, rosy neb of his. His eyes, too, small, dark and twinkling, are set close together, and the few pitiful strands of hair visible under the net are dyed an unconvincing ink-bottle black.

The boy sees all of this with that cruel regard which is to be expected at his age. More importantly, it is only a matter of a week or so since he ran away from his own very different world where someone like this would be the object of huge derision. But, then, hadn't he seen with his own eyes how those same locals come to scoff fell silent once The Great Man, made doubly grotesque by his stage appearance, had confronted them across the footlights? He'd sat there shivering with the rest of them at the sight of that terrifying, lit profile, nose puttied out for even more dramatic effect, and the sound, too, of the voice raising up the hairs on the back of his neck. "Truly, Trilby, you are helpless before my great and ancient powers. Svengali has you in the palm of his hand."

The distant generator hummed, moths kept striking the bare bulbs behind their tin shields along the edge of the stage and the audience, men, women, little children, sat like stones on the hard benches. Along the front ran a row of the "better" seats, a dozen broken-down old armchairs, legs sunk deep in the grass. The local bank-manager and his family, the teacher, the man who owned the hardware store, Tom McHugh with someone else's wife, a party of tourists down from the hotel – even they in all their finery and small-town sophistication were smitten.

On stage Rusty was laid out on a covered trestle while Max made passes over her limp young body, skin waxen, hair like straw falling as though weighted to the boards. She presented her lovely throat willingly, almost gratefully to those curving talons, it seemed to the watching boy. They were heavy with rings and ingrained with dirt, although only he knew that. He felt himself aroused, he was half in love with her already, and looking around hated the audience for sharing his feelings.

He felt something else as well. It was to change his life, set him on a course, as though tugged along by some invisible cord which would never relax its hold on him. Sitting there it came to him he was much more interested in what was happening to the people around about him than in the performance on the far side of those footlights throbbing weakly in unison to the distant pulse of the generator. All of these people, they were gripped by something, some power that could not be denied. Docile, they accepted their fate. And their fate, here and now, was to be taken over utterly by events on a raised, lit rectangle of bare dusty boards without the slightest pretence to any real, serious illusion of any kind.

Even the smallest child must see that. They had forsaken the cinema, after all, where all this was done so much better, for this old-fashioned fit-up show for one night and one night only – or so they thought – for they were to come creeping back again and again until the tent finally came down sighing like some great deflated animal carcase and nothing remained to remind them of what had happened to them inside but a pale, discoloured bruise in the middle of Bobby Clyde's big field. Gradually they would forget all they'd seen and heard, would go back to Boston Blackie, Johnny Mack Brown, The Three Stooges and the black and white newsreels heralded by the crowing cockerel. But he would not, would never, as long as he lived. His certainty was absolute on that score. Even then he possessed that same fierce self-regard and sense of being set apart.

And it was for that very reason while the others slept in the old lock-keeper's house by the river that he crept downstairs and let himself out into the watery grey dawn with only his cigar-box under his arm for belongings. But what else did he need? Not another thing, he told himself, as though modelling himself already on those same theatricals who travelled as light as air.

He'd caught up with them in the next county, following the posters, a strident, chemical pink with THE WALSH VARIETY PLAYERS PRESENT in black boldface drawing the eye first. Gus had laid the trail a day or so earlier in his old Ford van with the loudspeaker roped to the roof. *Thanks, Gus.* He loved Gus, fat and almost as foolish at times in real life as the country yokel he played on stage in his stand-up comic act. "Ach, whisht, would you . . . Shure, I'm deshtroyed entirely, so I am, I am . . ."

He'd never heard anyone talk like that before in real life. Neither had the people who sat there with him on that first night. None the less they laughed loud and long enjoying their imagined superiority over their poor, backward neighbours from the far South being parodied on stage. Yet whenever the troupe came to travel across the Border again deep into those parts where the audience did seem to speak in such a manner – at least to his ears they did – Gus continued delivering his patter without any change of accent. The crowd, he noticed, laughed just as uproariously as his own people had done. He'd quizzed Max about it for it made him feel genuinely puzzled.

"Don't fret yourself, dear heart. They don't recognize themselves. They never do. It's our little trade secret, don't you see, holding up a mirror that always reflects someone else. They're laughing at that man from the next village, or that poor creature over the hill, or that little old lady who's a teeny-weeny bit odd. It makes them feel good having a laugh at someone else's expense. Forgive me, but the Irish, I'm

101

afraid, are like that. But long may they continue to be so, for then, dear heart, we will always be in business. Don't you see that?"

To be honest he didn't. The Great Man chucked him under the chin, breathing cachou fumes all over him. "Don't concern your pretty head about it, Eric, there's a pet."

For his part he'd grinned back sheepishly trying not to let his true feelings show. All these terms of endearment, he was unused to them, and even if he hadn't been they still would have made him feel uneasy. It was like being enveloped by something clammy and highly-scented at the same time. He wanted to scrub himself each time it occurred. But he had no wish to antagonize Max and he continued to put up with his blandishments and sly, fleeting caresses.

Max, you see, had been the one to persuade the old woman to let him stay. He'd heard them talking together one day about it while doing his usual, invisible, skulking act around by the backs of the caravans like some cur snuffling for scraps. Max, indeed, had quickly christened him Dogsbody. It was one more expression he hadn't come across before but, though suspecting it wasn't entirely complimentary, it did make him feel he belonged which was all that mattered. Dogsbody. Most of them he quickly realized seemed to have nicknames, aliases of one sort or the other and, anyway, Eric didn't really have the correct ring to it. "Rajah" and Rusty, of course, were the obvious examples, as was Sonny, for certainly he couldn't have been born with that name. Even The Great Man himself he discovered was not as he seemed when it came to his own magnificent billing. But that disclosure was to come much later.

What he'd overheard was the tail-end of something, like so many of those other titbits of information he kept on snapping up so eagerly.

"But he's so much *prettier* than the others we've had come to us in the past. You must admit that, surely, now."

"Only if you behave yourself, Max. Remember he has a mother somewhere."

"But you're the only one we've got at the moment. Give darling little Maxie here a great big cuddle, there's a nice mummy."

The old woman laughed with that terrifying smoker's rasp of hers, more like a death-rattle than a cough. And he'd gone away pleased with himself, not put out in the slightest by Max's comments. Even then he had something of the whore in him.

But then all that seemed unimportant, so powerful was the desire to gobble up everything he could as fast as he could concerning this amazing new power he'd witnessed that night in the tent. More than anything he needed to share in whatever it was that held all those people spellbound in the half-dark. He genuinely felt he had found his vocation.

Looking back, he had also to recognize, painfully, perhaps, it was to be his first *real* and in some ways strongest spiritual experience. Some time later in a Belfast Exhibition Hall Billy Graham was to ignite him a second time with his own brand of pyrotechnics, but nothing could ever quite match that first evening under canvas in Clyde's great field with trampled meadow-grass underfoot. So much for the pure power of the Lord in contest with cheapjack melodrama. The message was not lost on him. Later, God forgive him, he made full use of it when the time came for him to run his own tent Crusade.

But, now, on this soft Irish morning in the year nineteen fifty or thereabouts his name is Dogsbody and he lies in his canvas kennel watching and waiting for the first signs of life in the other caravans. There are five in all, splayed out about the big green tent like a battered flotilla, each one berthed in its own individually ordered anchorage as befits such a variation in temperament of the owners. He must cultivate some of that himself, he has begun to realize, to set him apart, not only from the people paying to sit on hard seats but the others as well. Slap off, as well as on stage. Like Max.

"Always remember we're theatricals, they're not. And they give us the credit for being much cleverer than they are. Don't forget that, young Dogsbody."

But by this time The Great Man has gone to earth again in his rat's nest on wheels among the piles of old theatre magazines, drifts of costumes, hats, scarves, shoes, canes, squeezed make-up tubes and cold-cream jars, all lit by the feeble glimmer of a single oil-lamp. Its globe is smoked as well as cracked. Its reek permeates his clothes wherever he goes. The boy knows all this despite having never been inside the ogre's cave. Some sixth sense warns him against that. Instead he relies on snatched glimpses through windows and open doors for his information, eyes and ears working overtime.

A rising column of smoke from Gus's caravan tells him it's time to get up from his own bedding and go to the open flap. There's dew on the grass, inside the tent as well as out, one more of life's mysteries, and he hitches his trousers an extra inch to keep the damp at bay. He stands looking out waiting for Gus to appear. It's their private ritual, this pretence it's only coincidence they should both appear to one another at the exact time every morning.

Then the door does swing open and his benefactor is standing there in convict-striped pyjamas and his famous, wide-brimmed showman's hat which never leaves his head. He gulps the moist air allowing his eye to travel approvingly around the encampment. All is well with his little world, but then it always is. He manages to raise a laugh every time he comes on stage no matter what the part, that great, innocent, shining face of his as reassuring as some favourite uncle's.

They look at one another for a moment more, then the man on the steps rubs his great belly slowly, meaningfully. The boy heads across the grass towards him. Already he can smell the blessed aroma of frying bacon. Each morning he slips into the facing caravan as noiseless as a hungry ghost. No one pays him the slightest heed, not even the two toddlers erect in their high-chairs dabbling in their bowl of milk and rusks. Eyes screwed up against the smoke and heat of the stove, Maureen shakes a skillet over the high flame swiftly dishing up relays of food which he and Gus devour in silence. It reminds him of home, for meals were always eaten in that same fashion. The infants, twin boys, are tiny replicas of Gus. Their even temper is remarkable, as is their mother's as she sings her way through the housework. The extra mouth who feeds at their table often wishes he, too, were a part of this family.

After breakfast he continues to tag along close to Gus's heels. By now he's wearing a heavy, Western-style jacket in pale corduroy with darker elbow-patches, bib-and-brace denims and bright tan drover's boots. He revels in his showman's rôle, frequently lapsing into Americanese in keeping with the image and the outfit. The boy happily goes along with the conceit.

Today Gus is making a trip to the nearest town to publicize the show and Dogsbody is welcome to come along. So they set off in the old Ford van – Gus refers to it as "the pick-up" – which he drives one-handed, his other massive, leather-tipped elbow sticking out of the window. When the first houses start appearing a microphone is brought into play and his amplified tones stream out from the speaker above their heads hanging like chaff in their wake as, slowly, they work their way into the heart of town.

"The Walsh Variety Playhouse opens its doors in Byrne's field for one night only. One night only, folks, with a show for all the family to enjoy. Admission three-and-six and two-and-six. Children, half price, one-and-six. Curtain up, eight-thirty, local time. Drama, comedy, music and thrills, all in the big, green tent out on the Dublin Road. Ireland's oldest and best-loved travelling-show brings you the tops in popular entertainment guaranteed free from vulgarity. Nothing borrowed, nothing blue. Don't miss this chance of a lifetime, a night with the stars, and tell your friends . . ."

They're in the wilds of Cavan somewhere, some outlandish hole, dung steaming on the streets and a smell of turf-smoke on the wind. The people have that same backwoods air about them. They stare open-mouthed at their passage halting where they stand the better to comprehend the message. Already the boy in the cab is seeing them through Max's eyes. He feels genuine pity for them and the deadly monotony of their lives, particularly the ones his own age leaning up against shop-windows joylessly sucking on ice-cream cones or passing a single wet butt from hand to hand. He returns their gaze with something of The Great Man's own half-mocking, half-quizzical expression on his face.

At some stage they enter a public house together, Gus noisily breasting inside and he riding along on his coat-tails. It's a low-ceilinged, dimly-lit place with stolid drinkers sitting close together lining the tobacco-coloured walls. The bar is partitioned. On the far side the shelves are stocked with staples, tea, lentils, peas, flour, sugar, made up in two-pound, buff-coloured bags, and an old-fashioned bacon-slicer squats back there, a pile of wrapping-paper alongside ready to receive the rashers as they come curling off the circular blade. Without bothering to order a drink or offer a greeting Gus launches straight into a foretaste of what his comic routine that night holds in store.

"Listen, listen, I must tell you!" he bellows. "I ran into this fellow about a minute ago just up the main street there and we got to talking, so we did, and he says to me, he says – listen to this, will you – the wife keeps a goat in the bedroom, in the bedroom, so she does, and the smell is driving me crazy, *crazy*!

So then I says, why don't you open the window? Open the window, says he? Open the window? And let all me pigeons out?"

The great freckled paw slams down on the wet wood startling his audience into sudden, nervous mirth.

"Listen, listen . . ." And so it continues in relentless, machine-gun fashion for a good quarter of an hour or more. He, for his part, smiles dutifully as befits someone who has heard the jokes a dozen times before. He is perfectly content to merge into the background while still basking, of course, in the reflected glamour. Someone puts a full glass of something pale and golden in front of him. Gus is already well down his second pint of stout by this time. It looks and tastes like lemonade and he drinks as casually as he knows how.

Standing close to the rim of the bar he can make out the two of them reflected in the whiskey mirrors behind the publican's head. They make a fine pair, these two, he's thinking to himself as if it's a couple of strangers he's admiring, the big, ruddy-complexioned comedian in the cowboy hat and his partner, that slim, dark-haired youth modestly supping a mineral. Peeling off a poster from the roll under his arm he slides it across to the owner of the bar as if his own name is already on it. His face feels hot. He realizes he's smiling a lot, far more than normal. He gulps rapidly from his replenished glass.

"Then my mother-in-law. Last year she tried going on a diet. For six months all she ate was coconut and bananas. Coconut milk and bananas for six months! She didn't lose any weight but, by gum, she couldn't half climb trees . . . Then there was the time she fell asleep in the bath with the taps running. Didn't make any mess though, she sleeps with her mouth open . . ."

There's a low roaring in his ears while someone close by is laughing a little too loudly for his own good. The sound of that voice seems familiar for some reason. Gazing into the mirror, amongst all the gilded harps and shamrocks he can make out his own face, open-mouthed, eyes blurred slightly. As he continues to stare, intrigued, he studies more specifically the tumbler in his right hand – or is it his left? – and how it keeps rising to his lips over and over again as though powered by something mechanical. Never has he felt so perfectly attuned to the universe, life, as well as confident of his place here alongside this man in Western gear, elbow to elbow, the two of them playing to their audience. Partners, even . . .

Driving home some short while after he is violently and messily sick out of the window of the van. It seems it wasn't lemonade those sly farmers plied him with after all, but not before his loose tongue gives him cause for regret later. He recalls pressing Gus to let him have a part in one of the plays, a walk-on would be perfect, anything, for he knows he can do it, he does, honestly, but Gus merely smiles in that engaging way he has, telling him gently, "By and by, by and by."

He doesn't remember much more beyond those three little words which are to become hateful to him over the weeks that follow, reminding him cruelly as they do of his proper place in the others' scheme of things. All find the business of his being drunk hilarious, it being impossible to conceal it from them. And no one blames Gus for allowing it to happen either, not even Connie Carr, she with her sentimental and deep compassion for all forms of small animal life. If he'd been a dog or a cat, perhaps . . .

As for Rusty, well, she ignores the episode completely, bound up as always in her own affairs. He watches her move dreamily about the encampment, her old, pale, man's trench coat covering her skimpy costume. There's a hole in her tights far up one thigh the size of a half-crown which excites him unbearably – the audience, too – for one of the high spots is when she descends to sell raffle tickets during the interval. Sonny, his rival in love, watches her progress each night down below among the leering farm-boys through a chink in the curtain with a face like thunder. He's always been nervous of Sonny, not merely because of the feelings they share for the blonde beauty who seems not to know they exist, but because of his sullen, begrudging nature. It seems hardly credible he and Gus could ever be brothers.

"Well, I have to say, I am gravely disappointed in you, Dogsbody."

He and The Great Man are sitting side by side in the sun, deep in a couple of old armchairs moved temporarily outside for repair purposes.

"I really did think you were different, not like that other riff-raff we've attracted in the past. For all the wrong reasons, I must add."

For a moment he is tempted to ask what those might be, then thinks better of it. He's been avoiding this moment for some time but now that he's finally been trapped in this way, captive like the audience who normally sit in these seats, he knows there's nothing for it but take his medicine.

"No one cares about the occasional drop of nose-paint now and again. God knows, it's a hard enough old life on the road and we're all of us human – some a little more so than others."

Here he gives one of his wicked laughs baring the pale, pink roof of his dentures. Yes, he has seen those, too, reposing in a glass, beaded like some underwater relic, on his sneaking travels around by the backs of the caravans.

"As long as it doesn't interfere with the job, fine, but never, *ever* let them see you under the influence, offstage as well as on. Do you understand what I'm telling you? Do you, dear boy?"

And the hand comes creeping across to rest ever so lightly on his thigh. He watches it lying there, mottled and incredibly old, it occurs to him, compared to the rest of him. At this time of day, late afternoon, Max has finally shed his dressing- gown. Now he sports a burgundy-coloured corduroy jacket – he refers to it as his "smoking jacket" although he doesn't indulge – a loosely knotted cravat, horses' heads on a yellow background, and tight, thin, white cotton trousers clearly showing his well-defined privates. Tennis shoes complete the ensemble, a bizarre mixture of the drawing-room and sports field.

"It's simply a matter of keeping up the illusion, you see, dear heart. Once that is shattered and they begin believing we're just the same as they are then we might as well give up the ghost. Deep down, I suppose, we're more than a mite afraid of them. It may not seem that way, but they can do terrible things to you if ever you give them the chance. Believe you me, I do know."

He seems very serious for a moment as if on the brink of some dark confession, but then he brightens up once more. "Isn't the sun perfectly splendid today? A real Irish Indian summer."

Eyes closed, head resting on the worn leather, he soaks up the slanting rays as though on the deck of a cruise ship instead of a field in the sleeping heart of Cavan. From the tent come the strains of a piano. Connie Carr is practising her Ivor Novello medley. She drives Sonny demented with her habit of hogging the tent whenever he needs to run through his own musical programme, for he plays electric guitar to Rusty's vocals, although they never appear to have any contact except on stage. Most of her time seems to be spent stretched in the darkened caravan she shares with old "Rajah" her father. A creature of the night, Rusty appears only to exist to dazzle and excite when the lights go up, standing there deadpan and slightly doped-looking in her iridescent lamé sheath dress. With her long straight blonde hair she looks like a mermaid, or that Tuborg Gold girl on the posters. Just occasionally her glance might brush him in passing, but only for the briefest of moments. He knows he's truly beneath her notice but then so, it appears, is Sonny. Some day, he vows to himself. *Some day*. It's become his constant, unspoken refrain.

The man basking alongside also uses it, out loud, in much the same way as Gus with his "by and by". These are times when the boy despairs of ever being able to make these people alter their perception of him. As far as worth is concerned he feels roughly on a par with "Rajah" Brooks' little terrier bitch Rosie. But she at least does get her moment on stage "dying for her country" each night in a tri-coloured ribbon, green, white and gold, tied about her neck.

The final, sustained chord of "We'll Gather Lilacs" melts off into silence and Connie Carr edges out of the tent, a sheaf of sheet music held protectively to her bosom. She's wearing a buttoned-up quilted housecoat with a gauzy scarf covering her massed curlers, pink slippers with pom-poms, a final, surreal touch. Nervously she scuttles back to her caravan which the boy knows is stuffed with animal pictures, knick-knacks and frilly furniture. Even a budgerigar in a cage.

"Poor Connie," murmurs the man by his side. His eyes are closed, lids still brushed blue from last night's show. "She's a dear old thing, really. A warning to you, in the light of what we've just been saying." And here he raises his hand in a drinking motion.

"Oh, yes, indeed. Used to be quite a star in her heyday before she started lifting the elbow. You look surprised, dear heart. Well, don't be. We all have our darker sides here, I have to tell you. Join the club. Although you are a trifle wet behind the ears for any of that just yet. Still, we must do our best not to make you feel left out of things."

His ringing laugh seems to propel Connie the final few yards in a panic, at the door of the caravan turning a glance of terror on them before going inside.

111

"Never breathe a word, mind. She'd simply die, poor darling, if ever she were to find out I'd told you. But I always know when I can trust someone. It's written all over your innocent, Irish face. Come," says he, squeezing hard on his thigh, "it's time for you to join the elect. You can't be a Dogsbody all your life. Chop, chop," and he allows himself to be towed off into the musty, green twilight of the tent.

And as always he's struck by the silence as though a dome has come down over his head. Wavering discs of light dapple the trodden grass, arriving through roof and walls, for this is when the fabric is revealed in its true, tattered state. A ruined cathedral, he thinks, although he's only read about or seen pictures of such places. A setting for mysteries. His own initiation is very near. Never has there been a more eager acolyte, yet he's apprehensive suddenly now that his time has come. He feels resolve drain away, that which has sustained him this far. But then where did it all come from in the first place to make someone like him, never having known anything or been anywhere, be taken over so ruthlessly by the certainty of his own destiny?

"I want you to put this on," murmurs the high priest by his side in his shameless trousers and jacket of wine-red corduroy. He can smell its distinctive, doggy odour, but then that may just be The Great Man himself.

"Here, allow me." And his eyes are bound with a strip of some black, silky stuff, the scent this time that of mothballs with a dash of peppermint. Trustingly, he allows himself to be led up on to the stage and told to stand there. After a moment from somewhere down in the middle rows comes the voice of his instructor.

"Hold your head up and move it about a little. That's it. As if you're sniffing the air. Have you never seen a blind man? Of course you have. Now pay attention. For this, I'll be straight man. The stooge. You follow me?"

In truth he did not but he would have swallowed fire if commanded to, so eager was he to be a good pupil.

"In my right hand I am holding up an object. I want you to concentrate on that object. Can you do that?"

"Yes."

"Good. Now continue to concentrate very hard. *Harder*. Can you tell me what it is?"

"It's a scarf."

"Good. Now tell me what this scarf looks like. Describe it, please."

"It's yellow."

"Anything else?"

"With horses' heads."

"Excellent."

He stands there feeling a fool, still in the dark. Only he's not, which is the problem.

"You can take the blindfold off now." The Great Man is sprawled in an armchair in the front row.

"Not bad, not bad at all, for a beginner. With work and a good teacher, of course, you might even have a future – some day." The laugh again. "You seem a little put out, dear heart. Why the puzzled expression?"

The boy feels he's being tested and the thought of failing at this critical stage makes him sweat. He looks down at his tormentor hating that smile suddenly, the close-set, jet button eyes, the whole off-hand, mocking demeanour. All his resentments converge on that bright, canary-coloured band of stuff knotted loosely about the other's throat.

"But I could *see* it!" A cry from the heart.

"Of course you could. Don't look so shocked. Let's face it, they know it isn't the real thing. They actually *prefer* it that way. None of us are that good. Miracles cost extra, dear heart."

Miracles. One day, one day . . .

★

For the moment, however, it's a start, first rung on the ladder of apprenticeship to the higher illusion which will be his life. Such tawdry beginnings. But he shelves his reservations as though realizing even now something much more important lies ahead of him. So he watches and listens while this man coaches him. Greedy for every scrap he can get he quickly discovers there's more to it than simply standing there imitating a blind man. He becomes quite an adept at that, even pretending to stumble a little, palms outstretched to an imaginary and, supposedly, invisible audience. He also learns never to look too directly or too long at the "straight man" holding up the mystery object, a comb, a purse, a handkerchief, a cigarette-lighter, a set of rosary beads borrowed from someone below on the benches, but to cock his head to one side in parody of a person confined to the power of hearing alone.

Which brings him to the business of *codes*. Supposing he has now moved on to "reading" names which is the next grade in the mentalist's repertoire and the subject happens to be someone called Anne. His helper in the audience spells it out for him alphabetically, first letters of each sentence combining to complete the word. So after the customary flim-flam he calls out the following: "Are you ready? Now is the time. Hurry. Are you ready?" *Hurry* being the code word for repeat. He will then reply something like: "I see a name. A beautiful name. It's still blurred. It's something like Annette. No, no, it's much shorter than that. It's *Anne*!" Applause. Of course there are other systems infinitely more arcane involving words, gestures, even inflections, but for their present purposes the less sophisticated the better.

"Simple minds demand simple entertainment, dear boy. Anyway, why cast pearls before swine? Come. Now we must dress you to look the part. We can't have you appearing like one of *them*. I have just the thing over in my caravan."

So, finally, he is inside the ogre's cave – *what could he do?* – and feeling nervous, although about what exactly he has no real idea beyond that same old nagging sensation again that everyone knows something he does not. Standing in his only set of underwear doesn't help, but the curtains are drawn, at least.

"My, you country lads certainly are healthy specimens. A regular race of young Davids."

Mercifully his attention returns to the heap of costumes piled high over a chair, stirring up scents almost as disturbing to the boy's senses as the fabrics themselves, richly embroidered silks and satins, musty brocades and velvets, strewn now about the floor in an exotic, ankle-deep carpet. Poised there he feels like a tailor's dummy submitting himself to the racing hands of the older man as each relay of clothing is pulled on then scrutinized for effect. But the sensation is not all that unpleasant he's forced to admit and quite soon he abandons himself to the ritual.

He thinks of his mother for he must have stood just like this for her, too, once, being pulled and prodded, her mouth full of pins. For a moment a pang of something suppressed stabs at him. Everything from that other life he's put out of mind as though fearing some deflection from his purpose. A letter had been sent early on, brief, businesslike, telling them he was alive. Safe, *happy*, too, which seemed an odd addition for such a word was rarely if ever used in that house by the water's edge as though the very idea was an embarrassment, something beyond the expectations of people such as themselves. *If they could see me now* he can't help thinking, those silent ones alone with their thoughts around that kitchen table scrubbed bare as bone.

And then he's commanded to look in the long mirror and a spurt of excitement races through him as he realizes that even if they did he could never be recognized.

"So, what do you think, then, eh?"

Facing him in the fly-specked glass is someone from a far-off land, someone only glimpsed before at second-hand in picture-books or the raw, bleeding tones of Eastmancolor. He laughs out loud, he cannot help himself, and The Great Man joins in. And truly he is *great*, for the transformation is remarkable. Not just the clothes – the scarlet, thigh-length tunic, the baggy, white breeches and puttees, the turban, a single stone embedded in its brow – but his skin, too, for something vile-smelling and stinging has been rubbed in, turning him into Sabu.

The genie booms, "Farewell, Dogsbody. Welcome The Young Bamboozalem!"

And so the dream comes true. He has become one of the company. And all that sly observation standing him in good stead, for he quickly learns to be as they are living their double lives, the one on stage where everyone appears smiling, gay, and brimming with camaraderie, and that other, the daytime one, where they pass one another by in the field as though they'd never met before.

It isn't easy. Even Max seems more distant suddenly. But then he did make an offer to put him up in his caravan which he turned down as diplomatically as he could, saying he really did prefer to continue with the present arrangement under canvas, God forgive him. Something implausible about space and air and the familiar scents of his country upbringing. Those eyes, twin points of polished coal never missing a thing, dart quickly at him, then just as fast slide away again, the hand flapping up to dismiss the suggestion as of no real consequence. But he knew he had damaged things between them. Some things have to be resisted, even by a green-as-grass seventeen-year-old.

He and Maureen become a double-act. Their rôles should

really be reversed – that was the intention – but she's "breeding again", to borrow Max's crude expression, and is unable to get into the scarlet tunic. Moving among the audience like a sleep-walker she selects articles at random holding them up for identification. "There's no need to use them old codes, now, is there?" she informs him wearily. So he carries on with the primitive blindfold trick seeing the objects raised at head height as through a haze.

"It's a fountain pen or pencil, I think. Silver? Yes, yes, most definitely!" he cries out, the rehearsed accent a cross between Charlie Chan and Bela Lugosi. His feeling is that The Great Man is impressed although he doesn't care to show it.

More and more, off-stage as well as on, he becomes absorbed in his own world of make-believe, not bothering any longer to wash the make-up off between performances. His palms now are permanently stained with applications from the little brown bottle while his complexion stays a paler shade. When he looks in the triangle of mirror he keeps in the tent, each morning Elephant Boy stares back at him. The idea of being half-caste quite appeals to him and on the trips into town with Gus in the van he stays firmly in character.

"Meet our newest addition to the company, folks. All the way from a triumphant tour of the capitals of Europe. If you haven't seen his mind-reading act then you're missing out on something remarkable. I guarantee you'll go away amazed. Money back if you can detect the secret of his powers handed down from a long line of Himalayan mystics and wise men. I know *I* can't figure it out. Forgive him if he doesn't talk a great deal for I'm sure you'll understand he has to save all his pyschic energies for tonight's performance."

And he for his part smiles demurely back at them sitting there in their dark suits and collarless shirts fastened at the neck with the outdated single stud, taking care not to touch any of the lemonade in the array of glasses placed in front of him. It's

117

all a game, he tells himself, harmless, these people willing participants in the nightly charade, for he has seen them grinning at one another, slapping their thighs. It's the children and some of the mothers, too, who make him feel uneasy about what he is doing. Their eyes never leave him as he turns his bound head this way and that like something on a stalk instinctively seeking the light.

And then that evening arrives when something in him rebels or, rather, something outside himself takes a hand. Much later he is to see it in those specific terms, a touch of a Heavenly Hand, the way he describes it, giving his testimony of how a Power infinitely greater than he could ever have imagined reached out choosing him for its inspired purpose. Hallelujah . . .

On this particular night, a Friday, and almost a full house, the heat is oppressive. Hay-making is in full swing and the hot, dry scent of the fallen crop combined with the general airlessness has the senses reeling. With scorched faces the audience sit looking stunned. In the second row behind the town worthies a woman suckles her infant without shame.

At the time he is backstage perched on a hamper in full costume, his blindfold laid across his lap in readiness, a crack in the curtain allowing him to see without being seen. Connie Carr has just rounded off a medley of parlour favourites with her customary, tearful ode:

> "Little boy,
> Pair of skates,
> Hole in ice,
> Heaven's gates."

Old "Rajah", astride a kitchen chair, is playing "Roses of Picardy" on a musical saw. He wears an ancient First World

118

War uniform, forage cap, riding-breeches, and the high keening of the undulating blade has everyone's teeth on edge.

It is a time when there are still corncrakes. Their pulsing rasp sounds clearly from the fields outside. And another animal cry is to be heard as well, that of "Rajah's" little bitch Rosie, tied to her master's caravan until the time comes for her to "die for her country". The wailing saw must have set her off and that melancholy duet has the yokels at the back of the tent in fits. Max is down there amongst them in full make-up in his *Murder In The Red Barn* costume, arms carelessly draped about the shoulders of a couple of youths his own age. He whispers something to them, something outrageous he'll be bound, and their raw faces split open in sudden mirth. An odd mood seems to be abroad. He can feel it in himself as well, a distinct jumpiness. There are people out there he has an urge to inflict something on, something in the way of retribution, although why or for what he doesn't really know.

"Rajah" concludes his eerie recital – the sound is what one hears in nightmares, the howling dog merely reinforcing the notion. The audience sit as though they've put on an increase in weight. Their brains seem similarly affected. They can barely bring themselves to applaud. He watches, half-despising, half-fearing them through the pulled curtains. For the first time he's beginning to see what Max meant when he talked about them in that way.

And then it's Gus's turn to bound on stage, the boards groaning under his tread.

"Thank you, *thank* you, you're a darlin' audience! *Darlin'*, the lot of you!" he bawls without the slightest hint of irony, but then that's the nature of the man. He's wearing a chequered pantomime suit in bilious tan and yellow with a matching cap pulled on back-to-front. In his mighty grip the microphone looks slim as a reed.

"Ladies and gentlemen, every so often The Walsh Variety

Players have the great good fortune to secure the services of someone whose talents are so *remarkable*, so *amazing*, so *mystifying*, that mere words are inadequate to describe what you are about to witness."

By now his voice has dropped to a solemn, bass rumble as Connie Carr hesitantly picks her way through the opening chords of "In A Persian Market."

"All the mystery of the East, ladies and gentlemen, brought to you tonight in the person of our next performer. I feel certain you will agree with me when I say it's hard to believe one so young could carry so many secrets inside such a youthful head. Already he has appeared before many of the crowned heads of Europe. Ladies and gentlemen, all the way from a triumphant tour of the continent and parts adjacent, for a limited appearance only, I give you that master of mind over matter, that pyschic prodigy – *The Young Bamboozalem!*"

Each night Gus's introductions become more fevered in their invention. He, himself, genuinely has no idea what he will say next because nothing is ever rehearsed with these people, except for the "dramas", the words of which would seem to be as fixed as holy writ. And so the curtains come back revealing him centre-stage in all his young nabob's finery, bandaged eyes fixed on a spot slightly above the heads of those standing at the rear of the tent.

He's feeling confused and angry for some reason. Much of it he realizes is directed at the people out there and, in particular, The Great Man, who seems to personify on this night of all nights everything that is corrupt about this whole pretence. Through the fine gauze of the blindfold he fancies he can see him grinning at him as from a great distance. And as that sly, silent drip of venom continues to find its way into the ears of his two young companions the boy on stage convinces himself that he, and he alone, is the butt of that evil humour. In a way it's good to bring his resentment to bear on him out there with his chalky cheeks and vampire's lips for it means he doesn't have to feel quite so guilty about his own involvement in what is about to take place.

But now he must focus all his attentions on Maureen who is hovering nervously in the centre aisle. As his accomplice she wears white, transparent pantaloons, gripped at the ankle, a short, embroidered bolero covering her freckled, swollen midriff, while mouth and nose are hidden under a square of muslin, completing the harem effect.

"Ladies and gentlemen, I will now request certain amongst you to hand me selected personal items which The Young Bamboozalem will identify using his amazing supernatural powers."

No effort is made to soften her accent which remains purest Dublin. "Moore Street on a rough day," is how Max describes it, and although he has never been to that city he recognizes the cutting truth of the remark. The Great Man himself, of course, speaks like an English lord and has coached him rigorously in his own stage voice.

"Open vowels, dear boy, open vowels and, of course, slow everything down to a crawl. Every word a treasure in the mouth, a titbit to be savoured. Have you got that? You're really quite a quick learner, you know. We'll rid you of that dreadful ploughboy's accent in next to no time. All you have to do is place yourself in these old but expert hands. Repeat if you will, then, after me: How Now Brown Cow . . ." There was something else too about the rain in Spain falling in the plain and he dutifully practised the magic phrases alone in the tent, or while sloping about the field hugging the hedgerows every chance he could get.

Putting into practice what he has been taught, he intones, "I see something made of leather, dark brown or, maybe, maroon. A wallet, I think? Yes. It belongs to a young lady, if I'm not mistaken."

All of this is easily recognizable, he sees as much the instant Maureen holds up the schoolgirl's cheap pocket-book. But then as the applause boils up he is on the point of adding, "There's a photograph inside." For a moment the significance of what has happened doesn't hit home because a snapshot of some kind did imprint itself upon his consciousness and just as rapidly recede like some half-glimpsed actor's face on a cinema screen. Yet he also knows the face belongs to that of a boy about the same age as the girl. *He knows*.

But now Maureen has moved on to another victim a couple of rows behind. This time it's a middle-aged man in work clothes whose bald head gleams like an egg under the lights, for lights there are, slung in a loop along the ridge-pole to enable him to "see" the objects. Flirting crudely with the man Maureen strokes his pate then manages to extract a comb – metal, it catches the light – from the breast pocket of his dungarees, holding it aloft, and the crowd erupts with gleeful malice. And once more he delivers his findings in that fake, broken accent of his, the one he's worked so hard to cultivate.

More and more items are being thrust into the air for identification, people waving, scrambling to volunteer as a mood of gross excitement grips them. Maureen's breathing comes faster and faster, sweat running down her distended belly in a glistening, bisecting stream. Her flimsy muslin mask has come adrift, her harem pants cling revealingly. In the midst of all those pawing hands she is beginning to look like a sacrificial victim. As he himself is, it strikes him, raised up on his wooden altar. He fancies he hears Max's laugh booming out louder than all the rest and for a moment closes his eyes behind the soft pressure of the silk to gain a respite.

Lord, he finds himself murmuring, something he hasn't done since he was a child under the bedclothes on those black nights, the waters of the headrace roaring away outside, and the light of the candle throwing phantom faces on to the wallpaper of his attic room. It was always hard to decide which was worse, the spectres among the cabbage roses or the dark itself.

Those faded pink blooms, they float back now, falling ceaselessly, for he could never halt their slow, diagonal drift to the floor no matter how he tried. An optical illusion, of course, but real none the less, almost as real as what he's seeing suddenly right now behind the blindfold and behind closed eyes at the back of that. In the centre of one of those old-fashioned floribundae there appears for just a fleeting instant, as in the case of the photograph earlier, a burnished, metallic disc the shape and size of a –

"*Compact!*" he cries out above the din and, opening his eyes, he sees that Maureen has her hand resting on the shoulder of a second young woman. Maureen looks up at him, an odd expression on her face, half-angry, half-frightened, and when the young woman shyly slips something into her hand she glances quickly down at it as though wishing to keep it hidden from him. Sudden rage fills him.

"*Powder compact!*" he bawls. "*Silver! Silver!*" until Maureen finally, reluctantly, holds it in the air.

At this point she quickens her pace, snatching greedily at the objects people are waving, as though hoping to forestall further repetition of that last trick of his. But, of course, he knows now, as does she, no trickery is involved and his anger grows as he realizes he is to be given no chance to exercise this amazing new power he has discovered in himself. He's also finding he's suddenly terribly tired for some reason and so submits himself to the old cynical routines, calling his cues out automatically but without any real attempt any longer at acting the part he's up there to play. Still, he does manage to get in a few more stabs at the real thing, secretly closing his eyes and concentrating on the blood motes behind the lids. In every case but one a recognizable image appears matching the real thing. Various items of jewellery, a tiny pocket mirror, one Mickey Mouse watch, a lipstick, a pair of gloves, a prayer-book. All belong to young girls or women, he realizes – the one eluding him a cigarette-lighter taken off a brilliantined old toff down from the local fishing hotel. But by now he is too tired, clearly so, for Gus comes on stage to save him further pain.

"Ladies and gentlemen," he announces, a burly, chequered arm encircling his shoulders, "as I'm sure you must appreciate the mental concentration involved in this particular act is phenomenal. The Young Bamboozalem here" – a bear hug crushing his joints – "in spite of his amazing powers is human just like you and me. At this point, therefore, he must take his leave of you in order to re-charge his mental batteries for another time. However, I assure you he will be here on this stage tomorrow night at the same time with more of his amazing telepathic feats and extra-sensory magic. Tell your friends what you have seen and, in the meantime, please will you show your appreciation in the time-honoured fashion. The Young Bamboozalem, ladies and gentlemen!"

And applause swells, filling the tent. It seems louder, more threatening, somehow, with blinded eyes. Gus loosens the black silk knot at the back of his head. Freed of the gentle pressure, he blinks against the overhead lights, swaying slightly. It's as though something has been drained from him, a sensation he is to come to recognize. Yet no matter how often it occurs he will never quite get used to its slow, deadening onset. Like an epileptic or diabetic he learns to live with his disability – if it can be called that – yet each time always seems like the first.

Here, now, with the roar of the crowd in his ears – "*More! More!*" although not one of them, he knows, will ever realize just how well he has performed for them – his legs are like rubber. His arms tingle while a dull, throbbing band seems to have taken over from the blindfold.

Backstage, Max is touching up his graveyard mask in a square of mirror nailed to one of the tent-poles. As he stumbles past, the man in the rusty frock-coat murmurs, "Don't run before you can walk, young Dogsbody. You're playing with fire," with a wolfish flash of his dentures in the glass.

Maureen, too, has something to say, although, in her case, to everyone within earshot.

"I'm not going down among that load of feckers any more. My place is here, I tell you. Up here. And that's the end of it." But, of course, it isn't.

Next day a family meeting is called in the tent to which it's made clear he is not invited. Yet, trudging the dense perimeter of the field with lowered head, he isn't all that put out, despite the convincing show of melancholy. Inside he feels strong, resourceful, knowing what happened to him last night was no accident but the beginnings of something which might very easily take over his life. *Thanks, Lord*, he murmurs to the hedge, surprising himself for the second time.

Then the tent flap is drawn aside and he sees them emerge with stern faces, Connie first, in housecoat and curlers, fretful as always, then Rusty – it gives him something of a thrill to think of *her* discussing his future – followed by "Rajah", a slouching Sonny, then Maureen looking daggers, Gus mopping his brow and, finally, Max and the old woman together. She leans heavily on her brass-tipped blackthorn. It leaves vicious perforations in the soft earth. The rest of the company disperse to their caravans while Max continues talking, talking, his hand on her sleeve.

Staring straight ahead, she indulges him a moment longer. He makes her laugh, he has seen it, heard it, that chesty cackle that makes everyone within earshot fearful for her health as well as their own. But today The Great Man seems to have drawn a blank, for the creased old face remains set. The boy's heart sinks – despite having convinced himself his destiny lies beyond those patched canvas walls and dusty boards under bare bulbs. He's frightened suddenly. He's not ready to take the first step on his own. He still needs these people and the shelter of their ancient tent. And there's so much more he has still to learn.

Watching the old woman hobble off he feels despair. Max stands there until the caravan door closes at her back. Only then does he glance across to where he waits miserably. A long, crooked, yellowish finger is extended in the air and at the signal he trots dutifully across the field like a dog to his master.

"I think I've managed to persuade them to keep you on. For a wee while longer, you understand."

An arm compresses his shoulders as he allows himself to be gently guided towards the caravan he swore he would never set foot in.

"The family vote went against you – and I, alas – but the old lady swung it in our favour. Eventually and after a lot of hard bargaining on the part of yours truly. Amazing old bird, Fay. A head for business and a heart like granite. You happen to be good business, dear heart. The audience adored you and that's what's important, so . . ."

Inside the caravan the flame from the oil lamp with the cracked globe gutters and trails smoke although it is bright day outside. The reek of paraffin, liniment, cologne and unwashed clothes combines to form an almost suffocating aroma. They sit facing one another across a low, squat, stuffed object. It looks like a flattened leather toadstool embossed with pyramids and palm-trees. A pile of magazines lies strewn on top, foreign, at a glance, judging by the titles, and the boys cavorting on the covers in skimpy bathing-trunks certainly don't look as though they hail from this side of the water. The Great Man sees him eyeing them and gives a laugh.

"We can take a closer look together later if you like. But, in the meantime, you may find these almost as interesting, now that you've thrown in your lot with us."

Going to a wardrobe in the shadows he takes down an ancient shoe-box which he places on the heap of magazines.

"All that remains of my once extensive collection. You can see I was lucky even to rescue this much from the conflagration when it came. A piece of advice, dear heart, never, *ever* smoke in bed, although, in this particular instance, yours truly was not the guilty party. But that's another story. Here, have a look at this," and delving into the scorched shoe-box he produces a photograph of someone in doublet and hose holding a skull up to the light.

"Recognize anyone you know?"

The frame is trimmer, the hair more plentiful, but nothing can disguise that nose.

"Liverpool. The old Coliseum. Agate said my Hamlet was one of the most forceful and interesting he'd ever seen. Outside the West End, of course. The actual notice used to be in here somewhere."

And the box is upended, an entire lifetime shaken out for his inspection. The past smells musty, old scents emerging from a long sleep, as foreign as the sepia-toned faces staring up at him, refugees from another era as well as country. Cracow, Poland. A group portrait, the earliest, and centre-stage even then a young Max sits astride the family dog, a breed he has never seen before, as big as a small pony with heavy fur and a studded collar. There's snow on the ground and a mansion in the background. Max is two. But that's not what he's really called. Emmanuel Isidore Berkowitz.

"Hardly a handle to come tripping lightly off the tongue on Shaftesbury Avenue, dear heart. *Or* looking good in lights. And especially not at that particular period, that's for sure. So, hey presto, change of name as well as accent, although that did

127

come some time earlier. Now here's the new me all blacked up in the old Haymarket days. Max Buckingham lording it in *Othello*. They did so love the name, you know. The Irish, too. And still do. It was like rubbing shoulders with royalty, don't you see? Wrong side of the blanket and all that, but near enough, near enough. Poor deluded darlings, they'll believe anything if you tell them what they want to hear. As you seem to have discovered for yourself. Tell me, slyboots, as a matter of interest, one fellow artiste to another, just exactly how did you and Maureen cook up last evening's little spectacular between the pair of you?"

He manages to evade the question by plunging a hand into the shifting mound of old paper in front of them, stirring up more memories for his inquisitor. But The Great Man has never been one to be overly interested in anything or anyone other than himself as he has come to realize so there's no real danger of being found out. Which is an expression with an irony all its own, because, in truth, he hasn't really deceived anybody.

But right now those look like real tears in the eyes of the man across from him. He feels embarrassed, angry, too, as if the other has moved out of character without warning him.

"Look at me then. Just *look* at me."

The young actor in the photograph kneels now with a fist pressed to his brow. And here he is again in sandals and toga with an outstretched short sword, in a frock-coat and powdered wig, in cardinal's robes, as a pirate, beggar, Cossack, Indian chief. The guises are coming thick and fast like a swiftly dealt deck of cards, the features behind the make-up ageing before his eyes. The body is thickening too, nimble Jack becoming a portly monarch and then with no change of pace or warning a queen ousts them both. Rouged and padded, fore and aft, she pouts and preens in front of a succession of backcloths becoming progressively more garish

128

and tattered. Minor characters start appearing, dwarves and clowns and scullion girls, grotesques in animal fur.

Deeper and deeper into the pile Max delves, the yellowing stills building up in a drift about their ankles. He seems to be searching for something that isn't there, some image, a clue to condradict the evidence before his eyes. He looks old, sad, and the boy yearns to be somewhere else but hasn't the courage or the know-how to rise and leave the other to his grief. It seems peculiar to him at his age that a musty old hoard of souvenirs should occasion such distress, and especially in someone as cynically buoyant as The Great Man himself. Yet a part of him does sense something of what the other must be going through. It's only a feeling half-realized as yet, but he does give thought to his own little cigar-box, still almost empty at this stage in his life, but then puts it out of mind in the certainty that his career will be a very different one.

So there they sit in the ogre's den – only it's no longer that, more the retreat of an ordinary old man locked up with his memories. His own father was like that, although looking back it's hard for him to imagine just what they might have been. Solitary feats of daring on the weir, most likely. For he remembers how he enjoyed pitting himself against the suck and flow of the dark water as it tore through the cunning network of gates and sluices to emerge tamed downriver. At such times he would arrive home soaked through yet strangely content to sit smiling into the fire hands spread to its warmth while his patched old waders would drip silently from their hook on the scullery wall.

"Go, go now, it's getting late," murmurs the man hunched opposite although clearly that's not so for the sun is still high outside.

Stepping out into the hard light and glancing about him at the huddle of caravans and the tent where he sleeps, he sees all of it clearly as for the first time. No sign of life is present. Even

Gus's two little children are subdued and silent inside somewhere as though their difference from others their own age
starts early. Everything and everyone waits for night to arrive
and the throbbing necklace of bulbs, pink and green, blue and
orange, to prick the country dusk.

To pass the time until then he decides to make his way out of
the field and along the road which must lead somewhere. But
at the gate – it's been lifted clear off its hinges and laid flat
against the bank – he comes to a halt feeling apprehensive. For
some reason he convinces himself if he carries on he may not
be able to get back in again.

Instead he returns to the shelter of the hedge. In a quiet,
shady part hidden from view he finds a corner to curl up in
until the light starts fading from the sky just as everyone else
seems to be doing. Sprawled there, the smell of dock and
dandelion in his nostrils, it crosses his mind what he has
chosen is not much of a life for himself – that's if free choice
enters into it. But patience is a virtue and surely brings its own
reward. Quite genuinely he believes this to be true and so lies
in his grassy nest sucking on a stalk, confident that soon, very
soon, that special door of opportunity will open to him.

And so night finally arrives. The coloured lights deepen
against the blue blackness and the voices on those ancient,
scratched records drift out once more across the fields, Guy
Mitchell, Rosemary Clooney, Frankie Laine, Connie Francis,
drawing in the crowds. Like country people everywhere they
come in their own good time, women and children first,
young girls pushing, giggling, then the menfolk cutting a dash
in their Sunday suits or slouching half-drunk in dungarees
against the back canvas wall.

Tonight they all seem in boisterous mood. Rolled-up sweet
papers and, later, cigarette butts arc in the air to fall among the
shrieking colleens near the front. At one stage a scuffle breaks

out and the two combatants resolve their differences outside where they can be heard grunting and swearing in the darkness. The advertised acts run their course, The Laughable Sketch, the night's big Drama *Murder In The Marshes* ("If our play doesn't make your flesh creep, then it's too tight") the various musical items. Connie, "Rajah", Rusty and Sonny, everyone, receive their share of catcalls and barracking, The Great Man included, who comes off spitting.

"Animals! Farmyard filth!" he growls in carrying tones, tearing off his police-inspector's moustache. Then darting a venomous look in his direction, "Perhaps you'll be able to tame our lovable little friends out there with some more of your parlour tricks."

Gus, meanwhile, is standing with the blindfold in readiness. Even he seems to be far from his affable self and his touch with the band of black silk is a shade on the rough side. He's sighing deeply, tragically, as he knots it in place, great onion-scented gusts like the air from a bellows and the boy, feeling the blast on his cheeks, senses deep reproach.

All this is my fault, he tells himself. *Everything was fine until I arrived on the scene.* Yet he knows he must accept the rôle he has been handed, for something, or *someone*, he knows not which, has chosen him to be an agent of change. At this early stage it never enters his head to see any of it as divinely inspired but something of that must have been working through him, for, before the curtains are parted, he catches himself murmuring, "*Lord, Lord,*" as on the previous night, only this time with real fervency.

And it does seem to give him confidence. The crowd roar at the sight of him standing there, head cocked and ready to receive the first images. It's him they've been waiting for, nothing can deny that, and a warm sensation passes over him as though he's with friends, a big, boisterous family of well-wishers willing him on to even greater feats. *You can do it, you can do it*, he seems to detect in their cries and as Maureen's tones try to rise above the hubbub he begins swinging his head this way and that in the direction of individual voices.

Wallet, pipe, fountain-pen, spectacles in a metal case, water-pistol, a shopping list, a golf ball, two marbles, a set of dentures. The things people have in their pockets or about their person! One joker raises a clenched fist and he hesitates, for he sees, hazily at first but then with a rush of clarity, the undeniable imprint of a french letter in its little oiled sachet.

Keeping his sights on the grinning youth he tells him, "I really don't think you want everybody to share your little secret, now, do you?" thrilling to the confident note of rebuke in his voice.

The culprit lowers his great mitt, looking sheepish, and he passes on, concentrating on the younger females in the audience, for it's there his powers seem to be at their most vital. A girl in the fourth row engages him in particular, a freckled beauty with large, dark eyes and a mouth like a ripe fruit. Blushing, almost visibly palpitating under his scrutiny, she gazes up at him as though offering him her secret soul. And for a moment he is tempted to take advantage of all that young innocence, for it would be so easy to speculate on that crushed scrap she presses to her cheek.

"A man's tie. Silk," he's on the point of communicating with more to follow when he notices the way she keeps on glancing at someone among the toffs sprawled in their armchairs in the rows at the front. It's a man alongside his wife and he looks even more desperate than the girl for he keeps tugging at his shirt-collar as though it's begun to throttle him. In that instant the boy on stage feels himself suddenly much older and wiser than anyone else in the tent, a terrible burden of knowledge he hasn't asked for pressing down on him.

The blindfold is now squeezing his scalp, his eyes ache, he sways under the hot lights. He needs to get off stage right now but Gus is nowhere at hand to ease his exit. A terrifying image of having to stand rooted here with nowhere to turn takes hold. Although it's the wrong thing to do he pulls the blindfold up and over his head and the crowd goes quiet. Faces rush at him. He feels naked and exposed for it's they now who are drilling him with their deadly know-how and not the other way around.

The girl clutching her married lover's keepsake is weeping openly. The object of her grief crouches even lower in his chair while the wife, a hard-faced blonde, holds herself ramrod stiff. Despite the heat a fox fur encircles her throat like a high tan choker, its little artificial eyes malevolently reflecting the overhead lights, a match for the woman's own flinty glare. It's a triangle the boy has no desire to explore further, yet, even as he looks down on them more and more secrets tremble on his tongue. He senses trouble in store for all three, the girl in particular, for she bears an extra burden all her own it suddenly strikes him in that her stoutness may not arise from purely natural causes. More such terrible insights must surely follow, he tells himself, unless he can make his exit.

Looking towards the back of the tent he sees Rusty standing there, lovely face fixed in repose as always, long mermaid's hair falling sheer like a golden downpour to a point below the belt of her trench-coat. They lock glances over the heads. Silently he beseeches her. *Help me. If only as one performer to another. Please.* Cool as ice-water she stares back as though his entreaty has fallen short like a stone among the heads of the crowd. The moment stretches. *Just one*, he's telling himself, *that's all it takes. Just one to smell fear up here for them to turn on me like a pack of dogs.* He had seen it happen to the others, heard the baying for blood. And now it was to be his turn. He closes his eyes fervently wishing he hadn't unmasked himself. *Help me, Lord. Please get me out of this mess and I swear I will –*

But he never gets the chance to finish his vow for just then

133

the sound of solitary clapping breaks the silence. Opening his eyes he sees heads turning towards the back of the tent where Rusty stands as composed as ever, only now her hands are sending out a steady signal and, after a slow, dawning moment, her lead is taken up by the crowd on the wooden benches. The sound swells to a storm of applause and somehow it saves him as nothing else can for, like a great wind, it drives him weak in the legs and staggering backwards into the wings and safety before the sheer force of its vehemence.

Later. The empty tent and blackness. No stars are visible. He can barely make out the canvas dimensions of his vast bedchamber. Outside an owl is quartering the field. Wide awake under his weight of dusty velvet he lies listening to the cries of its prey, puny little squeaks of fear, but so diminished and so distant from his own preoccupations he hardly feels a thing for them. His brain still churns even though it's several hours since he came reeling off-stage before the onslaught. A triumph, really, if he were to be objective, but the cost to his nerves may have been too great. He can still see those open mouths eager to devour him. With love, as it turned out, with love, but it could so easily have gone the other way.

There's another reason why he cannot sleep. He's thinking of Rusty. *Rusty*. The name, the word, reverberates in his head until its syllables are scoured of meaning. Still, as a name, he has decided, it isn't appropriate, not for her, not for his beautiful mermaid. He must discover for himself her true name. That became imperative the instant she sent him that special look high above the heads of all those poor punters each with his own personal fantasy regarding her availability. Already he's hearing words, sentences, their first proper conversation, until in return she will ask him *his* name.

"*Eric?*" she'll say. "*Eric,*" repeating it softly. "*It suits you. Serious. Always so serious. I've watched you.*"

"*Really?*"

"*Oh, yes. I could see you were different.*"

And then she'll say, "*Would you think it terribly bold of me if I crept in beside you? Just for the warmth, you understand. I haven't a lot on under this coat, you see.*"

Dreaming happily away in this fashion and with something of an erection to boot, although his intentions are chaste as can be, he lies under his invisible canvas canopy breathing in the scent of trampled grass overlaid with ancient dust from his immediate covering. Another odour is present too, hardly one to attract the object of his desires, for he does smell a trifle gamey in his old vest and spare pair of underpants. He only has two to his name.

Up to now the nearby stream has been his only washing place. Submerged to the chin, he once startled a couple of local children who bolted in terror at the sight of a black man in their burn for, of course, his make-up had stayed intact. For an instant he has this delightful image of himself and Rusty taking a dip together. And each night when everyone is fast asleep she will come creeping softly to his bed. Like a couple of innocent woodland creatures they will curl up together, sharing warmth, their body scents mingling to become one, for everyone in the company, and Rusty is no exception, has the same free-and-easy attitude where the daily scrub is concerned.

In a relaxed mood of anticipation he drifts half-dozing, half-dreaming, in his nest of old stage curtains soon to be shared by an angel in fishnet tights.

At some point he must have dropped off for, suddenly, he is aware of a light approaching the tent. Heart pounding like a nervous bridegroom he sits upright in readiness. The approaching glow seems to be travelling erratically across the field at head height, which is odd, as is its motion, for now it hesitates, halts, almost going out.

135

Arriving at the tent this will-o'-the-wisp proceeds at the same nervous pace, hugging the canvas walls. He feels he should offer something vocal in the way of encouragement but all he can muster in the vast emptiness is a high, sissyish cough to denote his presence. In response there comes a muffled cry – it sounds like a swearword at this distance – as a guy-rope brings his night visitor up short. Simultaneously the light races perilously close to the almost transparent fabric. He holds his breath. The flap lifts. The yellow glare of a lamp rushes in.

"Cooee! Are we awake? It's only little old me!"

Even if the voice had not alerted him to the identity of his caller that great, beaked profile certainly would, for the light shines full now on that all too familiar and most unwelcome face still coated with greasepaint from his performance earlier.

"Come to pay his respects to the Great Bamboozalem. For –if the mountain won't come to Mahomet . . ."

He's quite drunk. In his left hand is a flat, silver flask, while his right can barely keep the oil lamp upright or steady. The boy watches as The Great Man advances swaying, broad-beamed in his grandee's dressing-gown, down the middle aisle of trampled grass.

He still cannot bring himself to believe the truth of what he's seeing. Some terrible mistake surely has been made. At any moment the true, expected guest must appear in her long, pale raincoat and stockinged feet, silently staring. He can see her face, read betrayal in those beautiful sea-green eyes as she stands there. What must he do to avert such a nightmare? For nightmare it is, the shadow-play on the tent walls the stuff of bad dreams, a grotesque, Punch-like silhouette keeping pace with its owner and both steadily closing in on him.

"My darling, *dearest* boy, do forgive the intrusion and the lateness of the hour but, being a creature of impulse, I felt I simply had to come calling for I've missed my Dogsbody, really and truly I have . . ."

The words trail off wetly as he fetches up hard against the front of the stage. For a moment he looks uncertain as if wondering just where in the world this obstacle has come from. The lamp wobbles, then manages to find even keel on the bare boards a few feet from his bedding. They face one another across the open, hot mouth of the globe.

"So, dear heart . . ."

A gusty sigh. His hair looks most odd for the plastered strands seem to have slipped sideways revealing a pale crescent of skull.

"Max," he appeals. "Max, please . . ." But already he knows there's no point. Nothing short of a bullet in the brain can deflect or cut short The Great Man once he is underway.

"A disillusioned man, that's what you see before you, dear heart. And more than a little hurt into the bargain, for I did get the impression, rightly or wrongly, that we were chums, you and I. I really thought we were, despite the generation gap. Not that a few years either way ever meant a great deal – at least, not to yours truly it didn't. Young people have always sought out Max Buckingham. He has had many young friends over the years – you're certainly not the first – and all of them, believe me, seemed more than grateful for his sympathetic ear whenever it was needed.

"But, alas, it seems you have decided to turn your back on old Max now that some modest little theatrical success has come your way. But what does it amount to? *Really?* Max Buckingham is not the man to take away from anyone's moment of glory, that has never been his style, but, *really*, just how important to you, dear heart, is the acclaim of a pack of howling hyenas who wouldn't recognize true professional talent if it bit them on the arse? Forgive me, forgive me . . .

"But, aside from all of that, it does not do to upstage your fellow artistes. Which, I'm afraid, dear boy, is what you have been about in your own funny, little, amateurish way. Poor

Maureen, for instance, even if she is a pathetic cow, doesn't know whether she's coming or going, thanks to your carry-on. Now I have not the slightest interest or desire to know the whys and wherefores of what it is exactly you get up to with those poor gulls out there, that's between you and them, thank God, but for your own sake I advise you to pack it in. *Pack it in. Please.* Believe me it can only end in tears, take an old thespian's word for it . . . Dearie me, I've gone quite parched with all this chin-wagging —" And he takes a long shuddering swig from the flask so cleverly shaped to fit precisely into a pocket.

The boy notices that. He also perceives the reason for The Great Man's curious, slipping hairstyle is that he is wearing a wig, and a badly fitting one at that. Why hadn't he spotted something like that earlier? He's finding it difficult to keep his eyes open. If he could only curl up in his snug lair right now, shutting down his brain like some machine that has exceeded its workload, in the morning, maybe, everything would be back the way it was, all of this nothing more than the bad dream he first imagined it to be.

Indeed he must have drifted some little way down that road, for an unexpected noise brings him back, making him start up, pulling the velvet drapes close about his naked shoulders. The oil lamp trembles on the boards, Max's palms spread flat on either side, where he has brought them down in a fit of frenzy. A fearful change has come over him, his face lit like something from hell, scalp naked and gleaming, the pretence of the hairpiece abandoned. Those are real, not imagined, tears trapped in the oily make-up about his eyes.

"Booing me! *Me! Go home. Go home to England.* You heard them. But where *is* my home? I've never had a home except places like these. Once I had them eating out of the palm of my hand. I was carried through the streets of Wexford. Did I ever tell you that? I was a god in their eyes, grown men wept to see my Lear and, afterwards, no end of young chums came calling round to my caravan. *They wanted to, wanted to*, I tell you. There was nothing to be ashamed of. *Nothing*. Horseplay, youthful high jinks. Country people know about such things. But then that busybody priest with his sick mind took it into his head to speak out against me. The most awful things, terrible lies, all of it lies, from the pulpit, too. What could I do? Threats were made. They were going to run me out of town. Never again, I vowed, never again. But it's such a lonely life, how could I help myself? You do understand that, don't you? You do, *oh, say you do*!" But of course he doesn't, how can he, as he confronts the reality of this bald, sobbing stranger face-down before him.

He looks out from his tangle of bedding feeling the unfairness of it all. He's still only young, he tells himself, it isn't just or proper to have this burden thrust upon him.

"Never get old, Dogsbody."

The voice sounds muffled and faint now as though travelling a very long distance.

"And never, *ever*, whatever happens, let them do it to *you*."

A fitful little wind rises outside the tent – it sometimes arrives like this just before dawn – the lamp flickering in response. The Great Man – only he can never think of him in that way ever again, not after tonight – shudders, sighs, slowly raises his pale, gleaming dome. It's exactly like a giant egg. Humpty Dumpty, the watcher thinks.

"Your face, Dogsbody. If you could only see your face!" He's laughing now. "A picture, as they say. Oh, I do so adore it when you just know you have them at your mercy. Putty. Pure putty. You see, dear heart, that's what makes some of us great and the rest greenhorns. Like your good self, I'm afraid. No hard feelings. Tell me now, really and truly, did you actually *believe* for a single instant that you could upstage someone like the great Max Buckingham? And feel sorry for

139

him? For that is what I detect. Good God! *Pity, is it?* From some raggedy-arsed little nobody I took under my wing out of the goodness of my heart believing I could make something of. Well, let me tell you, Master Country Bumpkin, Max Buckingham needs no one's pity, do you understand that? *He needs no one! Comprenez?*"

Halfway to the tent opening he turns to face him for the last time. Much of that closing speech has been directed upwards to an invisible audience under the roof. Squatting among his rags the boy shivers a little in the half-dark. He feels demoralized now, angry, too, for he burns to retaliate.

"One fine day, for your sake, I sincerely hope you find someone just *half* as inspiring as Max Buckingham. But I very much doubt it."

The tent flap is a matter of feet away, the man in the sumptuous dressing-gown determined, as always, on having the last word.

But from his lair the boy calls out, "I have! I have!" barely aware of what it is he's saying.

"Oh? *Oh?*"

The yellow lamplight illuminates a painted skull grinning at him.

"Do tell. Or – is it a secret?"

"I've found the Lord! I've found Jesus!"

"Really? Well, I must say, I haven't had much competition from that quarter ever before. Let's hope this new-found 'chum' of yours is half as much fun."

And he disappears into the night laughing like a demon leaving him staring at blackness and still pondering the import of what he's just blurted out.

How long he held that posture is difficult to say, but he must have fallen asleep for, in a dream state, he's conscious of something, some presence, then a voice, monotonous, low, dispassionate, with a warning to leave this place quickly before it's too late. He has the impression *flee* is the actual word used but, of course, that may well have been anticipation of what lies ahead and the language of his new career.

Whatever the reasons, he decides to take heed of the still, small voice, and when first light arrives he slips away, leaving nothing to denote his passing but twin tracks in the dewy grass, trusty little cigar-box under his arm.

FIVE

"And that was the last you set eyes on all of them, was it?" enquires Jordan in those soft, creamy tones. An accent from a vanished, rustic past. If ever it existed, save in the imagination of someone like Gilchrist himself. But that was how he did speak.

They were hunkered in the lea of a breakwater while further up the shingle Angie sits sunning herself, face presented sacrificially to the noonday rays.

"Max and Gus and that girl. What was her name again?"

"Rusty."

"Yes. I can just see *her* all right."

Without thinking Gilchrist said, "Poor thing, she had this awful birthmark. Could never disguise it properly, not even under all the stage make-up. She would always try to keep one cheek turned away from the audience. But you couldn't help notice them staring. People can be very cruel. Country people."

None of it was true. The invention had sprung to his lips fully-formed and, he was bound to admit, frighteningly plausible-sounding as if from nowhere. The truth of it was he didn't want to share her with anyone, the real Rusty. He had made her much too alluring for her own good and realizing it had concocted this falsehood, this fictional blemish. A little startled at his own deceit he crouched there on the soft dry sand, granules fine as caster sugar.

The beach was practically deserted today save for a scattering of well-spaced late sun-worshippers broiling on their mats, most barely worth a second glance. Closer at hand, bare, blackened legs planted in the sand, was a solitary gipsy woman festooned with cheap cotton shifts and loops of jewellery. She stood there looking disorientated, obviously badly put out by the emptiness of this stretch of the *playa*. For some little time she had been glancing over in their direction but seemed too demoralized to do anything about it.

Jordan said, "And you never ever saw them again?"

Gilchrist was taken aback by the other's persistence for he thought he had deflected this particular line of questioning. So, for the second time, even more surprised at his own duplicity, he heard himself lie.

"No, that wasn't the end of the story."

Hesitating for a bare second, he plunged into the hazardous deeps of his own invention.

"Much later I ran across them all when I had my own tent. A very different performance, as you can well imagine." He permitted himself a little laugh. "By a coincidence we happened to be in the same part of the country. In competition, if you like. One night I went along to their show. Nothing had changed, well, it had, or maybe it was just me, but it all looked so, so sad, so tawdry and down at heel. You understand?"

The other nodded. Recently he'd had a haircut, that ridiculous pony-tail shorn off, ending up on some barber's floor where it belonged. In Gilchrist's opinion he looked much better for it, quite handsome, really, in a florid way, but then an element of self-interest might be said to have influenced that particular judgement. Strangely enough, since they had first met – was it a week, a little more? – their appearance had become even more markedly similar as though proximity was working in some mysterious way to smoothe out any minor differences.

He, Gilchrist, for instance, had discovered in himself a taste for much more casual attire. Today he was wearing an old pair of cricketing flannels – now where on earth had they sprung from? – held up by an equally mysterious tie in vaguely school colours. A lavender polo shirt with a tiny snapping crocodile over one nipple completed the snazzy ensemble. And on his feet he had a pair of new navy deck shoes. The panama had been left at home.

Jordan said, "You never introduced yourself? Not even for old times' sake?"

Gilchrist allowed his mind to wander, his eyes, too. Angie hadn't changed position, squatting bare-breasted, palms upturned to the great ultra-violet god in the sky. Every opportunity she got she would offer herself in this way with a tiny sigh, even in the middle of a conversation. It seemed excessive, obsessive, even, but he supposed it must have a lot to do with her upbringing in that grey, permanently overcast, Northern town of hers.

But then he himself had been soaking up the morning rays in the privacy of his own balcony. Already he had taken on a pale, biscuit hue save for that bisecting triangle of white left by the imprint of his underpants. Despite his new-found laxity he couldn't bring himself to go the whole hog, even though there was no one to see him on his recliner. When he looked in the mirror that pale outline of untouched flesh somehow represented all the hidden repressions of the old life, a reminder of something that could, or would, never leave him. Perhaps he and Angie had more in common than either of them realized, except, in her case, he suspected that lean, lithe, little body had an all-over tan. Her nipples were like tiny, raised punctuation marks – *braille*, he thought a touch unwisely – while a column of bleached down inched its way clear of the waistband of her shorts, thinning out to nothingness across the spread of that taut midriff.

Sensing a slow and gradual restriction in the region of his own groin, hurriedly he went on, "No, I never did. Just melted off into the night along with all the other punters. Sometimes I do rather blame myself for that."

My God, he was thinking to himself for the second time, *what a capacity for lies and lying you really do seem to have.* Already he had an ending all mapped out and prepared, the perfect ending, if there was any justice in the world.

One night he would be looking out over the heads and there they all would be, Gus, Maureen, old Fay, Sonny, "Rajah", Connie Carr, even The Great Man himself, dressed to the nines, the whole crew sitting in a row, birds of paradise among a flock of barnyard fowl, come to shake their heads and say, *Isn't it sad, but I told you so.* And of course – what else? – he would have them at his feet in next to no time crying out for mercy along with the rest of those country sinners. Conversion of that sort would never be sweeter or more rightfully his. For a moment he found himself half-believing it actually had happened that way out there in the sticks on one of those emotion-torn evenings under straining canvas, for there had to be a wind.

"*Listen and tremble before the Lord's mighty breath. He is everywhere and arrives without warning at any time of day or night. And no one can hide from him whenever and wherever he makes his presence felt. Remember he is only the thickness of a tarpaulin away.*"

Jordan said, "I want you to meet a few people. They want to meet you," and Gilchrist felt suddenly relieved, for he might have been tempted into pursuing the fantasy into areas where retreat might not be possible without contradicting himself later on.

Angie called out, "Won't be a second, honey!" although she couldn't possibly have overhead what had just been said. But then she did seem to be peculiarly and nervously tuned into her companion's merest mood and reaction. A proper little crystal set and no mistake, thought Gilchrist, not unkindly, watching her pull on her singlet. It was dusty pink today with NO SWEAT stencilled across it in yellow, dayglo lettering.

Jordan sighed, murmuring, "That'll be the day – honey," for Gilchrist's benefit.

They watched as she picked through her bits and pieces on the spread towel. Walkman, paperback, lotion, comb, cigarettes, flask of Evian, her Snoopy keyring. One by one they disappeared into her leather haversack. Finally she peered in at them there in its dark, scented recesses. For a moment it looked as though her head was deep within a nosebag, a blonde, foraging pony, and Gilchrist couldn't repress a smile at the sudden bizarre image.

Jordan called out, "No sweat! No sweat, honey!" and when she glanced up they were laughing together.

"I'm glad you two find me so hilarious," she retorted, not in any peevish way, shying a pebble in their direction, the gesture itself so ineffectual, so *feminine*, that they continued to grin.

"If you could only see yourselves. Two, two –"

She broke off and Gilchrist thought to himself, *she's as much in the dark as we are*, for even though a week had gone by, not once had the burning issue been addressed. It was as though they had put it aside temporarily, perhaps even for good, for the curious thing was the more they saw of one another the less that amazing similarity seemed to matter, a private concern for them and them alone. He couldn't explain it even to himself, and if the truth were known didn't really care to any longer, content to allow life to slide by in his new company.

A stray cur came slanting towards them desperately sniffing the sand. He and Jordan studied it as if it were something from outer space, unable to relate to it even if they wanted to. Its dugs were swollen – there was a distant litter somewhere whose unheard cries rang in the creature's brain like a klaxon – yet they continued to watch indifferently, two potential exterminators. Then it went nosing off just as the gipsy woman had done. She was a distant blob by now, trudging after her moving shadow across the sand. The sky was oven-baked, metallic blue, the sun a throbbing white disc. To look directly heavenward was to tempt transferring that milky image to the retina for a long time, perhaps permanently.

Angie said, "Ready when you are," and putting on sunglasses they headed up the beach together for the distant elevator whose shaft had been hewn out of the rock. Along-side rose a flight of sixty-five stairs, the number printed on a noticeboard as a warning in four languages. Today only a solitary figure, predictably Nordic, toiled upward, ant-like in the heat. When the heavy doors clanged shut they leant against the moving metal walls, eyes still shaded, luxuriating in the sudden chill.

"I know the only place to be on a day like this." Jordan's voice came out of the blackness like some West Country genie's. "Coolest spot in town. Isn't that right, young Angie?"

She didn't respond. Gilchrist could feel her soft, breathing presence close by, the sensation somehow much more arous-ing in the dark. Then the doors slid apart and Jordan strode off into the glare and Gilchrist realized he was meant to follow with the girl. He felt suddenly nervous, left alone with her in this way, for the first time, really, since the three had met.

A fair climb still lay ahead, taking them through one of the

147

more picturesque parts of the old town, past cave-like interiors where old women sat with lace for sale, or the newer wave of hippies displayed trays of painted pebbles and junk jewellery. Gilchrist's legs had begun to ache. This was terrain more suited to mountain goats. Indeed, Jordan could be seen skipping tirelessly ahead despite his bulk from one flight of blue and white tiled steps to the next. As they watched he slapped outstretched palms with one of the bearded ones and something passed between them. This transaction, if it were such, took place at least three times on the ascent.

Angie said, "Maybe you can tell me what's going on here. I mean, are you two related, or aren't you?"

Gilchrist was concentrating all his energies on the climb. He had the beginning of a stitch as well as a blister on one heel.

"Could we rest – just for a minute?"

They sat down on a low, lime-washed wall. In the courtyard beyond purple flowers exploded from the shade and a cagebird sang. It sounded mechanical, like a toy, not real. He sat there listening to the frenzied outpourings until his blood ceased to pound. Angie lit a cigarette. She had one of those lighters on a thong about her neck. Smokers' hands were always busy, busy, he reflected. His own lay flat on his thighs brown and awkward like a pair of kippers. The liver spots were much more noticeable today.

"So," she said returning to the fray. "Are you or aren't you? *He* certainly won't tell me."

Right then Gilchrist was tempted to plunge into another of those instant inventions of his. It would have been so easy, yet it wasn't the same, somehow, not without his fellow-conspirator present. Instead he enquired innocently, "Not a word, you say?"

"Nothing. Says he doesn't care to talk about it. Far too many painful memories, according to him. Shit!"

"Well, some things do take time to heal," he heard himself collude.

In that moment, crazy as it might seem, he experienced genuine curiosity about something which he knew to be utterly bogus, without foundation. But then could he be really certain of that? Might there not be something genuinely blood-based between the two of them other than the merely physiological? This country, these people, were doing strange things to him, all those Northern notions of reason and restraint evaporating like so much mist under the hot sun. But if that were so, why then didn't he feel some alarm? Did he even *care*? *Take heed, friend, for you're driving down the road to Hell with the car doors open*. A favourite old stand-by from the tent circuit days.

"Fit to go on, are we?" enquired Angie, and he rose with mock alacrity. "Lucky I know where he's heading. Otherwise he'd just leave us like a couple of prats."

There didn't seem to be anything to say to that so they resumed their climb past open doorways where whole families could be glimpsed in the gloom munching silently together. The interiors were uniformly spotless, contrary to what he had been led to believe about this society, tiled floors, gleaming, cool, dark rooms leading the eye on towards leafy glimpses of courtyards beyond. It was like passing a succession of forbidden little Edens where people like himself and this girl would never be invited to enter.

"He is a right bastard, you know. Everyone finds him out. Sooner or later."

He said, "It'll all come out in the wash. You'll see," and she laughed for the very first time, he would have sworn to that.

"What a pair," she said. "Bet you're another Scorpio."

At some stage she stopped to buy cigarettes and he watched her rummaging through her haversack while the shopkeeper leaned on his counter reading his newspaper. She looked so vulnerable in that instant, a schoolgirl delving among her books for change, that he felt quite fatherly suddenly, keeping a protective eye on a teenager a little too under-dressed for her own safety. Waiting there in the heat outside the tiny shop – little more than a kiosk, really, and crammed to bursting point – the moment became frozen for him, the emotion instantly bridging time and distance.

He is remembering a day like this in September – *can it, then, only be a year away?* – and another resort, except there the sea is cold and the sun far from scorching. It's about seven in the evening, that dead time in England, the streets empty, that identical, bluish square flickering silently away like some electric icon in the corner of every room he passes. Each house also seems to have a VACANCIES sign in the window – the season has been a poor one, three in a row, so far – and he hurries past all those dead front parlours lit by television with no one there to watch.

He's in something of a panic, for *she* is on her own back in Elsinore and this "little trip to the shops" has taken him far longer than intended. A couple of times he finds himself retracing his route after sorties down side-streets which all look the same to him. He realizes by now he should have stayed on the broad Esplanade holding the statue of George III in view and, further on, the striped Victorian clocktower like something made out of the town's own seaside rock. But he's been nervous these past days about being recognized, even on his own. There may have been photographs in the papers by now, even over here – worse, something on one of those same television screens dogging him as he hurries past lugging his purchases.

Insanely he finds himself going through his shopping list, or, rather, hers. A packet of frozen ice-cream Mars bars, salami sticks, something called Tizer, more mysteries named

M&Ms, Hula-Hoop crisps. Trash, all of it, but what else was he to do? *Tell me*, he continues to invoke that chilly deity who seems to have turned his back on him.

For two whole days now she has been lying in her room face buried in the pillow not bothering to wash or dress properly. A sour, vaguely rank smell hangs in the air. She keeps the windows hermetically sealed despite the weather, another of her little habits. When he taxes her about it gently he hears her mutter something into the bedding about "the curse". Could he have heard her right? Half of him understands what she's saying, the other half shies away in distaste.

He's not at all happy with his behaviour. Every night he is on his knees on the far side of that flowery partition wall. She has persuaded him to buy her a pink, plastic transistor radio in the shape of an American diner – he recognizes the outline, classic fifties, from his trip – and as he prays it babbles softly away in concert like some half-witted imitator in the next room. Later he is to discover it's one of those imbecilic broadcast "chat lines" where young people ring up and yammer inconsequentially for hours on end, running up vast amounts on their parents' telephone bills in the process. At least, he thinks that's how it works . . .

At the boarding-house he climbs the sandstone steps and slips his key gently into the lock. He feels more nervous than usual about meeting Mrs Stacpoole in the hallway for there are small, scalloped-edged cards liberally thumb-tacked on almost every landing forbidding eating in the rooms and the carrier-bag plainly bears the name of a well-known grocery chain. Halfway up the first flight he hears the dreaded voice coming from the basement.

"So pleased to see the young lady up and about again."

Turning, he looks down on that startling figure emerging from below stairs, the burnt orange wig, slightly askew as always, the only fixed point in a constantly changing

151

ensemble. Today she has on a robe with a mandarin collar enlivened with writhing gold dragons. Her make-up also seems appropriately oriental. Is it his impression her eyes have been elongated with Conté pencil? He knows it's ridiculous but she reminds him more and more of Max Buckingham. Only he, Gilchrist, could have stumbled on theatrical digs out of all the boarding-houses in this Dorset town where there already is a Sharon, a Carmel, an Eden Vale, a Shiloh, even a Nazareth Lodge to choose from. But all this is irrelevant as he tries to take in what the landlady has just said.

"What do you mean 'up and about'?" he enquires, heart beating like a drum.

"Well, she did slip out of here not half an hour ago done up to the nines. Wouldn't have recognized her. Would we, Sylvester?"

Her husband, a melancholy coloured man with crinkly white hair and a gold tooth in the middle of his mouth, murmurs assent. Rarely to be seen – even now he's out of vision – he spends much of the time in the basement half-light like some homesick, ageing retainer brought back from Mrs S's colonial past. That's sheer fantasy on Gilchrist's part. He does have a pronounced Liverpool accent.

"She didn't say where she was going?"

That's a mistake. He realizes it even as he speaks. He sees her eyes sharpen momentarily, but his anxiety is much too great for him to be cautious.

"Young people," she murmurs looking at the carrier-bag in his hand, "can be so – impulsive. Inconsiderate? The Amusements have still another week to run. Beside the pier, you know. You could always try there."

"So she *did* leave a message."

"No, no, but it just struck me that someone from – from her background – might find such places attractive – exciting?"

"Thank you, Mrs Stacpoole," he replies, controlling himself, "you've been most helpful. She really should have told her old uncle where she was going. But she's a good girl and I know her far too well to have any fears about her getting into mischief. Poor mite, to lose both parents in a car crash like that at her age. Orphaned. She deserves some fun to help her forget. That's what we came here for, after all." And he continued on up the stairs with the reek of the woman's scent following him just as surely as he knows her coal-rimmed eyes are.

Once inside his room he flings water in his face until his rage is not quite so murderous. *The painted old bitch*, he mouths to the mirror, *that harlot with her dusky paramour*, for he feels convinced they cannot be man and wife despite the profusion of rings on her fingers. *How dare she patronize them*. For he knows he is included in her remarks about being Irish and by definition a bogtrotter. Just what makes these people behave so lordly with their pitiful pretensions to superiority, when it's obvious to anyone with half an eye that everything about them, *everything*, is one colossal lie, their history, politics, sexual habits, washing arrangements and, particularly, that watered-down farce that masquerades as their religion.

For an instant he's back once more inside the tent calling retribution down on the heads of an entire race. For, oh, that appalling creature with her autographed photographs on the walls and her endless stories of how Larry and Ralph and Donald and Harold – when he was an actor, and before he was a famous writer – shared a kipper and sometimes, even, a bed, and life was one merry round of theatrical tittle-tattle. He didn't believe a word, not one solitary word of it. Why should he? Max Buckingham should have been an object lesson in what to expect but, here, even at his age, he was still a greenhorn when it came to dealing with the English and their deceitful ways.

153

Eric, he murmurs sadly to his reflection in the fly-blown glass above the basin, *Eric, they have you as bad as themselves, these people*. It's true. Where else did that lie spring from and so easily, too, about death in a three-lane pile-up and a young girl left defenceless, alone, unable to fend for herself? He gives a loud groan at that point, darting out the bedroom door and downstairs two at a time through the miasma of stale perfume hanging in the passage.

Along the front he hurries under wrought-iron lamps hung with floral globes as big as moons. It is deep dusk by now. The sea murmurs softly to his left. Already there are shadowy humps on the corrugated sand where couples are staking out their territories for the long night of the senses ahead. He is aware of giggling, and cigarettes pin-point the gathering darkness.

The roar and lights of the fairground draw him on, his panic gathering pace. There's something truly hellish about that glare, he persuades himself. Already he may be too late, although what awful fate may have overtaken his young charge he daren't specify.

Only when he plunges into the carnival proper, eyes and ears assailed, are those fears realized in exact and human form, arriving the moment he sees the young fairground attendants clinging to their machines, predator eyes roving over the milling forms and faces below. His is a race against time to get to her first before any of those grease-stained monkeys do.

Pushing through the crowds, at any moment he expects to come upon that dreaded sight, the innocent, *his* innocent, in her pathetic finery – just what must she be wearing, anyway, for he feels certain he knows everything in that pink nylon holdall of hers – and the roustabout offering a joke, a cigarette, a free ride.

My God, she might well be aloft this very instant, head pushed back and screaming, while her seducer, all teddy-boy sideburns and tattoos, rests oily paws on her young shoulders. They all of them have that identical look, dark, gipsyish, the occasional flash of precious metal in an earlobe or about throat or wrist. Someone like her must be seen as instantly "available". He hates using such a vile word but he must be realistic and, of course, once that accent is heard then nothing can save her. These young jackals certainly can't be doing this for the love of it, or their pitiful wages. It's that other inducement, the nightly trawl for teenage girls that keeps them tethered to their merry-go-rounds.

He studies one such youth in a white T-shirt riding the rim of the dodgems. A bulging leather change-pouch covers his groin. Or is it there to focus attention on that ready masculinity? Once more Gilchrist is appalled by these ideas breeding inside his head. If he had stayed with that travelling troupe and hadn't received the Call when it came, he, too, might have been just like this same, cold-eyed youngster restlessly scouting the crowd for his prey.

And then he sees her, not in the company of some leering young fairground jockey, but all alone, as though protected by the invisible shield of her own innocence. She is holding one of those ridiculous confections on a stick spun out of air and sugar water and precious little else, and immediately his heart melts at the sight of that puny figure in jeans and skinny, ribbed, sleeveless sweater nibbling her pink froth. For a moment he watches her, unseen among the crowds. He really cannot help himself for he has become something of a voyeur as far as she is concerned.

He's sorely tempted to continue stalking her a little longer –*what harm can there be in it?* – until he notices her smiling at the antics of someone running the coconut-shy. He's old enough to be her father, this character in a Union Jack waistcoat and battered top-hat, but to him, in the state he's in, no one is exempt from suspicion. As he breaks through

155

the crowd she sees him, her face losing all that earlier, innocent anticipation.

Lord, forgive thy servant, if he has erred on the side of being over-zealous in his concern for this young girl. But then he thinks, *perhaps this is what parenthood is really like*, this constant, agonized vigilance. It's all been such a new experience for him – he has had to learn in such a fast and painful way – but in their better moments together they have shared some of that. *They have, haven't they?*

Unable to help himself he takes her by one of those thin, burning arms, hauling her back the way she came. She makes no move to resist him or protest, the candyfloss falling to the ground to melt, trampled and forgotten amidst all the other debris of that place.

Later that night he remembered how she beat on his chest, crying, "I'm not a baby, I'm not a baby!" Then, worst of all, "I want to go home!"

Exhausted, they wept together, kneeling side by side on the thin, scorched rug in front of the gas-fire they'd never learned to light and he had prayed, "Dear Lord, yet again hast thou delivered this child out of the yawning pit and the snares of those who would seek to corrupt her purity. Thou knowest full well the difficulties that beset us. Our enemies never sleep – even in this heathen place so far from our own dear, green land. But, like the Israelites of old, how can we return, while there are those who seek to persecute this young girl for her beliefs, even her own flesh and blood? Like that solitary lost sheep on the hillside, this little one kneeling now before you is more precious than a thousand saved souls. Continue in thy divine protection, we beseech thee, until such times as those who would harry us tire of the chase. Amen."

But, deep down, of course, he knew there was little hope of that. He recognized, however, that his words gave comfort to the object of all that hue and cry kneeling beside him before this dead gas-fire, a curious altar, surely, with its chalky filaments bared like so many ancient, brittle teeth. Persuasion was what he was good at. He could always tell if his powers were working well because then he would be carried along on the tide of his own rhetoric. And for just a moment he found himself actually believing in a safe haven for them both away from the bigots back home and their lying slanders.

Sadly, the following morning the dream had faded in the pale light coming through those high, narrow sash-windows overlooking the English Channel. Seagulls strutted on the deserted front as though they had the place to themselves and as he and the girl made their way to the railway station with their light luggage those same cruel-eyed scavengers paid not the slightest heed to them. He remembered that morning vividly, the mist, the smell of wrack and sewage, the cries of the terns combing the beach. Moreover, the girl was beginning a cold and the treadmill of his concern was starting up all over again.

Close by a voice enquired, "Smoke?" and when he shook his head automatically all those images from that past broke up, scattering like the pieces in a kaleidoscope. Angie lit a cigarette for herself from the cartridge lighter strung about her neck. She inhaled with closed eyes then blew out a soft jet of bluish smoke.

"You really should cut down," he said. "For your health's sake," then stopped embarrassed for it was as if he were back behaving like a surrogate parent again.

"I know," she said. "Jordan's always on about it as well, even though he has the odd puff himself. But then that's different, isn't it?" And she grinned mischievously at him.

"Now I've got two sugar-daddies to fuss over me," she continued, slipping an arm through his, and Gilchrist couldn't

157

be certain what disconcerted him more, the unexpectedness of the gesture, skin upon skin, like a sudden, delicious burn, or the way in which she seemed to be able to read his thoughts.

They were walking together up yet another incline – he knew the route so well by now, for it led to the bull-ring and beyond that the open-air Thursday market – and his acute awareness of this scantily clad slip of a thing pressing herself to him like this became more intense. He hated to feel power ebbing away in this manner for, somehow, she had managed to shift most of it her own way with just a few coquettish remarks. His legs trembled ever so slightly. He prayed she wouldn't notice and he thought, *what a soft touch you turned out to be in your harvest years, you old dope*, pushover for a certain rather obvious type of young hussy. Hussy. He liked the thought and sound of the word. There was something pleasurably titillating about it.

She said, "I bet you haven't a clue what to expect. Who you're going to meet, I mean."

He said nothing. The full force of her sun-oil had re-asserted itself, that strong and sweetish coconut aroma. He felt certain it would linger on his own skin long after they had separated.

"I call it – them – The Tall Story Club. But don't tell Jordan that. All boys together. I don't count."

She tightened her gaze against the harsh sunlight, dark glasses pushed up and resting above the hairline. It gave her the look of an aspiring model. His original impression of this girl was undergoing a serious change, he realized, no longer fixed and, frankly, patronizing. There was something immensely flattering about being in her company, on the receiving end of her attentions. Already he was beginning to feel regret about having that withdrawn, quite soon, too, judging by what she'd said.

They were passing a tiny row of food shops, *comestibles*, fish, fruit, meat, baker's, like a conspiratorial huddle, for on either side there was nothing but low, lime-washed dwellings, grilles on the windows, dark, heavy doors, those blue and white tiles covering every floor.

Angie said, "Here we are," outside what looked like a workmen's café. Through the open doorway he could see a few battered tables and chairs and three men in faded navy overalls, heads low over piled plates. He looked at her.

She grinned. "Follow me and all will be revealed."

They went into the café – there was a strong smell of frying oil, and flies buzzed, heavy and sated – through a door, past the stench of a toilet, then along a corridor and, suddenly, they were in a courtyard full of plants, roofed with an enormous vine like a living canopy. The sunlight poured through its screen dappling the white cloth of a large, square table and the heads of those gathered around it. Jordan sat facing him in the place of honour but rose when he saw them, extending both arms in his customary, lordly fashion.

"Welcome!" he cried. "Welcome to our humble gathering!"

There must have been a dozen bottles of red wine at least on the cloth in various stages of depletion. Gilchrist stood there, all his vaunted skills as a spellbinder fragile as a butterfly's wing. The faces stared back at him. All were male, as Angie had said, and waiting, it seemed, for some word or gesture to satisfy their anticipation. They were also regarding him with a certain amount of shock. It made him realize, despite everything Jordan must have told them, his appearance in the flesh like this still came as a surprise. Then Jordan was waving to him to come join him near the head of the board. Angie seemed to have disappeared, but to his shame he didn't seem to mind any longer.

"This is Bob and this is Mike and meet old Digby here and the one with the cigar is Dan, he's American, we put up with him because he's got a sexy young wife, and here's Dick the

159

Dago, for obvious reasons, and down there is Trevor, a boring Welshman, and that one there trying to look intelligent is Ken from Woking, God help him, and beside him is our legal eagle Carlos, any problem with your lease come to him, and that's Reg, and Mark is out in the loo. One more and we could call ourselves the twelve apostles."

After the laughter had died away, Ken – he was totally bald and wore a black eye-patch – murmured, "All present and correct from where I'm sitting. Now that brother Eric has joined us."

"Damn it, he's right!" roared Jordan, thumping the table. "One-eyed, he may well be, but our ex-pat from Sussex can count better than the rest of us."

"*Surrey*, old chap, Surrey. Get it right," corrected the Moshe Dayan lookalike wearily. "*If* you don't mind. But, then, somebody from Dawlish, I suppose, can't be expected to know any better."

There was to be a lot of such jocular sniping as the meal progressed, all those little morsels of class, education and background which the English so enjoy picking over like monkeys combing each other for fleas. Yet it did surprise him to find it reproduced here in such a setting with such loving dedication. It was as though distance did make the heart grow fonder of old ways and made them anxious to practise their skills on one another just in case they had lost their touch.

He caught himself thinking, *thank heavens no one, as yet, has homed in on my own place of origin*, realizing, of course, if he stayed here long enough it had to happen. But it would be so wearisome to have to explain, as well as justify it, all over again, then have it explained back to him as he knew so well to his cost. Protestant, Catholic, England, Ireland, troops out, troops in, the terrible tedium of all that hopeless, hopeless business.

At such times he longed to cry out, "None of that has

160

anything to do with me. I'm an innocent bystander to all of that. Someone caught in the cross-fire. I never wanted anything to do with any part of that, I assure you. Only when I tried to shield an innocent young girl from those same horrors did I become a target for both sides." He heard his excuses ring out in his head, so well rehearsed and polished by usage they arrive like beads on a wire.

Jordan was saying, "Yes, it was a sheer fluke that brought us together. Chance in a million. Something you read about," and Gilchrist realized everyone around the table was looking at him for some sort of confirmation. Their eyes met, he and his long-lost "brother".

It was a moment fraught with tension, and Gilchrist could have sworn there might have been fear in the other's eyes.

Then he heard himself say, "Yes, you could call it something of a minor miracle in many ways," and he was glad Angie wasn't present to hear his words, feeling he might have betrayed her in some inexplicable way. He was remembering what she'd said about The Tall Story Club. It looked very much as though already he had become a paid-up member.

Confident of his support now, Jordan continued, "I don't blame our mother, not after all these years. She had to do what she had to do at the time, God rest her, and I'm certain she would have been happy to have seen this day."

He beamed at Gilchrist, but for the life of him he couldn't muster a return volley, not just at this particular moment. He sat there watching his glass being filled with wine from one of the beaded bottles on the table. The pourer was the one called Ken from Woking, he of the hairless pate – it looked like a bathing-cap, pale, coffee-coloured, or a bank robber's nylon stocking mask, stretched like a second skin.

"Tell me . . . Eric," he said softly, leaning forward, his one good eye fastened on him in unnerving fashion. "Your accent. It isn't *really* West Country, is it now?"

Happily, just then, three young waiters in white aprons came bustling in with platters of fried fish and bowls of salad. There was a great to-do of passing plates and cutlery and calling out for, "*Pan! Pan!*" and more *vino* and Gilchrist sat there feeling the first trickle of the Rioja slide down his throat like chilled, slightly smoky blackcurrant cordial. He was an innocent when it came to drink and drinking but the taste of this was so light, yet so velvety, recalling autumn fruit and bonfires, that he saw his glass somehow almost magically retain its level even though he seemed to be supping away quite steadily.

He began to pick up fragments of conversation from the diners on either side of him. Talk of time-shares and apartments seemed to dominate the discussion. He got the impression everyone was involved or interested in deals involving the rent or sale of property. All decried the young bleached blond touts – of both sexes and always English, alas – who infested the downtown *plazas* putting the bite on confused, elderly tourists, but Gilchrist couldn't help feeling these people were in much the same line of business, a case of fleas living on the backs of lesser fleas, a pulsing pyramid of hustlers, some merely a little more discreet than others. He was surprised no one, as yet, had put out any feelers in his direction, then decided Jordan must have warned them off.

They exchanged smiles now – he really was feeling amazingly mellow – and the look was one of such unmistakable kinship that once again he experienced that old surge of affection for the man at the head of the table, the picture of flushed bonhomie. His own face must look just like that, he decided, without benefit of a mirror. But then, was there any need of one, when his reflection beamed back at him from across the table?

He ate more of the *pescado frito* and helped himself to salad. The plates kept on being replenished by the boys from the café, Pepe, Bernardo, Felipe – already he knew them by name – and the rising currents of conversation seemed to swirl about in the foliage overhead. He realized for the first time those were bunches of real grapes hanging an arm's length away, greenish-gold in colour, slightly dusty to the touch.

Woking Ken finally seemed to be losing interest in his pedigree. At some stage, he, Gilchrist, recalled telling him that as far as he was concerned – he couldn't speak for Jordan – everything was a closed book up until a week or so ago and that any real research into their past had yet to begin. It happened to be true, and for a moment the other's single eye, a watery, bloodshot blue, clouded over as though registering the shock of the unexpected. Gilchrist realized it was quite possible he might have broken the cardinal rule of the Club, namely, that of never, ever coming out with the bare, unvarnished truth. *Details* were the thing, those extra trimmings which kept the blood coursing and interest alive, even though everyone in their heart of hearts knew they were nothing but the gilt on the gingerbread lie.

A short time later he rose, excusing himself, although no one paid any heed, not even his bald companion, for the noise was at its peak by now, people roaring and gesticulating across the table at one another.

In the toilet he faced the cracked tiles, urinating long and luxuriously. He felt a warm glow of irresponsibility with no possible likelihood of remorse or regret. Even the stench of the open drain at his feet had no power to threaten his mood. All his senses seemed to have taken on some protective coating. He studied his stream amazed at such potency, such a healthy colour, too, the piss of a young man in his prime. As he stood there lost in such thoughts he was joined by one of the men from the table. Gilchrist had a feeling he was the one they called Mark, or he might have been Reg, he couldn't be certain, but, of course, none of that mattered, names were irrelevant now.

"Well, Eric," said the man companionably. Like Gilchrist, he, too, was cupping his cock in that ludicrously prim way men affect in such situations. "Hardly the time or place, I know, but I've been dying to meet you for ever such a long time. Heard so much about you."

Bullshit, thought Gilchrist, but not unpleasantly. Then – *cock, piss* and now *bullshit*, where were all these awful new words coming from? There was no mirror on the wall. For a moment he almost wished there was just to verify he hadn't become that slack-jawed, loose-tongued character which his present mood seemed to indicate.

"I see dear old Ken has been giving you an earful. Bit of a sad case, really. Used to be something tremendously important in ICI, they tell me, then the roof kind of caved in on him. Wife, job, house, company car, lost it all, the whole shebang. Just like that."

To emphasize the point the man at his side snapped the fingers of his right hand necessitating its removal from his thing and Gilchrist stared straight ahead as though his life depended on it. His companion was a man in his early forties, blond, his skin taut and glistening like that of a well-filled sausage, and with that puppyish look almost certainly retained from his schooldays. The accent was similar to the dreaded Ken's but with a touch more drawl to it. Also, Gilchrist couldn't help but notice, an acrid whiff of body odour which seemed out of character somehow. Or was that merely his naive misreading of the English class structure again?

"Tell me, tell me, old chap," the other continued breathily. He may well have been a shade drunk as well. "Come on now. You aren't *really* a man of the cloth, are you? For – have to say – we don't get too many of those out here on the old Costa del Sin. Mind you, could do with a spot of Hymns Ancient And

Modern. C. of E. myself, in another time, another place. Never really leaves you, you know."

In a high, artificially modulated voice, he began humming "Lead Kindly Light" and Gilchrist cursed the retention of his bladder for it meant he was captive to this idiot's opinions until it had emptied itself.

"That's all in the past," he heard himself murmur. "New beginnings, you know."

He was wondering just how much these people really did know about him and his affairs. He may well have relaxed his guard much too soon, he told himself. How much had he confided, anyway? More important, how much information had been relayed by the man at the head of the table?

He realized he no longer needed to pee and as he backed away buttoning himself – the cricketing trousers were of the old-fashioned sort – the other man loudly broke wind then said, "Oh, I do beg your pardon, padre," giving an unpleasant laugh. Gilchrist felt a sudden surge of anger. It would have been enormously satisfying to grip that fat schoolboy neck, leaving a lasting imprint, then apologizing in a similar offhand way. Sweating a little, he made his way out into the passage to come face to face with Jordan.

"Everything all right?"

They looked at one another. Gilchrist felt like blurting out, "Your friend back there needs to be taught some manners," but shook his head instead.

"Just give me the nod if you find all this too boring for words. We can always slip off into the night, you know. No one in there is going to notice." He gave a laugh. But Gilchrist merely smiled at him continuing on his way.

At the end of the passage he hesitated – it was like plunging into a noisy, green-shaded pool – and as he did so he could have sworn he heard what sounded like a sudden yelp of pain coming from the toilet he had just left.

In his absence his glass had been replenished and, sipping slowly, he allowed his gaze to roam about the table. He could do so with perfect confidence now. It was as if he were watching a play from the anonymity of a seat in the stalls. No, no, it was more like one of those very big old masters with a title like "Boon Companions" or even "Breaking Bread", a tableau patched with pools of light, an effect created by the overhead foliage. *Chiaroscuro*. That was the word, wasn't it? Heads, hands, faces, sudden vivid glimpses of clothing swam in and out of focus as their owners argued and gestured, but rarely listened, it seemed to Gilchrist, all the while drinking inordinately, it also struck him, despite his own steady intake. A voice began droning on in his ear about batting averages. It appeared there was a Test Match in the West Indies. He didn't even bother to turn his head to see who it belonged to.

Then he felt a palm fall on his shoulder and a different speaker breathed, "What's your little weakness, then, eh? Sex? Drugs? Rock and roll?"

Glancing up he encountered the slow smile of someone sporting the deepest, most permanent tan he had yet seen. In swift succession he also registered a stick-like form wrapped in a loose linen suit, pale, mocking eyes, a cologne as pungent as anaesthetic.

"Why don't you change places, Derek, there's a good sport," he murmured to the cricket bore. "Mustn't keep our guest all to ourself, you know. Share and share alike," and he slipped adroitly into the place the other man vacated without demur.

"Just kidding, of course. About the guilty past, I mean. Something of a standing joke, you might say. Keeping you topped up, are they?"

And suiting action to the words he emptied more wine into Gilchrist's glass. On the little finger of his pouring hand – he was left-handed – he had a signet ring set with a cornelian.

Gilchrist suspected it to be one of those Masonic rings that swivelled to reveal the T-square and compasses. He couldn't help himself, for why did he get the impression everyone here was either angling for information or trying to sell him something?

"I'm old Digby, by the way. Diggers. Founder member and all that. Rotting away quite happily out here since nineteen sixty-seven or thereabouts. You wouldn't have recognized the place then, of course. Sleepy little fishing village. All the old windmills still in operation. Three-course meal with wine all in for less than a quid. The old civil-service pension doesn't go far these days, I have to tell you." He gave a light laugh and pulled out a cigarette case. "Smoke? No? Don't mind if I light up? Sure?"

Gilchrist kept wagging his head from side to side like a mechanical dog, the motion leaving him strangely giddy, not unpleasant, more a gentle loosening of his faculties. He felt suddenly very hungry again and speared a large piece of hake from the platter in front of him. The man in the crumpled linen suit watched with an amused expression on his dark face.

"You may or may not realize it, but what you have around this table is quite an interesting cross-section. Not quite your average collection of blokes. No, really. All DPs, you see, in one way or another. Displaced persons, to use an old-fashioned expression. You follow me?"

Gilchrist did, unfortunately. His mouthful of fish tasted dry, unpalatable. Hurriedly he downed some wine trying not to gulp as he did so. The man by his side slowly twisted the ring on his smallest finger. The stone was the colour of dried blood.

"Tell me," he murmured, eyes raised to a rent in the overhanging foliage. "Tell me, if it isn't too personal, or too rude . . ."

And it was like being a child again as far as Gilchrist was

concerned, that well-remembered moment of terror and praying for a miracle to divert the inevitable. It could happen, he always told himself, if he willed it strongly enough, a matter of building up supplies of psychic muscle-power, whether he was quaking before some instance of family wrath or some crisis in the classroom, or facing the McQuillans on the way home after school. One rapturous day, Nelson, the most villainous-looking of the tribe – but then they all had shaved heads save for a tuft at the front – fell into the weir as he was heading, breathing threats, towards him across a fallen tree-trunk.

He remembered he felt a crying need to give thanks to something, *someone*, there and then for his delivery but couldn't focus on anything concrete. That was long before his conversion, of course, but looking back perhaps there had been some other more mysterious, more elemental force trembling there on that river bank waiting to show itself if he had persevered that little extra while longer.

Now, as he stared at his questioner, feeling as paralysed as he had been on that day forty years earlier, a pair of hands descended out of the air on to the other's shoulders. For an incredible moment he almost believed they might be about to tighten about that lean, mahogany-hued throat as in some amazing reaction to his prayers, but instead they began a gentle massage and their owner, Jordan – for it was he – said, "Young Angie just rang. Feeling very neglected, she says. I think we'd better be off, that's if I can drag you away from Diggers here."

But Gilchrist continued to be held by those kneading hands working away at that bony carcase under the linen in that weird, almost abstracted way. And when he looked at the face of the man on the receiving end of those powerful paws, for they certainly were that, all right, he saw that the other's smile was fixed, the teeth bared just that little too enthusiastically to be sincere. *These people are afraid of him*, he told himself. He was, of course, thinking of the man in the toilet, for he felt convinced by now that cry of pain he had heard had been caused by these same hands. *Perhaps, I am, as well*, it also came to him. But if that were the case there was something oddly pleasurable about the sensation which he couldn't quite explain.

"I don't seem to be able to . . ." he heard himself murmur in absurdly polite tones as he attempted and failed to get to his feet. His lower limbs had gone strangely molten as though all the wine he had drunk had flowed downhill and partially solidified there.

"Here, let me help," said Jordan. "It's what brothers are for, after all," and those wrestler's hands of his went sliding under his armpits and he allowed himself to be hoisted up out of his chair and on to his feet.

Digby said, "Would you like me to arrange a taxi? It would be no trouble."

"All taken care of, old bean."

"You seem to have thought of everything."

"You bet."

Gilchrist remembered thinking at the time he had never been in such strong, capable hands. Which was certainly true for now he could feel them steering him on his way out of that patio roofed with greenery, along the corridor, past a kitchen full of clatter and steam, dark faces turning and grinning out at him – he grinned back – until they reached a phone in an alcove. Jordan dialled the local six digits and he watched, entranced, at how adroit the other appeared to be at everything he tackled, even such a simple, mundane operation as using a telephone.

"It's me," he heard him say to the handset and when he said, "What's your address?" it took him a moment or two to realize it was not Angie who was being asked that question but himself. When he told him it was something of a shock to hear it repeated down the phone in that public way. It was as though he had handed over something very personal of himself which he had been guarding until that moment.

"Bring some booze," he heard Jordan say into the round, black mouthpiece, grinning at him as he did so. He smiled back.

All of this was most heartening, he told himself. He didn't deserve any of it. Really, he didn't. And to think he had been so, so desperately alone, so steeped in misery less than a week ago. His eyes were starting to prickle embarrassingly as Jordan put down the receiver.

"You know something," he said. "I'm really looking forward to seeing your place. No kidding." And Gilchrist was convinced he had the smile of an angel.

In the back of the taxi he heard himself insist, "We could have walked back. It's really only a little way," but they both knew – the driver as well, probably – his heart wasn't in it.

The liquidity in his legs seemed to be affecting other parts by this time. He sat there swaying to the rhythm of the springs as the car swept them through a maze of alleyways he had never seen before, yet must have. He had read that drink could produce such an effect on one, the famous carpet-ride sensation, where the familiar becomes mysterious, even threatening, although there was none of that, the reverse, in fact, for these sights now whisking past were alluring, exotic. Yet it was hard for him to believe those same troubled souls with twitching hands and deadened eyes who used to seek help as a last resort at his meetings had ever experienced any of this. *Much too good for them*, he caught himself thinking.

When the taxi drew up before the Miramar Gilchrist was surprised to discover that dusk had somehow crept up on them. Already the swifts were slicing between the buildings, and street-lights, too, were beginning to pierce the mesh of overhead foliage. Where had the day gone, he asked himself? He felt a sudden tremendous tiredness as though the very question had drained him.

"I'm in your hands," he said with a sigh to the man who had just paid off the driver, whereupon Jordan gave a great neigh of a laugh. "Not quite. Nearly."

Then he held out his palm saying, "Give me your keys."

By his side Gilchrist stood breathing in that heady mix which made this place so very unsettling to him, especially at this shadowy hour. He could detect burning charcoal from the kitchen of the Moorish café up the street, the lamb spitting fat, mint, the reek of those dubious cigarettes the customers smoked, closer at hand the overcharged scent of freshly watered jasmine and geranium, and, finally, those other nameless odours circulating at gutter level disturbing as rats in the dark.

"Come on, old chap," came the soft tones of his companion. "Hand them over, there's a good lad," and Gilchrist did so in a rush for, quite suddenly, he felt overwhelmed by it all. It was too much for him on his own, the smells, the heat, the night closing over him like an ancient, dampish, musty-smelling blanket whose origins were questionable, even, possibly, more than a shade hazardous to his health as well.

Inside, the foyer felt as church-like as ever. All that was missing it often occurred to Gilchrist were candles and a whiff of incense, but Jordan looked about him obviously impressed.

"*Muy elegante*," he observed, peering closely at the bank of mail-boxes set into the marbled wall. He seemed to be reading the names. But Gilchrist was already over by the lifts anxious to get upstairs. He had that swimming sensation in both legs again, although it seemed to have changed direction and was marching back up his trunk again like a column of ants, *inside*, not outside his skin. Perhaps if he had a chance to lie down they would take up residence in one spot. Somewhere in the region of the midriff seemed appropriate.

"I've often wondered what this block was like. On the inside, I mean. Do you mind me asking what you pay a month?"

Gilchrist stared out at the floors slipping past like silent, other worlds through the glass porthole in the doors of the lift.

"I bought my own place," he said modestly with barely a twinge now about revealing further secrets. It was almost a relief, in fact, to shed such information which he had been guarding so zealously for such a long time.

The Hermit Of Apartment Forty-Four, he thought, and then the lift moaned to a halt and they stepped out into that corridor which had never known natural light. Suddenly that seemed to him to be the most perverse aspect of all in a climate so ablaze with light. His head was full of the strangest connections today. If he could just lie down perhaps they would go away, along with this continuing yo-yoing sensation in his stomach.

"Double locks. Only the best, eh?" commented Jordan trying his keys and Gilchrist felt like saying, *Please don't expect too much*, for the other was like a small boy reacting enthusiastically to each fresh revelation. *Don't be disappointed when the door finally opens*. But deep down he really meant himself, not the apartment. Barely a week had elapsed since his and this man's paths had crossed yet already he was conscious of a dependence, a bond steadily hardening, fusing them almost, like twin elements in a single entity.

"Very nice, *very* nice!"

The words seemed to fill the space with unexpected noise after the door closed behind them and Jordan prowled about throwing out exclamations of delight over his shoulder.

Gilchrist stood in the centre of the living-room a little put out by it all for it was hard for him to see the modest layout in quite such rapturous terms. But then, perhaps, it was he who was being modest. After all it was something of an achievement to have found this place all on his own and financed its purchase without any real help or advice from anyone.

"You've got a terrific set-up here. Absolutely terrific."

"You really think so?"

"Would I lie to you?" Here he grinned broadly. "And the *view*!"

In a growing mood of exuberance Gilchrist slid back the glass panels. "The sea is directly opposite," he said, pointing. "Not that you can see it at this hour."

They stood on the balcony together facing the invisible Mediterranean, the night air bathing them in its soft, slightly clammy embrace. On the Avenido Montemar far below the lights of the cars, ambers and jewelled reds, pulsed and occasionally coalesced into smoking skeins which teased and tantalized, breaking up before the eye could follow or hold their shape. An arm encircled Gilchrist's shoulders and he felt choked by sudden emotion. For such a long time now he had been so alone, so alone. Surely he must have served out his penance by now. Some warmth, a little brotherly affection, he deserved that, he did.

Jordan said, "What you and I need is another drink – to keep those home-fires burning."

Gilchrist apologized for not having anything about the place and he did regret the omission, genuinely, but the other waved his excuses away.

"I told young Angie to bring a little something for just such a contingency. She should be here any time, as a matter of fact. You don't mind, do you?"

But of course he didn't. What a perfectly absurd notion. Already he was mentally re-arranging the furniture, another lamp here, some decent pictures there, a rug or two, a spanking new colour-scheme. Why not? For he had started seeing the place through the other's eyes. Like so many other things, he thought. *Why not?* Those two little words had a tremendously attractive ring to them, a motto ready-made for the new man looking back at him from the mirror on the far side of the room. It hung ever so slightly askew, only now he was noticing that, and had a crude gilt frame. My God, were those *cherubs*?

He was making a mental note to get rid of it as one of the first of his re-decorating decisions when another face swam in to join his own in the glass, two pairs of eyes regarding him now, enclosed by that tarnished, oval surround.

"The question is, dear heart – which is the genuine article? The real thing. Is there one? Something to think about, eh?"

He watched the lips move, heard them speak the words, yet it was as though they travelled from a very great distance, not a mere foot away.

"Furthermore, what if it just so happens there's two of everybody? I mean, everybody separated, floating out there like two planets miles apart in space and never, ever knowing about each other, never, ever finding one another except perhaps just that once. Once in a blue moon. Like now. A miracle, wouldn't you say? Something *you* would know all about, eh, brother Eric? You did tell me about it, remember? All that laying on of hands and that. And now it's happened to you. And me, of course. Mustn't forget that. If you don't mind me saying so, you don't look too thrilled about the whole business. Yet you should, Eric, you should, 'cause you and I, we have a lot of catching up to do, a lot of very interesting times ahead. Twice as much, you might say, as other folk. Think about it. *I've* been giving it a lot of thought, you see. A lot. *Mucho*. The old head is just full of ideas. Come on, don't look so worried. Cheer up. *Cheer up*."

Gilchrist watched himself being embraced in the mirror. He was stiff, that was plain, he should be giving more. It was like seeing a stranger perform. What poor, poor acting, especially as his partner seemed such a natural, too. What energy! What enthusiasm! Perhaps he could learn something.

Then the intercom buzzed and disengaging himself his other half, his "twin" – *had they resolved any of that?* – crossed to the contraption on the wall and released the lock downstairs. "Come straight up," he instructed his unseen listener. "Apartment forty-four."

He was grinning at Gilchrist as if to say, *see how easy it is for us to swap places.*

"Young Angie," he told him. "On her way."

He dropped into the solitary armchair extravagantly making himself at home while Gilchrist took the hard couch.

"By the way, what do you think of her?"

The directness of the question embarrassed Gilchrist. It must have showed, for the other laughed, cocking his hand like a gun.

"Got you! I know you like 'em young."

Breaking off, he leaned forward, face full of sincerity. "What I meant was – what I *mean* is – no secrets. Okay? What's mine is yours, and what's yours is – well, all that sort of stuff. *Comprende?*"

At that point the doorbell rang, but Jordan continued sitting there looking at him with that same knowing smile on his face.

"She likes you, too, by the way. Just thought I'd mention it. Thinks you're the nicer of the two – by far."

Opening the door Gilchrist received the full force of Angie's scent like a blast from a beauty salon. She was wearing a sleeveless black sweater, short leather mini-skirt of the same colour, equally tight, and white high heels. She had teased out her hair in some miraculous fashion so that it resembled a great, tousled, flaxen mane, more animal-like than human, making her face doll-like and very fragile. She also brought with her that intense cloud of perfume inside which she moved as though protected by some sort of invisible and womanly shield. Gilchrist felt his pulse quicken and a corresponding inability to look her directly in the eyes which were enlarged with blue eye-shadow to theatrical proportions. Jordan greeted her from his armchair.

"Welcome to Eric's *casa*," he drawled. "The *casa* of our dear *amigo*, Eric. We are privileged, for as you know an Englishman's home is his *casa* or, in this case, Irishman. Forgive me for saying so, Eric, but you don't come across as awfully Irish, has anyone ever told you that? In fact your accent is rather like that of my own. Wouldn't you say so, young Angela? Two ole country boys far, far from home? You can take the boy out of the country but you can never take the country out of the boy. Which sounds suspiciously like a toast to me."

Angie stood a little way inside the room exuding feminity to an almost threatening degree. In one hand she held a weighted, plastic carrier-bag which looked as though it might very well contain a concealed weapon.

Fixing Jordan with those ice-maiden eyes she said, "Well-pissed, are we?"

Jordan looked shocked. "Are we, Eric?" he asked.

"Not him – *you*."

"Oh, dear, do I detect a sourish note in the air? Perhaps Angela doesn't care for Jordan any more. Perhaps Angela has transferred her affections elsewhere. Never mind, what little surprise has she for us in her bag, I wonder."

"Just guess. What do you bloody well think?"

"So, okay, don't just stand there looking good enough to eat. Rustle up some glasses in Eric's nice, neat kitchen, there's a pet."

Gilchrist sat on the sofa listening to all of this like an outsider who has been invited into someone else's home, not his own. Yet he felt neither resentment nor unease, nothing but that same vague sensation of drowsing in a deep, warm bath of torpor, immune from anything resembling responsibility. He could hear Angie opening doors in the far room. There was something arousing in the idea of her hands touching his things, her scent being trapped inside drawers and cupboards. For a moment he allowed himself the unthinkable, her lingering imprint on the sheets of his bed, then she appeared clutching three tumblers.

Jordan said, "Clever girl," and Gilchrist felt like echoing his words for he had no idea he had so many glasses. They must have been left over from the previous tenancy, he told himself.

"A little pick-me-up, something to make the old ticker beat faster. Mustn't let the moment melt, as an old mate of mine often used to say. This will bring life to a dead man, you wait and see, Eric."

Angie poured out two generous measures and a smaller one for herself. The label on the bottle said *Fundador* but Gilchrist hadn't the desire for further investigation for at the first sip his stomach seemed to ignite and his eyes started running. Angie said, "I'll fetch some water," and he smiled gratefully at her through a tearful haze.

When the tap was flowing freely in the kitchen Jordan murmured, "Here's to long-lost connections," as though he didn't want her to overhear, something shared just between the two of them. Yet that may have been illusion on Gilchrist's part, for the moment Angie returned, back he was to the old mocking self again. But which was the real self, Gilchrist asked himself? Was there one?

He had this strange, unsettling image of layer after layer of disguises being peeled away to reveal absolutely nothing, all taking place in front of a mirror – *where else?* – and himself in charge of the operation, surgically masked, hooded and

177

rubber-gloved. Surreptitiously he found himself touching his own face as he sat there on the settee. It felt definitely mask-like, as though he had begun to lose control over its reactions. And as he proceeded to drink more brandy the gesture became something of an unconscious accompaniment to everything which followed.

At one point the poodle upstairs went into its jittery dance routine across the tiled floor – the unaccustomed sound of more than one voice must have set it off – then it began to howl and continued doing so without variation or cessation. Jordan listened intently. As they both watched from the settee he rose and began moving carefully about the room, his head to one side.

Angie said, "What are you doing? Leave it be."

"Ssssh," he told her, continuing his tracking of the sound and its source. He had the look of one intent on some private, gleeful mischief. Gilchrist wondered what form it might take, but, hazily, with no real involvement or personal anxiety about the matter. The brandy had, he decided, a definite, sweetish aftertaste. It reminded him of cough-mixture, although of a lighter colour and not as thick and, of course, without the unpleasant connotations. It, also, but much more forcefully, generated a warmth which sought out every living part. Swirling the inch or so in his tumbler as the others had done he waited for events to take their course.

"Now, don't, *don't*," warned Angie a second time. Again there was that premonitory edge to her voice.

Jordan had stopped and was staring at a point somewhere on the ceiling. He listened more keenly, then, throwing back his head, he directed a howl at that invisible target, mimicking the dog's cry perfectly. For a moment Pepe the poodle stopped as though listening to a rival in the flat below, but after a moment resumed his howling again until their cries rang out on two floors like some nightmarish canine duet.

Tiring of the sport, Jordan laughed loudly, then threw back the rest of his cognac.

"Now he has a playmate. The invisible dog, eh?"

Angie said, "Eric has to live here. Or had you forgotten?"

"Why shouldn't he have a dog of his own? Didn't it sound *real* to you, Eric? Didn't it?"

Gilchrist told him yes, it did, most lifelike, and watched his glass being topped up. Angie covered hers with the palm of her hand. They sat together on the striped settee, bodies touching. How could Jordan remain so impervious, he asked himself, for he had this powerful urge to caress that tan and golden forearm resting so close to his own.

"Dogs, chickens, horses, cows – seals. You name it. Didn't know I used to be an animal impersonator, did you?"

She looked at him out of fiercely scornful blue eyes. *Really*, thought Gilchrist muzzily, *was all this aggression necessary?* He felt so relaxed himself.

"Further episodes from The Tall Story Club, I take it? Pull the other one."

Dropping to his knees in front of her Jordan grasped one of her chocolate-brown calves, playfully at first, but beginning to squeeze.

"This one, darling? Or how about this little piggy-wiggy here, eh?"

She sat there almost primly, staring straight ahead of her at the old, orange sideboard against the far wall. Lazily Gilchrist wondered just how long she would be able to withstand the pain, for pain there had to be. He felt her body stiffen alongside his, yet was unable to react as he knew he should to stop what was happening. Jordan's face was a foot away. He could smell the liquor on his breath.

"Could I – ?" he said, holding out his empty glass, and his other self cheerfully obliged. Gilchrist watched him dispensing drinks from the top of the sideboard, so naturally, with such ease, then bringing the glass across to him as though this was his apartment and not someone else's. *Mine*, insisted Gilchrist, *mine*, with a brief but ineffectual attempt at self-assertion.

"Mother's milk," toasted Jordan, grinning. "Takes to it like mother's milk." *He means me*, thought Gilchrist.

"See?" he said triumphantly, turning to Angie again.

Her legs, Gilchrist noted almost casually, had practically reverted to their original, all-over hue. He felt a certain degree of shame at the sight, but then that seemed to fade just as rapidly as the marks had done.

Still holding the centre of the floor – they were his audience – Jordan proceeded to give another of his farmyard imitations, a cockerel this time, and the cry didn't sound bizarre or at all startling to Gilchrist in that setting, even though it managed to evoke childhood for him in that house deep among the Antrim fields alongside the weir a lifetime away in time and distance. But it was another feeling that melted as quickly as it appeared.

Angie said, "So many, many hidden talents. You just never know with you where the next one's coming from. Like that time we decided to take up art again, remember? That stall in the market? Hand-painted tiles? And that other time. Have your name printed on an authentic bullfight poster while you wait? Sure-fire money-makers. I wonder what ever went wrong."

"I'll tell you what went wrong," retorted Jordan, pointing his glass at her. "A tiny but essential element just happened to be missing. Something called trust. Faith in your partner's vision. Forgive me, Angie, dear, but lack of imagination happens to be a tremendous failing of yours. Just no imagination, that's all."

It struck Gilchrist this was how married people talked to one another, or so he imagined. And it also came to him he still hadn't found out if they were or not – married, that is. They might very well be. He knew so little about this pair, not even this elementary piece of information, yet his own history appeared to be an open book. He had never considered himself to be someone who wore his heart on his sleeve – it was for others to bare themselves to him – yet why did he feel so vulnerable, so transparent?

He sat back and listened as Jordan honed the cutting edge of his tongue on the person by his side. Again he had that urge to fondle her bare skin even though he knew it meant instant disaster, like touching a live current.

"Anyway, what do you know about what Eric and I did or did not do before you came on the scene?"

That was something of a shock, and he kept his eyes fastened on the tawny swirl in his glass. *Was this his second or his third?* He must be careful. But then, *why*, he thought?

"Let me tell you you don't know the first thing about either of us, apart or together. We're a mystery as far as you're concerned, a closed book, so don't go making judgements about either of us, do you hear? We don't care for it. And what is more, neither one of us gives a toss what you think. We know who we are and where we come from, not like little Miss Ponte-bloody-Fract with her short skirt and shorter memory who has the gall to tell us where *we're* going wrong. The cheek, the fucking cheek of it! From someone who not so long ago was handing out disco fliers for a thousand pesetas a day and as many hamburgers as she could eat. Well, you can go right back to the street any time you feel like it, any time you fucking well fancy. Be my guest. Fuck you, Angie! Do you hear me? *Fuck you!*"

The poodle upstairs started howling again but it was not the moment for duets. Gilchrist, too, felt in no mood for any further diversions. The room seemed to reverberate with the force and noise of the quarrel, his head, too, a foretaste of what was to afflict him so grievously on awakening the following

181

morning. He felt impregnated by scents and sounds not of his choosing. His apartment, his very existence, had been taken over by outsiders, he had to recognize that as a fact, despite everything which had happened between them so far and would go on happening. And that was the most worrying aspect for, sitting there, captive in his own room, he realized he had no proper say or control over subsequent twists in this scenario.

Angie said, "*You* certainly won't. Don't you ever put your hands on me again," and she rose and went to the door leaving an eddy of scent in her wake.

Gilchrist felt he should do, say something, but his limbs and tongue were not reliable any longer. Jordan leaned against the sideboard and watched, a smile on his face. He raised his glass, drank, and she let herself out cleanly without a backward glance.

Gilchrist felt a sudden sadness. *She didn't look at me, not once*, he commiserated. *She might have slid one farewell little flicker in this direction. Would that have killed her? For old times' sake?* He wanted to laugh at that – how ridiculous – but couldn't. They listened instead to her high heels clacking down the hallway to the lifts. Then there was the mechanism of the doors arriving and opening followed by descent into silence. The apartment was quiet as well, as though after an explosion.

"She'll come round, don't worry. She'll be back, she always does," said Jordan reading his mind, for he did suffer a pang of something – deprivation, he supposed. How lonely he must have become without even knowing it.

They sat facing one another, he and his reflection. Jordan had let himself slide down into the easy-chair opposite. He looked so – so at home – yes, that was it, like someone with an inalienable right to ownership. There was something terribly unfair the way he saw it about having to sit on one's sofa like this while someone else, a stranger, sprawled at ease just a few feet away across the room. Jordan looked at him and grinned.

"Women! Aren't they the pits? No imagination, no soul, man. Know what I mean? Anyway, who needs her? Tell me that. *We* certainly don't. Look, please forgive the language earlier. It sort of slipped out. I keep forgetting about you being a pulpit-pounder and all that. Less reverend father, more brother. Right? *Right?*"

Gilchrist nodded. He had given up struggling to make sense of what was happening to him. All of this could only be digested at some remove, he told himself. So he perched there allowing the conversation to wash over him without impedance like one of those old, green, timber teeth smoothed by the current and age from the weirs of his childhood. It was a powerful image to hold on to. Comforting, as well.

"What young Angie cannot understand is that I am someone who's looking way, way ahead all the time. For those possibilities. One of life's born optimists, that's me. Should I be ashamed of that? Angie certainly thinks so. But then she's a woman – aha, ain't she just – and like all women her natural instinct is to put a dampener on things. Mother Nature's little wet blankets. Always on about the straight and narrow and facing up to your responsibilities – whatever the fuck they might be. Sorry. Sorry . . . No, we're not married. I can see that look in your eyes, Eric. Just shacked up together for better or for worse. And lately it's been the latter, I don't mind telling you. Time for a shake-up. I may just seek your advice on that score . . . Another drink?"

This time Gilchrist declined and immediately felt like a traitor who had thrown in his lot with the female killjoys of the world.

"Something else? Up? Down? Just say the word, man."

Again he shook his head and his companion slipped

something out of an inner pocket and just as deftly into his mouth. He washed whatever it was down with brandy. Then he allowed his head to loll against the back of his chair. When he resumed speaking his voice seemed deeper, more measured. Or was that merely Gilchrist's imagination at work?

"I was about to say I'm never wrong about such things. Possibilities, I mean. Potential. But that would be a lie. Sure, I've made mistakes, but, okay, so what? The important thing is never waste it when you happen to have it. Unforgivable. And while we're on that subject, excuse me for saying so, but, Eric, in your case, I see somebody in danger of just that. Everything you've told me leads me to believe you could be doing a lot more with your terrific talents than you have of late. Am I right? Still, all is not lost. Here followeth brother J's great plan . . ."

Gilchrist started feeling very tired at this point. His concentration seemed to be seriously on the wane, gaps opening up in the gist of the other's flow like potholes in a roadway. He did try to focus on what was being lost to him – forever, it occurred to him – and despite what he felt must be its extreme importance, but this terrible lethargy was hard to fight. Phrases like "doubling up", "pooling our resources", "united front", repeated themselves with almost incantatory force and he realized he was nodding to their beat like some brain-washed disciple sitting there, still upright, instead of sprawled as he should have been like his mentor. He wanted, he *needed* to sleep so very badly now.

Then Jordan said, "I never ever told anyone this before," and suddenly rôles were switched. *This has to be special*, he told himself, *so please pay attention*.

"I had two brothers and two sisters, but they were never real blood to me, not in the true sense, because I was adopted, you see. They told me when I was fourteen, the family did. That was the bad part because how could they have kept it from me all that time? Because they all knew, that came out, and two of them were younger than me, little kids. It sent me off the rails for some considerable time. Oh, a real bad boy, not at all nice to know. Not the sort of person you would care to have in your congregation in that big tent of yours, Eric. The collection-box would need to be in a very safe place, I have to tell you. And as for conversion, well, you'd be wasting your precious time. Chalk and cheese. Yet look at us. There but for the grace of God, eh? In your case, I suppose, *He* must have played quite a substantial part. And maybe there is something in those things you call miracles after all. I mean, as I said before, just take a good look at us. Peas in a pod, chance in a million? And why here, now, in this dump? Sewage-on-Sea? I don't think we should just ignore it. Or, again, maybe we should. You tell me, you tell me – brother. But I can see you've had a long day. These family reunions can be hard work. Another time. Another time."

He laughed one of his great, rolling, West Country laughs. There hadn't been one for some time and the sound startled Gilchrist into something approaching alertness.

"Don't look so worried. Long-lost brother J has a terrific trip lined up for the pair of us. You and he will be travelling on the same ticket from now on. Isn't that something to look forward to? Come here," he commanded, but he was the one to rise from his chair and cross the room where he proceeded to take Gilchrist's cheeks in both hands.

For a moment they looked at one another. *One eye just a shade darker than the other, not blue, no, definitely not blue*, observed Gilchrist and the thought cheered him for he had himself almost convinced as he sat there that he had disappeared without trace into the quicksand of the other's personality, body as well as soul.

"Absolutely certain you don't want to go on to a club somewhere? Further your education? No?"

But Gilchrist shook his head and as he did so Jordan came forward suddenly and kissed him on the mouth. Then he withdrew laughing and walked to the door. Gilchrist's lips continued to retain the sensation while the rest of him felt numb as though all other feeling had raced to the spot like blood leaving a corpse. His laughing familiar surveyed him one last time.

"Know something?" he said. "I really, really hate to leave this place. Feels just like home sweet home already. No kidding. But I must, 'cause you look dead. Don't get up. I can let myself out."

He looked around the apartment with Gilchrist in it. "Yeah, I could have picked this place myself." Then, "Listen, I'll be in touch. Rely upon it. Remember what the song says, eh? The best is yet to come? *Adios, amigo*."

The door swung shut behind him but his feet made no sound on the tiled corridor outside as Angie's had earlier done. Bolt upright on the settee Gilchrist strained until he heard the whine of the elevator followed by the sound of its padded, metal doors opening and closing, but even then he could not relax. He was in a high state of nervousness. Nothing could be taken for granted any more, nothing, not even the fact of the other's departure from the building.

He kept waiting for the bell to ring and with it the next turn of events in his penance which had its origins that day in a heated, public swimming-pool on a chill, Sunday afternoon nearly a thousand miles away.

SIX

The Maltings,
Sutton Scotney,
Hampshire,
England.

Dear Eric,
You said I was to write to you if ever I needed anything no
matter what you said and now there is. Would it be possible
do you think for you to maybe come and take me away
from this place? I don't want to be ungrateful after all you
and your friends have done for me but I'm not sure if I can
stick it much longer being here with Mrs Allardyce and all
her wee girls. Quite a few don't speak English did you
know that? You told me once it would be like Coming
Home To Canaan Over Here In Beulah Land for I still
remember those hymns we used to sing together but I'm
still waiting for Joy, Joy, Joy, To Break Through. Once or
twice lately I've even been thinking that maybe being put
into a convent mightn't be all that much worse than being
cooped up here like this. Now don't be offended I know it's

for my own good until all the fuss dies down over there I do really and Mrs A. even though she is very strict is fair I'll give her that but the truth is I'm feeling very homesick. Also I keep wondering about some of those things you once taught me. For instance does Justification mean *all* sins are forgiven you? Is it like taking confession? That wee book with the pink cover you gave me isn't very clear or is that just me? I just wish it was you I could turn to and not Mrs A. although to tell the truth I wouldn't dare ask her anything. Am I being a great big nuisance? You used to call me that remember? GBN for short. It seems such an awful long time ago and so very far away as well. Has there been any more fuss about my leaving home like that? There's nobody here I can talk to and I feel so stupid sometimes. I still haven't discovered what a Malting is. Ha ha. Well I must run now because I hear the downstairs bell for evening Bible Study and Mrs A. is a desperate stickler for punctuality. It's the Healing of the Centurion's Son tonight. I hope this reaches you safely. One of the maids, she's from Fermanagh, will put it in the post for me although it's strictly against the rules. Like so many things here. Please please be in touch.

> Yours in Christ
> Donna.

In his cigar-box he has three mementoes now in that same rounded schoolgirl hand. Two are picture postcards, their shiny views pinpointing the sender's route south from Ayr to leafy Hampshire. Burns' Cottage. Winchester Cathedral. This particular letter concludes the correspondence.

Sitting in his hired car – its metal ticks in the heat – the single pink page spread on the seat beside him, he is not to know this. Yet why has he been reading and re-reading it as hungrily as a lover ever since its arrival just four days ago enclosed, mercifully, in a plain envelope with the address similarly disguised in capitals? The postcards came incognito as well, for he can easily imagine his housekeeper's excitement if something rosy-coloured in a feminine fist were to come through the letter-box on Slemish Drive.

Wilma Clyde. He can see her now, raw, prawn-pink nostrils a-quiver for any whiff of impropriety or backsliding. She had been foisted upon him when he first arrived among the Brethren. Her cattle-dealer brother Archie, as gross as she is gaunt, and a big wheel on the committee of ten, arranged it. He won't go as far as to accuse him of being a hypocrite and a thief – like the rest of them he manages effortlessly to combine the laying up of wealth with a "good living" example to all those outside the sacred circle – for if he did where would that leave him? He has always kept his mouth closed on the subject, except on the Sabbath when he's given rein to rage and rant about greed and sharp practice like a mad mullah knowing full well he will never be able to bend those stiff-necked elders or their ways. They tolerate him as some sort of holy, shouting fool – it's something he recognizes – the lash of his tongue fading the instant the Sunday serge comes off and the real weekday world of barter, cunning and penny-pinching resumes its routine again.

Wilma is the sister the family could never marry off. No dowry would ever be great enough. God help him, did they actually believe he might be the one, the "catch" they had given up hope of ever finding? Was that why they moved her into the house on Slemish Drive? He shudders at the thought of it, of the two of them under the same roof on a more intimate footing, all that chapped boniness wrapped in coarse calico. Her hands are like half-thawed meat. Poor Wilma. Damaged goods. Like the house itself, with its leaks and draughts and poor drains. It was like living in a Norwegian wood, so unrestrained was the use of pine polish and disinfectant because of her creed of open windows as well as open bowels.

Was, he thinks to himself. Was. The tense of his existence has changed to here and now. It's like being on the brink of something, something momentous, and all because of a sheet of shocking pink notepaper in a childish hand. *"Don't be offended . . . for my own good . . . great big nuisance . . . all you've done for me . . ."*

Allowing his head to fall forward on to the steering-wheel, he gives a groan. *My God, what have we done? What have I done?*

According to his map Sutton Scotney and The Maltings should be a little under a mile away, the last village he passed a place called Egypt. *With a strong hand hath the Lord brought Thee out of Egypt.* Turning the key in the ignition Gilchrist pulls out from the hard shoulder on to the empty A30 and heads south, remembering, as he drives, that sequence of events which first drew him into all this like a moth to an open flame.

Or was it the other way round? Certainly she was the one who had the look of someone doomed that night she turned up on his doorstep with her pitiful clutch of belongings. The porch light, he recalled, seemed to pass straight through her pale skin as though it were paper. It made him want to shield such fragility from the cruel glare and he quickly turned off the overhead light. There was also the neighbours' response to think about. A visitor such as this arriving at such a late hour – the tidings would be gleefully relayed to Wilma at tom-tom speed.

Fortunately she was not at home that night – God was good – the sickbed of some up-country aunt having called her away. He suspected a legacy might be involved. He could imagine her gathered in that grim farmhouse along with all the other relatives waiting for the death-rattle. They would then strip the place – he had seen it with his own eyes – outwardly respectable people playing tug-of-war with pictures, clocks, jugs, china dogs, fire-irons, canteens of cutlery, like vultures straining at carrion, while in that inner room the corpse barely had a chance to chill. It was like servicing savages.

But this was different. This young girl with her refugee air and pink nylon holdall was what true ministering was all about. He did feel that, genuinely, then, and it seemed an emotion as unalloyed and pure as anything he had known.

"Come," he said as though he had no need to ask a thing, closing the front door and leading her down the hall to the back kitchen where the Aga exuded heat and a certain down-to-earth comfort which the parlour, the room where he normally received visitants, could never provide. An upright piano stood there, locked lid permanently shrouded with a linen runner like a coffin-cloth, six straight-backed chairs arranged like those of a doctor's surgery, and a set of Old Testament engravings on the walls, uniformly dire and threatening. Giving her Wilma's chair he felt as though they were conspirators already, two children in an empty house with the grown-ups away.

Her trainers were sodden. He made her take them off and prop them up against the range to dry. She was wearing yellow ankle-socks and a livid green get-up he understood was called a shell suit. The papers kept reporting the material had a horrifying tendency of catching fire, youngsters combusting like human torches almost as frequently as they appeared to be savaged by the more ferocious breeds of foreign dogs.

She said, "I can't go back there. Never. I'll kill myself first. They locked me in my room. Three whole days of it. I had to climb out through the window."

Indeed her hands were grazed and there was caked mud on the knees of her tracksuit. He poured tea from the big cream enamel pot and the homely ritual appeared to calm her.

"Donna," he said. "Donna, please begin at the beginning. No one is going to harm you here. You can see that, can't you?"

191

Her eyes filled with tears and he reached over one of his stiff, white handkerchiefs. Wilma always starched them to board-like consistency.

"It isn't fair. Three against one," she moaned. "Praying, praying over me night and day. They brought in three priests. The old bald one is the worst. Father Ambrose, he's called. He threw holy water over me. They won't listen to a word I say. I don't want to be a nun! I don't want my head shaved!"

It was that particular image which was to haunt him. Each time resolve wavered, and it did, oh, it did, the thought of that pale, freckled globe as defenceless as a newly hatched egg or a baby's skull stiffened his determination to protect this innocent.

"Tell me precisely what happened. From the very beginning, mind." But, of course, how could she? It was like asking a frightened animal to walk a circus drum. Instead there came an outpouring of accusations and terrors, imagined or otherwise, all centred on that house in the slums of Waterside where his own particular influence had never prevailed. Until now, that is. The realization gave him no satisfaction.

As far as he could make out the seeds of all of this were sown some time ago in her workplace, Ardmona Poultry Products, a sprawl of low, reddish, brick buildings outside town on the main Dublin Road. Once it had been an army base and still retained the chain-link fencing, its gatehouse, and the weighted, red and white painted barrier like a barber's pole, permanently raised now, of course, for who would want to raid a chicken factory? The employees, all women, wore overalls and white nylon mob-caps. From a distance they looked like laboratory technicians instead of butchers.

Donna had liked wearing the uniform because of this. It made her feel part of something and in a very short time she had managed to work her way up the conveyor clear of the blood, the boiling water, and jerking carcases on hooks to the final oven-ready product. She described in detail and with some pride how she would place the trussed bird squarely on its little polystyrene tray, then encase the lot in a clear film of fine-gauge plastic. Her stop-watch time for this operation was three-and-a-half seconds.

Pouring out more tea Gilchrist regretted what he'd said about starting from the beginning, not because he wasn't interested in the specifics of her nine-to-five existence – my God, he was, he was, suddenly, like an eager parent – but because of the sights and smells her words conjured up for him. For some reason he couldn't get the image of rubber gloves out of his head. He could see them so clearly, discarded along with all the other animal waste at the end of the day like bloody udders from some other slaughtered species. The thought of those small, pale, childish hands sheathed in such things was an obscenity. He found himself hovering protectively as she talked, her mouth filled with shortcake from Wilma's tartan tin.

She told him of the lunch-hour gospel meetings some of the factory women attended and of how she had gone along one day simply out of boredom or, again, maybe curiosity. They had made her very welcome even though she was a Catholic. Loneliness may also have played a part because there weren't many like her on the workforce and those that were kept their heads low. The usual thing. Then a party of missionaries from the Emmanuel Pentecostals turned up one day to talk to them and their message seemed so simple to her, so free from dread, unlike that of her own religion, that she had felt a stirring and a desire for deeper understanding.

Gilchrist listened to the familiar expressions rolling out of the young mouth and felt depressed. It was at times like these he doubted everything his work stood for. *Work!* Nothing much had altered in his career since those nights in that old green tent in the middle of nowhere. He was still peddling lies and short-lived miracles. He wanted to say to this child, *forget all that parrot babble. That's for dried-up spinsters and those old jinnies who accompany them. Hopeless cases. You're not like that, you're, you're* . . . His hand trembled on the smooth enamel knob of the teapot. She told him of Harold Drummond's involvement, how she was directed to him by one of the women at the factory, eventually deciding on his advice to take the plunge, literally, that Sunday afternoon at the swimming-pool by giving herself to Jesus.

"And now I'm saved, Mr Gilchrist, washed by the precious Blood of the Lamb. He *will* look after me in my time of trouble. He *will*, won't He? I mean, if I am His, and He is mine?"

He said, "Yes, Donna. That's what the Good Book says. But, tell me what happened at your home?"

"They were waiting for me when I got back. Damian had told them, my brother – he was there, remember? – but I was going to, myself, anyway. But they wouldn't listen. They were all hitting me, Mr Gilchrist. Then they locked me in my room upstairs and that's when the priest was sent for, first Father McGreevey, and then when I wouldn't give in, the other two. I heard them talking about sending me to a convent across the Border, somewhere in the Free State, and that's when I decided to come to you. There was nobody else to turn to, you do see that, don't you? You won't send me back to them, will you, Mr Gilchrist?"

The rain had left her hair in rat's tails, the face diminished, an urchin's face. There were crumbs, too, about the small mouth. Even now as she spoke her hand kept straying compulsively to the plate. *My God, have these people tried to starve this poor child into submission as well as abusing her?* Her account had all the elements of the worst kind of religious horror story. Personally he always steered clear of such lore in his sermons. Others in his calling did not and many in his flock, he realized, felt cheated when he didn't lay into the Scarlet Woman of Rome or the Great Whore of the Seven Hills. But he had decided early on to leave that sort of thing to the Bible-bashers and bigots, for, frankly, he didn't care passionately enough about such stuff. Hearing it from the victim's own lips was a very different matter. He burned at the injustice, the barbarity of it.

"They'll be searching for you," he said. Then, "Does anyone know you're here?" for that canny old part of him still advised caution.

No, no, she assured him, she had told no one, not a soul, not even the women at work.

"How did you come by my address?"

Turning a worldly look on him she replied, "Everybody knows about *you*, Mr Gilchrist. It's an awful nosey wee town. Sure, they'd be able to tell you what you had for breakfast."

They were sitting facing one another across the shiny, checked, American cloth of the kitchen table. The grandfather clock in the hall ticked lugubriously away while, close at hand, the Aga roared through its consignment of wetted slack. Outside, a westerly freighted with rain rattled the windows. It was like being in a cabin at sea.

Then self-interest made him enquire, "Tell me, Donna, what age are you?"

"Sixteen-and-a-half," came the reply in a low voice. "People say I'm small for my age."

Lie number one, he thinks now as he goes through the gears of his rented Ford. A continental juggernaut, French number plates and canvas sides billowing, has slowed him to a crawl. And the proof is in the newspaper inside his suitcase on the back seat, a photograph showing her with some of her factory mates grinning in a group. She has a printer's halo about her head and underneath, "Fifteen-year-old Donna Brady who

195

went missing from her Waterside residence three weeks ago. Have you seen her?" *Residence*, he thinks to himself wryly.

The paper is one week old. A whole month, he calculates, thirty days since that rainy night and all those phone calls he kept making while she sat munching in his kitchen like some rain-soaked little rodent. She has child's teeth, tiny, pearl-like.

So, what other lies has she told him, then? The question is curiously irrelevant for, to be honest, he doesn't much care. With his own strange logic it somehow makes them even, any falsehoods on her part cancelling out those on his, for, yes, he did deceive or, rather, flee his responsibilities. Otherwise why would he be here like this now with the dusty English hedgerows sliding past? He might as well be watching cut-out cardboard through the car windows for all the impact this new terrain has had on him so far. He travels inside a metal, as well as mental, cocoon of his own making. But back to that night . . .

At nine o'clock he placed his first call but it wasn't until ten-thirty that he got through to the one who was to mastermind Operation Bulrush as it was to be called. Yes, it *was* exciting then. There was a mighty adversary to out-manoeuvre and, of course, right was on their side.

Sandy Dinsmore wasted no time in pleasantries. After a brisk catechism in a catarrhal Scots accent, referring to his visitor throughout as "the puir wee lassie", he instructed Gilchrist to "guard her well" until such time as he could arrange to take her off his hands. *And just when might that be*, enquired Gilchrist a trifle nervously for he was thinking of Wilma due to return the following day, clutching her funeral booty, no doubt, but unlikely to be softened by any of that.

"Dinna fret yourself, man, speed is of the essence, you don't have to tell us that. Our wee bundle of joy will be transported safe to salvation like Moses in his basket before you know it. Yon Papish idolators won't get sniff of hide nor hair of her where she's going. Not while we have the God of Israel on our side."

And as he stood there bemused by all of this Gilchrist heard the voice on the other end of the line launch into a brief but impassioned prayer for their mercy mission. Casting his eyes up the hall he could make out the subject of that petition. Her head was flat on the kitchen table, she was sleeping now, exhausted, innocently unaware of what was being planned for her over the phone.

That night Gilchrist took her up to a spare room at the top of the house. No one had ever used it before, at least not in his time, so he stripped the bed, replacing the blankets and chill linen with aired bedding from the hot-press while she stood there sucking her thumb and trying to keep awake until everything was ready. In the midst of it all he caught a sudden, unsettling glimpse of himself in the cheval glass, the room's only other article of furniture save for a small, white, painted, skivvy's chest of drawers. This man had his arms full of bedclothes, even more strange, was prattling on about towels and toilet arrangements like some fuss-pot landlady, yet none of it sounded odd or unnatural. *Gilchrist*, he was to tell himself later when the house was silent, *you've played some strange rôles in your day but never, I think, that of a mother hen before.*

There was to be no sleep for him that night, his mind was far too busy with recent events and, of course, their consequences, for already he was worrying about what he might have let himself in for. But each time his terrors got the better of him the thought of that young charge in the attic upstairs sent a tender wave of something over him leaving him weak and womanly. The temptation to creep upstairs and listen outside her door became very strong at times. He kept watching the telephone on its bog-oak table in the hallway, in his imagination connecting its invisible wiring to a frenzied web of organizers all busily ringing one another. *Why wasn't he part of that network*, he asked himself? Never had the house seemed so still or quite so ghostly. He listened now as if it might be possible to monitor breathing three flights of stairs away or, more alarmingly, some change in its shallow cadences.

At six in the morning the telephone finally broke into life and he darted from his chair to still its ring. It was one of those ancient, ebony-hued creations with a plaited lanyard cord and a mouthpiece smelling of dust. The bell continued to thrum long after he had picked it up.

"Yes? Yes?" he croaked – his voice sounded rusty like an old pump – and after a listening moment the phone went dead in his grasp. He stood staring at the vile thing, Bible-black, in keeping with Wilma's fanatic sense of the fitness of things, then it jangled a second time and he snatched the receiver from its cradle.

This time someone said, "Just checking, laddie, just checking . . . Is the coast clear?"

Quickly he whispered assent and after a pause the by now familiar voice continued.

"Listen carefully. Here is what you must do. Ensure the consignment is all wrapped up and ready for immediate shipment. Do that now, straight away, for our carriers will be calling to take delivery in approximately thirty to thirty-five minutes. Have you got that? Aim for half an hour at the outside, for the timetable is a very, very tight one."

The message appeared to end there even though the line continued to hum.

Gilchrist cried, "*Hello? Hello?*" Then he heard the old Scotsman intone, "Whosoever shall give to drink one of these little ones a cup of cold water, verily, I say unto you, he shall in no way lose his reward in Heaven. Matthew Ten: Forty-two."

"Can't I make her breakfast even?"

He heard his own rising voice ring out with the ridiculous query even though the connection had already been severed. Did he really say *carriers*? Could it have been *couriers*? Such conjecture was almost as irrational as his concern about breakfast.

The slow, inexorable tick of the grandfather clock finally brought him to his senses and made him head for the stairs. Already light was beginning to seep through the hall curtains. But his knocking at the door of the room under the eaves brought no response and he forced himself to twist the brass knob, thrusting his head into the room.

"Donna, Donna," he whispered. "Time to get up. You have to get ready."

The room smelled of – it was unfamiliar, something close, warm, moist, unsettling – a young animal's smell.

He heard the bed-clothes move then a voice ask, "Who's there? Damian, is that you? Who is it?" and in a sudden new rush of concern he switched on the light.

She had the coverlet up over her chin. All he could see were eyes, mouth, that shocking red hair like, like – Little Orphan Annie's! He almost laughed out loud at the revelation. Those old American comics from his childhood arriving like contraband inside food parcels – it was the time of the war, after all – then passed from hand to hand until the folds fell apart. The coloured inks were startling, almost psychedelic, he remembered, just like Annie's own electric bush. But was it really that Titian shade? It may well have been sandy, even bottle-blonde. He hung there, half-in, half-out of the room with this ridiculous moot point gnawing at him.

He heard her whisper, "What is it? What's happening?" and he forced himself to be that comforting figure of authority, a bit like the one downstairs in the oleograph entitled "The Light of the World", except he wasn't holding a lantern above his head.

"Trust me," he said. "Put your clothes on and I will explain everything downstairs."

Only he didn't, did he? For she was sitting with a round of toast and an untouched egg in front of her and still not a word of explanation out of him when this car drew up outside, headlights raking the leaded lights of the front door: He felt relieved in a sneaky sort of way. He was after all merely an intermediary in this whole business, he reminded himself in justification, a human halfway house. He had carried out his part, and at no little cost, either, to himself and his reputation. He still had to live in this town after the caravan had passed on. If word of this ever got out or was relayed back later in some fashion he could expect bricks and bottles through his windows, perhaps, worse, for the people down Waterside way had a brutally direct mode of retaliation in such cases.

"Are you coming as well? Where they're taking me?"

The eyes beseeched, the colour of sea-water, as big as those of the legendary waif in the funny papers.

"Unfortunately, no. But these are fine people, good people, Donna. You'll be safe with them. All they care about is your welfare, you must always remember that." *God forgive him. Pontius Pilate.*

Then he let the visitors in, a man and a woman, fifty-ish, respectably dressed. They looked like bank employees, although the woman wore a hat. She appeared the more serious of the two, almost stern, in fact, and his heart sank. They introduced themselves, Robert, Emma, and he led them to the parlour which at that hour had an even more funereal air about it than usual. To his surprise the man glanced about him almost approvingly. She, too, appeared to soften a little as if the surroundings had set their minds at rest. He left them sitting there side by side on Wilma's ladder-backs in their two-piece suits for the woman was also wearing worsted, although in a finer texture and fuller cut to accommodate her rather buxom figure. *Matronly* was the word he would have used himself, but more nursing than maternal in definition. Yet that was what the plan actually involved, it appeared, for Donna was to travel with them as their daughter to avoid suspicion.

He brought her in to meet her new "parents" in that cheerless room with its pictures of prophets calling down doom and destruction and listened to his own stumbling introductions before leaving her to their attentions. She had a smear of butter on her chin, he noticed, as she stood vainly trying to hold on to his darting eye, frightened, a wild animal poised for flight, and when the door finally swung at his back he felt as if he had slammed a cage shut.

In the kitchen he sat staring at the egg in its china cup. She hadn't touched it. He thought the reason might be she wasn't sufficiently confident about slicing the top off cleanly, something of a knack at the best of times. Then he thought, *pull yourself together, all this self-reproach is totally misplaced.*

A short while later the man, Robert, emerged from the parlour and marched outside to the car returning after a moment carrying a small, new, cheap-looking cardboard suitcase. He had a purposeful air about him as if he had done this many times before. Curiosity tinged with some alarm was beginning now to gnaw at Gilchrist. *What was going on*, he asked himself? *What was in the suitcase?* Inflamed by lack of sleep his imagination raced through the most outlandish possibilities. *Some sort of exorcising paraphernalia? Bell, book, candle – evangelical style?*

Then the door opened and he appeared once more. Closing the door quietly on those within he stood with his back to it as though on guard staring straight ahead of him. Gilchrist felt even more of a stranger in his own house yet all he could do was sit gazing guiltily at the untouched breakfast on the table.

Finally the woman came out, a satisfied expression on her

heavy face. She had Donna by the hand, a new Donna, even more victim-like in demeanour than previously, for they – the woman – had dressed her in schoolgirl uniform, navy Burberry, knee-length pleated skirt, white blouse, beret, ankle-socks, sandals. She looked at him. He looked away.

The woman said, "I don't think we'll need to be bothering any longer with that awful pink thingy, will we, dearie?" motioning towards Donna's nylon holdall. It was lying in the hall where she'd left it after coming downstairs.

"Totally unsuitable. Anyway, everything we need is in here," and she patted the ugly brown suitcase. *We*, he noted, with rising resentment.

"No, no," he protested, "she really should take it with her. It won't take up much room and, anyway" – here he seemed to lose all his resolve – "can't it go *inside* the case?"

The man and the woman exchanged glances. "There can be no harm in the odd wee keepsake," he murmured. "Surely, now?"

"As long as it's nothing frivolous. Lay not up for yourselves treasures on earth where moth and rust doth corrupt," was her reply, but by this time Donna had already gathered up the bag and was clutching it to her breast. It looked startling against the drab blue of the belted Burberry, but then that was what it was called, after all, he reflected, "shocking pink", her favourite colour as he was to discover.

The woman said, "Shall we pray?" and the three of them lowered their heads. "Bless our enterprise this day, O Lord, and our young sister here who has chosen the shining path to true redemption. Watch over her and we, thy humble servants, who would convey her to a place of safety and Gospel refuge. Confound her enemies who would seek to return her to the snares and delusions of Rome and all its hateful idolatries. But, above all, cleanse her from any lingering taint or stain still present from a mistaken creed that she may be a worthy candidate for blessed salvation in the wonder-working power of thy Blood. Amen."

Gilchrist stood listening to all of this in his long brown hallway, first light seeping through the stained glass in his front door. A burning bush was the dominant motif, *Ardens Sed Virens* on a curling scroll underneath just in case the symbolism was somehow overlooked.

More and more he resented this mausoleum of a house. It was like living in a religious way-station for there was nothing here he could call his own or feel concern about. Really it was Wilma's house, not his, and the more she indulged her penchant for the monotone and the morbid the more he yearned secretly for undiluted colour, noise, light, the sound of raised voices, all of which, thank goodness, could still be found inside the big tent in that mired field on the outskirts of town. Whenever he led the singing in "There Is A Green Hill Far Away" – ironic image, at any time, in the context of those boiling Palestinian wastes – he liked to convey the setting as being here, now, in Hugo Patterson's big ten-acre even though the reality of all that churned-up mud outside worked against him. Just how much longer could he go on peddling his suspect imagery?

"Are you sure you can't come – Eric?" He looked up startled by the sound of his first name. "Mr Gilchrist? On the boat? As well?"

A moment of embarrassment followed. At least he and Robert reacted that way. On the other hand, the woman in the hat – vaguely Tyrolean, he noticed, for the first time – retorted angrily, "Completely out of the question. Pastor Gilchrist has already discharged his full Christian duties in this affair. His place is with his flock. And you, young miss, have no call to go mentioning details of the arrangements which have been made for you. As I've already told you in there the less anyone knows about our plans the better. Considerable risk is involved for far too many people. People who have been working tirelessly away on your behalf most of this night regardless of the consequences. Do you understand? Do you?"

"Yes."

"Yes, who?"

"Yes – mother."

"Good. Now thank the pastor for all his kindness and we'll be on our way. The Lord's work awaits." And that was when he finally found his courage.

"I'd like a brief, personal moment with Donna, if I may," he told the woman in the feathered hat.

For an instant she stared at him as though she had no intention of moving, fleshy nostrils a-quiver just like his housekeeper's, scenting delinquency, no doubt, then Robert ventured, "I'm sure that's in order. She is one of his flock, after all, and of course we must bear in mind Mr Gilchrist did baptize her."

Gilchrist waited until the front door with its livid, flaring bloom had closed on the two of them.

"Go into the kitchen and warm yourself," he told the girl. A schoolgirl now, it came to him, in her camouflage of blue and grey wool mixture.

"There's something I want you to have." And quickly moving upstairs to his bedroom he stood there looking about the glacial wastes of all that bare, brown linoleum at a loss as to what he could find as a keepsake. He thought of a Bible, but then decided against it for she would see enough of those where she was going.

On top of the wardrobe well away from Wilma's prying eyes and hands was his old cigar-box. Taking it down he blew the dust off and emptied the contents out across the bed covers. It was a pitiful collection after all these years, more like a child's hoard than that of a grown man who preached regularly to others of the virtue of putting away "childish things". But then he thought, *that's just what she is*, and he raked through the assortment of odds and ends, not releasing memories, as expected, but, rather, genuine puzzlement. For where had most of these objects come from, he asked himself? Why were they here at all? He held a spent cartridge to his nose, the reek of cordite faint but still there after – twenty, thirty, forty years, was it? How did that happen to be here? And this miniature green bottle and this pebble, a domino, the skull of some tiny animal, a mirror from a birdcage, a farthing, a single round spectacle lens, King George's melancholy bearded face on a shard of china. Everything scaled down as if from a doll's house.

As he stood there handling each worthless object he heard the car horn outside, a single, short, peremptory bark. He could just imagine *her* leaning across to stab the button. Defeat stared at him from the debris on the counterpane. There was nothing, *nothing*, he despaired. Yet he had promised her. A noise rose from the foot of the stairs and, barely aware, he grabbed up a piece of driftwood, the size and shape of a crooked little finger.

She was waiting for him in the hallway, her hand on the bannister, a worried look about her.

He said, "It was difficult to find something appropriate, but you might well appreciate this little memento. From – from the Holy Land."

He placed the fragment of dead wood, light and dry as pumice, in her moist palm and kept it hidden there, his hand cupping hers. She stared up at him in awe.

"No, no, put it in your pocket," he told her. "Look at it later. When you're by yourself."

Then he added, "From the shores of Galilee. Something private and personal, just between you and me." God forgive him, but it may have been his first step towards seduction: a lie usually is.

"I just wish you were coming too," she sighed.

"So do I," he said, lying. It just slipped out. *Or was it a lie?*

"Will I be all right, do you think? With them, I mean? She is very – very . . ."

He continued to hold the hot little paw. "Only because she wants the very best for you. Remember you must do exactly as she tells you, no matter what, if you're to be smuggled away from here to a place of safety."

"Smuggled?" she queried with the first sign yet of a smile. He laughed with relief.

"Yes, yes, think of it as an adventure!" he cried. "And it will be exciting, I promise you! New places, new friends, a new start. You still want that, don't you?"

"Oh, yes, yes, my heart is full of the Lord Jesus Christ."

"Well, then, cheer up, and don't be a GBN because no one cares for one of those." She looked at him in puzzlement.

"Great Big Nuisance," he translated and she grinned back, repeating the initials over and over like the delighted schoolgirl she had suddenly become.

"Come," he said, picking up the pink holdall, "we mustn't keep these good people waiting any longer. There's a boat to catch. Ever been on one before?" She shook her head.

"See? What did I tell you? An adventure," propelling her in front of him like a package on legs and, indeed, already that's what she had become to all of them in Operation Bulrush, "the package" or "the shipment", whenever any future mention was to be made of her over the phone or by letter.

He watched her climb into the back seat of the car, a dark grey Volvo estate, and as it pulled away the woman in the passenger seat shot him a parting look of suspicion. He waved, ignoring her. In the rear window a small, anxious face was turned to his and he held it until it disappeared out of his life for good. As he thought.

Then he went back into that house closing the door behind

him with its scriptural message snaking below the bush that blazed but never burned. There had been a text across the back window of the Volvo as well. Suddenly he felt sick of his life, these constant admonitions to do this, be that. Yet here he had just sent off another soul to be shackled by those very same commandments.

He sat in the kitchen watching the flame in the Aga licking at its porthole of toughened glass. *Caged, too*, he thought. The whole house was like that. A prison. Restless, prowling now, he climbed the stairs, not to lie down, even though he'd had no sleep, but on, further, right to the top of the house. He sniffed the air in the attic room for some trace of her presence but everything had reverted to its former mustiness, the smell of old hymn-books, he decided, obsessively, for he was in an unshakeable mood of depression by now. It was like being deprived of something potentially transforming which now he would never get to experience, perhaps enjoy.

Crossing to the rumpled bed he found himself touching the sheets. Cold, dry, barely creased. The temptation to examine them even more closely was strong but he stopped himself. There was something unhealthy about continuing with this business, whatever it was. But wasn't the dread in which he held his housekeeper equally sick in someone of his years? As the thought hit home he was in the process of re-making the bed, returning it to its former, lifeless, untouched state. When he'd done he looked around the slope-ceilinged room one last time, then he switched off the bare, hanging bulb and locked the door behind him, consigning it to oblivion.

But he hadn't been able to get rid of the memory of that night quite so easily, the memory of that schoolgirl in her navy Burberry and beret. *Had there been a school tie? If so, which one?* Inconsequential details of that sort continued to torment him long after Wilma returned, empty-handed, as it turned out.

Her face remained set in a mask of grim reprisal for days on end and she embarked on an orgy of spring-cleaning which took in the house from top to bottom. He listened to her demoniac progress with bucket, mop and dust-pan, waiting for her demand for the key to the locked attic, but it never came. In an odd way he almost wished it had for he burned to confront someone, anyone, with the burden of his secret.

On several occasions he sat down and rang those same numbers he had dialled on the night itself but no one answered or, if they did, they sent him off down blind alleys of polite evasion. It was as if he was no longer involved, yet he was, in a way which he could never have imagined possible.

He took to driving out towards the chicken factory at lunch-hour, past the women perched on the lowered barrier like fowl – or white birds poised to migrate – but he stopped all of that when some of them began waving at his car.

Once he made his way on foot down past the houses where he imagined she might have lived. Posy Row was the local name and once, a very long time ago, perhaps, it had presented a picture of semi-rural charm, gardens bursting with holly-hocks, red-hot pokers and the patriotic orange lily and Sweet William, but all of that had gone long ago. Broken-down cars lined the lane now, hedges and fences trampled flat, while dogs and packs of children roamed the open spaces united by their scavenging.

He increased his pace, for he felt about as conspicuous as a debt-collector or social worker. Even the urchins stared at him in the same hard, quizzical way as their mothers who leaned gossiping and smoking in doorways, folded arms supporting breasts the size of footballs. Continuous suckling still pre-vailed here, he made a mental note in his newly acquired welfare-worker rôle, so very different from his own part of town where the offspring were spaced almost as carefully as the houses.

One cottage he passed had the curtains drawn and on an old, wrecked bus seat in what passed for a garden three children with fiery red hair sat swinging their legs. They had a restrained air about them as though tethered by some invisible force emanating from the house. He found himself slowing and staring a little more closely than was wise. *That same hair*, he thought, and his heart raced violently. One of the trio, a boy, nine, ten, thereabouts, picked up a stone and glared at him with what he took to be threatening intent. The eyes were hard, the colour of seawater. Gilchrist walked quickly on.

And then the postcards and, eventually, the letter arrived, saving him from further insanity of that sort.

He had freed her from that awful place, that slum, that family, he tells himself, and now here he is going through the same process a second time. It seems to be his fate.

The Maltings turns out to be one of those very large, very old, russet brick establishments he has seen countless times before in a certain type of English movie. And as he drives up the curving, gravelled sweep, indeed, he does feel a little like an arriving suspect in a country-house mystery. He looks at his watch. Perfectly on time, as befits someone of his calling.

There is one other car – well, more a small mini-bus. It is parked facing the steps leading up to the paved terrace which is empty of chairs or umbrellas despite the marvellously sunny weather. He tightens the knot in his tie and climbs out into the soft, scented air. Ring-doves gurgle eerily in the yews. No other sound disturbs the peace. For a moment he stands gazing up at the old house. It seems much more stagey, more exotic, up close like this to his Northern eyes, but then all those old films did tend to be in black and white.

For the first time the full foreignness of his surroundings hits home. He feels intimidated by the lush setting, the heat, the unfamiliar soft glare of the light. He might well be in

France – abroad – but then that's where he is, after all. They might care to call this the Home Counties, but not to him it isn't, nor that young girl, either, he has travelled so far to rescue. *The power of words on pale pink paper*, he tells himself as he prepares to do battle with whatever forces lie in wait.

The high double front doors are ajar and, almost furtively, he doesn't know why, he moves through and into a bare hallway suddenly chill after the heat of the open air. Facing him is a long receptionist's counter with a bell and beside it a sign saying Please Ring Once If Unattended. Beyond, through a glass door, he can see a corridor stretching to infinity. There's a strong smell of Jeyes' Fluid and the sound, also, of singing at some remove, girls' voices, a piano, a hesitant tambourine. The tune is not immediately recognizable but, no matter, he is back once more in that old familiar atmosphere again of cheerless observance and denial, that vintage black and white film he was fantasizing about earlier replaced now by depressing reality. The setting may be a disappointment but at least it holds no surprises, and that may be an advantage when confrontation arrives.

He presses the bell expecting to hear it peal but nothing seems to happen, so he repeats the process. Still no result. But then the singing falters and stops in mid-chorus and he realizes he has misread, or disobeyed, the instructions on the card propped facing him. To his horror he spots that the word Once is underlined in red. He stands there waiting for nemesis. Although there is a staircase curving off to the upper floors he feels certain when it comes it must surely appear along that corridor and his instincts prove correct.

A door opens near the end and someone stout and female emerges and begins marching towards him. Squinting a little, for the light is poor at that distance, Gilchrist prepares to be chastised for his transgression, for that striding figure means business, he doesn't need glasses to tell him that. Her own spectacles glint, rimless, cruel, reflecting, miniature suns as she bears ever closer. There's something familiar about that girth as well as gait, the set of the mouth, the mannish, shaved nape. He superimposes a hat, a business-like suit, dark shoes, stockings, and suddenly it comes to him. But it's much too late for that for the glass doors are pushed outwards in an explosive rush as though aimed at him and a voice announces, "It's good of you to call at our little refuge like this, Pastor. Casual callers aren't encouraged as a rule but, of course, in *your* case – "

The rest of the sentence hangs in the air as the eyes, magnified slightly, survey him behind oval lenses. His tie is throttling, his palms slippery with sweat.

"My sister has told me all about you." Again a pause as though testing him via his reactions. This time he no longer can conceal his surprise.

"Sister?" he ventures a shade croakily.

"Aye, you met her at your house yon time, remember? Some people say we're very alike. People who don't know us well, that is." She smiles at him as though inviting confirmation but he's still too shaken for diplomacy.

"Emma never married, of course. My Alec now, the late Mr Allardyce that was, passed over some wee while ago. Gave his life on the mission field. Are you a family man yourself, Pastor?"

He starts as though at something improper.

"No, no," he protests and catches her smiling again.

"Our little friend is expecting you, and thinking of nothing else ever since I told her. But I imagine you know what young girls of that age can be like."

Again that arch look and, panicking now, God forgive him, Judas that he is, he blurts, "I hardly know her. Not really. She came to me out of the blue, as a last resort. At the last minute. Still, as I was in the neighbourhood, I felt it would be un-Christian of me not to look in on her. To see how she was settling in, I mean."

"You did the right thing. We rarely get visitors. It's a strict policy, we must protect our anonymity at all costs, for the girls' sake, you understand, but sometimes a new face can be a tremendous tonic. There are times when we would hardly see a strange face for months on end, certainly not a *man's*. But then, you're not – "

Breaking off she slips a hand over her mouth and he stares unbelievingly. *That wasn't a giggle, was it?*

"What I meant was, *you* are no stranger, Pastor. Certainly not to us."

They are moving down the long corridor now past the array of inspirational prints on either wall, scores of dusky faces smiling out at them all with that depressing sameness of expression bordering on simple-mindedness. At least such scenes have always depressed Gilchrist. Such tirelessly sunny gaiety, and always that missionary figure in white surrounded by his adoring circle of piccaninnies. What a bore. Fraud, too, he shouldn't wonder. *Like yours truly*. For some reason the thought no longer has the power to disturb. He has changed, is changing, he tells himself. *Let it happen, let it happen . . .*

They go past a glass door and, glancing inside, Gilchrist sees a classroom with perhaps a dozen young girls in pale blue gingham, heads bent over their Bibles. Many are dark or olive-skinned just like their counterparts in the pictures on the walls outside and his eyes dart instinctively towards those paler faces hoping for a flash of that remembered, electric red hair, but he draws a blank.

"Our numbers are down at present, but even if only one solitary soul seeks sanctuary, then our duty is clear. It's not the ninety and nine, after all, that concern us but the one who's out on the hills alone and far, far away, as the hymn puts it. Isn't that so, now, Pastor?"

For a moment Gilchrist convinces himself that this woman turning her gaze on him behind her stern spectacles has penetrated his defences. But then why should she suspect him? He hasn't done anything yet, has he, other than make his way here in response to a private letter? He experiences a sudden and unexpected spasm of gaiety despite his dreary surroundings, and at that very same moment Mrs Allardyce – can she really be that strict disciplinarian described in the letter? – emits a little whiff of lavender water as though protesting her disputed femininity.

"Only last week we opened our doors to three new converts all the way from Manila. What a time they had in getting here. But, truly, it was worth it just to see those wee, brown, happy faces once they realized they had reached the Hallelujah Side. What a terrible, idolatrous country that is. And as for that Imelda Marcos! Potiphar's wife, that's what I call her. All those shoes! The world today is a dreadful place, wouldn't you say, Pastor, for the young and unprotected?"

"Indeed I would," he agrees, nodding sagely.

He's quite without shame now. It's like being back on that platform again under spread canvas looking out over the upraised faces of the faithful and knowing he cannot be challenged. Winning, winning, all the way.

At the end of the corridor Mrs Allardyce comes to a halt before a solid wooden door unlike any of the others they've passed.

"This is my own office," she tells him. "You can be private here," and again that sideways, artful smile, or what he imagines to be one. Carved in the mahogany in ecclesiastical gold script are the words Knock And It Shall Be Opened Unto You and he waits for some sort of compliance. Instead, she produces a key from the pocket of her loose linen smock. He marvels at the yardage of material needed for such a garment. It's as voluminous as a small tent, setting up eddies of perfumed air as she moves, and he watches as she inserts and turns the key in the lock. He follows her inside.

There doesn't seem to be a lot worth locking up at first glance, for it's a remarkably austere room with a small window and little or no sign of that feminine touch he felt he had detected earlier. He sees a simple desk, a chair, a filing cabinet in the usual sludge-green, a couple of other straight-backed chairs pushed up against one wall for rare visitors like himself.

"Just make yourself comfortable and I will fetch the little lass. A face from home can be so terribly welcome, you know," she says sighing, before turning at the door. "I won't intrude for there must be so much the two of you will want to share. Not forgetting a wee prayer, I hope? For her continued fellowship here with us? That would be so nice, and a great comfort, too."

He smiles reassuringly at her, hands clasped behind his back in best clerical mode. More and more he is begining to realize just how enjoyable it is to play a double game. Not only playing but *winning*, he tells himself. *Winning souls*. It's what he is cut out for.

"Two minds with but a single thought, Mrs Allardyce."

"Oh, call me Rebecca, if you please, Pastor Gilchrist."

"Eric."

This time the giggle is unmistakable as the door closes releasing a tiny eddy of lavender scent into the air like a hint or promise of unfinished business. The essence of that homely lilac flower follows him wherever he goes, it seems, his religion's own peculiar odour of sanctity. Very possibly he may carry some of it on himself for his housekeeper, he knows, seeds his drawers with sachets of the stuff as though to ward off the Tempter. Protestant garlic. Remembering the cheap perfume *she* was wearing that rainy night when she came to him in his house, he wonders whether they've made her get rid of it.

214

He's still standing there abstracted by such thoughts when, suddenly, unaccountably, he becomes nervous about their meeting. He drags the chairs out from the wall and arranges them to face one another in the middle of the room. He pulls them close, apart, then closer again, as if mere inches have become crucial. His hands are damp. He wipes them with his handkerchief then does the same to the top rails of the chairs as though getting rid of evidence. Now, should he be on his feet or seated, or, perhaps – ? Rehearsing these ridiculous niceties in his head he hears a hesitant knock and calls out, "Come in!"

The door opens and it's her at last, looking frightened and, yes, much younger somehow. She's wearing the regulation, summer, short-sleeved, blue gingham, plain white ankle-socks and sandals, and he's thinking – almost a running refrain now – *what have they done to her?* It's the hair, of course. They've tamed it somehow, making it appear *ordinary*, something unimaginable as far as he is concerned and with shock he realizes it's the image of that flaming mop which has sustained and excited him ever since he saw her that first time advancing towards him across the wet tiles of the swimming-pool that Sunday in March. Nervously. Like a lamb to the slaughter. But shorn now.

The door closes and they look at one another, then at the two chairs holding centre stage and Gilchrist recognizes just how unreal they must appear that way almost as if already exchanging confidences in their own mute, wooden fashion and not their occupants.

She speaks first. "Eric?" Questioningly. As if he's the one who has changed *his* appearance. Perhaps he has, he doesn't know.

Touching his own scalp he begins. "Your hair – it looks – " when, to his horror, she starts sobbing, not out loud but in a horrible, cowed whispering which makes him melt.

"Sit down. Please," he gently commands, moving her

across to one of the chairs, remarking as he does so that same remembered, young animal heat. At least they haven't been able to change or interfere with that. He reaches her his handkerchief. Is it his imagination or is there the faintest whiff of the dreaded scent? Then thinking – *that hellcat of a housekeeper daring to imprint her spoor on me, even at this remove –* and kneeling before the weeping teenager, he tells her, "I won't let them harm you. I'm here now, I'm here," renewing the promise he made that first time in the swimming-pool and knowing then, as now, he might live to regret his words but not caring, not caring.

She tells him of everything that has taken place since they last met, the sea-crossing with her "parents", the journey down through the mainland by bus, then train – car numbers might be traced – the succession of "safe houses" on the way until, finally, she arrived at The Maltings. The first part had seemed like an adventure just as he had told her it would and already the tears have dried, remembering, as she does, all that mystery and her at the centre of it guarded like young royalty. But then things changed as the reality of her new life spread before her.

"Do they ill-treat you? *Have* they?" He finds himself glancing across at the door as though Mrs Allardyce might be breathing out there close to the wood.

"No," she whispers, shaking her head and leaning near like a fellow-conspirator. Her breath is not as sweet as he might expect but then that's a tiny and very human flaw which only serves to reinforce her vulnerability.

"Everyone's awful strict, but then they have to be, haven't they, for our own good. It says so, doesn't it? In the Good Book?"

"It also says, Suffer The Little Children."

"Do you think I'll ever be able to understand all that? Being a Catholic, I mean. I never realized before what terrible things

216

they were getting me to believe. It was all wrong. It was, wasn't it, Mr Gilchrist? About the Virgin Mary and trans – transubstantiation and everything."

Never has he felt so inadequate. What a sham he has become. Years of evasion and ready answers, half-truths, platitudes, when what people desperately craved were the certainties. Stones instead of bread was what he fed them.

"Do you want me to take you home? Is that what you really want? If it is, then it's not too late, you know."

She stares back at him and the tears suddenly are there in force again. He studies those lustrous, rolling beads, marvelling at such fecundity. When was the last time his own cheeks were wet?

"Well?" He's still on his knees. Really it should be the other way round.

She continues to look at him, lips quivering, eyes awash.

"Well?"

Part of him wants her to have changed her mind since writing that letter, but then that other less altruistic side worries that he may have burned his boats in vain for there's no way he can go back, not after what he has done to that bank account. It comes to him suddenly that, really, he's the supplicant, not this bare-legged child in her uniform of blue and white, and that his posture may be appropriate after all.

"Can they stop me?"

He hands over his handkerchief a second time, she takes it, he rises from his knees, pulling forward the other chair. No longer the supplicant, more the seasoned plotter now, he questions her.

"Have you signed anything? Anything at all?"

"I think they might want me to."

"Once you're over sixteen you can go where you please."

It's unworthy, he knows, but she *had* lied to him. He'd decided to keep the newspaper report for later, and there will

217

be a later, that seems a certainty now. Quickening to the possibilities in his head – perhaps they are fantasies and on the sick side at that, but he no longer cares – he asks, "You really meant what you wrote in your letter?"

Surprise makes her mouth drop open. Pearly, spotless, baby teeth. "You got it?"

To prove the point he pulls the folded sheet of pink stationery from his pocket. In the instant she is changed utterly. Giggling now, she grabs his free hand and for one heart-stopping moment he believes she might actually kiss it. *Gilchrist*, he tells himself, *you may not emerge exactly unscathed from all of this. In fact, you may not come out at all*. But it no longer bothers him. Bridges and boats have been burned and in such cases one must never, ever look back. Who wants to turn into a pillar of salt anyway? He's surprised at his own skittishness.

"You're positive you want to go home now?" he asks, returning to priorities.

Her face changes. "Home?"

"Where else?"

"I thought maybe – "

There's something sly about her suddenly, some calculating, female thing that excites him, oddly enough.

"Well, maybe a little holiday might be in order. Before anything is decided. Before rushing into things." *God forgive him*.

The eyes light up.

"Oh, *could* we? Could we, do you think?" Then she adds, "Just the two of us?" with more of that same archness, and pretending to be authoritarian he tells her, "As long as it's understood you are in my charge. At all times. Is that understood?"

"Oh, yes, yes, *yes*!"

"Good," he says. "And now let us pray," reaching out to take that small, hot hand in his.

218

His farewells to Mrs Allardyce some little time later are cordial in the extreme.

"Oh, such an awful pity you have to rush away like this," she gushes. "Just when we were getting to know you. You never even got a chance to see our lovely grounds. They're quite extensive, you know. You're absolutely sure now we cannot offer you a cup of tea or something equally refreshing?"

She's standing at the top of the steps smiling down on him, her powerful, pillar legs outlined through the light linen of her smock. He throws a bogus glance at his watch. His eyes, he realizes, were noticeably fixed on those great thighs and their terrifying confluence.

"I mustn't miss my Sealink ferry," he lies to her. Second nature now. "France, Switzerland, then Germany. Luther's birthplace, you know? A little pilgrimage."

"Oh, I do so envy you. Truly inspirational. Next year I myself hope to take a small party of the girls abroad. Only those who will benefit from the experience, of course. Who knows but our little red-haired friend may be one of the lucky ones."

"I don't see any reason why not. As I just told you, she seems to be settling in admirably, admirably. All due to you, of course, and your sterling efforts on her behalf – Rebecca."

At the mention of her name she appears to sway as though overcome with emotion, a fleshy colossus in billowing linen, and he moves smartly backwards to the safety of the gravel. The wood-pigeons are still cooing in that decidedly creepy way of theirs. The sound makes him uncomfortable. The whole place, he has decided, has all the cloying charm of a cemetery.

"Have a nice crossing! Bon voyage! Don't forget us, will you?"

She's waving to him now, framed in the doorway, meaty

guardian of all those children half her size and weight. Monstrous mother-hen. *But one little chick will soon be fleeing the nest*, he tells himself with grim satisfaction as he slides his car key into the lock. *One little fledgling with reddish fuzz, so soft, oh, so soft to the touch.* His, it comes to him in realization. All this time he has been longing to touch, to fondle, and hadn't the insight or, perhaps, courage to admit it. The thought makes him shiver even though the inside of the car is oven-hot. He drives away, gravel spurting from under his tyres.

Three nights later he is back, but parked outside this time in a small but convenient lay-by. A few feet away he can make out a sign prohibiting dumping By Order Of Hampshire County Council, yet someone has laid an old mattress at its base like an offering, alongside a collection of smaller, household rubbish. He sits there making silent inventory. One rusty lawnmower, an umbrella, a venetian blind, one bicycle wheel, assorted plastic plant-pots, a roll of carpet, a birdcage, a gutted TV, a bound pile of magazines. Somehow they don't look disparate, these items. Why does he form the impression they all derive from the same garden-shed? To come sneaking along here after dark with such a cargo surely denotes desperation, extreme bravado, or how about – no possibility of being disturbed? The last appeals to him very much for although he has been sitting here a good half-hour without a single car passing his nerves are beginning to twitch.

I'll give her another fifteen minutes, he tells himself, yet knows he won't, he will wait until dawn if necessary. The thought of that whey-faced runaway creeping out through those gates and finding no one there is far too unbearable to contemplate.

As he sits there listening to the night noises of the English countryside – furred and feathered things stalking and devouring one another by the sound of it – a single, wavering light appears in his driving-mirror. In a panic he watches and waits, for it could be someone on foot with the leisure to observe and take note, a rural bobby, perhaps, if such still exist, but then he recognizes a cyclist and not a very sober one at that judging by the way his machine wobbles and swerves from verge to verge.

Sliding down in his seat Gilchrist follows the drunk's progress until his ruby-red tail-light winks then fades from sight like a tipsy firefly. Why can't his own life be uncomplicated like that, meandering home with a skinful on a Friday night like everybody else? *Why?* Closing his eyes he wills his thoughts to be quiet, to let him be, just this once.

The plea seems to work, he must have dozed off, for next thing he knows he is bolt upright, listening, eyes straining in his head towards the distant gates. He hears a noise at the side of the car. A pale face swims up close to the glass. Pushing open the door he peers out and there she is, dressed in the shell suit, clutching the pink holdall to her chest.

"Nobody told me they locked the gates at night," she's babbling. "I had to climb over the wall, so I had."

He keeps forgetting she's still the slum child with all that ingrained expertise in getting through and over fences, into gardens, orchards and hay-barns, ravening packs of them fanning out after school to pillage the surrounding farms and farmers. He looks at her soiled hands and then at his own soft, lily-white specimens clasping the steering wheel, but then as the image of the pair of them illuminated in a bubble of light like that takes hold he cries, "Get in, get in. *Quickly!*" and she scrambles into the car pulling the door behind her.

He accelerates away and continues driving at speed, the hedges racing straight towards them down the blanched tunnel formed by the beam of the headlights.

After a while she says, "You're not annoyed with me, are you? Everything was great until I got to the gates. Honestly."

"No, no," he tells her, "I know that," patting her knee. The material feels odd, rough yet smooth at the same time, some new twist to man-made technology.

"Would you like a mint?" She's holding out a tube of Polos now and he takes one off the roll, his heart paining him with, oh, such a sweet ache.

Some miles later he realizes she's asleep at his side thumb in mouth and the ache threatens to become permanent. Slowing down fractionally so as not to wake her – it's well past her bedtime – *good God, why hasn't that struck him before?* – he drives through sleeping hamlets, past equally lifeless filling-stations keeping to the dark minor roads as planned.

A little after one-thirty he arrives at the entrance to the caravan park and, turning in, bumps gently up the track leading through the trees. A light is still on in the bungalow beside the communal toilets and wash-rooms but the owner of the site seems singularly uninterested in the comings and goings of his customers. In a compound by the side of the house he keeps a couple of lolling Alsatians, but Gilchrist suspects their presence is more a gesture than a threat. They look overweight and listless like their master, with his beer-drinker's belly and a gammy leg that hints at redundancy, or perhaps, compensation money.

"My daughter will be joining me in a couple of days," Gilchrist informed him when he first arrived. "From her college, you understand. She'll need her own – " hesitating over the words " – sleeping arrangements."

"In that case you'll be wanting one of the Wayfarer de Luxe mobiles. Cost you another twenty."

He was wearing his customary soiled Jethro Tull T-shirt, an inch of exposed flesh above his belt, navel embedded like an extra closed eye in hairy lard.

"Number twenty-six. Can't miss it. Need anything just give us a shout."

It was as simple as that, money handed over, no questions asked. And nothing to sign, either. They could disappear without trace in this country, two minnows in an ocean of apathy. The image appealed strongly. Sometimes drifting, sometimes darting, as the currents took them, a voyage of discovery. Second chances for the pair of them.

Switching off the engine he sits there for a moment before deciding to wake her. It seems such a brutal thing to have to do. She looks so defenceless. He wonders if she's dreaming. *What do young girls dream about?* There's so much suddenly he wants, needs to know about this sleeping stranger. He studies her in the amber glow from the lamp outside. He may not get such a good chance again to observe without being observed. That excites him. Like a burglar working fast for fear of being disturbed his eyes plunder the sleeping shape by his side.

The face, of course, is what draws him, the closed lids – he thinks of pearls, that same slightly moist transparency – their pale fringe of lash, the ear-lobes pierced but innocent of jewellery, the cheeks, nape, upper lip, all coated with blonde down. He has read somewhere every square inch of the female form is covered with fine, in places, almost invisible, hair. *Dear God, where are his thoughts taking him.*

"Donna," he whispers, "wake up. We've arrived."

Instantly she opens her eyes, yawns, stretches, all in the same sinous movement, the way an animal might, it occurs to him.

"Are we? Are we, really?" She smiles at him then, turns to look out through the car window, her hand shading her gaze.

"Was I asleep long?"

"Not long."

"Where are we? What is this place?"

"It's called The New Forest. Have you heard of it?"

She shakes her head still trying to make sense of what lies beyond the glass.

"Let's go," he tells her.

There's a light on in the third mobile home along the row. Some have got television aerials. One of those late-night movies, he decides, that ghastly will-o'-the-wisp blue. With exaggerated consideration for the neighbours they creep inside, she taking her cue from him with a compliance which he finds deeply reassuring.

Her innocent delight when she sees the interior is just as disarming. He watches as she moves about on tiptoe excitedly opening doors and cupboards. There's a stove, sink, table, fridge, a bathroom, toilet as well, all hidden away when not in use. There's also two bedrooms – well, one, for the room they're in doubles as a sleeping-area.

"Is this *ours*? Our very own?"

Her thumb is in her mouth again as if all the excitement has suddenly become too much. For a moment he's sorely tempted to lie to her. He's in a position after all to stay as long as they like, even buy the place outright if he so wishes. Anything is possible. *Isn't it?*

Instead he says, "You must be dead tired. Why don't you take the other room? The bed is already made up. We can make plans in the morning."

"Plans?"

"Yes, plans."

The word has suddenly become magical. They stand there, minds busy with their own interpretation of what it means. And for that moment Gilchrist believes in fate, two minds in harmony, or, if not that, at least converging towards unanimity. Just a matter of time. *Give it time.*

He watches the door close. He sits down on the settee, listening until all sounds of movement cease on the far side of the thin partition. To be on the safe side he gives her another ten minutes – *is that a gentle snoring?* – then he leafs over the sofa-bed and unrolls some bedding, silently undresses and pulls on his blue and grey striped pyjamas. They smell of camphor. He had forgotten that other odour of righteousness. Millions of mothballs rolling around inside drawers and wardrobes in all those godly households, those toxic marbles diminishing in that mysterious way as though by some nocturnal will of their own.

His brain is in turmoil again. He lies there staring intently at the ceiling. It has a granular, porridgy texture he never really noticed before, threatening to run. He switches off the bedside light.

Dear Lord, who knowest all things, past, present, but particularly future, continue to direct thy servant's faltering footsteps. Only thou can see a path through this dark wood. Lead two poor runaways to that promised Higher Ground where refuge can be found, where their pursuers cannot reach them. Above all, guard the slumbers of this young girl in the far room that she may wake refreshed to a new day and, most importantly, a fresh start. Needless to say if some of that same bountiful rain should fall on the head of thy humble servant despite all his shortcomings then his cup would, indeed, runneth over. Amen.

The following morning he is slow to wake, a struggle towards consciousness as though weighted down, yet the bedclothes are light, basically a single, covering sheet. There's an enervating airlessness about this climate he finds it hard to get used to. When he can focus a little better he makes out a seated presence across the darkened room and, as though fearing he might call out, it identifies itself.

"It's me. Don't you remember? Donna." Small, tremulous voice.

In the instant he realizes nothing has changed, his authority has survived the night, may even be a fraction stronger if that is possible. Still, he cannot help being conscious of his disadvantaged position, spread like this in pyjamas, his private bumps showing through the thin sheet.

But then she says, "Do you take tea?" and when he says, yes, milk, no sugar, if it's not too much bother – he sounds like a visitor and not the host – she rises from the armchair and goes through to the kitchenette. She's wearing a white, outsize T-shirt with writing across the front he can't quite make out in this dim light. It reaches to mid-thigh. Her bare legs look like blanched stalks of celery.

All this enforced intimacy he has let himself in for – will he be able to cope? A part of him is apprehensive, but another is excited, too, in some as yet unexplained way. Surveying his bump – it breaks the flow of the sheet exactly half-way like a marker or a mound in that snowy landscape – he decides not to dwell on the subject further if he's wise and, rolling sideways on to the floor, makes a grab for his trousers.

By the time the kettle is whistling he has dressed himself after a fashion and has had a quick look outside. The morning is overcast, the trees drip silently. Rain is something he hasn't bargained for. A wet day spent indoors, their first together. Can they survive it?

Miraculously they can and do. Better than that, they come to inhabit their new-found space, basically nothing more than a single room, with an ease which surprises and delights Gilchrist. Time passes in a smooth rush. They read together. Both have a soft spot for the Centurion And The Sick Servant and, of course, little Zacchaeus hiding in his sycamore tree, another favourite. She teaches him a game called Twenty-One. In one of the drawers they find a pack of playing cards along with a corkscrew, a paperback book by Jackie Collins and an empty cigarette packet.

They have a good laugh together at this hoard, the collected vices, as it were, and encouraged by his mood she sings:

"There is one thing I will not do,
I will not stand in a cinema queue.
There are two things I do detest,
A painted face and a low-backed dress.
There are three things I will not do,
I will not gamble, smoke nor chew."

To his surprise, hers as well, he finds himself joining in, some buried remnant stirring from his own childhood. *How can there be any harm in it*, he asks himself.

Still in playful mood, that evening they drive to Winchester, and after a meal and breaking one of the song's taboos – *again, why not?* – go to see the latest Hollywood epic about an android. She makes the choice. As always there's a sugary message underlying all that mayhem and rending metal to do with fragile but ultimately prevailing humanity. But why do the film-makers bother? Who do they think they're kidding? Man's infinite capacity for self-deception? But he's no longer in the sermonizing business. The revelation comes as something of a shock. Question: does he have anything to put in its place? For a moment, sitting there in the popcorn-scented dark, Gilchrist experiences a descent into the void. *What have I done?*

Driving home – *home*, he feels like crying hysterically, for he's still in a manic mood – she says, "I like your car, Eric. It's new, isn't it?"

"Rented," he replies somewhat ungraciously.

"What about your own car? The one back home." *That word again.*

"It was never mine. *They* owned it." He hears the bitterness in his tones, self-pity as well.

Then she says, "This is much nicer," brushing the

upholstery lightly with her hand. "The seats go all the way back – they *recline* – don't they?"

"I'm not sure. I think so," he replies.

"If I was able to drive, you could have a wee sleep. Maybe you could teach me. You look tired, Eric."

"I do?"

"Yes," she tells him and touches his cheek fleetingly with a butterfly caress, no other word or words will do, making him long to close both eyes and allow the rushing car to race on into the night under its own weighted volition. Bliss to let someone else take charge for a change, even a fifteen-year-old, popcorn and Cola scenting her fingers, steering him towards some sort of – he doesn't quite know what – longed-for state. Just something suitably amnesiac would fill the bill.

Next day the rain has gone. Northwards, to their own changeable climes, according to the radio weatherman on long-wave. It sounds odd hearing him refer to "the eastern counties of Northern Ireland." As far as they're concerned it might as well be "Faroes, Heligoland Bight or Tyree." Remember, he reminds himself, she's been here well over a month now. He feels travel-hardened himself.

Over breakfast they make plans. First things first, he tells her, she must be kitted out, no arguments, no discussion. He loves the way he sounds. So different from his uncertainty of last night. He supposes, secretly, he longs to see the back of that shellsuit. Every other part as well. It's begun to lose what little shape it ever possessed, grease-spotted, smelly, too. The fabric seems to retain the odours of every meal they've eaten together, a sort of virulent, green, mobile menu.

"What about money?" she asks. "The expense."

"No object," he assures her. "I have plenty."

"Oh, we have, have we?" She's grinning at him suddenly. Reaction on his part is automatic, predictable. "Lay not up for yourselves treasures on earth where moth and rust doth corrupt."

"Money is the root of all evil!" she throws right back.

"The *love* of money," he corrects her. "The *love* of money. First Timothy."

On their second visit to the famous cathedral city he spends lavishly on her. It's a rare experience for Gilchrist, even rarer to find himself sitting there in all those "boutiques" – *are they called that still?* – piped music pulsing, while she tries on "outfits" behind drawn curtains a few feet away. There's a space at the bottom, to deter shoplifters, he imagines, and it's hard for him to ignore those frail white shins and underclothes piling up around them in a drift while she wrestles into yet another garment from the rails.

Every so often, looking flustered, she pops her head out, followed by the rest of her, mouthing silently at him for approval. But what can he say, do, except try to limit the damage? Everything seems either too loose or much too tight. He doesn't know which is worse, the enormous, slogan-bearing sweatshirts and building-site jeans or the skinny sweaters and leggings cruelly cutting into, and exposing her junior sex. She has breasts like flattened baby pears, only really apparent for the first time. Perhaps the sweatshirt and denims would be for the best, he thinks to himself.

In the late afternoon, heading back in the car, Gilchrist feels exhausted. She seems drained, too, by all the traipsing and shopping, head slumped up against the window-glass. Behind them the seat is piled high with a slithery mound of carrier-bags. He has no idea how much he has spent, doesn't really care, either, there's more where that came from, his pockets are stuffed with notes. Just like those cattle-jobber elders back home. The thought delivers an invigorating dart of malicious satisfaction.

"Tired?" he asks. She nods sleepily.

"But – happy?" he pursues. More nods.

He drives on along the perfectly drawn roads, past trees on either side, clusters of tents and holiday caravans showing up every so often like giant outcrops of man-made fungi between those skinny trunks. The New Forest so far has been a deep disappointment. Like so many things in this country its former grandeur seems to exist more in peoples' imagination than in reality. He gives silent thanks he's not a tourist. He also takes satisfaction in how the day has gone. Tomorrow should be even more painless. There's no earthly reason why they shouldn't continue in this same easygoing fashion. The idea appeals, a slow, indulgent drift in tandem, making up for so much denied enjoyment. Two on a spree. As he drives he finds himself humming the tune of that little song of theirs. How does it go? *There is one thing I will not do . . .*

But later that same night those innocent words are to take on a more serious meaning, an indictment and affront to his conscience which is to haunt him like a steady ache. It comes about in this way . . .

When they return to the caravan site and after eating the take-away she's chosen for them – Kentucky Fried Chicken and fries out of a cardboard pail – she insists on trying on the clothes again. *For his benefit*, she tells him. Sitting there, captive, he feels the food he's swallowed lie heavy on his stomach, a nightmare-inducer for later if ever there was one, but still he smiles indulgently as each new combination of garments is unveiled. He tells himself to look upon it as an education, one of those experiences missing from his life up to now, but still he finds it hard to stifle his yawns.

Mercifully she also begins to show signs of weariness and abandons the fashion show having tried on a long white T-shirt like a shift, the words MATERIAL GIRL stencilled across the front, the title of a popular song he finds out later. It is what she intends sleeping in also, he is to discover. Soon after they retire for the night to their separate quarters and rapidly he falls asleep.

In the small hours an electric storm cups the counties of Hampshire, Dorset and parts of Sussex. Sheet lightning of a kind he has never experienced before irradiates the sky. Thunder follows and, fully awake now, he lies counting off the seconds to determine when the flashes will break directly overhead. Nearer and nearer they come till they coincide with a clap that rocks the caravan. He feels the bed move under him – *how can it be possible?* – a sort of slewing motion like a car skidding on ice, and the pots all rattle in the kitchen.

He hears a voice cry, "Eric! Eric! *Eric!*" in ascending pitch and a body hurtles towards him across the darkened room – a moment earlier it was bright as day – seeking him out under the sheet in a flurry of hot, twining limbs which burn where they touch.

"Oh, Eric, Eric, Mrs Allardyce told us it could come at any moment, any time, but I'm not ready for it. *I'm not ready!*"

He's holding her in spite of himself. He tells himself it's to keep her still because she writhes like a demon, a hot and sweaty little demon.

"What did Mrs Allardyce tell you?"

"The heavens would open up. There'd be the Crack of Doom. Listen. *Listen!* Do you hear it?"

Her hand has found its way under his pyjama jacket. It makes him speak faster, *yet why doesn't he attempt to remove it?*

"Thunder and lightning. A storm, Donna. It's only a storm. You mustn't believe everything people tell you. They may mean well, but that doesn't mean what they say is the gospel truth. Look, listen, it's passing already."

They lie there, entangled still, and Gilchrist suspends all his faculties except the physical. Her breath on his neck, her hands on his chest, the smell of young sweat. *This is wrong*. He knows it. Already he has gone beyond the bounds of decency. They both have. Does she know it, too? If not, then his conscience is in double jeopardy.

Eventually he says, "You should go back to your own bed now, Donna, really you should." His voice sounds strange, a recording played at the wrong speed.

She says, "I'm still scared, Eric. See, I'm shaking." Indeed there is a tremor, her palm palpitating against his midriff now. *How did he allow that to happen?*

"I'm not used to sleeping on my own. We all used to be in the same bed at home."

He has a sudden disturbing image of that red-haired lout of a brother of hers. What was his name? Damian? The two of them . . .

They lie together until morning. *Babes in the wood*, he tells himself in one of his more deranged moments.

But, as the light breaks, he tells her, "We mustn't be like this again. You understand that, don't you?"

She looks at him, thumb in mouth, and nods.

"Good," he says. "Good. That's settled, then."

SEVEN

"Little drops of water,
Little grains of sand,
Made the mighty ocean,
And the pleasant land."

He was on the beach again alone with his thoughts. Soon it would be dark. Already the sun quivered eager to slide into its nocturnal, cooling bath. It was his favourite time of day. Or so he used to tell himself. Something he had forgotten – or conveniently mislaid – like that business with the Dutch woman. Just about here they'd met, he, standing with his panama in hand and, she, hunkered on her straw mat, a yogi, mahogany-hued. He had made a remark about it and she had replied – what was it now? *Such a sad time. The blue hour.* Or that may have been something he'd picked up somewhere else. Blue – as in grey.

On his wanderings this far he had collected about a dozen or so small pebbles, oval, round, mottled, striped, or as smoothly uniform as metal, each unique to this time and place. Sermons in stones. They filled the hollow of his palm so satisfyingly and thus, every so often, he would jettison one to keep the numbers and balance correct, the feel of them curled in his palm just perfect. He would stop and examine carefully, carefully, before casting the reject away with something akin to regret and it seemed to him to be about as serious a judgement as any he had ever had to make.

Head bent, he trudged on, eyes fixed on the washed carpet of stones. And now the light was going in earnest and he began picking up more and more in a rush as if he must gather as many as possible before they lost that stunning uniqueness as dusk descended. His pockets began bulging. He could feel his booty bite through the thin lining, cold, wet too in places, for some had been plucked from the tide. Water always had that power to enhance. Once when he was young he very nearly drowned because of it – remember?

What else is left for you, old man, but remember? At least he can still laugh a little at himself. He hasn't reached the stage, not yet, anyhow, of holding loud, passionate debates with himself like those people he had seen on the English beaches. So many, too, arguing into the wind with only the gulls for listeners. Drifting overhead, nerveless legs dangling like limp, orange laces, they kept pace with their chosen crackpot, that cruel, narrow head to one side, those terrible glass eyes. *Tell me more, tell me more*.

He begins humming a little tune to himself – that was permitted – and the words flow silently in parallel in his head. "Living on the shore, living on the shore, I'm living where the healing waters flow . . ."

He's five years old again and back in the charge of Charlie and Tom and he can tell they resent having to watch him while they trap spricks in a jar. They coax the shoal towards the open end where it lies anchored between two stones on the bottom, invisible, a cord looped about its neck ready for Charlie's slow

234

and carefull pull. Charlie would never jerk, never. It's not in his nature.

He is unbearably excited by it all. They look like two giants, so deadly serious. The jam-jar had to be spotless, gleaming. Charlie scoured off the Robertson's golly with sand and water. He holds up the pound jar full of air until Tom nods approvingly. His silent brothers. Even now they're forging the future patterns of their lives together. They do it out of spite, he tells himself. To shut him out. He believes that, seriously, he does.

The flat rock where he's been marooned is surrounded by water. It's the middle of August and the river-bed is drying out, a shrinking necklace threaded by thin, trickling streams. He sees a kingfisher's sudden, jewelled dart and shouts out in excitement but they ignore him and the bird both. He hates them for it yet loves them too with an ache that catches him in the middle of his chest. Yet he tries so very hard to make them accept him.

He knows he must sit here on this rock and endure for as long as they care to stay. They might so easily forget about him, leaving him on his table-top. *Forever*, he thinks, feeling the tears prickle. *Or until the river rises*. Already he can feel it licking about his bare feet and ankles, then gently rolling him off, *he'll let it, he'll let it*, he won't struggle, and carrying him down to the weir and McCutcheon's mill to fetch up bobbing in the foam on the far side of the race with all the old tins and bottles and that dead grey and white dog he'd once seen, teeth bared in a hideous grin, stomach the size of a football, giving off a fearful stink. They would be sorry then. His mother would be crying floods of tears and his father would take down the razor-strop hanging under the stairs and whack them, whack them, whack them.

Tom holds up the second jam-jar to the sunlight for Charlie's inspection. Four, five, six inside already, magnified, lips pushing against the glass, a belly-buster among them, red-breasted, heavy with eggs, a prize. They'll all go in the rain barrel. They never live long, though. Then the cat gets them. He hates that part.

Legs outstretched, he perches on his island rock, bareheaded in the glare. *If he catches sunstroke* . . . He craves martyrdom.

The water makes a lovely, lulling sound. This is his favourite spot in all the world. When he's bigger he means to build a hut here and live in it, better still, a raft floating on four oil-drums. He knows how to do it for he's watched Charlie and Tom make theirs. Just how long must he wait before he can do things like them?

A wagtail alights on a stone nearby and he watches it bob like a toy with a weight in its end. He has a book of birds at home and although he can't read yet he knows all the drawings off by heart. His mother is teaching him his ABCs. she reads every night to him before bed from the big family Bible with all the names and dates inside. It's over a hundred years old. It will be his one day, she tells him, and then he'll be able to write his own children's names in it too. It smells as though it was in a fire. Sometimes he's allowed to leaf through it to look at the pictures, Moses at the Parting of the Red Sea, David smiting Goliath, Elijah and the Ravens, Joseph in his Coat of Many Colours – just like the quilt on his bed.

The one that affects him most profoundly, however, is Isaac on the Altar with Abraham his father, knife poised, glinting and terrible. When he looks at that picture he feels a powerful accord with the boy, bound and helpless, waiting for the blade to fall. It doesn't, of course, but who could ever trust their parent again after that? He can't help having doubts about his own father. If he had to he might easily do it to him, mightn't he, he being the youngest and least likely to

236

be missed? Snipe Island, further downstream, would be the ideal spot. Plenty of dry kindling to hand and no onlookers. Charlie and Tom are never away from it.

He looks at them now bending over their invisible jam-jar. Charlie is so slow, so careful, like an old man sometimes. What are the two of them doing catching tiddlers at their age anyway? Charlie is nearly seventeen and Tom fifteen. He can't wait to overtake. Even then he burns with impatience for his reign to begin.

On the right-hand side of his rock the water lies still and heavy as molten metal. Unlike the other pools this one seems to have no inlet, no overflow either, yet remains at the same constant level. He can see clear to the bottom. He trails a hand across its warm, liquid skin. When he takes it out it has that smell he loves. He leans closer until his face is inches away from the surface.

He sees a mysterious, submerged terrain, shrunken, scaled down, heights and hollows, thickets of algae hiding invisible creatures, hunters, armies, castles made of shells. There are bright plains of sand to be crossed, caverns to be explored, ramparts to be scaled using ropes of water-weed. It beckons, drawing him down into its enchanted, underwater world. He sees something glitter in the depths. Precious. A ring? He stretches towards it watching his bare arm swell. His mouth skims the water. Wet, warm, brown, he tastes them all at once. He still can't reach the prize. It's been waiting so long for this moment, an eternity, *for him*, wedged in its vault. All it takes is a touch, he feels convinced of it, a touch from him and it will be his. He can feel it between forefinger and thumb already, imprinted on the skin.

Charlie and Tom are still dabbling in the shallows, birds call, a distant tractor in a duet with a farm dog, it's all sharpened, intense, somehow, as if these might be the last sounds he might ever hear. The silver ring on the bottom entices, winking in a shaft of filtered sunlight. He takes a deep breath for he has decided now and like that boy in *The Water Babies* he lowers head, then shoulders, then chest into the pool breaking the transparent, air-tight seal that protects this magic world. It reminds him of the covers his mother uses when making jam.

There's a gentle roaring in his ears, his nose feels strange, but he stretches deep, deeper towards the prize. Yet now it seems much farther away which is curious. He feels himself going under but he's not shocked or afraid in any way. *I'm swimming, see, I'm swimming*, and a bubble leaves his mouth as though bearing the words the way it does in a cartoon. He's made a marvellous discovery, anything is possible as long as you're not afraid! He must remember that. Anything, *anything* can be within your grasp.

He studies his outstretched fingers. They feel as though they belong to someone else, hard to control, cold for the first time, all sensation gone as though sandpapered the way Charlie had scoured the jam-jar. He's almost there, his chest feels tight, that same taste in his nose when food comes up the wrong way, but he's nearly there, one more thrust, it must be worth hundreds, no, *thousands!* And then just on the point of success his ankles are brutally grabbed and he feels himself being hauled out of his underwater world like a cork from a bottle.

Charlie is holding him upside down and shaking him. Tom is watching. They both look angry. Charlie *feels* that way because he can't see his face from this angle but his hands tell the tale. They grip him the way they would a rabbit, or a plucked chicken. He feels puny, worthless, he needs to cry out – *why? why?* – but holds back because Charlie and Tom hate noise, especially that kind of noise.

They peel off his vest and trousers taking it in turns to rub him briskly all over with handfuls of hay. Then they dump him on his rock again until his clothes are dry. Not a word is spoken, they merely glance at one another in that sidelong way of theirs, returning to their fishing. He crouches on his rocky prison, hands clasping his knees, covering his nakedness. *Some day, some day.* The ring is forgotten, probably only an old washer, anyway, but that isn't the point. *That's not the point!*

He's shivering now as his back and shoulders feel the hot, flat blade of the sun. His wet duds steam slightly, spread on a stone like cut-out doll's clothes. His mother is sure to find out what's happened, she'll question Charlie and Tom, she's bound to, but they'll just shrug as usual and go on eating as usual, heads low over their heaped plates. They're a law unto themselves, he's heard her use the expression a million times – *but what does it mean?* He needs to pee badly now and lets it leak out in measured spurts feeling it run warm down his inner leg. He wonders if it will show up, a tawny stripe in the water.

Something else took place that day in summer all those years ago – his memory of it is sharp-etched and clear – an additional humiliation as far as he was concerned. A gang of girls from the village arrive to watch then stay to jeer from the farther bank. He has seen them before, big for their age, barefoot like boys, bold, fearless. *Hussies*, his mother refers to them, *those hussies from Mill Row*. The two McCabe sisters, Alma and Nan, Myrtle Balmer and Pearly McKnight, who has a lazy eye and a tight, black cap of frizzy hair and whose father, they say, was an American soldier. In some people's minds the two are connected.

At first Charlie and Tom choose to ignore them. Most of their taunts are directed towards him, naked on his rock, anyway. They dare him to show them his willy, his "wee willy winkie", as they term it. The word "wee" affronts him deeply for some unexplained reason. The elder McCabe offers to expose her own parts in return and as proof of her *bona fides* hitches up her frock far above the knee while the other three roll hysterically around in the long grass. All the while he's hiding his head to make himself as small and insignificant as possible on his baking platform.

Charlie and Tom are looking distinctly odd, both very red in the face by this stage. Something unspoken seems to be racing between them, a connection producing strong emotions. For a moment he believes it to be on his account, blood being thicker than water, another of his mother's puzzling sayings, but that idea is quickly scotched. He may be young but he senses things instinctively, the way an animal might, by observing the world and those in it from a low vantage-point, close to the ground. He sees himself as a fox sometimes, or a badger, those sly ones, and his particular favourite in these river haunts, the otter.

Then Charlie picks up the first stone and Tom follows suit. He would, too, if they let him. Charlie hurls it upstream to land in the shallows where the McCabe girl has been doing her cheeky dance for their benefit. Tom's stone flies after in perfect duplicate. She takes a second drenching. At this point she turns away baring her backside to them like a true hussy. Knickers of pale, washed-out blue. Charlie stoops and gathers a handful of pebbles rolled by the current to perfect weight and size for throwing. Stranded on his rock, he yearns to be involved. He watches the hail of stones start flying as deadly as sling-shot in one of those old books about battles long ago.

Alma McCabe covers her head with her hands and runs, bent over, ducking, from the shore. She's bawling loudly now, all bravado gone, and he thrills to that. It excites him. To his surprise his little willy is standing to attention hard and straight as a spigot. The other girls are screaming now as they come under fire too. On top of his rock he dances in a state of tremendous exhilaration. It's a war dance, his nakedness no longer an affront, for he's a warrior, a brave, red Indian chief and this is *their* territory, *theirs alone*, all this water, these pools and streams, these round-backed boulders drying to stepping-stones in the sun.

As the enemy run fleeing through the fields back to their village, he stands tall on his rock – it's no longer a prison, but a fort, a fortress – and directs a triumphal arc of piss after them. It curves through the air, a rainbow falling as golden rain in the water. Charlie and Tom join him, they seem just as excited as he is, laughing, even, and unbuttoning their trousers they, too, shoot twin streams at the retreating backs of the foe.

Their willies are proper willies, however, not like his pencil stub. For some reason they look bigger and redder than usual and the amount they are able to discharge is also phenomenal. Envious, he watches them compete for height and distance, pinching the foreskin until it balloons with the pressure, then releasing it for the jet to rise up, up and out to fall far downstream. Now they swing them back and forth like hoses, intersecting, matching streams to form patterns that sparkle in the sunlight. As a variation Charlie plays his on the jam–jar holding the catch. Tom does the same. The water boils suddenly, the tiny captives swirling like the snowflakes in his little seaside paperweight at home. He wonders will it poison them. *Only if the water turns yellow*, he tells himself.

Charlie and Tom are engaged in some other form of contest now, one he doesn't understand. They've turned their backs on him, arms pumping faster, faster, the napes of their necks reddening, punishing themselves in some odd way. Then they stop abruptly and he can hear them panting, both staring across the river towards the trees on the far bank. Looking in the same direction, he can see one of those village girls, Pearly McKnight, it is, the one whose father is supposed to be a GI. She's on her own, not doing anything, just standing there watching. He shakes his fist but it has no effect. Why doesn't Charlie drive her away like he did earlier? But he just stands there still with his thing in his hand. She can see it, *she must!* He cups his own miniature sprout from view.

Then Charlie slides Tom one of those famous, sidelong looks of theirs and the pair of them begin wading across the river towards the waiting hussy under the trees, black hair, eyes like sloes, that swarthy complexion. Everyone calls her Darkie to her face. Some say the soldier her mother went with was a black man. It's a concept he finds hard to take in, much too foreign for his limited experience. There's so much he doesn't understand. People will never tell him things.

A heron flaps past downriver but he's feeling far too betrayed to take any interest in its gawky flight. It probably sees him as pathetic as well, the small, insignificant, naked thing on its rock not even capable of fishing properly. *Please God, why can't I be an otter?*

Now the three of them are standing close together in the shade of the trees. He watches Charlie hook something out of his shirt pocket, something small and white, then hand it to the hussy. It looks like a cigarette. She takes it from him and he experiences a renewed rush of rage at such treachery. Then they go in amongst the trees where he can't see any longer.

He waits and waits on his rock. The sun nibbles a track across the top of his bare shoulders. He'll have a raw back because of this, because of them, he just knows it. *Please God . . .* He's unable to finish it, just something spectacularly punishing, *please*. He concentrates all his spite on that concealing clump of alder. *Let it be consumed, God, an electric bolt torching it and them with it.* Like the one in that film about the monster and his mad scientist master, zig-zagging down through the open skylight on to the operating table. When he closed his eyes in terror he felt certain he could smell burning in the cinema.

He does the same now and when he opens them again Charlie and Tom are racing towards him out of the trees pulling up their trousers as they go. A crimson-faced man carrying a bucket with a collie at his heels is chasing them. He looks like a farmer in a boiler suit and wellingtons. *Did* he *do that?* Charlie and Tom have a frightened look about them, which is surprising, shocking, too, for he always believed nothing or no one could put fear into them. *Did* he *do that?*

Knees high like a horse Charlie comes splashing through the pools and grabbing his clothes in one hand he snatches him up off his rock with the other. Barely breaking stride he continues to run holding him under one arm like a baby, a bare-bottomed baby, but one too proud to cry, Tom bringing up the rear, equally desperate in his haste even to pick up their mother's precious jam-jar. That worried him more than anything else, oddly enough, as he watched the ground race past below, a five-year-old, naked, human parcel.

Did he ever tell, he wondered? And he burned to blab so badly with a rage for retribution that stayed for weeks afterwards. But then what was there to tell even if he wanted to? He was too young to imagine, or put into words, what must have taken place among those trees, the girl on the ground, dress kilted up, a look of breathtaking passivity on her face – thinking of what? the cigarette? *two* cigarettes? – for Tom was waiting his turn on top after Charlie had his go. But did Tom ever get his turn? Did Charlie?

Such a long time ago. Water and sex. Always the two have been connected in some mysterious manner in his life. He lost his virginity in a swimming-pool. Well, took the first plunge in that direction, anyway. A man of his age. By the time the Dutch woman had taken him in hand – literally – he knew what it was for. The crude expression, previously unthinkable, slipped out as naturally as a breath.

Others follow as though liberated, cunt and fuck, prick and tits, a scalding litany ringing out in the silence of the darkening beach like chain-shot. He covers his ears with his hands – it should have been his mouth – but they continue to run on inside his head, fanny, dick, hole, cock. All those barnyard epithets . . .

He can't see the pebbles clearly any more. They're beginning to merge into a shadowy, mottled carpet stretching to invisibility. How long would it take to reach its end if he were to keep on going? The idea seems an attractive prospect, simply to walk away from one's past and all its mistakes, leaving everything and everyone behind, a diminishing, human dot. To his left an even quicker, obliterating solution . . .

But he's forgetting the crowned headland with its luxury hotel of one hundred bedrooms. At this hour in this light it has the appearance of pink nougat. Blocking his escape route, it looms up ahead, warm seas breaking over the boulders at its base. They look like debris left over from some catastrophe. But before reaching that rocky outcrop he must make a detour.

Already the pebbles give way to shingle, then soft, powdery sand which muffles and slows the feet. He's beginning to puff slightly, his lack of fitness as evident as it was then, not made easier by the weight of stones in his pockets. Yet he cannot bring himself to part with his treasure, not yet, not even if it alters the accuracy of his re-enactment. For that is what he has in mind, like some detective painstakingly going back over the scene of the crime. *But then again was one ever committed?*

These past weeks he's felt like a sleepwalker, fact and fantasy battling it out for supremacy inside his brain. He has the beach to himself but the ape on his shoulder is with him still, that voice in his head running commentary on every move he makes, every thought, no matter how private or how painful . . .

So. Back for seconds, are we? Another bite at the cherry? If – as we say — we're still not totally certain how it went first time around. Really, you do disappoint me, Eric, you a previously paid-up man of the cloth, too. Still pretending you didn't fuck that woman. Okay, she did it to you, then. That randy Dutch divorcee undoing the reverend's pants and having her way with him. While he just sits there in her living-room watching it happen to "someone else" — so he says — in a mirror on the far wall. Not a mirror? Glass doors? Amazing how good one's memory can be when we put our mind to it. Two minds, Eric, two, as I keep on having to remind you. First proper blow-job, was it? Young Angie does a very respectable French, by the way. One of her spécialités. Do anything for me, that little slag would once upon a time, anything for a close friend, one of the family. Just think what you missed, Eric. And I bet you thought of it, too. I saw you watching her. Relax, it's not a punishable offence, they can't lock you up for it. Speaking of which . . . Our other young friend, our other young under-age friend, Eric. Now, that was naughty of you. But nice, eh? So, how was it there? And don't tell me you can't remember too much about any of that, either. Her first time, was it? Bet she said it was, even if it wasn't, lying little cow. They take it in with their mother's milk. That time at the river when you were only a sprog with Tom and Charlie? That girl? Remember? That's what they're like, Eric, our little redhead included. And when you fucked her she couldn't get enough. Wasn't that the way of it? Wasn't it? Wasn't it?

"No, it *wasn't*, it wasn't like that! *She* wasn't like that, *wasn't*, I tell you!"

He heard his denials ring out in the silence, for it was about that time, the sea flat, unmoving. Any moment now the sun's livid lower rim would flatten as it met the horizon. His voice was that of a five-year-old again, enraged, impotent. Yet this time it seemed to produce an effect for a light came on in one of the beach bungalows. *Hers*, he told himself with a tremble of anticipation.

His excitement began to mount at the thought of all of this

245

duplication, a replay of events and sensations which had plagued him so. This time there would be no ambiguity. It didn't occur to him she might not be waiting there for him naked under her blue and white robe, that same look in her pale eyes, so arousing despite, or because of, its lack of emotion. Like that other girl that day on the riverbank? Was that the sound of a shower? Standing, listening there, his only regret was he didn't look quite so presentable as on that first occasion.

The slatted blinds were tightly closed but the living-room light was still visible as a fine yellow rim about the edges of the big seaward facing window. She must be paying a pretty penny for such a view, he told himself. As well as the seclusion. *A rich divorcee*. The phrase carried a powerful, erotic charge. He was trembling again.

Halted there, ankle-deep in sand, he ran his hands over his hair and clothing in a final, futile attempt to make his appearance a little more appealing. He really had let himself slide these past weeks. Ever since Jordan had moved into the apartment, in fact, for he could put a day, a date, a time, almost, on that first, fatal slackening. It was like watching another person go downhill before his very eyes. When was the last time he'd shaved properly? Or taken his things to the *lavanderia*? God knows. *But does he? Does he care?* He felt as if great, enervating waves of apathy were flowing from him, affecting everyone within touching, seeing, distance, even reaching as far as that ultimate observer. *When last had he actually attempted to pray?*

Yet there was one who appeared to flourish as he rotted, inversely. *Perversely*, he thought. Someone who whistled and sang as merry as a lark or, jay, come to think of it, for the more his own appearance deteriorated the more of a dandy that other seemed to become. It was a startling metamorphosis. His bathroom shelves were now crowded with oils and unguents no decent Englishman would dare put near his skin. Gaudy shirts and pastel-coloured slacks jostled his own dull dun things for space in the wardrobe. He'd even started carrying one of those underarm purses, more like a woman's handbag. And all the time his skin glowed, his hair cut closely to the scalp, pomaded like a local's. Even more miraculous, that flabby drinker's body had grown lean and taut.

The latter transformation was flaunted before him at every opportunity. He realized it was meant to shame him out of his torpor – he wasn't that far gone – but the more the other posed and exercised, press-ups on the balcony, or on the living-room rug when the weather was cold or damp, the deeper his own mood plunged. Dully, he watched this strutting, preening other self shed pounds and years before his eyes, noted the high-fashion garments taking up most of the hanging space in the one wardrobe.

Other purchases were made on an almost daily basis – pictures, rugs, lamps, a near life-sized ceramic leopard for some reason, a modernistic clock whose soundlessness was more worrying than any tick, new white goods for the kitchen – everything bang up to the minute. Gradually the tired old fitments which had come with the apartment disappeared and one day when he went out to escape from all this hi-tech glare he returned to find two workmen painting the walls a paler shade of the blue of their boiler suits. They ignored him. He went out again to the beach.

For some reason the expense of it all didn't seem to involve him even though he imagined it had to be coming out of his own pocket. But then again he felt far too jaded even to examine the state of his finances. He did, however, begin carrying his cigar-box about with him wherever he went – today it was hidden behind the wash-basin – yet somehow knew that the documents and pass-books it contained had been bypassed in some fashion, that his signature, like so many things, no longer counted, in the same way he no longer did. Part of him felt relieved at being rid of what he had appropriated in the first instance, for no longer could he pretend, even to himself, that his motives had been other than fraudulent. The truth spoke calmly to him, ignoring his tired rebuttals.

You stole that money, it said in flat, slow, ponderous tones, *as surely as if you'd rifled a till. And for your own selfish ends, too. Namely, to impress and seduce a girl young enough to be your daughter, while masquerading as her religious and moral mentor. What have you got to say for yourself?* The policeman conscience had now swapped helmet for a wig. *More to the point, how many other offences do you wish taken into consideration?*

"Where do I begin? Where?"

He heard his shout ring out once more like one of those loonies let loose on Weymouth sands. One had a metal detector, he recalled, which should have given the lie to his derangement but didn't for he kept waving it at the gulls to warn them away from his territory. He also waded off-shore unlike other treasure seekers as though possessed of some secret knowledge, an invisible, underwater map only he could read.

Standing there, one of those same shouting ones – *touched* was the expression, wasn't it? – he saw the light go off in the beach bungalow facing him. He had done it with the sound of his voice! For some reason the phenomenon seemed perfectly natural. He felt like giving it one more try for luck.

Luck, he thought, *luck*, and came back to some form of normality. The stones in his pocket felt like stones. *What was he doing here?* And at this hour, too. Nothing remained of the sun but a shrinking sliver of orange resting on the surface of the waves. At his back a necklace of lights had sprung up, pricking the darkening sky, and the wailing of a police siren presaged the onset of the resort's lively night-life.

Shivering a little he began emptying his pockets until nothing remained to betray his presence but a tiny scattering of pebbles on the soft, grey sand. All their magic had vanished the moment they touched ground as surely as any fantasies he might have had concerning the woman waiting in the dark for him behind drawn blinds.

Turning away he began to make tracks back along the beach staying as close to his original set of footprints as the light would allow. It had long been his habit, after all, and there is always something consoling about old habits no matter how childish or irrational. Already he felt calmer, less fraught, much better able to deal with the demons within.

EIGHT

"Who made you?"

   "God."

   "For what were you made?"

   "To glorify God."

   "In what state was Man created?"

   "In the image of God, holy and happy."

   "Did he continue in that state?"

   "No."

   "How did he fall from it?"

   "By disobeying God."

   "How did he disobey Him?"

   "By eating the forbidden fruit."

   "That's enough for one day," he tells her, shutting the little Sabbath School Society *Shorter Catechism*. Appropriate point at which to call a halt for some of those same illicit juices still linger from the night before. *Peach? Pear? Apricot?*

   He's quite beyond redemption now, he tells himself, too far gone even for that little pink booklet on the table before them to help him.

   "Do you think will I ever be able to get it off by heart? Mrs

Allardyce said I had a head like a sieve." She laughs. "Allardyce. What sort of name is that?"

He smiles. Secretly he loves this collusion, this game that they play. Now she takes it a step farther watching him the while.

"Man-mad, that one."

He mimes reproof.

"*Honestly*. You should have seen the way she would carry on whenever a man came near the place. The way she looked at *you*."

"Oh, I'm sure that can't be correct." *Hypocrite*.

They sit there allowing their brief little flurry of animation to settle. Outside the English beeches seem to be closing ranks as the light fades. Their leaves are like massed copper coins. He can just make out the winking sign in green neon that reads Timber Tops Trailer Park and a picture of a Christmas tree without the decorations. It all looks and feels like some other planet. Does she feel that way, too, he wonders.

"I bet she'd have a purple fit if she could see us now."

Then she does a startling thing, for she puts her hand over his and says, "Don't worry, she wasn't a very nice person. None of them were. Her awful sister, or that wee, grey-haired man who came over on the boat with us. I didn't tell you. We don't need them. We don't need any of them, Eric. Do we?"

The heat of her touch never ceases to surprise him. It's hard not to flinch from that first searing shock but, then, steeling himself, his skin absorbs and, finally, embraces it and soon he's longing for contact to last forever. Last night while the storm raged and she clung to him it felt as though their blood temperatures had coalesced in some miraculous way to a feverish degree.

"Tell me again."

"Tell you what?" It's another of their games.

"You know. Come on. *Please*."

"Oh, that. Well, if you'll put the kettle on."

Rising from the dainty little table – it folds up almost invisibly into the wall when not in use – she goes forward to their kitchenette. *All these diminutives*, he's thinking to himself. There's also a dinette. It's like living in a doll's house. Perhaps they're really playing house, he and his little friend. He hesitates in his head for it's something which still hasn't been satisfactorily resolved. Ward? Niece? Daughter has a ring of being far too – incestuous? *Lord, steer thy servant clear of dangerous waters.*

When the tea has been poured, the milk, sugar, a plate of bought shortbread fingers – wherever did she acquire such graces? – he begins with the Episode of The Burning Tent. Already it has taken on epic quality, the great turning-point when first he heard The Call. Her eyes shine brightly in anticipation. He finds it hard not to embellish yet he knows danger lies there for she seems to recall details better than he does, certain little grace notes he'd put in originally without thought for the consequences.

"What about the birds," she'd say. "You left the bit out about the birds."

"Oh, the magpies."

"One for sorrow, two for joy. Remember?"

"So then I stopped on the road and as I did so I looked back and saw – "

"The tent on fire! A Sign From Above."

"Or – behind."

"And the Voice. Tell about the Voice. Please. *Please.*"

"Leave this place, it seemed to be saying. Put everything behind you. All the lies, the cheating, the deceit." *What a young prig*, he thought.

"Your own Crusade? Your own tent? Right?"

"Right."

"Oh I wish *I* could have a Vision. Hear a Voice. Do you think I ever will? You were about my age, weren't you?"

"A fraction older."

God forgive him but he can't remember what was true and what isn't any longer. Had he made *all* of it up? Yet why shouldn't it have happened the way he'd told it – as she believed it? Where was the harm? Max Buckingham could so easily have set that canvas ablaze that night. Certainly he was drunk enough, crazed enough. And he was sure he had heard something in his head on that dark, Irish, country road in the back of beyond. Something or someone had spoken. It had happened to others, or so they claimed, why not to him? Didn't he deserve it? All those subsequent, thankless years of service to an absentee Master – why not a little sign, a little voice? *Why not, for heaven's sake? It wouldn't hurt him, would it?* He had started haranguing inside his head again. Next thing he knew it would be the seagulls on the beach for him if he weren't careful.

"And after you left those people with their show – but no tent – " she grinned suddenly, maliciously at that. "What happened next?"

Each time it's as if she's hearing it afresh – how can he resist? So he tells her about working for the farmers for a month, sleeping with the animals, eating kitchen scraps and leftovers, his "Calvary in Cavan", as he was to describe it later to his Gospel audiences. Enough parables to last a lifetime.

Back home then and it's as if he has never been away from that silent house and those three munching mutes at the bone-white table. Only his mother looks directly at him, sighing, but then she did a lot of that, something he always associates with that house and the ever-present, soft roar of the river, great melancholy mewings, female whale-music.

He reads all the time now from the big Bible with the broken brass clasps. It lies across his thighs in bed like a hinged door. Sometimes he buries his face in the cleft, smelling ancient lands, the dusty robes of prophets. He's with them on their journeys, enduring extremes of heat and cold. Walking, he transfers his imaginings to his own lush corner of Antrim. A mossy well becomes an oasis, a bare ploughed field a corrugated dune. Ash, elm, oak, alder, they turn to date-palms before his eyes, a hawk remains a hawk, quartering desert wastes only he, and it, can see.

He starts attending outlying gospel halls, those tin-roofed, country tabernacles with their hard benches and wheezing harmoniums. He thirsts for Meaning, Knowledge, Truth. They give him homespun platitudes, drab imagery, stones instead of bread. Those part-time preachers, they depress him with their bad grammar and rotten technique. He sits near the back burning up with his own arrogance. He longs to leap up and astound them with something from his old fit-up repertoire. Instead, hand on breast, eyes to the rafters, he gives his Testimony.

"Once I joined a travelling troupe of painted play-actors. Pretty soon I was as bad as they were. I lied, drank, gambled, I cheated humble farming folk who paid good money at the door for the privilege of being hoodwinked. I was a willing apprentice to all those wiles. Mind-reading became an open book. Deeper and deeper I was drawn down, more and more I interfered with Nature's laws, those of the Good Lord himself. But he took pity on me and sent me a sign and, like Lot, I turned my back on that life and those misguided people. And that is why I am here with you all tonight, brothers and sisters, able to tell my story."

It flows from him like Water from the Rock and soon he is something of a star turn on the gospel circuit, sharing the same platform as the reformed drunkards, the gamblers, fornicators, wife-beaters and embezzlers. His fame begins to spread in line with his imagination. More and more "grace notes" get added to the recital. But then everyone else is doing it.

One night in a remote, upcountry hall, the speaker

following him, inflamed with competition, confesses to having once been tempted into relations with a farm animal – breed unspecified – but the shock is still so devastating in that tiny, airless place that the man, a whey-faced townie, his appearance only reinforcing the enormity of his claim, flees in mid-sentence as from a possible stoning.

Soon after that he gives up breast-beating in public for a while, but not before rediscovering those persuasive powers he seems to possess, particularly over the females in his audience. It's like being sprayed by an invisible haze of yearning, scent of a thousand illicit desires.

"And then I heard Billy Graham for the first time and went to Bible College in Kansas and then I started my first Crusade in Antrim."

"And then you saved me."

She says it so softly, and he's reminded of those other women from his past – *his past career*, he tells himself – devouring him with their eyes and all with that same unspoken word there as well, *Me, me, me. Choose me.*

Then she sighs like a child who has just heard her favourite bedtime story. There's something unhealthy about all of this, he decides, nursery games, the two of them in their snug Wendy House spinning fairy tales. But how can he deny himself these pleasures?

"Now you know everything about me. How about you?"

She looks at him. "What's there to tell?"

For a moment he's tempted to shatter that shell of seeming innocence. He has the power, the secret knowledge, but he tells himself, *no, it will keep, why spoil things?*

"Would you like to eat out?" As if they've done anything else.

"Somewhere nice?"

He has constantly to remind himself he's treating himself as much as her on these occasions for denial has for so long been part of his life. They do have that in common. Menus in French can still agitate him, however, but then she is easy to order for and he always gives the impression to waiters his own choice matters far less than indulging his young companion sitting opposite.

Tonight she plumps for sirloin of steak – well done – garden peas, and, of course, chips, followed by Pavlova. He has the Dover sole, green beans, boiled potatoes, but joins her in the dessert. They also share a half-bottle of Blue Nun, a touch of forbidden fruit, it's true, but where's the harm in it? They grin across the table at one another delighted at their daring. As though in on the joke the waiter, a sly-eyed Spaniard with sideburns like scimitars, suggests a Benedictine to follow, but he declines and orders white coffees, instead, to finish off. As always he pays with cash.

That night he lies waiting for her to come to him although the trees outside barely stir and the moon rides anchored in a cloudless sky. He's in terrible turmoil, half of him relieved she prefers her own bed, the other half wracked by desire for the unthinkable. He turns and tosses as if on a spit.

At four, sweating, cinder-eyed, finally he falls asleep and when he awakes the light has almost reached as far as the heading on the curtains. She's lying next to him. He feels that warmth seep into his, the humid body heat of a child – an appalling image – but he suppresses it like so much of late. He is stretched on his back, face averted, thankfully, for his breath must be far from fresh. As usual he amazes himself at being distracted by such considerations at a time like this.

His thoughts continue racing. If he can manage to stay like this long enough, feigning sleep, she might return to her own room. How long has she been beside him, anyway? Minutes? *My God, hours?* More important – is she or isn't she awake at this moment? All his senses strain after the information. As he listens he realizes he cannot detect breathing and starts to sweat. He is on the point of turning when her hand brushes his hip. Light as a leaf it rests there, unmoving, then, as though by prior knowledge, stealthily, thrillingly, it advances until it finds the opening of his pyjama trousers. What follows seems also governed by familiarity. Eyes closed, he lies on his back, not merely shamming sleep but also pretending this isn't happening, his mind, his body refusing to accept responsibility for what is taking place below his waist.

Freed of involvement he floats in a warm stream of sensations back in time to that other river where perpetual summer reigns, a cloudless sky high above, and him lying, a naked starfish, basking in the deepest of its pools. Half-submerged, he floats in its tepid embrace. He has it all to himself today for now he can swim, no longer needs Charlie and Tom to watch over him. The water is his friend, he would give himself up to it willingly if the need ever arose.

Nothing breaks the surface but the soft, gleaming curve of his thing, his willy, as that girl called it. Thinking of her now, more specifically, of her companion who had gone into the trees with Charlie and Tom that time, gradually it straightens to the perpendicular. It feels like a rod now. He closes his eyes to allow it to surprise him further. Now it's growing hot. Soon he must touch, *soon, must*, but he holds back, willing the water to do it for him. He moves his outstretched arms, creating tiny, lapping waves. They break over the prow of his prick – another of those words he's heard Charlie and Tom use. Harder and harder he concentrates, feeling the blood throb, and thinking of the girl with the black hair and what Charlie is doing to her.

He can visualize it in his head just like a film, that one he once saw but wasn't supposed to, two people violently kissing, then opening each other's clothes in a rush, finally falling, the man on top, on to a pile of hay. Was it Jane Russell? Everyone has seen her breasts but what is she like *below*, down there? He can only fantasize, as he does now about the girl among the trees. Dark, dark hair. Curly? Straight? Coarse? Fine? His own is like dandelion down.

But now Charlie is putting his thing into hers. Does she hold it? Oh, yes, yes, *please let her hold, please, oh, let her touch, please*! Even as he feels himself come he holds back from groaning aloud, pretending to the bitter end.

His face is turned towards the plywood panelling beside the fold-away bed. The wall must be little more than an inch thick. To think of all this happening – a criminal offence, no less – with only a thin, aluminium membrane shielding it from the outside world. He can hear a dog being shouted at, a car coughing into life, a fretful child, a radio tuned to some music station. The monotonous, pumping bass notes have some-how managed to penetrate the very metal of the trailer itself.

Still shamming, he waits to find out what happens next. The rage in the blood subsides, the patch of wetness across his front turning cold, then gluey. So much of it, too, but then hadn't he been saving it up for such a very long time? *Saving himself*. A virgin for Jesus. Just when had been the last time? That Sunday in the swimming-pool when he'd clutched her to him, the water-level mercifully covering his shame? *My God, she must have felt it. Must have*. Now there's a thought.

"Another pair of your good white trousers ruined," his housekeeper had complained. "What do they put in that water, anyway?" Albumen. *The white of an egg ran down her leg* . . . He can't remember the rest. One of Charlie's little rhymes. Devil's ditties. At times it seems his head is full of filth.

He lies studying the varnished wall a foot away. All the fitments have the same honey-blond finish. Swedish pine. It says so in the brochure he came across in one of the drawers, along with the playing-cards and that paperback novel with the lipstick-red title. *There is one thing I will not do . . .*

He feels drowsy now, all that hot constriction of a moment ago diffused, so that when her grasp finally loosens and the hand withdraws – *for it must, mustn't it?* – he's not really conscious of it happening. Or is it, perhaps, just more proficiency on her part, the work of an adept? The idea slips through his defences leaving a nasty residue, something with which to torment himself later.

The small, warm hand retreats finally and he senses the rest of her poised to follow. And then she does, oh, so delicately, so sweetly, scarcely disturbing the covers, sliding out from under and away, the mattress barely registering her passing. And then he has the bed to himself and his thoughts once more. *My God*, he's thinking, *my God, maybe, just maybe I can get away with this.*

What a monster of depravity he has become, and in such a short space of time, too. Yet the notion won't go away. It continues to slither seductively about in his head like a snake that has entered through a grille. A game. Which two can play. Allowing it to happen. While pretending it isn't. But why not? For far too long he's been groaning under the burden of his own rectitude. And for what? Eyes prickling, he remembers slights, injustices, those sons of bigotry and mean-mindedness back home and their treatment of him.

To his tremendous surprise he feels himself stiffening again. Then another revelation. *What if he's not alone, not the only one.* For he has a sudden and startling image of a multitude of strangers similarly engaged, partaking in this same "game" all over the place, everywhere, the great Bedroom Mystery. One partner lying doggo while the other . . .

He thinks of his own parents in their brass bed and the

progression stops dead right there, for certain doors will always remain, for him, locked.

Outside, he hears someone whistling, accompanied by the clash of empty milk bottles. The daytime world awaits – the world of Southern English order and restraint. But before getting up and the two of them face one another across that little folding-table over another breakfast – the last time was really yesterday, he tells himself, for the dark has become another country now, a place where they meet as intimate strangers – he repeats to himself his newest commandment. *Thou shalt not touch*. God have pity on him, he actually did believe it then that if he didn't initiate or reciprocate in any way, somehow he would stay inviolate, uninvolved, more importantly, blameless, a wise monkey playing dead in the dark.

NINE

Returning from the beach he took the long way home, up all sixty-five steps. Anyway the lift was locked at this hour. At the top he clung, panting, to the telescope jammed on its swivel. A fifty-peseta piece would release the mechanism – but what was there to see? Yet even in the dark he could tell the bay made a perfect unbroken arc below, the demarcation between land and sea, hot and cool, registering as a kind of vague fluttering on the retina.

Somewhere the scent of jasmine fought the man-made one of exhaust fumes. One of those mopeds must have passed by earlier, for the town's teenagers, he knew, enjoyed coming up here to rape the peace with their racket. He thought he could make out a small tribe of them chasing each others' tail-lights a very long way off on the wasteland beyond the distant bull-ring. They looked like fireflies stitching intricate patterns in the blue blackness. And such blackness. Dropping like a cloak where it fell beyond the limits of the streetlamps, it had the impact of a curfew, and so he pushed on towards the resort's blazing heart.

*

Its streets were more crowded than expected as if the *paseo* had started earlier than usual, but then he caught sight of a clock face in a shop-window, one of those digital affairs, the final number flickering at heart-beat speed, and he realized it was far later than he had imagined. Time, on the beach, alone with his thoughts, must have sped faster than anything that little lighted dial could express.

The shop itself was one close to the Miramar, small electrical gadgets on display, and spotting a figure in the distance he thought he recognized he pushed his face close to the glass as though intent on a shaver, a new transistor, or even that hairdrier in deep emerald, favourite colour of the Spanish. He sees it everywhere. Señora Guzman from the apartment above is walking her poodle or, rather, Pepe is leading her in and out of the palm-trees in the gardens across the way.

Waiting his chance until the dog has lifted its leg – both appear to strain in concert as usual – he scuttles rapidly over to the entrance of the block. Hands a-flutter – *why, what has he done?* – he spends some time searching, then finding his keys, and pushes the larger one home. It feels unfamiliar, un-smoothed by usage, they both do, and he has to concentrate on guiding it into the lock to get it to catch.

Inside in the dim entrance hall – that familiar mortuary atmosphere as usual – he not only continues fingering the keys' metal but sniffs them as well as though for clues.

The night Jordan first came back with him his keys had gone missing, he recalled. He had got drunk, there were more than a few blanks, and in the morning, head pounding, he had searched his clothes, the apartment, everything, to no avail. But then Jordan had arrived with the keys dangling between forefinger and thumb. They had turned up in one of his pockets, he'd told him – *now, how could that have happened?* – the famous grin providing its unsettling counterpoint as always.

He had made duplicates – why be coy about it? – for the proof lay in his palm. And now he didn't even care if he found out or not.

"Look, a minor embarrassment has arisen," he'd confided casually to him over a glass of something bitter-tasting that same day – hair of the dog, Spanish-style, according to his new-found familiar.

"Young Angie has turfed me out. Don't ask me why for we've had our barneys before – you may even have noticed as much – but this time it looks like curtains. *Her* place, you see, not mine. But then I suppose it had to happen some time or other. To be honest – " and here he reached across and laid a finger lightly on his wrist as though to underscore his sincerity or, he was to decide much later on, as a quack might gauge a patient's bank balance while pretending to take his pulse "– I don't really give a – " Another hesitation, the grin unashamedly boyish now.

Gilchrist felt like a fish being played gently towards the shallows but didn't care. Perhaps the fish felt the same, weakening in that curious, almost pleasurable way now that the struggle was almost over.

"As I said last night, who needs it? Who needs *her*? There are things in this life far more important. Friendship, for instance? Blood-brothers?"

The gaff gleamed, the mouth of the net yawned, the tired trout gave up the ghost.

"It'll only be temporary, you understand. Somewhere to lay my head for a while till I get settled. I give you my solemn word, you won't even know I'm there."

The lift now was bearing him silently upwards to his waiting shadow, the one who had taken over his keys, apartment, finances, his very life itself. The metal doors finally slid apart and he stepped out into the faintly perfumed corridor still bearing the scented traces of Mrs Guzman, or so he liked to imagine.

Mrs Guzman, dear, sweet Mrs Guzman, please tell me how to get back to the simple life like you with your little dog and your visits to the hairdressing salon and that boring, beetle-browed spouse of yours. Could we have an affair, do you think? To break the bonds that bind yours truly to the memory of someone young enough to be our granddaughter?

His head was throbbing. He felt as if he had started drinking again. Perhaps hell was really like this, a custom-made pit of his own devising where he jerked and spun from one crazed indecision to the next.

When he opened his front door – again the key felt scratchy in the lock – he saw that all the lights were off and for that brief instant his heart soared. Perhaps he had come to the end of his purgatory after all, his inquisitor taking himself back to wherever it was he had come from in the first place. He stood there luxuriating in the unaccustomed silence. Even the radio was silent, first time in weeks.

Quickly bolting, then chaining the door, he leaned his back up against it. The wood felt reassuringly solid, built to last, built to withstand a siege. All he had to do was lie low, play dead in his tomb until any danger of a return visit had passed. Those miserable weeks of isolation he had endured when first he arrived seemed very attractive in retrospect suddenly.

But then retribution swiftly struck – how did he ever imagine he could get away with it? – for out of the darkness a voice enquired, "And just where the hell have *you* been?"

The lamp beside the new armchair came on and his shadow was sitting there in the flesh as always, glass in hand. Blinking against the cruel retaliation of the light, Gilchrist hung in the archway. For some reason he found himself unable to take his eyes away from the other's outstretched, bare ankles – socks were for the likes of people like himself he'd discovered. There was something supremely decadent it occurred to him about those twin glimpses of tanned flesh between the expensive moccasins and the fine gaberdine of the trousers. Once again there seemed to him to be some sort of correlation between his own deterioration and the burgeoning elegance of the man stretched out in the chair facing him.

As if to drive home the point he heard the other say, "My God, just take a look at you, the state you're in. You're not fit to be let out on your own, you know that? Apart from which, of course, we were meant to be at the bank. Remember? I sat in all afternoon waiting for you to turn up."

Without batting an eyelid he added, "An extra set of keys wouldn't be too much to ask," and Gilchrist felt a sly and sudden, delicious stab of vindication, first in an age.

"Well?"

"Well, what?"

"Notice anything different – new?"

He couldn't, in all honesty, but then there had been so much recently which apathy on his part had turned to invisibility in a matter of hours.

"The VCR. Arrived this afternoon. Just as well one of us happened to be here."

VCR, he's thinking, *what in God's name does VCR stand for?*

Jordan heaved himself up from the chair – *another acquisition paid for by my money*, he thought – black leather, chrome, serpentine in shape, and appeared to sway a little. His face looked flushed. For the first time Gilchrist noticed the bottle on the floor nearby was more than three-quarters empty.

"Want to show you something. Something you'll *really* appreciate."

A plastic bag was on the table and he went over and took something out of it, holding it close to his chest so that Gilchrist couldn't see what it was.

"Be a patient boy. Nice things come to those who wait. Who was it said that?"

He was kneeling in front of the television set now as though in obeisance to a household shrine. That, too, had appeared as if by magic.

"For the love of Christ," he called out over his shoulder. "Sit down, would you, and pour us a couple of snorts. And cheer up. Talk about a creeping Jesus."

The dead grey screen came alive, imparting a ghastly jollity to his features. Hands clasped in front of him Gilchrist sat obediently on the settee watching the particles of static hiss and rage until they coalesced into a bluish rectangle. *Video*, he thought, *he wants me to look at a video. He's gone out and bought one of those new machines. A VCR.* The realization registered dully, no more than a minor blip, like one of those same space-age dots on the screen.

Shakily Jordan rose from his devotions. He took an empty glass from the sideboard and half-filled it with whisky. These days he drinks only Chivas Regal. "Here," he said, pushing it towards him. "Party time."

Although he had no intention of drinking, Gilchrist took it from him anyway.

"Tell me something, when was the last time you took a shower, Eric?"

After replenishing his own glass he subsided with a grunt into the snakish embrace of the armchair. The light from the table lamp cast a soft glow across his profile. He looked young, healthy again. Soon they would be able to pass as father and son instead of brothers.

"You've no idea the trouble I had getting my hands on this tape. While you were mooning about God knows where. Just take a look at you. I happen to have friends in this town. Business associates. What must they think when they see you in this state? What must they think of *me*, for Christ's sake? From now on I don't let you out of my sight, *comprénde*? Do yourself a favour, Eric, get your act together. You're your own worst enemy. Maybe this will help you see what you're missing out on. Show-time!"

And at that the screen came brilliantly alive with a collage of overwrought faces in close-up in a frantic mime of singing, praying, swooning, while a gospel soundtrack invaded the room they were sitting in like a thunder-clap. Gilchrist allowed the images to swamp him as they were meant to. The barrage beat on his tired brain, cameras cutting faster, faster, music responding in kind, the worshippers in that distant stadium – *it was Earl's Court, wasn't it?* – abandoning restraint like a mob of crazed idolators. Which they were, for, at the peak of their frenzy, the Great One himself appeared, beneficent face replicated a dozen times or more by the battery of screens about the hall so that all could see and worship, even those in wheelchairs or manacled to alloy crutches. The roving cameras browsed on their misery imparting a kind of sheen to deformity and disease.

The Great Man beamed from his ascendancy, a short, stocky figure with dyed black hair, head vaguely disproportionate to the rest of his body like all the great performers, and waited for a break in the delirium. People were keeling over already even though the main event had yet to commence. The ushers, big, black and burly, for the most part, shuttled them as they fell slack-mouthed and twitching back to those darker reaches of the arena where the cameras couldn't, or wouldn't, venture.

But an opening finally did present itself, a still moment in all that tempest of revivalist zeal, and the Great Man raised his arms and into the space shouted, "Faith is a Fact! Faith is an Act!" and the crowd howled even more manically.

The words appeared subtitled in Spanish and Gilchrist fixed his gaze on that pale ribbon of print as though the true mystery was being revealed there and not above it on the rest of the screen. It was like watching a travelogue, one of those filmed reports bearing no relation to anything normal or civilized. Yet, every so often, he caught himself recognizing things which seemed familiar, but then before he could get a fix on them they would alter before his eyes to something else entirely, something barbaric, a televised glimpse of hell.

Across the room Jordan's lit face appeared transfixed. With his free hand he beat his thigh in tempo with the music, laughing, calling out "Hallelujah!" at each fresh new excess.

A commercial break came up, only it took place in the same hall, on the same stage, emptied suddenly of the Great Man's presence as though he might be embarrassed while money was being mentioned. A new face – he was called Financial Director – exhorted the faithful to pledge their "love-offerings" to carry on the important work and, to illustrate, held up a slip of paper which grew in close-up until it filled the screen. On it donations for ten to one thousand pounds had boxes ready and waiting to be ticked but, naturally, Visa, Master Card and American Express would be acceptable if more convenient. As the ushers harvested the waving crop of folded pledges in plastic buckets up and down the aisles a choir sang "Bringing In The Sheaves" and Jordan whistled in renewed admiration. "Praise the Lord! I've seen the light!" he called across the room.

Soon after the tempo of proceedings was cranked up even more brutally. "An incredible Anointing is taking place here tonight, my friends!" the evangelist cried out in his loudest tones. "Can you feel it? Can't you? It's all around! Feel it! See it! Hear it!"

And suddenly the stage was filled with young and old aching for that healing touch. They queued to be "slain in the spirit" and when he laid his fingertips on their foreheads, then pushed, with that seemingly tender yet at the same time oddly dismissive gesture, turning quickly away as he did so as if in distaste, they went down on the spot as though felled. The young white men in suits and crewcuts helped them up and bustled them away still twitching and drooling to the side of

268

the stage where another aide with a clipboard rapidly noted down details of their particular "miracle".

Gilchrist sat on the couch incapable of any real feeling save a kind of numb depression. Was this what he had once wanted for himself, this choreographed exercise in humiliation? Was this the man he had striven to emulate? He watched him now as his features expanded to fill the screen, for he was appealing to a much greater audience now, everyone out there watching, in fact, in the privacy of their homes, all those ill or sick at heart or crippled, and he urged them oh, so sincerely, so compassionately, to place their palms against the TV screens and receive the electric charge of the Redeemer's merciful, healing power, "the Mighty Cathode Ray of the Lord seeking out and destroying the Dis-ease in all of us that only He can cure." Finally he begged them to lift their telephones during the next break and ring their friends and beg them to tune in so that there might be a Mighty Power Surge of new viewers across the network and the nation for Jesus and His Mighty Works. Amen.

As the choir broke into a full-throated roar of rejoicing, above the din Jordan called, "Do you know how much this guy pulled down last year – him and his organization? *Twenty-seven mill! Dollars!* And you know something else, he started out just like you did. Maybe even smaller. He may not even be as talented. Think of it, just think of it. I don't have to draw you a picture, do I?"

But another and very different image from the one intended was gathering speed and pace now inside Gilchrist's head. For all his harping about evil and the physical face of evil, deep down he had never really, *fully* believed in the concept. Not wholeheartedly. Here, now, for the first time he felt conversion might be possible. Grinning at him from across the room, in his image, but younger, better-looking, seemed to be its raw embodiment.

That side of things he had always left to others, those down in the cheap seats, their feet firmly earthed to the soil with all its old, elemental superstitions. And, of course, they *wanted to*, desperately *needed to* believe in a bogey-man, horned or otherwise, just as a child creates his own personal monster on the shadows of the bedroom blind. But now he had one as well, custom-made, as though from a likeness, his own private demon sitting opposite in a maroon and lime Hawaiian shirt with crossed, bare, brown ankles. He shivered – the damp lining of his pockets felt clammy against his skin – and for a second almost believed he could detect a sulphurous whiff in the room.

"Well? What do you think of it so far?"

The tempter in his easy-chair spoke softly to him. He had pointed a little matt-black box of tricks at the set and, miraculously, the volume dropped to a whisper. On the screen the performance continued unabated, yet it seemed much less blasphemous now without sound, the actors decidedly second-rate, amateur, even. A negro woman wearing a lurid, orange *muu-muu*, grossly overweight, her eyeballs rolling upwards, couldn't be hoisted from the stage where she had fallen and the camera lingered on the drama as though paralysed by its sheer *grotesquerie*. But then a more uplifting tableau presented itself, a mother with angelic child – again they were black – gazing rapturously up at the Master.

"Well, what do you reckon?"

"Not a lot. To be frank."

The other slapped his knee triumphantly. "Didn't I tell you? I *knew* you could do better, *I knew it*!"

"You don't understand," Gilchrist said, hardly recognizing his own voice, so calm, so *honest*, was it for the first time in weeks. "I thought it was truly horrible. Is." For the Great-Little Man continued to mouth from the screen in huge close-up – they could see his fillings – his message scrolling sentence by sentence across his glistening jowls in accented script. *Deo*, Gilchrist kept on reading, *Deo* and *Salvacion*.

"Exactly what are you saying?" An icy note had entered the other's tone and Gilchrist felt his courage desert him.

"It may look impressive," he argued mildly, "but, really, it degrades those it seeks to uplift. There's no real truth there."

"And you would know all about that, would you?" *He seems to be taking this personally*, Gilchrist found himself thinking.

"Imagine silly old me thinking there just might be the tiniest flicker of enthusiasm, gratitude, even, that I went out and busted a gut getting hold of the damned tape in the first place. *And* the VCR to play it on. Oh, you don't have to worry, it's only rented."

Now, that's unfair. But the protest only registered with the force of a gnat landing. Jordan was on his feet now, striding back and forth, the whisky in his glass slopping alarmingly. He could smell its fumes from here. His own glass he'd put aside.

"Of course, I should have known. Perfectly pointless. Pissing into the wind. Oh, I'm so terribly, *terribly* sorry, I should really watch my tongue, I keep forgetting we have a true man of the faith in our midst, the proper article, not some jumped-up amateur like our friend on television with all that awful fame, followers and so much of that horrible, *disgusting* money! Okay, be a loser, then. Throw it all away, all that experience and expertise. All that, that – "

He struggled for the word, his forehead bulging with the strain. He seemed to have grown much larger suddenly, pumped up by some emotional pressure.

" – vocation!" The word came spitting out like a venomous cannonball.

Gilchrist sat gazing at the television screen without really seeing what was going on. He was being harangued from two quarters, two missionaries intent on conversion, and both seemed to be getting angrier by the minute.

"Look, let's cut the crap – again, if you'll forgive the expression."

A change of tack, sincerity now. After the storm, the calm. He'd done it himself. It seemed to be happening on the small screen too for the Great Man was beaming now as well.

"What we're talking about here is a clean slate, a fresh start – for both of us – because I can help you if you only let me. Trust me. I didn't tell you this, Eric, for I didn't feel you were ready to see and hear some sense but I've already made a recce. I know, I know, perhaps I shouldn't have but, believe me when I tell you, you could build yourself a terrific little power-base here. Simply terrific. Lots of pensioners crying out for that gospel light at the end of the tunnel, lots of lost souls. Lots of ailments, Eric, lots of ailments. Take it from me, you could cut a mighty swathe right here, brother, in Senility-on-Sea – if you put your mind to it. I've had one or two preliminary notions already. For instance, to get the word out, put our name on the map, how does a telephone prayer-service grab you? Sort of Hotline To The Hereafter, eh?"

He was laughing and Gilchrist noticed that the preacher on the video must also have cracked a joke for his entire stage crew, clean-cut youngsters the lot of them, were roaring their heads off in mime.

"Well? What do you think? Pretty neat, eh?"

He had dropped into the recliner again stirring up a scent of new leather. With his free hand he gestured, pointing the little remote control directly at him and Gilchrist jerked into speech as though triggered by those invisible rays.

"I can't do it any more," he said. "It's gone. Finished with. I've lost my – " he almost said *nerve* " – vocation."

There was a silence that felt like the lull before a bombardment. The television screen flickered brainlessly, a distraction now, an embarrassment. Jordan cut it off dead with a tap of his forefinger and the beaming, evangelistic countenance dwindled to a tiny blue fireball.

"Well, goodnight and farewell to the pair of you, then." The accent had reverted to his native West Country, a brutal, mocking drawl.

"Dear, dearie me," he went on, "if that ain't a terrible shame. Lost our vocation, our spiritual bottle. First sniff of hair-pie and he wants to throw it all up. Makes *me* want to throw up, an' all. 'Cause I had great hopes, great plans here, ladies and gentlemen, for this particular partnership. Spent a lot of time and effort, I did, but all to no avail, it would now appear. Wants out, he says. Doesn't care to know. To say I'm disappointed would be an understatement. More like fucking furious, brother Eric, 'cause I made a commitment here, can you understand that? Can you? *Can you?*"

His shout started the dog off upstairs.

"And don't look at me that way, please, as if you don't know what the fuck I'm talking about. Of course you do. You just don't build up all a person's hopes and dreams, worm all their secrets out of them, then expect to walk away. A person's life we're talking about here. This person's life!"

He thumped his chest – it made a sound like a drum – then downed more scotch as though genuinely thirsty and not just for the taste either. How far gone was he, anyway? Pretty far, Gilchrist decided. Yet under all the boozy invective lurked something far more disturbing than just the drink talking. It had to do with being *taken over*, and he was the victim, not the man across the room from him glaring into his glass, despite what he'd just said. A switch had taken place, but any transfusion of secrets had been from *him*, not the other way.

All his life Gilchrist had locked that precious sense of self inside for safe keeping like a fragile heirloom which couldn't face the light. Sometimes it even had a recognizable shape to it in his head, transparent, like blown glass or a delicate clock of rare provenance with its workings on show, but only ever to him. How, then, had a drunken, abusive replica of himself somehow succeeded in breaching those defences? How much had he really told him in his unguarded moments? Or perhaps – and here came that chill again, that imaginary whiff of sulphur from a dark place – he already knew everything about him there was to know without needing to be told a thing? Over in the far corner of the room the china leopard's eyes appeared to gleam in the dark now that the TV had gone dead. It seemed to be watching him. Perhaps he had become transparent to everyone, every thing.

In a quiet, and he felt, perfectly reasonable tone, he said, "I think you may have some keys of mine," to be answered by a derisive laugh.

"These, you mean?" Holding the duplicates aloft between thumb and forefinger, he shook them the way one might summon an underling with a tea-bell.

"Mine, did I hear you say? *Mine?* Oh, surely not. *Ours.* After all, what's yours is mine, and vice-versa, of course. Haven't you recognized that by this time?" He leaned forward and the buttery glow from the lamp bathed his features in a coating of the purest adoration.

"Like it or lump it, you're stuck with me and there's not a thing you can do about it. See?" And again he tinkled the keys before slipping them back into a trouser pocket.

"Relax. Go with the flow. We're on the same side. Two of a kind, remember?" He laughed, stretching lazily, and the light somehow made his arms impossibly, inhumanly elongated.

"After all, what could you do about it even if you wanted to. *Report me?* Who to? Let's face it, we're made for each other, Eric. You *can* see that, can't you? And now I'm going to take a shower and I suggest you do the same." Rising to his feet he moved towards the bathroom, then paused.

"To keep you from being bored while I get ready, how about another video? Don't fret, it's not our American friend again. This is much more – shall we say – lively? *Mucho exotico*. Might even be another first for you. In fact, I'd be prepared to bet on it." And taking another cassette out of the plastic bag he hunkered down and switched tapes, slotting the new one into the letter-box mouth of the machine.

"You see, Eric, I hate to be the one to have to tell you this, but, you know, all those years you were laying down the law on sin, temptation and the perils of the flesh you didn't really have a clue what you were talking about. You didn't, did you? Little Miss Carrot Top may have helped break your duck, but all in all you did lead a very sheltered life. I mean how did you ever expect to fight the devil and all his pomps if you never even got to see the colour of his drawers? Scarlet, Eric. Scarlet."

The video he found himself watching while the shower ran in the next room was entitled *Swedish Teenagers Love To Love* with subtitles in English this time. It started off conventionally enough, boring, even, with three flaxen-braided nymphets lying around someone's bedroom discussing their boyfriends. All were wearing tiny satin shorts and vests as if they'd been out jogging together and now had returned to throw themselves down all sweaty and flushed. Indeed, presently, one of them complained about feeling hot – the word in Swedish sounded almost identical – and the other two giggled at that, extracting much girlish fun out of the word, daring her to take something off. She giggled in return – he liked this one best for there was something lumpen and housewifely already about the other two – then one of her friends pulled down her pants which led to retaliation in kind and then the third girl not wishing to be left out of the fun slipped off hers as well and in a trice all three were gambolling around naked except for their short white sports socks.

All this time the camera had kept its distance as if out of politeness, but now it lunged in voraciously, so that the screen swarmed with pale flesh punctuated by those sparse, little, triangular tufts of maiden-hair. The nuzzling, slavering, sucking and eye-rolling gathered pace, a smooth white object like an ivory tusk was introduced and almost reverentially brought into play, the accompanying groans on the sound-track became even more frenzied, yet Gilchrist sat marble-eyed throughout, dully noting the puppy fat, the occasional spot on back or buttock, the glimpses of raw, pink, inner parts.

At some point in the proceedings a handsome young plumber showed up, bag of tools in hand, and after the barest of preliminaries the "orgy" proper got under way. Yet that word, somehow, hardly seemed applicable, for where was the purple and gold, the houris, the clashing music one read between the lines of the old books, or used to see in those wide-screen epics in living Technicolor?

What he did see was the young man's great thing, massively erect, like a blanched tuber, being massaged in loving close-up by each of the teenagers in turn, then all together, as though it were some form of religious object, in much the same way they had earlier handled that other pale plastic substitute. While they ministered to his engorged manhood he lay back on the carpeted floor, face expressionless, ox-like, his blond hair oiled in one of those ridiculous footballer's perms like a damp poodle's pelt. His name was Dirk.

Once more the doorbell rang and a second young plumber stood there, swarthy and stockily built, for a change, the magic of film quickly relieving him of his overalls and inserting him into the sweaty tangle of limbs in a minute flat. Yet although he didn't seem quite so spectacularly endowed as his mate the same amount of loving care was lavished on his "plunger" by those flickering, rosy tongues.

276

Gilchrist had read somewhere, perhaps even heard – although where? – the expression "foreplay". Was this it, he wondered? Jordan, too, had used an expression earlier. "Hair-pie." He thought that might be what he was seeing right now for the menfolk, finally, were reciprocating like a couple of eager labradors on all fours, while the neglected Trudie dreamily played with herself.

Ingenious permutations of coupling were now taking place. One girl lay like the filling in a sandwich between both thrusting plumbers while her two friends nibbled at whatever titbits they could get hold of around the edges of the repast. In the middle of all this Jordan appeared in the doorway towelling his wet hair, wrapped in his silk dressing-gown with the gold dragons.

"Got to the juicy bits yet?" he called out. "You can always re-wind, you know. Your turn for the shower."

Gilchrist dutifully rose and made for the lit bathroom. Steam had started rolling out. Jordan was combing his hair in front of the big oval mirror over the non-existent fireplace. For the briefest of moments Gilchrist glanced at the burnished figure of a bullfighter on a side-table. He could almost feel it, cool and weighted in his grasp, the delicious lustre of it. He looked at the back of his familiar's head, that shampooed sheen, the curling licks, the matador again, the head again – the exact configuration of his own, he told himself, underneath all that healthy thatch. But before a connection between bone and metal had time to merge he managed somehow to get as far as the bathroom door. *Dear God, what is happening to me?*

He took a last backward look at the screen, a final glimpse of his humiliation, his penance. The first young plumber had disengaged himself from his partner and, encircling his great circumcised root in his fist, proceeded to pump his awesome discharge on to the upturned face and over those pear-shaped, teenage breasts.

He could still hear his yelps after he bolted the door.

The shower was set to much hotter than he thought he could bear but he bowed his head beneath the fierce jet regardless. He wanted to scald away the memory of all he'd just seen, and for a moment of pure fantasy, even that stuff from the girl's face, leaving her clean and innocent as she must once have been. It was the one he'd liked best, the thin, freckled one, for she reminded him of another. And as the water streamed down his tears mingled and were diluted in the rushing torrent of heat.

TEN

They enter a dream-time together, two refugees – no, not even that – merely shuttling numbly from one dead West Country resort to the next barely knowing any longer what or who it is they are fleeing from.

He changes rail routes at random now, travelling to half-remembered destinations from old geography lessons. It was all lists then, wasn't it? Capes and bays, rivers, lakes, towns grouped under what they manufactured, coal, chemicals, wool, cutlery, glass, carpets. Axminster slides past featureless and forgettable as a yawn. They sit across from each other, faces half-turned to the sidings gliding backwards. Men in orange tabards freeze as though caught at something illicit.

At some point and, without speaking, she rises and makes her way up the swaying aisle towards the toilets between the carriages. Today she wears acid-green leggings, a hooded sweat-suit top – so he understands – and the new trainers, unlaced, tongues lolling, almost as big as the boxes they came in. He watches her shuffle towards the automatic doors. Her legs are like two lollipops.

Fields slide past, fields he'll never see again, but then there are enough to outlast lifetimes, each so different, variegated, at least to his countryman's eyes, unique as pebbles on a beach. On such occasions he feels swamped by the sheer spawning multiplicity of things, places, people, events, thoughts – particularly his own. He yearns to be under last night's sheets, needing the refuge of that moist, young presence again mere inches away, for always there's that tiny gap between, that no-man's-land, rigorously observed by both except for the small, expert, ministering fingers bridging the divide.

Last night when she came gliding like a somnambulist into his room – there have been times when he pretends she really does sleep-walk and in his turn he only dreams what takes place – he lay trembling with the usual mixture of guilt and anticipation. *Lord, this is so wrong, I know it is, I know it . . .* But then for the first time he breaks the rules of their night-time game together by moving away. She slides closer, he rolls over on to his stomach flattening his "unruly member", for that has become as responsive as a dog's ear by now, alert and straining even before the doorknob has turned.

This new liveliness is an embarrassment, not just in the dark but at all sorts of odd times and places during the day as well. It's as though he has sprouted an extra limb with a will and appetite of its own. Yet he has to admit to a certain fascination, too, with all of that unexpected blood flow, those sudden, lusting hydraulics. For example – to be crude, for a moment – how does he compare with other men? And what about staying-power? He does seem to reach completion rather speedily. He tries to invoke the image of Charlie and Tom that fevered day at the river-bank.

Does family resemblance, he wonders, apply below the waist as well as above? It feels strange to be discovering for himself at long last what most men find at a very early age, namely, that life-long fascination with their own cocks.

He groans aloud at the word, still shocking to him, or it may have been the painful constriction in his groin. Anyway, he hears her murmur something as to a half-asleep child. "Eric? Eric?" And, then, very softly, "Turn around," it sounds like.

How easy to obey like that same drowsy infant, or a docile patient, perhaps, for she does tend to handle him in a distinctly nurse-like way, he's noticed, a further cause for jealousy of her past. Instead he remonstrates in muffled tones, "We mustn't. *You* mustn't."

Silence. Then, in a pitifully small voice, "Don't you like me any more?"

He lies with his face buried in the landlady's sprigged cotton pillow-case seemingly doused in cologne of some sort. Had he got the wrong room by mistake, the more feminine one?

"It isn't that. It's, it's – *this*."

Outside on the deserted esplanade a car full of late-night revellers rampages past. The music from the radio pours forth setting up a momentary distraction. Does she recognize the tune, he wonders?

"Am I not doing it right, is that it? Damian always – "

He feels aggrieved suddenly at that distant, yet ever-present, sibling abuser – at her for filling his mind with these images – at himself most of all. Wanting to retaliate in the cruellest way he knows he says, "Why did you lie about your age?"

"What do you mean?"

"You said you were sixteen. I know you're not. You lied to us. You lied to *me*, Donna."

"But I tell you I *am* sixteen, Eric."

She continues to use my first name. Why not stop all this before something is damaged now, irreparably. But something else makes him want to continue twisting the blade.

"Donna, it was in the local paper. I saw it. I have a copy to prove it. In my suitcase."

He's thinking, *see how easy it is to destroy a dream with a few well-chosen words.*

But now there follows the worst possible reaction to those words for he hears her sniff, feels her start to tremble, finally begin sobbing quietly, and, yes, even apologetically, as though wishing to cause the minimum offence. The sound of it, plus the awful muffled throb of it, combine to cut through him like a knife.

Turning quickly he draws her towards him and her open mouth clamps on the well-washed flannel of his pyjama-jacket. He's conscious of so much scalding wetness soaking through. It's accompanied by another sensation far more shocking, as that other part of him, stiffened and conscious-free, despite everything, seeks contact of its own on its own terms. As he comforts her, God forgive him, *it*, that damp dog's nose he seems to have inherited, continues questing.

She's wearing a T-shirt in what seems a man's size, nothing else save a tiny pair of pants – it's her usual night-time attire, he's noticed – but the T-shirt has ridden up, as has his own pyjamas, and flesh now collides with flesh, adhering in a film of sweat. Here in the dark like this age somehow miraculously has become irrelevant, the great leveller. He's filled by a sudden tenderness and, yes, gratitude, which makes him feel like weeping too. Arms entwined, torsos fused, they lie together. Then, tears notwithstanding, her hand inches its way down seeking him out in that by now familiar routine.

He closes his eyes, pretending he's floating river-borne and free, despite being tethered by the lightest, gentlest of con-straints. And now a thrilling variation, for he feels himself being guided towards a soft, warm anchorage he's never been before. She encloses him in a triangular nest of smooth, inner thigh and damp cotton and all the heat they've generated seems concentrated in that one part of him, that throbbing, doggy snout. He feels that centred itch grow and grow, she clasps him tighter – or is it he who swells to fill that baby-soft, imprisoning space? – he has one final stab of panic, of remorse, but before he can act on either, even if he wanted to, he achieves tremendous, flooding release, groaning once into the damp, scented pillow. And it's as though he has cast off for real now, afloat, face down, the sound of blood in his ears like that of weir water.

The sweaty bond of their bodies breaks first, then arms, finally that shrinking, wet nose, no longer such a bully. *What a deluge*, he's thinking, *she must be awash. Is that how women feel? Where did it all go? My God, what if some –*

Lying in the dark, he hears her murmur, "I never thought you had it in you, Eric." His brain is in such a state of jelly, limbs, too, that at first he misunderstands.

Then she says, "Keeping it to yourself. Not letting on all this time. Sneaky, just like the rest of them."

He feels he should offer some sort of defence. But how can he tell her he went along with the deception, otherwise it might spoil his fun? Instead, he lies there, circulation easing, waiting for her to slide away and back to her own bed in the adjoining room. But she continues stretched by his side, the two of them that, by now, almost statutory distance apart, and he, as usual, waiting for intervention in some shape or other to – intervene. Although certainly not Divine. It feels strange to discover oneself abandoned and not feel as bad as expected. All along his faith must have been wafer-thin to have been pulverized so easily by the attentions of a sixteen-year-old. *Fifteen*, he corrects himself, sticking to his guns.

"My birthday was last week," he hears her murmur from her side of the bed as though reading his mind.

"Why didn't you tell me?" But, of course, it's obvious to them both. Deception is mutual. He has the feeling they may not be able to get out of this, this time. Too deep, too far, too –

"Can I see it?" A second time he misinterprets grotesquely

for, of course, she means the newspaper from home. By now she has snapped on the bedside light, a dainty crinoline lady with the bulb buried discreetly beneath her petticoats – *he's definitely in the wrong room* – and is sitting up, T-shirt drawn down over her knees like a tent.

"*I'll* get it. Just tell me where it is."

For an instant he's tempted to lie, tell her he hasn't got it any more, but her face is so alive, so open and trusting once more without a trace of resentment now that he points to the suitcase flapped open across the armchair.

"Goody!" she cries, bounding from the bed. *Did he really hear her say that? Goody?*

He watches her root through his shirts and underthings. The money-belt is buried in there somewhere. Who would have believed such a lightweight cummerbund could carry so much in notes? He never allows himself to think of an actual amount, it's far too distressing, like a confession in open court.

"Is this it?"

But both recognize it for what it is, their home-town tabloid crammed with Rotary Club photos and driving offence cases. Each Thursday on Slemish Drive it would squeeze through the letterbox like a flattened carcase, his housekeeper gloating over each reported lapse or wrongdoing with a zeal which appalled him. His own name is regularly displayed in the Church News section inside a bordered box paid for by the Mission. Not any more, though. Had he moved forward, yet, through all that dense newsprint to share the headlines with his young bedmate?

"Oh, I can't read it," she complains bitterly and leaps in beside him again holding the out-of-date paper up to the pink glow of the lamp.

"My God!" she shrieks. "I'm famous!"

He watches her lips move as she digests the front page. Never has she looked so – so *wholesome*, yes, that, for he's

284

realizing for the first time she has put on weight. All that rich restaurant fare, he's thinking, fattening steadily under his care, his tutelage – may God forgive him. Maturing before his very eyes.

Then she asks, "Can I keep it? Can I?" even though she's already folding it in two, then again, until it's the size of a paperback. He looks at her dumbly – what can he say? – for he knows he's lost her already.

She wriggles out of his bed and goes towards the door, the wad of newsprint clutched to her breast like a Sunday-school prize. *Why, oh, why, did he have to hold on to the evidence?*

She looks back at him one last time, a cool, quizzical glance, weighing him up as if seeing him for the first time, pyjama–clad there in bed. Just before the door closes, soft, discreet and sly, somehow, he catches a quick, tantalizing glimpse of freckled, upper thigh, the white, bisecting slice of pants, then he has the lonely bed to himself.

At the far end of the hallway a toilet flushes and he tries not to think of her hunkered there under the hanging light discovering her name in print over and over again. How long does it take a thrill like that to lose its appeal?

The whole house gradually quietens and he lies there listening to the weary, grating growl of the pebbles on the distant beach. He is so very far from home, so very far . . .

At breakfast they have the dining-room to themselves. The landlady looks a little oddly at them as though she may have heard something the night before. All that commotion, he's thinking, girlish squeals, bedsprings, doors opening and closing. These places are like echo–chambers. It's time for them to move on. But where? He's beginning to lose heart as well as direction.

They munch silently, conscious of the unseen listener beyond the open hatch. Craving comfort he has the full breakfast – English – while she orders muesli. She can pronounce it now. Will she ever appreciate just how much he's taught her? She sits watching him slice into his egg. Then, abruptly, she excuses herself and leaves the room. To look at that paper again. One more time.

When she returns her eyes are puffy and red. "You should have told me," she hisses at him. "What was going on. Back there."

He can't help glancing over at the hatch as she says it. It's closed now as though out of respect for an imminent confrontation. But none occurs, nothing. She merely studies him as he finishes off every last scrap on his plate. *Waste not, want not.* He can't help himself. Then upstairs they go to their respective rooms to pack.

The train they're on is a stopping train, every hole in the hedge, as yet another station detains them. This one looks suspended in time like a film location, flowers bursting from baskets, even a vintage bicycle propped against the waiting-room wall. Nothing moves on or off the train, which should be steam, not diesel. What a curious country this is. Just as you always imagined it to be, as of now, then minutes later jolting you with something foreign, unsettling, unexpected. Like a mini-bus load of Sikhs in turbans and saris shuttling past up the motorway. Or that Fast Draw Wild West Competition, all those ordinary men and women dressed to kill as gunslingers. Or bungee-jumping . . .

A whistle shrieks, the wheels turn, the ancient, never-used waiting-room glides past. Beyond the white painted fence, glistening spears – *repelling air-borne invaders?* – he sees a car-park crammed with cars baking in the sun, heating up then cooling down again in time for their owners coming off the six forty-two. Commuters. Another unforeseen curiosity.

Beyond all that alien, shimmering bodywork the open

countryside again and in a field alongside the tracks a cricket match in progress, paunchy men in white, galvanized suddenly into action, chasing an invisible ball as though staging a show for their passing benefit. He looks over his shoulder to check if they've reverted to statuary the moment the train pulls clear.

He's not completely certain if he imagined the scene or not, it's still only ten in the morning after all. His eyes feel gritty through lack of sleep. For a moment he closes them and the next thing he knows the train is drawing into another station. Across from him the facing seat is empty and in a panic now his glance darts to the overhead rack. The pink holdall is still there.

Even though he's nervous about leaving the luggage unattended – the money-belt crosses his mind – alarm forces him out of his seat and up the aisle towards the connecting doors between the carriages. Both toilets beyond are vacant and so he passes on to the next pair. One of these has the Engaged sign across and, pretending nonchalance, he leans staring out of the window at the countryside flowing past. He looks at his watch but it can't tell him anything. *What in God's name can she be doing in there all this time?*

He goes to the door and whispers, "Donna, Donna," to the painted metal, loud enough for her to react to the sound of her own name while not alerting any stranger who might just happen to be in there. He waits and as he does so the full outlandishness of his actions strikes home. None of this can, could ever, be explained away, and a sudden image of a blank-faced jury staring back at him as he stammers out some sort of desperate, botched rationale assails him like a blow.

Then the toilet door emits a click, the sign changing to Vacant, and a middle-aged woman, fiercely made-up, emerges in a haze of scent. She looks suspiciously at him despite his respectable demeanour and he smiles reassuringly back as she waits for the connecting door to slide sideways. *Another railway pervert*, she's probably thinking to herself, for he has read that the network, especially in the South, attracts them for some reason, some deep-seated, national deviation stirring to the sound of the iron wheels. The cases keep appearing regularly like drink-related ones do back home.

Back home, he thinks, and groans loudly in that chill, rattling space. He presses his face close to the window to relieve the symptoms but the wooded landscape now racing past merely aggravates his terrors. What if she's lying back there broken and lost at the foot of an embankment?

Feeling desperate he follows the woman into the carriage, yet, even as he does so, realizes this is the last one on the train. There are no more toilets beyond this point. He moves up the aisle towards its dead-end barely knowing why or what he's doing except to be methodical, for he may have missed her somewhere back there or – a sudden lift of the spirits – she may have gone the other way!

He quickens his pace and then, heart stopping, he sees a familiar crop of red hair like a small, rosy cloud above one of the seats. Another head, wild, dark and braided in that Negro way, like soiled pipe-cleaners, lies alongside. He draws abreast bending solicitously like a ticket-collector for some reason. She's smoking a cigarette, as is her companion, a youth in a khaki greatcoat buttoned to the neck despite the stifling heat.

"Donna?" he enquires as if it might still be a case of mistaken identity on his part. Both stare back in similar, quizzical fashion.

He has an urge to make his apologies then retreat for good for he feels exhausted suddenly, the strain of past weeks finally catching up with him here on a train to – he realizes he doesn't know the destination, if he ever did. Then, without a word or sideways glance at her companion, she rises and stands there waiting for him to do something. It seems he still has some authority left.

The moment stretches. A businessman across the aisle looks up from his papers and stares. He has a fountain pen between his teeth like a bit. Gilchrist lurches into sudden movement and with her trailing at his heels he leads the way back to their own carriage noticing for the first time it's a Non-Smoker. *There are some things, I will not do, I will not gamble, smoke nor chew . . . Why didn't she tell me*, he's thinking?

They sit facing one another just like before as if nothing has happened, only it has, something momentous, enormous, like an earthquake or an explosion, and his legs are still trembling from the after-shock. She stares out of the window but, try as he will, he cannot keep his own eyes away from that pinched little face. All of that earlier, childish filling-out seems to have disappeared. She smells of cigarettes. Something else as well like damp hay. He has a feeling it must come from that army greatcoat which looked as if its owner had slept out in it. He itches to ask her about it, about him, but can't bring himself. His tongue fills his mouth like dough. He may never be able to talk again.

As he watches, a single tear forms and courses slowly down the side of her nose, a snail track among the freckles. He puts his handkerchief on the table equidistant between like a crumpled flag of truce. She stares at it for a second then, to his horror, bursts into proper, flooding tears accompanied by a choking, animal noise which causes heads to turn. He leans forward, she pulls back, a look of hate on her face.

"Don't," he entreats. "Don't, Donna. Please." It comes out thick as treacle, but he has actually managed words, four of them.

"What do you want with me?"

He looks at her. Everybody in the carriage knows they're having a row by now, he's convinced of it. *Irish, as well. Wouldn't you just know.*

"Why didn't you leave me alone?"

Stung, he snaps back like a child. "Maybe *you* should have left *me* alone." It sounds laughable. If she would only laugh right now this would all be forgotten, swept away. *Please Lord, let it be swept away.*

"I want to go home," she moans.

"Is it the paper? Is that it?" She glares at him with contempt.

"What is it, then? For Christ's sake, tell me!" The oath slips out like a betrayal.

"Now," she says primly, her mouth set in a tight thin line. "Today."

"Today? Now?" He is a parrot now, an elderly, infatuated parrot. "It's impossible. We can't go back."

A woman diagonally across from them stirs restlessly as though about to intervene. She has that over-bred English look, face like a horse, no qualms whatsoever about speaking her mind. Already he can hear that interrogative bray, "I say . . ." Distracted momentarily he almost misses Donna's reply.

"*I* can," she murmurs.

The treachery of it hits him like a blow. "Okay. Go then. See if I care."

He's infantile now, regressing by the minute. She stares at him as though she might want him to reconsider, but that's wishful thinking on his part. *Was it because she saw me asleep, with my mouth open? And got frightened, disgusted, horrified at the sight of an old man, an old man she'd somehow got entangled with?* It's only the young who look good when they're asleep. Small things like that can and do change lives instantly. He truly believes that.

She stands up, her tiny bump of sex pressed hard against the edge of the table. *Last night he was enclosed there.* Not quite inside but near enough. Is there a fine line to be drawn? If so, who draws it? Almost coolly now he watches as she stretches up towards the overhead rack. *Shouldn't he be doing something to stop this?* But a terrible lassitude continues to press down on him as if he's watching a stranger. Those baby buttocks. *Two eggs in a hanky.* That old playground jibe.

The famous pink holdall – it's like an integral part of her now to him, an extension – drops in a limp heap to flatten out on the table-top. Once when she was asleep he went through it like a sniffer dog searching for something to slake his suspicions, feed his jealousy, anything, for he *was* jealous then, remember, of every other male her own age. He thinks of that young hippy further up the train, those dead eyes in a parchment face. She probably finds all that world-weary posture attractive, the acme of sophistication, calling everybody "man" and being "cool". Isn't that the expression?

She's wrapping the straps around those thin wrists of hers, now, yet, oddly enough, remains standing, her attention fixed on the fields slipping past. It's as though she's waiting and watching for a sign, a landmark to appear and he's still trying to work out this puzzling new dimension when she tightens her grip on the holdall and slides out from the seat.

He watches her walk off up the aisle away from him – *is this how it must end, then, between the two of them? So brutally?* – but it's only when a station pulls into view outside and realization hits him with a sense of outrage at this planned treachery that he jumps up and hauls his own suitcase down. He charges after her, seeing the doors swallow her up.

Already the train is slowing, another prim platform and waiting-room drawing into view, the name meaning nothing to him yet it should and will for he will remember in years to come it was at Tidsbury that this young redheaded heart-breaker literally ran out on him.

Theirs is the only door to swing open on to the peace of the platform. Birds sing with a forced zest that mocks his misery, but she is far ahead racing off to where green fields lap around

291

the tiny station like soft, rounded billows. He hurries after, lugging his suitcase with the money inside. Does he imagine it or has it been getting weightier of late?

They're in the country proper now, the sheer profligacy of it filling him up the way it used to when he was young, grass, dung, wind, a dog, burning stubble. He pants for breath, shirt soaked already, his right foot aching every time he lowers it to the ground. She's about thirty yards ahead striding on as if she might well keep going until she reaches the distant sea. He longs to call out to her but can't, the indignity is too much, this is bad enough as it is, this manic route-march in pursuit of a crazy, spoilt child along an English country road.

But she isn't that any longer, is she? Can people mature overnight, becoming sly, calculating, adult, on the precise stroke of a birthday?

Much later he is to marvel at how it all was to end – for it had to, how could it be otherwise? – on a stifling October day, an English Indian summer, so the papers said, in a lonely part of Wiltshire, more specifically, field, for that is where eventually she turned in like an animal at bay.

At the splintered wooden gate he hesitates as if she might, indeed, be waiting to jump out on him, vicious, maddened, vengeful, because of something he had done, taken from her, but couldn't work out what it might be. Instead he finds her lying face-down in the grass, the pink holdall by her side like a livid, chemical flower against the greensward.

"Donna?" he ventures. "Donna?" repeating her name as he moves cautiously forward avoiding the cowpats. He feels delicate, vulnerable, like a ballet-dancer. He can't help glancing around him. Only city-dwellers feel confident about strolling across other people's fields. Country-bred folk need the reassurance of a gun or a dog to carry it off.

He comes closer, lugging the Samsonite. It feels as if it contains ingots. She's sobbing into the grass. He puts his suitcase down and sits on it a few paces away, hunched forward like a doctor by a patient's bedside. Once more he softly speaks to her but this time it provokes a spasm that sends her legs convulsing like threshing green snakes. She turns her face towards him, eyes raw with crying, grass stems sticking to her mouth and cheeks.

"*Go away!*" she screams. "*Leave me alone!*"

"You don't mean that," he tells her. "How can I leave you this way? You need me, Donna," almost adding, *we need each other*.

"No, I don't! I never should have let you talk me into going away with you in the first place." The field feels suddenly chill with the shadow of dark wings.

"But it was *you* who wanted to be saved, Donna. *You.*"

"And you only wanted to save me for yourself!"

He sits there looking at her, stunned by such perfidy. "I only wanted to help you. *You* came to me." She buries her face in the grass again, spreadeagled like a starfish. She looks as though she's sleeping. Overhead clouds move slowly, great orderly battalions heading towards only read-about cities in the Midlands. He feels quite calm now, spent. One of them must depart this field leaving the other behind, no hope of reconciliation, none, never, barring a miracle, and those are only fairytales out of an ancient book he once used to believe in.

Finally he says, "Take some money. You'll need it," holding out the contents of his wallet, enough for several return tickets, but the amount means nothing to him. She ignores him, but by now he knows she will never speak to him again. He looks for some place to tuck the wad away for safe keeping, his eye resting on the waistband of her lime-green leggings. The sweatshirt has ridden up as always, exposing an almost shocking band of pale flesh. But, with a gulp, he decides against it and, unzipping the holdall, pushes the money deep down inside.

Then, taking up his suitcase, he walks away, zealously following his tracks in the grass back across the field towards the broken gate. Somehow it seems out of character in this rich, well-tended landscape. The pasture, too, looks fallow, starred with dock. *All this time it was waiting for this to happen. For them to happen. He'll remember this field always*, he tells himself.

On the way back to the station he passes the hippy leaning over a fence pretending deep interest in the crop beyond, yellow rape, blinding in the sunlight. They ignore one another, seemingly preoccupied with their own concerns. But about a dozen or so paces on Gilchrist turns and looks over his shoulder just to let him know that *he* knows. The young "traveller" – *they call them that, don't they?* – stares back at him. He's moved away from the fence and stands there, a scarecrow in filthy army surplus, hands hanging by his sides. Between the buttons of his greatcoat protrudes the head of a little dog, a terrier, like the other half of some mythical, two-headed beast, and both sets of eyes, hard, calculating, seem fixed on Gilchrist as though knowing him inside out, past and present – perhaps future as well.

Turning his back on his two critics he continues on towards the next stage on his downward descent.

ELEVEN

Some time after midnight they left the restaurant and the first thing Jordan did was head unsteadily for an alleyway so he could relieve himself while Gilchrist hovered at its mouth, a nervous replica in his parrot-patterned shirt, lightweight stone slacks and white shoes with their foppish little gold chains bridging the instep. They pinched, but, like the rest of the glad rags, he had been forced to wear them at the other's insistence. *I insist, I insist*. It had become a petulant, running refrain which he bowed to for the sake of a quiet life, an expression meaningless by now, yet still surfacing in his consciousness like something from a forgotten language.

His throat and stomach burned. It had been his first real encounter with Indian food. Jordan had laughed when he told him. It seemed to soften his mood. The strange, pungent dishes kept arriving with disturbing frequency while overhead the fans, giant, lazy propellers, sliced the heavy air. The waiters wore starched white ship's stewards' uniforms and purple turbans.

The restaurant was new and very expensive. He choked in disbelief when the bill arrived on a silver tray – for *him*, naturally – while Jordan enjoyed a Monte Cristo, pigtail-thick. Gilchrist was reminded of those banded torpedoes fat men always used to puff in the American comics. Most of the other customers were dressed as they were but with expensive, blue-black tans and medallions gleaming in their chest hair. The accompanying women were similarly bronzed with great, combed-out, candyfloss manes which caught the light.

Jordan appeared to know everyone, back-slapping, hand-shaking, cheek-kissing. At one point a bottle of champagne was sent across to their table even though up to then Jordan had insisted on drinking pints of icy lager, and Gilchrist regarded it with genuine trepidation, swaddled in its bucket. His glass was filled to the brim and he sipped as frugally as he dared without bringing down the other's ire.

"Feast your eyes, Eric. This is where the *real* money is." His double had leaned close and his breath blew on him, lion's breath, hot and scented with spices and herbs he had never ever dreamed of.

"See that little chunky guy under the palm-tree? The one with the Toni twins? Who said crime doesn't pay? But, then, again, no one's ever beyond redemption. Are they, Eric? No matter who they are."

The eyes were bloodshot and a little bleary and Gilchrist imagined he could see his reflection in those glistening pupils. *I'm drowning, Lord, going under. Throw thy servant a life-line before the waters of corruption close over his head.* But still the insinuating, soft voice of the tempter continued in his ear.

"All that business earlier about the geriatric set – forget it. Stuff them. Go for the hard cases, the luxury trade. The jackpot, Eric, the jackpot. As I said, no one's beyond redemption, even the hardest cases of all."

He grinned across the table at him, that malevolent, knowing grin of his.

"Am I getting through to you? Am I, brother?"

And again Gilchrist sensed something lightly caged, the smiling beast beneath the silken shirt. The question is, he asks himself, just how long can it be contained? *Soon, let it be soon*, for, by now, he's weary of waiting to take his medicine, knowing it must only come from this quarter. Yet still he cannot imagine or even guess at what form retribution must take, although violence cannot be ruled out.

Into his head there drifts up a sudden disturbing image of the young Angie. A few days earlier by sheerest chance they had come face to face in one of the San Miguel *calles*. For an instant their eyes met, even though she was wearing dark glasses despite the day being overcast, and when he saw the bandaged arm, the general air of neglect, he convinced himself they must be there to cover bruising. In one hand she clutched a sheaf of gaudy circulars and he remembered what Jordan had said about her ending up on the street as she had begun, just another bleached blonde drifter touting time-shares. He started to call out to her – he was genuinely concerned – but she moved swiftly off down one of the densely packed alleyways.

Standing there, jostled by German tourists, he thought suddenly of Donna, recognizing that same frailty, the same look of furtive vulnerability, all the fight and fire knocked out of her. *We did that*, he told himself, *my shadow and me*.

Then he saw his own appearance reflected in a shop-window. What stared back at him was the missing member of a trio of victims. A sudden flicker of anger flared in him and for once was directed not inwards at himself but at something, someone else.

And that same someone came lurching out of an alleyway buttoning his flies, belching, and the resentment was still there and Gilchrist hugged it to himself the way one might cup a candle flame.

Jordan belched a second time then laughed. "Bleedin' birianis. The Empire strikes back," a joke which Gilchrist didn't catch. *Was it one?*

"Well, where to, my love? He who pays the piper . . ."

They stood facing one another under a sign which read *El Calvario* for they were close to the old rocky heart of town where the windmills once turned in the *levanter*. They gave the place its name. His tormentor swayed drunkenly, grinning, taunting him as if he could sense that little spark of resistance sheltering deep inside.

"No ideas? No inspiration? Not even of a divine nature? Ah, well, it's up to me then. As usual. Tell you what, let's take a turn down by the sea-shore, where the healing waters flow. You used to be quite keen on that. Who knows we might even run into that Dutch lady-friend of yours. What was her name now – Rita, Renée, Renata?" And he set off, expecting him to follow. Which, of course, he did, breathing in the drifting fumes of his cigar.

Their route took them through the Plaza Costa del Sol where the painted ones plied their trade, swinging their handbags like *bolas* at the passing cars. One of them moved away from her mates, for they huddled together like exotic, chattering fowl, and confronted Jordan. Removing the cigar from his mouth he halted, exhaling a plume of smoke directly at the emaciated, ambivalent creature – for it was a *he*, wasn't it, anatomically speaking, below the waist?

"Not tonight, Gloria, sweetheart. Not right now, *if* you don't mind," Gilchrist heard him say and then confusingly, "Business hours. You always know where to find me."

The gaudily-dressed beanpole pulled a handful of banknotes from a white leather purse, thrusting them at him. He/she/it looked distraught, the great mascaraed eyes fluttering like frantic butterflies.

"Do me a favour. Please fuck off, Gloria. Okay? If you want

us to do any business, that is, on any future occasion. Can't you see I've someone with me? Show a little respect for the cloth. *Comprende? Clerigo? Mi amigo clerigo.*"

For the first time the tottering figure in the platform shoes seemed to notice him standing there. "*Clerigo?*"

"*Si, clerigo. Mi hermano.*"

"*Hermano?*"

The panda-painted eyes darted rapidly from one face to the other, then, with an equally swift motion the right hand began making the sign of the cross and Jordan walked off laughing at the hen-like flurry he had managed to create.

They continued past the underground rail-station with its crowd of young back-packers strewn like debris over the marble steps – some were snatching a little sleep before the police arrived to move them on – and still Gilchrist kept his distance from the man in front. It was as though an invisible but powerful cord held them together. What if he decided to sever that connection, slide off at a tangent down one of the darkened side-streets? But where could he go, he had no place to hide any more. The tiny glow of anger within continued to grow. He directed it at a spot midway between the other's shoulderblades, taking aim on the largest sunburst in the pattern of that gaudy silk shirt.

Now he trailed him along a canyon between two silent, windowless blocks. A stench of kitchen waste mingled with the other's head-high Havana, for they were threading their way past parallel hotels and this was the side the tourists didn't see, the sweat and heat of the kitchens and boiler-rooms the mere thickness of a breezeblock wall away. Underfoot, warm asphalt gave way suddenly to soft, dry sand and the man in front floundered almost losing his footing.

An oath floated in the air, changing to laughter, then, "Safe in the arms of Jesus, safe on his gentle breast."

"There, by his love o'ershaded, sweetly my soul shall rest," Gilchrist found himself whispering into the tainted air.

Ahead he could make out a break in the darkness, a horizontal bar of softer, paler blue, then without warning his double seemed to disappear as though the earth had swallowed him. Quickening his pace – *why should he feel concern?* – he came out between the towering, concrete book-ends to find himself on the beach. Fifty yards off the sea gently murmured, although it was difficult to judge distance in this light. He could make out a bump in the blackness at ground level and, presently, this stirred and a voice crooned in a mocking, child-like lilt, "Only a few more trials, only a few more tears."

He moved closer until he was standing by the side of the figure sprawled on the sand.

"You'd really like that, wouldn't you, Eric? Only a few more tears, eh? But you don't get off as lightly as that. Why should *you* be special? The Lord's Anointed."

Gilchrist hung there thinking, *Do it now, this is your chance*, but he could come up with nothing more specific than a raw, unfocused longing to rid himself of this burden, obliterate this stain from his existence for good.

"What gives *you* the right to be better than anyone else – the chosen one? Better than *me*? Don't stand there looking down from a great height, *damn you!*" And the inert bundle came to life and he felt his ankle gripped, then yanked forward with such surprising force that he fell back on to the soft sand, shocked but unhurt, to lie beside his tormentor.

"That's more like it." He heard the murmur up close now. "Equals. The way it should be. For I never said *I* was superior, did I, now, Eric?"

Somewhere out to sea a passing tanker lowed mournfully, a great, invisible sea-cow ploughing on, oblivious. On darkened beaches everywhere humans wrestled and despaired while the world went about its business. Why should he be any different? But, coming out of the darkness, hearing it from those other lips like that, only made that bud of resentment swell, and so he lay there hardening himself as though preparing for redress if and when it came.

"Do you believe in miracles, Eric? Maybe I asked you that before. Have I? You're looking at one, if you don't mind me saying so, a walking miracle – well, a lying-down one right at this moment."

He laughed at his own joke, but Gilchrist steeled himself. He was in the presence of evil, he told himself, *it exists here and now*, for it lay only feet away, a shape a shade darker than the surrounding air and from it trickled a voice, soft and seductive as silk. And as he continued listening to what it was telling him the greater his conviction grew that he must not let it prevail.

"Have you ever heard of the King's Cross Fire, Eric? Terrible loss of life, inferno in the Underground, November '87? Did you read about it, see it on television? All the bodies accounted for. All except one, Eric. They did a reconstruction of his face, it was in all the papers, but no one came forward to claim him. Man about your age and build, trace of heart-disease. Heavy drinker. The one that got away.

"I was in that fire, too, Eric. And you know something else? I saw him. We crawled past one another on the Down escalator. He was going up, unfortunately, straight into the very worst part, the upstairs ticket-hall. Four hundred degrees, Eric. Hotter than the flames of hell. But I came through it. I came through hell, Eric. It could have been *my* picture in the papers. That plasticine head. But very lifelike, bloody clever these boffins. I mean I recognized him straight away. He didn't say a word, just kept crawling the wrong way to his doom, up instead of down. Something told me, go down, go down. A voice, Eric. I was singled out. Do you realize what it is I'm saying? This – us – it was meant to be. Ordained. Isn't that the word? Why I'm here with you now.

So now you know why you can never break free, even if you wanted to. But you don't, do you, any more."

And again he felt his ankle gripped tightly. This time he pulled clear, scrambling back to his knees. He wasn't quite ready yet, that little, hot bud of hate was still furled within, yet he sent forth a first hesitant salvo of rebellion. "What more do you want from me?"

"Why, nothing, Eric. Not a thing."

"You've taken my money, my flat" – he felt like adding, *my memories, too*.

"But you *gave* them to me, Eric. Don't you remember? You wanted rid of them, taken off your hands, all those reminders of what you'd done. Can't you see that? I'm your conscience, Eric. Surely you can see that by this time. Then, again, perhaps I'm only in your mind, Eric, an invention. Maybe I don't exist. Go on, touch me. See if I'm real. If I really exist. Go on. *Go on!*"

But Gilchrist drew back from that sudden prodding and heard the other's laugh ring out as though he could see the sorry spectacle he made shuffling backwards on his knees on the sand, a startled cripple.

"Oh, don't fret, Eric, I'm only having my little joke. That's allowed, isn't it? We still can have fun, can't we? When was the last time *you* had fun, Eric? With little Miss Muppet, right? Our little redhead? Bit of a giggle, eh? Let's have some fun. Come on. *Come on!*"

And he was on his feet and swaying for Gilchrist could make out sideways movement in that blur outlined against the night sky.

"Come on, race you to the briny. Last one in's a sissy. You're not a sissy, are you, Eric? A *maricón*?"

Then he was pulling him up by the arms on to his feet and he could smell the drink on the other's breath, sweet, slightly corrupt. He let himself be dragged towards the white, murmuring ribbon of surf and, docile to the last, took his shoes off at the other's command and then they were wading ankle-deep in the water. The man gripping him by the hand seemed to be getting more and more excited instead of lulled by the soft, cooling wash about their naked feet. He began hauling him into deeper water until, soon, he was high-stepping alongside as the waves soaked their trousers.

"*Come on, come on!*" and the white foam splashed and roared. Gilchrist was trying his best to resist but the hand holding him was iron-hard. He was panting now, blood beating in his ears, legs trembling beneath the damp constriction of the cloth, face and arms salt-wet, eyes stinging from the spray. *I'm being harried to my death. Please, Lord, do something.*

And as though the thought had coursed between them like a small electric charge, or dye in the bloodstream, the pace faltered and the roaring of the spume gradually died to a murmur again. Gilchrist allowed himself to be towed towards the shallows, almost tenderly now, as though that temporary madness had been fantasy on his part. He felt the other's arm slide through his and now they were strolling entwined through the ripples towards some distant, invisible destination.

"What about our shoes?" he heard himself ask.

"What about them?"

It was silly, a ridiculous question, he realized it the moment he'd said it.

"You must learn to enjoy life. Give in to it. Don't fight it. Don't fight *me*, Eric. I tell you what, let's take a sail. The night is perfect for a sail. Don't you agree?"

Gilchrist felt his arm being squeezed for acquiescence and responded with just sufficient reflex, he felt, as though humouring a madman. Then they were in among the pedaloes, a beached shoal of them, twin torpedoes drawn up in neat, slightly skewed rows on the sand. Their white hulls gleamed like fish, almost fluorescent.

Jordan said, "Take your pick," and Gilchrist hesitated. *This was illegal, wasn't it? Interfering with private property – Spanish property.*

"Oh, for Christ's sake . . ." came the other's bark and there it was again, the barely restrained rage. He had felt it earlier burning his bare arm, longing to rend and tear, but holding back, banking down those fires from the pit. Now, single-handedly, he was dragging one of the pedaloes to the water's edge.

Obediently he clambered aboard up over the nearest fat metal tube, already wet, into a rusty seat while Jordan held the thing steady. Then he joined him, two tennis umpires side by side facing the ocean, searching the dark waters beneath their feet for the invisible pedals.

"Ready?"

The paddles slowly began to turn, clumsily at first, then picking up speed as their legs learned the knack of working in unison. The pedalo headed out to sea, Jordan steering with a rope, and the noise they made was strangely comforting, a gentle clopping like the sound of butter being patted. The moon had come out of nowhere, a great milky globe coating the pontoons with frost. Between their legs a calm rectangle of water kept pace with them, magical like a moving pool. Gilchrist stared down entranced. There were tiny darting fish there glittering like scraps of silver foil. Their existence seemed perfect, unhurried, natural.

Then Jordan grunted, "I need another drink," breaking the spell. Gilchrist felt the tiny seed of anger unclench itself. Deliberately he increased the forward pressure on his pedals, their roughened wood as natural beneath his soles now as an old pair of shoes. He was in his element, it struck him, *water, of course*, and when his companion lifted his legs clear, lazily,

304

crudely, producing a flask from his hip pocket, he thrust down even more powerfully. The pedalo began veering to the left for the man drinking by his side had abandoned the steering-rope as well as pedals.

"Here, have a snort. Come on," he ordered, shaking the flask at him.

Gilchrist ignored him. It was as if the years had fallen away and he was back once more on his beloved river, thrashing yet embracing its currents at the same time, that delicious sensation both languorous and invigorating.

"Slow down, old man. You'll do yourself a mischief." But the insult only made him stronger.

"I said, relax. *Enough!* You hear me?"

On either side of the twin tubes the water continued streaming past, boiling in their wake. Then there came a change in rhythm as the other regained the pedals, trying to force them about in a wide sweep towards the shore. Gilchrist fought back. "No," he said, resisting.

"What do you mean, no?"

"I said – *no!*"

Jamming his soles down hard against their flat, wooden stirrups, he felt the craft buck then come to rest, disabled by their opposing thrusts. *Water had evened the score*, he told himself.

Jordan ceased pedalling and said quietly, "Fuck you." He said it twice. From his mouth issued a soft-voiced but scalding torrent of abuse, obscenities such as Gilchrist had never heard, ever could have imagined before, sexual accusations beyond the bounds of shame or human ingenuity. The old Gilchrist would have covered his ears – this truly was the language of the pit – but, instead, he sat there unmoving on his rusty perch allowing it to pass over, through him, as though insulated by the magical power about his feet. He didn't feel anger any more. The bud had flowered, releasing its rancour, its place taken now by something calmer like that still pool between the floats. And so when the tirade of filth died away and they rocked together in silence once more and Jordan finally said, "Let's go back now," in soft, and, yes, pleading tones, he heard himself reply, "No," a second time.

Becalmed, the pedalo sat on the ocean bobbing ever so slightly. In their struggle, somehow, it had drifted about until now it faced the crescent of lights from where they'd set out.

"I'm asking you for the last time. We have got to go back."

Idly he wondered how long this stalemate could continue. He felt like advising the other not to fight it, as he had been instructed earlier, but before he could consider the matter Jordan struck him on the side of the face with his clenched fist. Then he was grappling with him, two wrestlers trying to unseat one another above that still millpond framed by the floats. The blow stung, his left eye had gone cloudy suddenly, but nothing mattered but giving as good as he got. In the midst of it all wild elation gripped him. He was smiting the foe finally, manfully, *Lord, how manfully*, for the other seemed to be giving ground quite rapidly, cowering, clinging to the metal arms of his chair. "Don't, don't!" he heard him exclaim.

In the moonlight the face of the man he pummelled appeared white and terrified as he kept up his barrage. *He looks nothing like me. How could I ever have believed in that resemblance, allowed myself to be taken in by it? How sweet, Lord, are the fruits of retribution. Eye for eye, tooth for tooth . . .*

The last time Gilchrist had used his fists had been in a playground while brothers Tom and Charlie watched from the sidelines with a callousness he never forgave them for. He had taken a bad beating that day before finally they stepped in. They told him it was for his own good, he had to learn to "take care of himself". Now, in the midst of this, his second blooding, where things were going in his favour for a change and so sweetly at that, he began planting his blows instead of squandering them, each one payment for every slight, every humiliation, each confidence betrayed. The moon stared down, a neutral observer, lighting up his target who whimpered now, and it seemed to Gilchrist that years of insults, not merely the score of these past few months, sharpened and directed his aim. Finally, one splendid right to the temple worthy of a professional – he could tell the instant it landed – caused his adversary to throw up both hands and losing balance as well as his grip on the metal supports of the chair he toppled sideways into the water.

From his victor's chair Gilchrist looked down as the other disappeared then emerged spouting. The formerly calm expanse, his beautiful pond, was now thrashed to an ugly black broth. Ignoring the outstretched hands he crouched there in the grip of something as cold as the water stirred up by the other's exertions. It was like studying some lower form of life. *Why was this creature behaving in this way? Why so terrified?* And then it came to him, as simple as a light coming on in a dark room. *Because he cannot swim!* But why would he venture out this far in the first place – a mile, was it two from dry land? Because of vanity, that's why, the unwritten commandment, but the most dangerous, most corrupting of all.

Gazing down on that pathetic figure Gilchrist experienced a surge of feeling he had forgotten existed, a re-kindling of an old zeal from a time dead and gone. Trusting some buried reflex he leant down and, for the briefest second, closing his eyes to gain maximum power and inspiration, he placed a palm lightly, even lovingly, on the drenched scalp below. Wide-eyed and fearful, his reflection stared up at him. He was clinging precariously to the slippery sides of the left-hand pontoon so that when Gilchrist pressed down hard, once, he went under without a struggle like one of those same willing converts from another time and place.

And there it so easily could have ended like that, in that

floating, watery cage far from a foreign shore. But as Gilchrist continued bracing his arm and with it his resolve to quench the fire of evil in the one below for good – hadn't he boasted how he had come unscathed through that inferno five years earlier like a salamander, and now only the blessed, slaking water of redemption could purge such a monster – he sensed his will start to weaken. The skull beneath his fingers felt like a child's suddenly, that soft, vulnerable pliancy. There seemed no fight left in the flailing arms. They drifted palely beneath the surface like seaweed. Bubbles broke.

"In the name of the Father . . ." Removing his hand as he said the words Gilchrist watched as his double emerged from the depths – but how shrunken, how aged! Pawing blindly, his hands found the base of his perch and clung there. He began retching.

Gilchrist stood up until he was balanced on the seat of his chair. The craft gently rocked beneath him but he moved in tune with it, bare feet gripping the weathered wood. First he removed his playboy's shirt, then the rolled-up trousers, then his shorts – none of them belonged to him, not even the underwear – allowing them to slither free into the depths. For a moment he held himself naked and aloof, gazing at the sea, shore lights winking like an unhooked necklace where the land began, as though seeing all of it for the first time. *The last time*. Then he took his wristwatch off and watched it slide into the calm pond below. It wriggled like a fish until it disappeared from view.

The man penned in the water below looked up to where he stood poised. "You can't do this," he gasped. "How can you? You'll never get rid of me. You hear me? Never. *You're my* – "

But Gilchrist didn't hear the rest for he had dived into the sea beyond the torpedo floats, such a clean, beautiful dive, as perfect as any he'd ever made with his brothers, knifing down through the warm surface waters until he felt the deeper cold assail his limbs and then, and only then, did he turn and rise to the surface. His head was a bobbing dot in the vastness – as he was – paltry, insignificant, and the thought filled him with a peace he thought he had forfeited forever.

The tiny, caressing waves broke about his face, and using the old-fashioned breast-stroke of his youth he began swimming easily, effortlessly away from the pedalo.

Just once he thought he heard a voice call out, "The wrong way! You're going the wrong way!"

But of course he wasn't, he was swimming back home, back along those cool, dark, remembered streams of childhood, letting them wash away each stain, every accumulated transgression with each stroke he took. His troubles had been born in water. They should end there too.

SILVER'S CITY
Maurice Leitch

WINNER OF THE WHITBREAD PRIZE FOR FICTION

While Belfast is torn apart by a vicious, undeclared war, two men are engaged in a bitter and equally destructive private battle for vengeance.

Ned Galloway, a street-wise hired gun, has abducted loyalist folk-hero 'Silver' Steele. His purpose: to prove who wields the real power in the city's battle-torn streets. While Galloway believes his anarchic skills can buy him a kind of freedom, Steele discovers that he no longer understands the mechanisms and principles of the city for which he once fought.

Together they are dragged into a final, terrible confrontation – where all who believe they pull the strings are proved dangerously, murderously wrong.

'It's not the action of the novel which stays in the mind so much as the precise delineation of the two personalities, both alien and criminal and both finely and unsettlingly rendered.' William Boyd, *Sunday Telegraph*

'Leitch is a powerful writer handling urban rot and confessional brutality with great technical competence, while not quite concealing a basic personal gentleness and, in spite of everything, an essentially romantic imagination.' *Irish Press*

'A tight-lipped and tautly-bound venture into the destitution of modern Belfast. The urban wildness of Ulster . . . is well caught. But more, so is the spiritual desert of the embattled Ulster mind.' *Observer*

POOR LAZARUS
Maurice Leitch

WINNER OF THE GUARDIAN PRIZE FOR FICTION

Yarr is teetering on the edge of madness. Not so long ago he was the biggest womaniser and tearaway on either side of the Border. Now what remains of his sanity is threatened by the terrible isolation he feels as a Protestant outsider in the Catholic village of Ballyboe.

His spirits are lifted momentarily by the unexpected attentions of Quigley, a Canadian film producer, who enlists his help in gathering material for a documentary. With this unexpected assistance, Yarr eagerly escapes from his pregnant wife, the girl assistant after whom he uselessly lusts, and the failing, tumble-down shop he runs.

But the Canadian's attentions are destined only to weaken Yarr's already feeble grip on reality as he hurtles toward the final disaster in his disintegrating life.

'By sheer vitality, by knowledge and an undeniable love, Maurice Leitch shapes this sodden clay and sets the figures leaping with life.' *Hibernia*

'Mr Leitch's achievement is to make the agonies of this finely conceived central figure real, and to infuse his miseries with a kind of painful comic poetry.'
Sunday Times

'[The] writing is full of sap: pungent, vital, total and passionately engrossed in its material.' *Listener*

A Selected List of Titles Available from Minerva

While every effort is made to keep prices low, it is sometimes necessary to increase prices at short notice. Mandarin Paperbacks reserves the right to show new retail prices on covers which may differ from those previously advertised in the text or elsewhere.

The prices shown below were correct at the time of going to press.

☐	7493 9044 1	**The Book of Evidence**	John Banville	£5.99
☐	7493 9979 1	**Ghosts**	John Banville	£5.99
☐	7493 9077 8	**Kepler**	John Banville	£5.99
☐	7493 9179 0	**Down All the Days**	Christy Brown	£5.99
☐	7493 9177 4	**My Left Foot**	Christy Brown	£5.99
☐	7493 9183 9	**Wild Grow the Lilies**	Christy Brown	£4.99
☐	7493 9168 5	**The Commitments**	Roddy Doyle	£5.99
☐	7493 9735 7	**Paddy Clarke Ha Ha Ha**	Roddy Doyle	£5.99
☐	7493 3614 5	**The Snapper**	Roddy Doyle	£5.99
☐	7493 9990 2	**The Van**	Roddy Doyle	£5.99
☐	7493 9732 2	**Langrishe, Go Down**	Aidan Higgins	£5.99
☐	7493 9718 7	**Lions of the Grunewald**	Aidan Higgins	£5.99
☐	7493 9829 9	**Ulysses**	James Joyce	£5.99
☐	7493 9658 X	**Poor Lazarus**	Maurice Leitch	£6.99
☐	7493 9657 1	**Silver's City**	Maurice Leitch	£6.99
☐	7493 9868 X	**Death and Nightingales**	Eugene McCabe	£5.99

All these books are available at your bookshop or newsagent, or can be ordered direct from the address below. Just tick the titles you want and fill in the form below.

Cash Sales Department, PO Box 5, Rushden, Northants NN10 6YX.
Phone: 01933 414000 : Fax: 01933 414047.

Please send cheque, payable to 'Reed Book Services Ltd.', or postal order for purchase price quoted and allow the following for postage and packing:

£1.00 for the first book, 50p for the second; **FREE POSTAGE AND PACKING FOR THREE BOOKS OR MORE PER ORDER.**

NAME (Block letters) ....

ADDRESS ....

....

☐ I enclose my remittance for ....

☐ I wish to pay by Access/Visa Card Number

Expiry Date

Signature ....

Please quote our reference: MAND